MW00720665
THE
PARADISE
ENGINE

For Mrs. Gregory, aka, Sally

Thank you for your
support, and for
many lovely memories
of Beach Elementary!

Becca.

THE PARADISE ENGINE

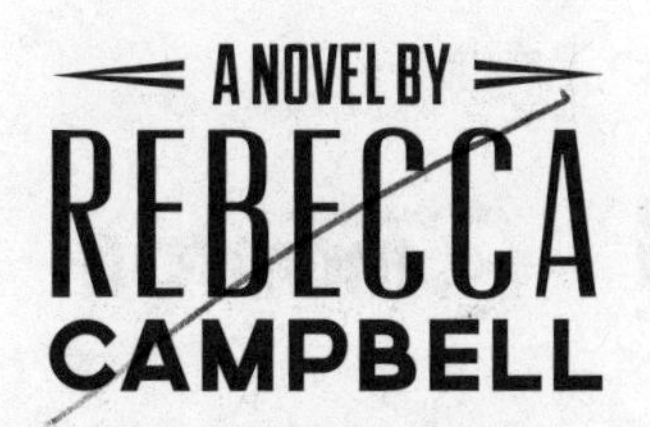

R Campbell

FOR MY PARENTS

LIBRARY AND ARCHIVES CANADA CATALOGUING IN PUBLICATION

Campbell, Rebecca, 1975-

The paradise engine / Rebecca Campbell.

ISBN 978-1-927063-25-5

I. Title.

PS8605.A5483P37 2013 C813'.6 C2012-906595-1

Also issued in electronic format.

Editor for the Board: Anne Nothof

Cover and interior design: Justine Ma

Author Photo: Jill Promoli

Government of Alberta ■

Canada Council for the Arts | Conseil des arts du Canada

Canadian Heritage | Patrimoine canadien

NeWest Press acknowledges the financial support of the Alberta Multimedia Development Fund and the Edmonton Arts Council for our publishing program. We further acknowledge the financial support of the Government of Canada through the Canada Book Fund (CBF) for our publishing activities. We acknowledge the support of the Canada Council for the Arts which last year invested $24.3 million in writing and publishing throughout Canada.

NeWest Press

No bison were harmed in the making of this book.

Printed and bound in Canada 1 2 3 4 5 14 13

No. 201, 8540 109 Street, Edmonton, Alberta T6G 1E6

t. 780.432.9427 **w.** newestpress.com

"

I feed too much on the inward sources; I live too much with the dead. My mind is something like the ghost of an ancient, wandering about the world and trying mentally to construct it as it used to be, in spite of ruin and confusing changes.

GEORGE ELIOT

MIDDLEMARCH

PART ONE

BLUEPRINTS FOR SURVIVING THE COMING DARK TIMES

PART ONE

A GHOST STORY

The first ghost appeared at the end of August, when Jasmine had already been gone for months. That was too bad because she was the only person Anthea knew who would recognize a ghost when she saw one, or know what to do about it.

Anthea didn't know a ghost when she saw one, though she was the one haunted. She also didn't know what had happened to Jasmine, but whatever *it* was, *it* was probably over. She knew only this: Jasmine was last seen just northwest of the city, on a highway that curled uphill along the coast and the mountains. She was last seen early in June, in the company of a bearded Caucasian male apprx. 30 yrs of age, who carried an army surplus backpack and was otherwise without distinguishing characteristics. Anthea *could* determine, then, that Jasmine was last seen facing southeast, hitching northwest along a highway that grew pineapple weed on its shoulders. Pineapple weed smelled like chamomile tea when it bruised, as it would do under Jas's runners when she stood for long stretches, one thin arm reaching out into the traffic and the other propped on her hip. Given how hot June had been, Anthea also knew Jasmine was kneecapped by heat waves that rose from the highway, so she seemed to float above the asphalt. To the drivers who did not pick them up, they might have been a mirage, or ghosts from the early '70s.

Jasmine would have enjoyed being mistaken for a ghost, especially one that smelled of chamomile. She and the man walked northwest all day. Sometimes where the shoulder was narrow, she slithered halfway down the ditch and he'd turn around to help her to her feet. They were still walking when the sky turned purple and rusty orange over the mountains. Jas's arms crossed over her chest. She shivered with dehydration and the sun-ache in her temples, the tight wrinkle of a burn on her nose and forehead. After that night no one saw anything, and so Anthea is unable to determine how much longer they walked north and west. This little film plays out in her head sometimes, unresolved.

That was months before the haunting, though, which had its start very early on a Sunday morning at the end of August. Anthea was asleep when it began, and she mistook the first visitation for a dream. In the dream a dark-haired man told her something very important she should not forget in a voice that had the texture of a shellac 78 on an old turntable. She listened politely to the man for a long time, unable to grasp his words though she felt their urgency. Just as she began to understand what the man wanted her to know, the squirrels in the attic started fighting, as they often did in the early morning. Half-awake and still listening to the distorted voice in her dream, she sat up and hit the angled wall above her head, and then stood and thumped the ceiling with the heel of her hand.

By the time Anthea was fully awake—still hitting the plaster, the squirrels still fighting overhead—the phone was ringing and she forgot even that she should not forget the antiqued voice of her dream, and so the second supernatural event of Anthea's life passed her without remark. She picked up the phone beside the bed, but no one was there.

She lay down again, and found herself thinking of the same thing she'd been thinking about when she went to sleep: that he'd been seen again, the bearded Caucasian male apprx. 30 yrs of age had returned from his pilgrimage up the highway. That was all she knew, so far. She wondered where he'd been spotted, if it was by the wall with the mural that says "Jesus Saves." That was the first place she'd seen him; Jasmine had taken her there and told her it was his corner. He'd looked a lot like the Jesus in the mural. He stood outside the recyclers where they lined up with returns, and he talked about tithing, standing at the exit like that, and some of them dropped toonies in his palm in return for a blessing or a little laying-on-of-hands. Once Jasmine had told Anthea, as though she was the first to realize it, that the poor and lowdown are always the first to recognize the truth. That's why you look for spiritual revolution in neighbourhoods where nice people lock their car doors as they drive.

Lying on her bed, listening to the squirrels, she wished she'd been the one to see his return. In the last month she had often watched the sidewalks for a Caucasian male apprx. 30 yrs of age with no distinguishing characteristics. This particular indistinguishable male would be pastiching reiki and biofield manipulation and exorcism on morning commuters, if he could make them stop long enough. If they just avoided him, he'd do it covertly, waving his hands over them as they passed, adjusting their auras and leaving—Anthea imagined—fingerprints. He was the sort of man who always had dirty hands.

The first full day of Anthea's haunting was a Monday. That morning she was late leaving her apartment, which was bad because on Mondays there were always meetings. While she waited at the bus stop, a woman walked toward her, first on the sidewalk, then in the gutter, then on the sidewalk again. When she reached Anthea, the woman stopped and smiled in that carefully conventional way women have when they're wasted in the early morning and don't want anyone to know.

"Hello, honey."

"Hello."

Under her arm she held a torn plastic bag full of socks. "See?" the woman said. "I found these. They were just over on that bench, hey. You want a pair?"

"Thank you," Anthea said. "That's very kind." The woman pulled two bright new socks out of her bag.

"Yeah-yeah. I saw you standing there and I said to myself, I'll give you a pair cause you're waiting for a bus like I do when I don't have a car. You look after yourself, hey? And don't spend all your money on crack!" The woman laughed nice and loud.

Anthea laughed too and took the socks. "Thank you," she said, and the woman nodded and walked away. Anthea wanted to say something more, to warn the woman, or tell her to be careful, but by then she was already down the sidewalk, then the gutter, then the pavement, carrying the rest of the socks under her arm.

On the bus Anthea took a window seat and watched for a Caucasian male, apprx. 30 yrs of age. There were lots standing on street corners, some were barefoot, some in worn denim with long hair. She was half-way to campus and worried about making her meeting when the express stopped at an intersection and there he was, crossing in front of the bus. He was attended by a blonde woman—not Jasmine, though for a moment Anthea's stomach tightened. He carried no backpack, but a drum hung over his left hip. His hair was longer, blonder at the tips, the curls more luxuriant than they had been in the spring. He was shirtless and bare-foot. She pressed the button on the bar beside her once, then twice, then went to the door.

"Please could you let me out here?" she asked. "Just here?"

The bus driver said nothing.

"Please!" she said. "It's a red!"

As she said it the light turned to green. The bus was in the intersection. "Please!" she said.

"Ma'am," said the bus driver, "this is an express!"

Anthea walked away from the door, down the crowded aisle and up the steps to the back window. She looked toward the street he had crossed, attended by another of his blonde sylphs. The window was dirty. What she could see of the intersection was hidden by construction, by other cars, by the slope of the street down which they drove.

She was nearly late for the meeting. She ran from the campus bus loop across dead, summery grass toward her building and then around to the back. Her entrance was on the damp side, half-buried in the earth down a cement walkway surrounded by juniper. She slipped in the door and ran down the half-basement corridor with the low ceiling, the one that smelled of synthetic carpeting and, when it rained, of MSG and powdered chicken soup from one of the tiny break rooms. She ran toward the Kilgour Institute along corridors that opened on tiny rooms a little bit like what you'd see in an industrial henhouse, and through the walls Anthea heard voices and footsteps.

The Kilgour Institute was an unusually well-funded local historical society devoted to the preservation of the Kilgour Legacy, and with it the city's recent past. It occupied a suite of offices on the main floor and a number of storage rooms in the basement and sub-basement of a secondary library. They shared the building with poorer faculties and satellites of the university: two doors down from the room in which she worked the Department of Gnostic Antiquities had its main reading room, and on the other side were the offices for the university's *Arkham Studies Journal.*

At the far end of her run the door to a conference room stood open. She was breathing a little heavily as she approached it, and when she reached it everyone was seated, with one chair remaining in the far corner, where the table was nearly jammed up against the wall.

Brynn shuffled in her chair. Anthea guessed that the meeting had begun a few minutes before, and it continued around her as she squeezed into the back corner. She tried not to look over Dr. Blake's head to the long window just below the ceiling. The needles of an ornamental juniper pressed against the glass, with a sliver of blue sky among its branches.

"Miss Brooke," said Dr. Blake.

"Dr. Blake," said Anthea.

"How are you? We heard you all the way down the hall. You were moving pretty fast."

"Sorry I'm late."

"We're just talking about the proposal from the Temple Theatre folks."

"Okay."

"You don't need a minute? Catch your breath?"

"No, I'm good. I'm good."

Dr. Blake turned back to the meeting. Anthea didn't look at the juniper, or the copper-coloured needles piled against the glass, the dead ones from last year. Instead, breathing as quietly as she could, she slipped a file out of her bag and folded her hands in her lap. These meetings were compulsory and monthly for the remaining staff of the Kilgour Institute: Blake, and Brynn, who had been a Canadian History postdoc, and a few stalled grad students. And Anthea.

Anthea was a fresh and average History M.A. from the department on the opposite side of the concourse; she was also somewhere near the sub-basement in the university's hierarchy, even at the brutalist end of campus. She had been hired the year before to work on the Institute's new digital initiative, which would see the entire contents of the archive catalogued and made searchable to the public. She had been assigned to the domestic papers, and was happy to find she liked Mrs. Kilgour's cookbooks and household accounts, mostly because she enjoyed thinking about food. Before the First World War they liked things boiled hard and long, then sieved. She wondered sometimes if they all had bad teeth, since they puréed even nice things like strawberries and baby spinach and black beans. She also wondered why they didn't mind people touching their food, because often the recipes called for a kitchen maid to shove overcooked carrots through a sieve with her fingertips. That probably explained the attention Mrs. Kilgour paid to her maidservants' hygiene, and the ledger dedicated to random inspections of fingernails and handkerchiefs. The best part of the whole thing was that Anthea's work at the Kilgour Institute required no analysis, only the management of detail, so she could enjoy without frustration the mysteries of watercress, Calves-foot Jelly, White Soup, Roman Punch. She understood the phrases "cut nicely" and "fast oven," and knew the price of candied ginger in 1910.

But while she'd been thinking about candied ginger, which was delicious, the meeting carried on. The slight film of sweat raised by her cross-campus sprint cooled beneath her clothes. She shivered. She wondered how she smelled.

Brynn was talking. "—a really exceptional opportunity, but I worry about our mandate. What do the by-laws say about outreach in the case of—"

"—be right, yes," Blake said some time later, "yes, but I think if you look at the original constitution, the Temple project—"

They were still talking about the Temple. It was okay then. She was on the database, not the Temple or the Biography. As she waited, she thought about Jas's Prophet and his attendant blonde. Above her head the juniper pressed against the glass.

One of those Ph.D. candidates—Kostantina?—said, "charitable work was well documented in the early—"

"—true or not. And I think we can at least do some initial survey work in our own archives. Speaking of which. Anthea, how are those cookbooks?"

"Yeah. Okay," said Anthea. She looked away from the juniper. She pulled a stack of paper out of her bag and set it on the table. "So," she said, "I know it's late, but here's what I've got for 1900–1920. There're a couple of spreadsheets, yeah, but I stuck in some scans of her menus, too. You know. If you're interested. For the website."

"Menus?" That was Brynn.

Anthea flipped to the appendix and read, "Formal, family, summer, luncheon, winter, breakfast, garden party, tea." She flipped the page and took another breath, "dinner, picnic, buffet, supper, spring."

"Oh," said Brynn.

"Autumn, wartime, ball."

Blake looked at the file on the table, though he did not open it.

"Children's party, peace. That's in chronological order," she said.

Blake said, "You've been really thorough. That's going to be some database." He reached for her nice little précis of the Kilgour Kitchen Archive, 1900–1920, and added it to his pile of buff folders. "But have you started on the scrapbooks? I think we talked about the scrapbooks last month."

"Oh. Yeah. Totally," Anthea said. "Scrapbooks. Next month I'll totally have something for you."

Brynn looked like she wanted to talk some more, but then the other three were wriggling out from around the table and toward the beige metal door that always made Anthea think of bunkers. People chatted and picked up their coffee cups and Kostantina said, "Drinks later?" and then they were gone.

Trapped in her far corner, Anthea waited for Blake to say something.

"There sure are a lot of cookbooks," he said.

"I think she liked entertaining quite a bit."

"I think she did. I really think she did. So you're sure you'll have time for the Temple work? It's not like the database, there's a bit of a rush."

"Yeah. It'll be okay."

"They're going to want photographs. They say they want other material, but it's always photographs when it comes down to it. Some portraits. Exteriors maybe. And some captions. They'll want captions. Next week?"

"Okay."

"Great! Let's have something for next Wednesday, 5 PM." Then Blake looked down and said, "Your shoelace is untied."

He was gone and Anthea was alone in the low-ceilinged room, wondering why she'd been given an assignment for which she had no obvious affinity, and in which she had shown no interest, especially since Brynn had been talking about the Temple Project since the beginning. The Institute hadn't done culturally relevant work in living memory, so people who cared about their mandate, like Brynn did, were pretty excited about a return to public history. The Project would reclaim one of the city's early vaudeville theatres from the wreckage of the eastside, preserving local arts history and developing a new venue with the texture of age, something precious and unusual in their youthful city. Or that's what the memo said. Of course, Anthea liked the theatre, had visited it a few times, but now she would have to contribute, and while a handful of photographs and some captions didn't seem like much, the thought of synthesizing nuggets of historical interest made her cranky.

She reread the original memo describing the Temple Theatre Project, then spent an hour with the old catalogue, leafing through typescripts on soft paper dating back to the first years of the Institute. They tore under her fingers if she wasn't careful, like the pages of old *Life* magazines, and left the same patina on her skin. After that, she requisitioned a key and walked down the stairs to the basement, then the sub-basement and Rm 023 with its stiff lock. The room was small and lit by fluorescent squares in the ceiling. Anthea shut the door behind her, then sat down on the room's single chair and pulled a box toward her, scuffing the dust that bloomed on its lid.

She should be working. Before her sat the box she had marred with her fingerprints; to Anthea's eyes it seemed to have been unsorted since the early days of the Institute. She started a list, which was pretty much all she knew how to do at the Institute:

1. One (1) program from one of Mrs. Kilgour's interminable musical evenings, introducing the Misses Fladd, who will play Saint-Saëns' "The Swan" for harp and piano, and including a recitation by Mr. Stephen Noyes.
2. Two (2) pieces of sheet music: "Oh Do Not Ask! Oh Do Not Weep!" by Francis Harold Fleming, America's Armless Baritone; "Wrap Me Up In My Tarpaulin Jacket," Traditional Air, arranged by Hubert Bentley.
3. One (1) photograph of Mrs. Kilgour dressed like a prima donna, including spangles and ostrich feathers.
4. One (1) dried, brownish-pink rosebud.
5. Three (3) black beetles, dead.
6. One (1) photograph of a man in a tight collar, the name *Mr. L. Manley, tenor* in yellow typescript on the back.
7. Seventeen (17) programmes for other ladies' Artistic Evenings (1910–1915).

Number 6 stopped Anthea briefly, on account of *Mr. L. Manley, tenor*'s Valentino eyes. But then she looked at 2 and 1, and she couldn't think what to do with them, so she sat beside the box, all its contents around her, for five minutes. Brynn would know what to do. Brynn would have a new spreadsheet already tied into her database, keyworded, its cells slowly colonized by tidy chunks of information. Anthea thought about throwing out the beetles and the rosebud, but how long had they been there? They might be pre-war.

Holding items 5 and 4 in her left hand, she thought about Jasmine's Prophet with his acolyte and his drum, and how he might know what had happened.

She considered repacking the box. Then she said, "Fuck," and flicked *Mr. L. Manley, tenor* into the air where he cartwheeled and fell in a far corner, with the beetles. He missed the box she'd aimed him at. She'd never been able to do it with hockey cards either, even though her brother Max kept telling her it was all in the wrist, and tried to teach her on too-hot summer afternoons in elementary school. But then, if Jasmine's Prophet had returned to the city, Jasmine might too. At the very least it meant that if he was found she could ask questions. Someone could ask questions. There were questions.

She picked up the next photograph in the pile—of *Mr. L. Manley, tenor* and Mrs. Kilgour, this time—and held it, thinking of everything Jasmine had ever tried to explain to her about the infinite, invisible threads that link all events into a unity of human action and experience, and about how those subtle associations made prophecy possible, and magic. They were called correspondences, and what people called spells was just the exercise of esoteric knowledge regarding the interconnectivity of all reality. She closed her eyes and said, "If this one hits the box, that's a sign."

It did not hit the box. She picked up the next one.

"Okay, actually, this one is the sign."

This one landed near the corner with the open box she'd been aiming at, though not in it. She dropped off the chair to sit cross-legged on the floor and thought about percentages—if more landed in the corner than didn't, that was a sign, allowing the subtle forces of Jasmine's cosmology the opportunity to act over a number of trials. Working on the flick of the wrist, though, she emptied the box of photographs and lost track of which spot meant what, and what the sign was, anyway.

When Jasmine walked away, did she find it, the thing she wanted? Did she get where she was going?

The next box down was wooden and older and smaller than the others, and had a torn paper label printed with the logo "OV" in an Art Nouveau font. It was the one she needed: inside there were shellac 78s stored edgewise in brown paper sleeves. No pictures in this one, which ended the little oracle in the corner, though for a moment she considered that 78s would fly straighter, like Frisbees. She pulled one out and read the label, published by some Kilgour Coal subsidiary called "The Orphic Voice." The aria was from Massenet's *Le Cid*, "Ô Souverain, ô juge, ô père," performed by Mr. Liam Manley and the Orphic Quartet.

Anthea checked her watch. It was ten. She lay down then on the only scrap of floor the overstuffed room afforded. *Consider your situation*, she thought: vaulted in at the bottom of the bottom, in with the junk drawers of a crazy dead coal baroness, and Jasmine. And Jasmine's Prophet, who was back and carried a drum over his left hip.

But what was it Jasmine's Prophet had over girls, who were the only acolytes around him? Never men. Never, Anthea guessed, women either. His congregation was distinctly girlish. The one with the blonde dreadlocks she'd seen that morning wasn't at all like Jasmine on first glance—Jasmine avoided white girls in dreads—but they shared some quality Anthea could not describe, something pliant, something that looked like "yes."

If Jasmine didn't want to be found it was one thing, but if she was out there, lost. If she was. If she.

LIKE HARRY HOUDINI

Anthea spent the rest of the morning in Rm 023 flicking photographs into the corners and then picking them up again. Her aim improved. That afternoon she left work early, but did not join the others on that West Side patio they all liked. On her way out, Brynn asked what Blake wanted when he kept her back after the meeting, and Anthea wondered why Brynn cared whether she worked on the Database or the Biography or the Temple Project. All she said, though, was that it was just more work and then she smiled and said, "Take her easy today, hit her hard tomorrow," which was something her father used to say when he didn't want to talk about it.

She returned to the intersection where she'd seen them, him with his drum and the dreadlocked blonde. She sat at one of the little tables outside the Starbucks and watched the street for an hour. She watched fratboys, and men in suits, and sharply dressed girls from Hong Kong, and skateboarders, and kids who could be K-pop stars, and handsome shaggy men who looked like artists. She watched construction workers and backpackers and barefoot old men with long, grizzled ponytails. She watched skinny eastside lesbians on bicycles, and elderly women in dust-coloured pantyhose and orthopedic oxfords. He did not return.

Though she admitted it was unlikely she would see him that day—this was not his neighbourhood, after all—she didn't really want to go home just then, not if the squirrels had started fighting again in her attic. Instead, she found a new thrift shop a few blocks from her apartment, already congested with pilled sheets and matted plushies. Inside she knelt down to dig through a Canadian Club box full of someone's high-school mix tapes: *91 Party Mix. Dance Hits 89. Party Party Grad 92*! A bloom spread over her fingers, from someone else's dust mites, gorged on someone else's skin.

As she rubbed at the dust on her fingers, she recognized handwriting and the faded collage of one cover, half-hidden in the box. She dug around, and when she found it, she thought of Jasmine's crappy car stereo from years ago, the one that still only took cassette tapes. And how the speaker on the right cut in and out, so when they listened to bittersweet pop from the '60s and '70s she only got Simon or just Garfunkel. At that moment she realized that she had never heard all of *Pet Sounds*. The tape she held was covered with pictures of Audrey Hepburn as Holly Golightly, dating from Jas's temporary collage period, all those afternoons when she cut classes and sat on the floor of her darkened dorm room, leafing through back issues of *Vogue* and *Spin* and *Entertainment Weekly*. Jas had called that one the *SadGirlMix*, and they had listened to it in the car while they cruised around the city on summer afternoons in first and second year.

Anthea crawled through other boxes, looking for the *MadGirl-*, the *FuckMeNow-Mix*, which she would also know by their carefully themed collages and their familiar playlists. There might even be other things—the books, the clothes, the costume jewellery—a scattered stratum-of-Jas in second-hand stores across the city.

Had she possessed even a rumour of etheric sensitivity, Anthea might have recognized that she was the subject of a haunting, one that operated not only through dreams, but by way of the objects around her, the words spoken in earshot, the birds that flew through the sky overhead, the Caucasian man, apprx. 30 yrs, she saw crossing at a busy intersection beside a blonde girl who was like Jas, but not Jas. She must have felt something, all the same, because she found herself wishing she and Jasmine had made one of those pacts people make about death, where you arrange a signal to prove that the dear departed persists in another, subtler form. The winter before, Anthea had heard that Harry Houdini made one with his wife, and had meant to mention that to Jas, but by then it was too late, and Jasmine didn't listen much anymore. Of course Jasmine might've made such arrangements with someone else: she had always remarked on Anthea's psychic opacity. Or possibly Jas had been bombarding her for months with the arcane communications of the dead: changing how blossoms fell from a cherry tree, or giving her significant dreams. Possibly Jasmine was not dead.

She bought the *SadGirlMix* for a quarter and left the store thinking of him, again, and how he used to stand on street corners with a sign that read "fRee ReiKi" and correct the clouded auras of Saturday afternoon shoppers, or 5 PM commuters.

He had been doing these guerrilla initiations—clarifying and attuning auras even when people ignored his sign—the first time Jasmine took her to see the new guy. Literally see him, it turned out, and not speak. Jasmine led her to a corner and told her to watch across the street, where a blondish man stood barefoot, seeming to preach, though there wasn't a crowd. They were too far away to hear, but Jasmine said it was prayer, the real kind, spontaneous and inexplicable. As they watched, a girl stopped in front of him, and he began what Jasmine called his real work, the subtle manipulation of bodies that he called initiation. He had initiated thousands—*literally thousands*, Jasmine said, *thousands!*—and it would be even more, when things were counted, because any one attunement could ripple outward from the point of encounter like a wave of salvation. He never knew where it might subside, only trusted to the Veiled Father to guide his hand, and set a spark moving in the darkness. That was why he liked to do stealth initiations for whole crowds at the International Airport, Jas explained. The ripples go even further that way; they fly.

"He's so thin," Anthea said. "Does he get enough to eat?"

"Sometimes. Most of the time." Jas was still, and then in a mutter, "It's about energies, you know. He does it all on these subtle energies."

Anthea had thought of saying something about him having Christly abs like starving desert prophets get, but she found she couldn't. Instead she said, "Mm-hm?"

Jas kept talking, looking at him rather than Anthea: "And it works, that's what's so good for me—I see it working in him and through him. He lays on hands, too, you know, though he doesn't need to. People pay him for that sometimes."

"Okay. Yeah. But what does he believe?"

"It's complex," she said. "It's really complicated. When I really get it and I really know what I'm talking about, I'll tell you. I promise." They kept standing there watching him until Anthea shuffled and cleared her throat. Jasmine glanced at her. "You want to go? You can go. I don't mind."

"No. Yeah. But. Do you want to go for a tea?"

"I think maybe I'll just stay a bit longer." After the words stopped, her lips still moved, but Anthea couldn't make out what she said and had to look away. It was her turn to speak too quickly, not liking Jasmine's opaque, prayerful face.

"Okay, but we could take him with us? I could buy him a cup of tea? Or coffee? Would coffee be better? Shade grown coffee? There's that fair trade place with the spelt scones. And organic. Stuff."

Across the street Jasmine's lovely Prophet finished his work and kissed the girl on her forehead. They stood close together for a long time. He released her, but she dawdled, diffident, looking up at him through her lashes.

Jasmine said nothing. Then she did: "Don't worry about it."

Yes, something strange happening even then, that goosebumped the skin down Anthea's spine, even though this wasn't the first time Jas had gone looking for answers. When they first met, Jasmine had carried her tarot cards everywhere, then she had talked incessantly about Joseph Campbell and tried to use him in all her term papers, then the same with the White Goddess thing, and then Wicca and I Ching and Kabbalah, and she still followed The Aquarian Centre, which was apparently compatible with this new Gnostic-street-reiki.

But rather than thinking about the cold that crept beneath her skin, Anthea just kept talking, because she was embarrassed, and because she wanted to just go and drink coffee and talk about anything in the world but that man across the street. Since she'd just started on the Kilgour Domestic Archive, she said, "I've been working on some Edwardian stuff. To do with social conditions." She didn't mention that it was social conditions as expressed by household accounts, or really just the sauces chosen by Mrs. Kilgour for family dinners, 1901-1909. Mrs. Kilgour liked hollandaise. She had wanted to tell Jas that. There had been a time when she and Jasmine would have talked about it, and at the end of their conversation gone looking for one of those restaurants that still served instant hollandaise on their frozen spring vegetable medley, and imagined Mrs. Kilgour in her dining room.

"Institute?" Jasmine said, and for a moment Anthea thought she would say more, but her eyes were still turned on her Prophet. "I'm glad you're enjoying yourself, but it sounds like a distraction from what's real. We shouldn't be so attached to the things we can see. We should release," Jasmine stared at him another long moment, "the corporeal hallucination."

"Okay. Sure."

"That means the material world."

"Yeah, I gathered. But maybe they do good work, too?" Jasmine smiled. She looked sweet and sad. Anthea really didn't like it when Jasmine looked sweet and sad, so she kept talking, though her voice squeaked slightly: "But I kind of want some coffee?" What she wanted was to not be there, watching Jasmine watch her Prophet as he mumbled and prayed on the other side of the street, and caressed the aura of a fair-haired girl who looked up at him, her face an open flower beneath his hands. Anthea crossed her arms over her chest.

"You know, you really don't have to stay. I'll talk to you later. I'll call you."

Anthea withdrew, an apology on her lips, though she said nothing. It was stupid that she wanted to apologize. As she made her way to a coffee shop, she thought about how once Jasmine had been a big Andrew Lloyd Webber fan, and she hadn't even been embarrassed to admit it until she lived on campus in first year. How she'd silently thrown out all her original cast recordings and the *Cats* poster, but once when they were together in the car, "Starlight Express" came on the radio and she sang along good and loud. Anthea hadn't said anything, but she'd noticed. She'd liked that Jas knew all the words and that for a moment she hadn't been embarrassed.

That day came to be an event horizon in Anthea's memory. In the beginning she had assumed the Prophet was just another of the temporary infatuations which constituted Jasmine's spiritual education, which looked a bit like this:

List of Places Jasmine Looked for Answers:

1. Auras
2. Automatic Writing
3. Campbell, Joseph. *The Hero With A Thousand Faces.* Princeton, N.J.: Princeton University Press, 1968.
4. Estés, Clarissa Pinkola. *Women Who Run With The Wolves.* New York: Ballantine Books, 1992.
5. Graves, Robert. *The White Goddess: a Historical Grammar of Poetic Myth.* New York: Creative Age Press, 1948.
6. *I Ching: the Book of Changes.* Translated by James Legg. New Hyde Park, NY: University Books, 1964.
7. Kabbalah
8. –mancy

i) cartomancy
ii) necromancy
iii) oneiromancy
iv) ornithomancy
v) stichomancy

7. The Prophet
8. Scrying
9. The Aquarian Centre
10. Theosophy
11. Wicca

This was just off the top of Anthea's head and incomplete, but it helped her to think about Jasmine's trajectory. It should end with the Prophet, since he was the terminal point on Jasmine's descent, but then it wouldn't be alphabetical. And actually, "descent" was Anthea's word: when Jas described her initiation into the Prophet's circle, she suggested upward movement, the ascent of some sharp mountain face, toward clearer air at the summit.

Of course, from Anthea's point of view it didn't look anything like that. Jasmine—once so carefully groomed, so *dressed*—grew blurry, then invisible in the crowds on the east side of the downtown core. Like for instance the hair she once got from carefully applied bleaches and dyes, the hair turned from gold back to her original frizzy honey. Her clothes had lasted a little longer, but then there were only T-shirts and jeans and ugly runners. No modish miniskirts, or Mitford-esque tweed, tortoise-shell, pincurls, Jackie Kennedy sherbets or glamour girl rhinestones: no retro where she was going, and no vintage.

During those latter days Anthea sometimes saw Jasmine when she was out walking, or in a cab on some late night. She'd look down from the windows of the train to the intersection where the squeegee kids worked, and there was Jas, dishwater hair and backpack and greasy rag in her right hand. There she'd be, stringy in polar fleece, watching him lay hands on girls lined up outside some bar. And every single time Anthea caught sight of contentment, and if he was there she turned her own eyes on him from across the street, or the train windows, and wished that she could see what Jasmine saw. She'd turn to whomever she was with and tell the story of Jas and her Prophet, and make it funny, or sad, or creepy depending on her feelings at the time, and how much she'd had to drink.

One day Anthea noticed that she hadn't seen Jasmine for a while, and it occurred to her that Jas might be gone in some new way. She kept looking, though, going out of her way to cross and re-cross the familiar intersections, the mural that read "Jesus Saves," the recycling place, the corner by the library. As she walked, she thought through again and again the last time she had seen her friend, and how on that day she didn't know it was a last time.

It was a weeknight. She was walking alone, and found her way to the Temple Theatre's boarded-up windows: the Institute had just officially joined the reclamation project and the theatre was on the gentrifying edge of Jas's new neighbourhood. Anthea spent a long time in front of the old vaudeville house looking at the façade and trying to imagine it without the dull brick-coloured paint, and with the broken faces on the columns rendered whole, and the broken leaves on the lintel, too. She thought about her grandmother as a little girl, going to hear Fritz Kreisler. She thought about her father, Colm, seeing *Butch Cassidy and the Sundance Kid* and *Midnight Cowboy*, back when it was a movie theatre in the late Sixties and served all the dropouts near the waterfront. He had liked it a lot, and talked about the fancy plasters inside and the *egyptienne* paintings on the ceiling of the auditorium, and Anthea had wished she could break in with a flashlight and explore what was left before the Kilgour Institute and the provincial arts board remade it into a World Class Venue.

Back then the Institute's work seemed relevant. After a long look at the building, she wandered west again, toward the posh shops that were also, indirectly, part of the Temple reclamation project. She was ready to go home when she looked down the block and saw Jas with another girl, a skinny teenaged blonde. They were standing at the corner, the girl silent and Jas calling out to the people who wandered in and out of the expensive shops and cafés, people who didn't stop, but texted with their eyes downturned or just looked away.

Across the street Anthea looked at a display of Scandinavian furniture, all tweed and blond wood. She kept Jasmine in the corner of her eye, watched her hands alternately outstretched in blessing or cupped in the Buddha's begging bowl. After a half-dozen tries she succeeded and stopped one man in a group, so that his friends hung back in a semicircle around the two of them.

Anthea looked at the next window, with its three mannequins in black and grey and chocolate. Cashmere. Linen. Sometimes a Merino-silk blend. In her peripheral vision and reflected in the plate glass she watched the little knot of men around Jasmine, something she had seen quite often before, though never before in the context of street evangelism. With her eyes still on the asymmetrical hems, she planned things to say, how she would be kind, or clever, or just tell Jas to call her mother forgodsake. While she rehearsed, more people joined the little group on the corner, and then Anthea had to cross the street to keep watching.

"The Father," she heard first, "you might call him God. He gave us the way to healing in the laying on of hands. I saw you walking down the street and I knew that you've been hurt. Someone put the evil eye on you. It's here." Jasmine laid her hands across the man's neck, then down either side of his spine. She plucked at the man's left shoulder blade, then worried at it with her fingers until she held something heavy Anthea could not see, and cast it from her with a great effort. When she was finished, he turned to face her and she held her hands together and bowed, "Namaste," she said.

Anthea waited in back of the little crowd and she thought maybe Jasmine spoke extra carefully and clearly even though she also seemed to avoid looking in Anthea's direction. The blonde girl made a mark in the little black book she held.

"Haruna ke felach. Spiritus Sancti!" Jasmine said. "Parach me Laruna Mundi! You are the five hundredth—is it the five-hundredth, Steph?—soul I've attuned! Parach mo parach! I feel something about this moment, about you, too. Are you a Seeker?" And Anthea watched Jasmine take on another familiar attitude with the man, something she had seen her do many times before, with her head inclined and her eyes upturned, one hand on his bicep, the other resting against her cheek. He smiled at her, a new initiate though he might not know it. That was when Anthea let her own eyes drop and walked on, pretended she wasn't being cut. She didn't even know the crazy lady either, who picked up stinky men right on the street, with her laying on of hands and her speaking in tongues that wasn't Reiki, or Wiccan, but a more recently made-up practice. But then when she was past, still feeling the crowd behind her and wondering whether the man would go with Jas, to some place where money would change hands, then she'd felt all shuddery through her legs and her mouth was dry. And she thought, *that horrible, mean woman, who did she think she was?*

And that had been her chance. She'd gone and spent the toonie she'd had ready in case Jas was begging, she'd gone and spent it on more tea for herself instead of thinking of her friend, whose bones stood out in her face, and whose skin seemed thinner than it should be. She told herself that if Jasmine had winked, even blinked, waved a hand, she'd have given her the toonie, at least. She told herself that if she had known it was the last time, she would have done something, anything, differently. She did not always believe her own story.

ESCAPE ROUTES

She liked to watch the flight of crows each evening at sunset, the commuter birds who spent their days by the water, but roosted inland. They crossed overhead from the west kitchen window to the east-facing bedroom, earlier and earlier as the summer ended until it was fall and they crossed while she was still at work. She watched them against whichever sunset she happened on; the crows were constant where the colours changed, sometimes pearly, sometimes layered from pink to gold like a Shirley Temple. The crows spilled like black beans across the west, but when they were close she saw that they were crow-shaped holes, little glimpses into the void behind the sky.

She probably loved the crows so much because she knew that they could survive the *comingdarktimes*, a phrase she used to describe the unspecified misfortune that awaits the world-in-decline. Of course, it was not always unspecified, though any name she applied to such a disaster was necessarily inadequate. Sometimes it was distinctly nuclear. She has seen past the first flash and the dust cloud, and after that the wasteland of the fused city. When she saw these things, she remembered the crows, because she imagined that the time after the flash will belong to them, that the city will be reclaimed by their forward-backward-forward migrations through the rubble. Of course there were more than just crows. Her mental list of survivors also included dandelions and Queen Anne's lace. And what else: brown rats, and rattish black squirrels; raccoons and skunks and coyotes. And cats, too, she thought, and ants and spiders, and broom that will cover the melted metal and glass of the detonation's heart, and underneath it will be the territory of scratchers and biters and scamperers, who eat and fuck and bear blind, pinkish babies in the razed city.

This is not to say that Anthea stored up water and astronaut food in some exurban cache, or bought gold or contemplated prophecies in order to determine the date of the coming apocalypse. She left that kind of thing to Jasmine. Her private Kali Yuga was not so epic. It was something that accompanied her, rather, like the decaying hum in an overheated engine or the regular, sub-aural twick-twick of a bit of loose plastic hitting the edge of the turntable each time the disk goes round.

Insubstantial as it was, the hum, or the twick-twick sound can be traced to one night when she was seven years old, eating golden raisins and sitting on the counter in the kitchen of her parents' house in Duncan's Crossing, two hours north of where she now lives. She was listening to a radio documentary about the impact of a nuclear strike on the city. In her memory the house was empty. Her feet did not touch the brick-coloured battleship lino of the floor, not even when the fire in the stove died and it grew cold.

It would begin with a high elevation burst above the hospital at the centre of the greater regional district. The resulting EMP would still traffic and trains and streetlights and pacemakers. So it's five o'clock in the afternoon, and the boats in the harbour drifting, the stock exchange frozen, and all across the city people climbing down from buses, or leaning out of windows to look up and to the south. All of them poised for flashblinding as the second missile detonates the water in the harbour and the skyscrapers and the piles of yellow sulphur on barges that line the northern shore.

"In the centre of the city," said the CBC announcer, "some will have taken refuge in bomb shelters or wine cellars. They will be crushed or suffocate as the earth above them liquefies, then sets in a hard crust."

Outside the blast site, perhaps fifteen kilometres from the centre of the city, those who hid in basements of reinforced concrete will emerge, if they were not trapped, and upon them falls the fallout. This descending sky, Anthea decided as an adult, would be the green of smog at sunset.

Those who are still coherent, though adrenalized, flashburned, endorphined, walk east, along the river, to escape the city. The prevailing winds are westerly, and these refugees will be on foot; they will not outrun the cloud which creeps eastward from the coast at wind speed. Some will make it out of the city, but find that the EMP has destroyed all electronics west of the mountains. Doctors perform amputations without anaesthetic, prepare solutions of sodium bicarb for the radiation sickness that will level survivors hours after exposure.

It is unreasonable, and the memory contains no explanation for her focus, but in Anthea's mind the story ends with the refugees walking out of the city. She explained this to Colm, long after she listened to the radio program. He wanted to know why she had to sleep with the hall light on and the door opened just enough to cast a yellow beam across the foot of her bed. All night, she insisted, not telling him at first that it was a way to know about the EMP, which would approach them silently, she knew from the CBC.

But when Dad asked about it, she could not explain at first, too dreadful were the ragged survivors walking out of the city to Hope. She thought they would have to travel a very long way; she knew they wouldn't all arrive. She could see them walking at night when it was very dark and the hall light did not entirely convince her that the blast had not hit somewhere, silently, far away beyond the shroud of mountains that separated them from the two likely targets. Her brother Max had explained about these two targets: the submarine test range north along the coast, the port city. You want to stop them from fighting back and destroy infrastructure, he said, you want to cripple reconstruction. *In-fra-struc-ture,* she had sounded out. *Reconstruct. Cripple.* Max was twelve and understood these things.

They wouldn't see the blast, Max further explained, except if they were looking that way and it was cloudy out and then they'd see the light hitting the cloud. They would hear it, of course, but much later, as sound travels at 340 m/s. Then if it was at night they might go outside and look south and see an ugly glow on the horizon, like sunrise. That was the city burning. So in Anthea's mind there was the flash, something you could miss unless you were looking up and to the south at the exact moment it reached you. But then there'd be the lights suddenly gone, the radio dead, and it would be like when a storm knocked out the power, and suddenly the sound of the fridge died in the kitchen, and the TV stopped downstairs. And you knew that night you would be eating wieners and beans heated up on the woodstove, and then playing gin rummy by lantern light.

But on that day it would be the end of all wieners and beans, all steady yellow lights, all sunshine. *Nu-ku-lar Winter,* Anthea sounded out. "Nuclear," Max corrected and told her what *that* was.

So when Dad came in to say goodnight, and as he was leaving she reminded him again to leave the hall light on, he stopped, silhouetted in her bedroom doorway. "Panther, what is it?" Panther was his special name for her.

She couldn't say it out loud.

He tried again. "Did you see something scary on TV? Were you watching *Twilight Zone* again?" She shook her head. "Did you read a scary book?"

She looked up at Colm, her covers pulled right up to her chin, and her hands and feet underneath, because no matter how hot you were, you couldn't put anything out of the covers, if you wanted to be safe. "I heard on the radio," she started, then stopped, then started again really quick, like she was running, "I heard on the radio about what would happen if they dropped a bomb and how we would all have to walk out of the city if we weren't killed and then and then." She stopped.

"Bomb?" Colm asked. "What kind of bomb?"

"And there wouldn't be anything in the hospital and we'd all be burnt and have no clothes 'cause our clothes were burnt."

"Oh, buttercup," Colm said. "Oh, sweetheart. I don't think we'd walk out. Maybe we'd stay here. Or go to Grandma Hazel's house on the beach. Then maybe we could eat fish, and grow vegetables in the big garden."

He figured they'd work it out, when it happened, and she shouldn't worry just then. He got her a glass of water, and then pretended to trip and spill the water on her, only the glass was empty and that made her laugh. Then he promised again not to turn off the hall light.

What she remembered after was that he said: "I think it's *unlikely,* Panther," which sounded like he had thought carefully about the problem, and determined that her worries were unreasonable. Later, she realized it *was* unlikely—and she hoped this was what Colm meant—because there would be substantially more damage done than that described in the radio story, which accounted for the effect of only three nuclear warheads: the first high-elevation burst; the detonation in the harbour; the detonation over the suburban hospital.

Even though his voice was cool and kept its distance from fear—it was a voice like the one in her own head when she wanted not to be scared—he could not stop the figure who now walked through Anthea's imaginings. This figure walked along an empty road out of the city, one that passed between ashy mountains, and there was no sound but the wind. And this figure accompanied Anthea in dreams, or emerged in the darkness behind her eyelids when she was half-awake and always unprepared for the familiar silhouette.

And later the figure resolved a little, as though in the intervening years it had begun to draw near to where Anthea stood: she was a woman whose dark hair hung down into her eyes, where it was not burnt, and whose eyes were also dark, whose feet were bare, and in whose arms rested a bundle, that might be a child or might not. Anthea did not like to think about what it might be, and when she dreamed it, did not like to imagine unwrapping the bundle and discovering what it was that lay under the dark rags, what child, or thing, might be carried in the woman's arms.

ON THE BRIXTON CIRCUIT

The dark-haired man at the back of the car was too tall for the second-class seats. He could not stretch his legs and in the cold they had begun to cramp. Twisting slightly to unbend them, he rested his knuckles against the window to his left and watched telegraph poles flick through the reflected interior of the train. He did mental arithmetic—subtraction, as he set possible grosses against inevitable nets and came up with a red tint to his numbers, as he had done quite often on this circuit.

While he'd been embarrassed for months, the present crisis went back to that patch of unwellness in Portland one week previous, when he'd been cut to 3/7s pay ($64.28) for missing twelve shows. It could not have been helped, his lungs were that bad and singing out of the question, even for a crowd as undiscerning as the one at the Portland Palace Theatre. He thought now he had been so ill as to be hallucinating, because in his memories the air in the communal dressing room was textured like glass, through which floated bubbles of viscous yellow stage light. The nice lady with the ballerina dog act had touched his face and said that if one of her pups had a nose that hot she would send him right home to his basket and give him ginger tea. He had taken that as permission and crept out in the dark and rain and found his way back to the boarding house.

Now much better, thank you, but unable to sleep for counting and recounting, he endured the same rain as it seeped in through the window and up through the soles of his shoes. Still in the slight grip of fever, he found this train indistinguishable from the many he had ridden in the last months, from this city to the next. Stopping his count for a moment, he reflected that his days—or his weeks, for he thought now in terms of engagements—were a handful of grubby beads. Not pearls, as he had once imagined when he was the sort of boy who aspired to apposite sentiment. Definitely cheap glass beads, probably hung round the neck of some aging tart.

He shrugged into the collar of his overcoat, resting his chin against the velvet for a moment and liking its texture, though that velvet was the other reason for his current obsession with numbers. He had paid cash for it in San Francisco (the exact price did not bear thinking), enjoying and regretting the sensations of a rich man almost in the same moment. The coat and his illness had forced an uncharacteristic fit of asceticism: he took a cheap ticket ($4.63) and nothing but a cup of tea (5¢) before this night spent sitting up, rattled like a bag of bones by every crossing. He had in his pocket seventy-four cents to see him through to his next payday. Though he could depend on a week's credit at the hotel (which catered to theatre people), that was still only one and a half meals each day, as the establishment served the thinnest of breakfasts and no lunch. There was laundry, as well, and the occasional glass of rye. There were his shoes, which badly needed resoling. He had got so thin he did not like the way his one good suit hung from his shoulders.

He did not wish to panic, and when he felt the rising financial claustrophobia, he disciplined his mind and turned away, picking up the book he had dropped into his lap one hundred miles earlier: Caruso's *The Art of Singing,* which was elementary but soothing in its familiarity. He imagined a scale that ran to the elusive C. *In ascending the scale the furrow in the tongue increases as we come to the higher notes.* Noiselessly he allowed the *cavities of the head free play* with his breath. He imagined perfecting the throb that escaped him at the top of "Ô Souverain, ô juge, ô père," and knew he wouldn't sing it on any of the stages he was visiting this quarter. "I'll Take You Home Again, Kathleen" maybe, or if he was lucky "The Rose of Tralee." In his mind, though, "Ô Souverain."

In reality, he was careening into another wet western city, for another eleven minutes before the intermission, billed *Liam Manley: Sweet Singer of Sweet Songs.* In fact he'd spent the night watching whistle stops through the glass. Sometimes among the larger crowds there were legless and armless men. Blind men, half-blind men from whom he averted his eyes, though they couldn't see him, blind as they were, hidden as he was in his car. He tried to suppress a cough.

He awoke in the tiny, yellowish room. He was not sure how he came to be there. The night before was populated by insubstantial memories of his early morning arrival. Like the previous night's journey, these memories had the quality of dreams, so he forgot his room number but remembered the lobby's thin carpeting, and the brass door handle under his fingers, how it was dull but for a thumb-shaped spot where a thousand hands had rubbed it bright.

He turned over and the bed squeaked. His shoes were below the steam register; his only remaining clean shirt hung above it. He got up and reached under the mattress where he had left his trousers in an attempt to re-form some sort of crease. They were appalling, but he set about picking off under-mattress lint. For a moment he regretted his belief that one could tell a gentleman by the crease in his trousers or the care he took with his shoes (he would have to get at least a shine in the next day or two). He could imagine that natural aristocracy shone through fustian (*well-cut* fustian, of course) but not, somehow, through cheap gabardine.

He made his way downstairs in the afternoon, counting off the meal he had missed and deducting it from his bill. In the hallway he passed another theatre man, a dancer, judging by his tight trousers and the pretentious, syncopated flourish as he took the stairs two at a time. Liam nodded as he passed and the man—he was sure of it—the man gave him a peculiar look. On the street outside he wondered whether it was something he had forgotten? Someone for whom he had been mistaken? He stopped short in the middle of the sidewalk just a block shy of the Brixton Palace Theatre, and the woman behind him said "Pardon me!" and pushed past. No, he had seen that look before. He must have been talking in his sleep, and the man had heard. Or worse, he might have been dreaming, and—he did not like it, but he must admit he had occasionally done so in the past—shouting in his sleep. The man had heard, and not knowing what to think, had dismissed him as a madman or a drunkard. He thought the man had stepped unnecessarily wide in the hall, as though Liam were someone to be avoided.

He wanted to go and find the man and explain to him. He wanted to make the point that he was not mad, just unwell. But in the past he had tried explaining, and it had left him feeling even more peculiar, and the person to whom he explained would grow very quiet, and then when he finished the silence was unpleasant.

The theatre was old, but not yet old enough to be picturesque. It was still a frontier sort of place, with raw boards in the collective dressing room and an ugly plush curtain. From the stage door he walked a narrow, cold hallway to the manager's office, and then found his way to the stage. It was still early, before the matinee, and he sat on a scarred chair at stage left and watched all the men in shirtsleeves walk up and down the aisles after their brooms. Above them the smoke-brown walls were stencilled with crooked lozenges in brick-coloured paint.

Colonials, he thought.

Even so, the stage was deep and black and still. When the men spoke, their voices were lost in the hollow of the huge room. It was cold. His nose dripped. He smoked a cigarette and thought of rye whiskey. He thought of how he'd look incandescent and singing, and how stage lights would hide the ugly stencils and render the empty space around him a luminous dark. He allowed the *cavities of the head free play.*

After that it mattered less that outside the air was a clammy suspension of coal smoke, and every surface on the east side of the city bloomed with that floating particulate. The theatre was beyond all that: if he measured it, he'd find it larger inside than out. He'd find that corridors and insufficient forty-watt lighting ran for mile beyond mile on either side, emerging in other theatres, dressing rooms, stage doors.

And if he began walking along those corridors what would he find? He would find an exit somewhere among the doors that opened on other doors, a final threshold that would lead somewhere else entirely. In search of such an exit Liam had sung in dull, flickering halls from Portland to Seattle to Edmonton and back again, avoiding places where people knew a damned thing about music. Therefore condemned to places where his perfect tenor's name and face—like Ivor Novello! Like Rudolph Valentino!—was more valuable than what was left of his voice. Liam crossed the creaking boards of all those stages, stood before frayed red velvet seats, or garish fresh velour. He clasped his hands as though crossed in hopeless love, and in every audience he knew which women smiled wetly and imagined themselves the object of his song. He always knew the ones who would wait outside the theatre for him, who would introduce themselves, and say "yes" when he asked them to take a walk. They always smelled like *Quelques Fleurs.*

On the morning of the fourth day of his engagement, Liam lay on the lumpy chesterfield in the hotel drawing room, breathing the sweet, whitish smoke of the magician's pipe. The magician sat in a wingchair beside the fireplace, reading a newspaper. Liam hadn't recognized him without his turban (which was purple silk with an enormous ruby fastener), and had only realized who it was when they'd been sitting in silence too long to be politely broken. Liam was nearly asleep, with his jaw unhinged and a bead of drool forming in the corner of his mouth. He stayed in the lobby because it was the least chilly room in the hotel, though he had never seen a fire. Instead of a fire, the grate held a fan of shiny, orange paper.

Somewhere far away a door opened and closed, followed by a murmur, then footsteps fast and sharp, driven like the blows of a hammer right through the thin carpet to the floorboards. Liam opened his eyes and his heart hiccoughed. He wiped his mouth free of the drool, then he sat up quickly and the blood left his head. A voice cut through in his momentary disorientation: "Mr. Manley! I have been looking for you!"

Liam coughed. "Oh—yes?"

"Yes. Mr. Manley. It is absolutely crucial that you and I discuss the details of a great undertaking and waste no time, for your presence is imperative for our success!" The man who stood above him wore a bowler hat and carried a furled umbrella. He was immaculately dressed, his face so clean it shone.

"My. Presence?"

"But in my excitement I have pressed too quickly, and offended your sensibility, no doubt, for which I apologize. My name is Goshawk, and I am here to present you with an opportunity." They shook hands. Goshawk's was small and cool.

"Please sit down, Mr. Goshawk."

"Thank you, Mr. Manley, I will! Now I feel I must speed to the heart of the matter, as there is no time to waste! You, sir, are a man of high culture and real European sensibility."

Liam ran one hand over his hair and his fingers came away oily—a nervous habit he had long endeavoured to break. He could not wipe them in the open, though, and let his hand rest on his knee, palm up. Some men wiped them on their shirts, at the back under their jackets, but he thought that a dirty habit. A response seemed necessary, so Liam nodded.

"Are you familiar with the local benefactor, Mr. David Kilgour?"

"I have heard his name."

"Then perhaps you've heard of my employer, his wife, Mrs. Leticia Kilgour. She is a woman of remarkable sensitivity who, due to the straitened conditions of her youth, never benefited from a complete education—at least, not as a young person. However, being a woman of superior character and dedication, she pressed on in the face of all obstacles. She has now determined to pursue a course of action in keeping with her early ambitions. She combines a prodigious will with a fine natural sensibility, Mr. Manley. Truly—a great woman made greater by her early difficulties."

Here Mr. Goshawk paused to contemplate Mrs. Kilgour's personal greatness.

Liam felt he had to ask, though he was not sure it was polite to be so direct: "What course did she wish to pursue?"

"She was gifted with a fine soprano, and through dint of effort she has improved on nature! Her goal in contacting you is threefold. First, for the simple joy of singing with one as gifted as yourself. Second, to enlist your help in support of the Arts, and arrange a tour through the west, a tour for the benefit of those not commonly exposed to the more cultivated pleasures of the European concert hall. Finally, a series of recordings."

"Recordings?"

"Solos and some of the historical duets—the great moments in German and Italian opera that call men's hearts to better things! My employer believes strongly in the improving nature of fine music. It is her goal that others should benefit as she did."

"She'd like to sing duets with whom?"

"With you, sir! She is aware of your gifts, as well as the years you spent in Paris under the best masters! She wishes to work with you, sir, the aim being a performance that would present the greatest moments in the recorded catalogue."

"I must. That is. I must think this over." He wondered how he should ask about payment, and looked down at his hand. The slight film of hair oil was not visible, at least.

"Of course. Mr. Manley, there will be some small remuneration involved, though I do not wish to upset you with such worldly matters." Mr. Goshawk mentioned a sum. For a moment Liam didn't breathe. Then he thought about new handkerchiefs and bespoke shoes.

"Well, I'd better meet your employer, then."

Three minutes past the appointed hour, Liam brushed his coat for the second time, and adjusted his tie. In the foyer he studied the only decent mirror the hotel afforded, and with a careful ceremony placed his hat upon his head. Mrs. Kilgour's car stood at the curb. He had seen it from his window, and when the message came, he had sent back that the driver should wait. Then he had counted to sixty before he opened the door. He left the hotel, careful not to make eye contact with the man in grey serge who stood beside the car in the rain. Liam had decided earlier that the driver should recognize him as a gentleman, and open the door. He slowed slightly, to give the fellow time to do so, looking at the silver figure—a winged woman—on the car's hood.

"Sir," the man said, with a lazy little tap on the brim of his hat. Liam acknowledged it with a nod he thought would be called "cool."

Once inside, Liam relaxed a little, and examined the black leather and walnut interior with curiosity and pleasure. He had imagined quite clearly what it might be like to sit in this sort of car, though in that version of events it was his own automobile, of course, and a grey Lagonda. But this black Rolls-Royce did very well. The car passed the railway tracks and the station, the city's low, sprawling business district, and then neat, suburban houses just going up. Neighbourhoods came and went, the lots grew larger, now fenced and gated, pointed and curlicued towers rising over the shrubberies. There were grey-green rhododendrons piled up against the stone and brick walls; there were rose gardens behind iron railings. There were black-frocked women marching children, airing babies in huge perambulators. If one had to settle at the end of the world, he thought, this might not be bad.

The car slowed and drew up to a grey stone gatehouse. The chauffeur exchanged a few words with the shirt-sleeved man who opened the gates, and they drove through a small park full of bare rose bushes, a drab little army encamped around squares of grass. He did not know whether to be impressed or horrified, especially when he saw the monster at its heart— Craiglockhart Castle—a sham baronial manor in coastal granite, squatting in the garden like an ogre, shaggy with towers, points, a cupola, and medieval arches.

After the chauffeur dawdled a moment, Liam slid out of the back seat, and approached the massive, bronze-studded doors in the *porte-cochère*. Using the same tactic he'd employed outside the hotel, he stalked up the steps without hesitation, and again (miraculously) the doors opened.

The hall was grand, but it lacked the texture of age that had so impressed him in the large houses he had seen in London. Stained glass (pictures of King Arthur, he thought, and knights and ladies) tinted the grey light a flattering gold. His hat and coat disappeared in the hands of a maid, and he was shown to a south-facing drawing room, decorated with pre-Raphaelite paintings of St. Cecelia, Orpheus, and the nine muses, one half of it occupied by an enormous piano. Alone and not sure where to stand, he went to the windows that overlooked the rose gardens.

He heard her footsteps first, and then her voice, "Mr. Manley!" Her accent was common Canadian, carefully refined by long vowels and a drawled "r". Mrs. Kilgour wished to speak with elegance.

When he turned to face her, he saw a tall woman—grave and handsome, dressed in dull purple, as though in a late stage of Victorian mourning. Her chin was weak, but she countered it with a powerful jaw. Her fingers were white, thick, folded neatly when she was at rest. Her skirts hung below the ankle, but beneath them he detected enormous feet. "Sit down," she said, "and talk to me of music!" As though no one ever did.

Five minutes later he did not like to admit that he was out of his depth. She watched him closely, and had he been a few years younger, he would have blushed under her long gazes and smiles, though she was of such an age that he could not regard it as impropriety. He had expected a coquettish denial of her ambitions, had come prepared to draw her out, press her to sing for him. This was not the case.

"I am very glad of the opportunity to labour beside you, Mr. Manley," she said very businesslike as soon as they had properly introduced themselves. He was scandalized, though a little relieved that he would not have to flirt it out of her.

"Mrs. Kilgour, I'm flattered, but I'm not sure why you've chosen me when there's a fine opera company in town that would welcome you." He was not sure he wanted to know how she had come to hear his name.

"But Mr. Manley, it is only a little bit of a company! And as to where I found your name, well I heard you sing once in the home of my great friend, before the war." She mentioned a name, a place he had sung in the early spring of 1914, in a room full of conservatory roses. He had been there half the night, because after the contracted hour-long recital, the ladies had requested sentimental Scots ballads (he remembered transposing them so that he need not face the high B or even the A) and he had not known how to withdraw politely. Around midnight they dismissed him and he had gone home with his scarf wrapped twice around his throat. He had taken away a rose for his lapel, and warmed it in his bare hands so that it would not wilt in the cold of his homeward walk across the city.

She went on. "I can't think why you take such work, Mr. Manley, and in vaudeville! When I saw your name, I thought I had been sent a gift. I remember how sweet you sang 'My Luve is Like a Red, Red Rose.' There are few men alive that can sing that song as sweet as my father did, and you are among them. And I thought, I'll send for him and we will do this work together!"

"What work is that, Mrs. Kilgour?"

"Why, there are men and women up and down this coast with not a note of music in their lives! And some of them with a natural feel for it, I'm sure—but no opportunity for the God-given pleasures of the human voice raised in song. We must do something, give them wholesome food of the spirit on which to sup!" Liam found himself nodding. "We will start in the coal mines. There are good people there, who will welcome us. After that, we will see what is needed farther north, among the fishermen and the poor Indians."

Liam shrivelled, but pressed on. "Did you have a program in mind? I imagine recital pieces?"

"Yes, I had thought on the great inspiring duets. Wagner and Verdi, of course. No hymns, we don't want to frighten those that come in search of entertainment, either. You'll catch more flies with honey." She nodded like a female Machiavelli—no, Liam, corrected himself, as though she thought herself to be one. He pitied the men in her husband's offices, the women in her service. "But also some of the homely songs, such as they would have heard as children. To soothe them, and remind them of wholesome things." She smiled, carnivorous and maternal. "You look like the sort of man who appreciates wholesome country melodies."

Liam swallowed, resisting the new image he had of himself in a shabby Girl Guide hall, beside a battered piano, singing "And Let The Rest Of The World Go By" to a shuffling crowd of coal miners and their wives, all done up in Sunday suits and hats with cherries on them.

He thought a moment, and then said, "You have the advantage of me, Mrs. Kilgour. You have heard me and I have not yet heard you. Will you sing for me?"

Mrs. Kilgour proceeded silently to the piano and stood beside the bench where she could see the music that she'd placed there before he'd set foot in the house. He waited, and then realized what she wanted and joined her at the piano. By some unpleasant chance the music was "And Let The Rest Of The World Go By." He rippled through the opening bars. It was a fine piano, warm, with a pearly treble.

Her singing hurt, more than he had thought it could. He had assumed that she would be amateurish, but not this. She stood at his left, and as she approached the sentimental final bars, her fingers closed on his shoulder, so he felt them to his bones through the layers of suit and shirt and flesh. He glanced up and saw that something was expected of him, as she smiled at him, then shut her eyes and raised her head. But what, what could she possibly want more than that he listen without throwing himself from the window? Oh—there it was. He joined in harmony—or what would have been harmony under conventional circumstances: *a place that's known to God alone and let the rest of the world go by.*

"Oh fine, fine!" she said, clapping her hands as they finished. "Oh Mr. Manley we will raise the heart of any who hears us!" She sat beside him on the bench. She smelled of peppermint and a sour stomach. "I will say, though, Mr. Manley, that I think you struck wrong on the dying fall. I like an even tone withdrawing there, so that the listener might have a moment to think on the meaning of the song, not just end it, plunk!" She struck his knee to show how she did not want it to end, and demonstrated her own ideal with a diminuendo honk. "But we'll go to work before the concert series."

"When did you have in mind for this—?"

"Oh, no more than a month or two, I think. January at the latest. I have thought on this a great deal, Liam, and I am ready to act!"

"But do you think, Mrs. Kilgour, it's time enough—?"

She looked stern, but said gently, "We are artists, Liam, and it is a great, godly thing we do. We cannot help but be ready."

PRODUCED BY THE ACTION OF LIGHT

There were no contracts. Mrs. Kilgour mentioned that some of the musicians had asked for them, and she had thought better of involving such worldly men. Instead there were large, irregular cheques, and he moved into a better hotel. Mrs. Kilgour was happy that she could now visit him in the afternoons, and even remarked that he was much healthier-looking since he had moved into the CPR establishment. By a kind of passive adoption he joined her circle, or her clan, more accurately, which orbited Craiglockhart Castle. He was often there for meals, and met her friends and the collection of cousins, nieces and nephews who appeared and disappeared by Mrs. Kilgour's desires. In spring he thought he would play tennis on their courts, if he could learn how, and take a boat out on the little ornamental lake in the park, or go to their hunting lodge north of the city. He met the city's fast set and went with them, once or twice, to the one nightclub the provincial little place afforded.

There was work to do, however, lazy rehearsals often interrupted by short sermons regarding the Power of Music, and photographs for the posters, the programs and the newspaper. He had already given a few minutes to a man from the society page, and quite a good picture had shown up in the paper. He liked it; he looked like a gentleman, though a bit threadbare. He didn't yet have his new suits then and been forced to make do with old charcoal gabardine, but it was not so shabby after treatment in the hotel laundry.

She had wanted the photographs taken in the conservatory, but there he had put his foot down. It was no better than a wedding or engagement then, he said; if we are to set out as artists, we must begin as artists. She had fluttered, then submitted girlishly to his demand. Her secretary, Nora, hired the Temple Theatre for an hour in the morning before the first program, and made arrangements with her photographer, a nice man who worked for the theatre and photographed weddings around the city.

Liam approached the Temple, which had until the month before been the pinnacle of his aspirations. His *immediate aspirations,* he corrected himself. There was still the grey Lagonda and the contract with a large company, though it might not be New York or Milan. San Francisco, perhaps, or Buenos Aires. Now he stood at the theatre's great doors, which were made of glass and copper, glimmered with vines and arched like the Alhambra. It was nine o'clock. He wore a new suit, charcoal broadcloth with a midnight-blue tie, purple socks, and jade cufflinks. He was to meet the photographer at nine, precisely, but it did not do to be kept waiting by a photographer, so he thought it better to be a little late.

The doors gave, and he was in a hideous lobby again; it was one of the new kind, meant for lounging and circulating, with gold plush benches and pink granite pillars. The steps were pink granite too, with a brass handrail and a carved pink granite balustrade.

He climbed the steps to the double doors that opened into the theatre itself, walking briskly, ignoring the janitor who looked at him, and seemed about to ask him his business. Liam raised his chin and the man did not stop him.

Inside, the photographer attended to his equipment, and at first did not seem to notice Liam. Liam waited a little longer, determined that the man should acknowledge him. He smiled what he thought of as his laconic smile, the one he had recently adopted for shopgirls and desk clerks.

The photographer looked up, and when he saw Liam standing in the centre aisle, he stood up straight, one hand at his tie, the other resting on the accordion-pleated cardboard of his camera. "Mr. Manley?" he said. "Is that Mr. Manley?"

"Yes."

"My name is Walter Lyon. I was to meet you here." He looked down at his watch. "I was to meet you here at nine o'clock."

"Indeed."

"I understood it was to be Mrs. Kilgour as well. I understood—"

"Later, Lyon. You're to take my portraits first." Liam felt expansive, warm, putting the man at his ease like that. He might have been chilly and superior. He might even have been rude. He could have reported badly to Mrs. Kilgour, if he had wished it. He was so happy to find that he did not wish it, that he smiled at Lyon, and at the little girl beside him. Liam could not guess her age, but she seemed reasonable, and sweet in her little white smock.

On the stage, Lyon had stopped. "I hope you aren't bothering Mr. Manley, Hazel. I bring my daughter with me, sometimes. It's a treat for her as she loves the Temple. I hope she doesn't trouble you. She is a good girl."

"Fine, fine," he said, and Lyon returned to his preparations. With more of that *laconic* grace he had so lately cultivated, Liam walked the length of the apron to examine the caryatids that supported the proscenium, their substantial and nicely-shaped bosoms drifting high and round, clung all about with plaster drapery that looked like wet cheesecloth.

In a moment Lyon was with him again, standing at his elbow. As he turned to face them, Lyon bit his lip and said, "If you are ready, Mr. Manley, would you join us at the piano?" Leaving the caryatids and their impressive bosoms, Liam returned to the piano and leaned on the music rack, his legs crossed. He wished he had a slim, black cigarette between the fingers of his left hand. As Lyon and his assistant busied themselves with an extinction meter, then the cameras and the last of the flash powder, the little girl lolled on her chair and stared silently at Liam.

"Your name is Hazel?" he asked, pleased to condescend to a little girl, after the fussy, overdressed children at the Castle.

"Hazel Lyon," she said.

"Are you here to help your father?"

"I like to watch him take pictures." She was staring at Liam now, not having realized his condescension. He had forgotten that children could stare so steadily and openly.

"How old are you?"

She raised her right hand, the fingers spread wide. "I'm five. Pretty soon I'll be six." Now she stuck up her thumb.

"You should be in school, not hanging around in theatres. What does your mother say about it?"

"She doesn't know. It's just Dad and me." The little girl smiled, then set her steady gaze on the stage, examining it with what seemed to Liam un-childlike intensity. "Do you have a little girl?" Hazel asked.

"No," Liam answered, "but I have a little sister. Much older than you, though." And Liam wanted, suddenly, to say more, and tell how he had not seen his sister in years and years, but Lyon and his assistant Berezowsky had finished their ceremony and made their invocations, and he did not even have time to tell her Ella's name before Lyon looked up.

"Hazel, leave the gentleman alone." And then, "If you would face Mr. Berezowsky, Mr. Manley, I think I could capture your profile adequately."

Once properly at work on the portraits, Liam was himself again, finding comfort in the grave attention of the two men as they manipulated light and shadow around his face, and composed their frames by laws intriguing but unknown to him.

Liam was used to being watched. What success he had, he did not like to admit, was often due to pictures that appeared in local newspapers on the first day of his engagements, and he kept a greater variety of promotional photographs than most men of his profession. As Lyon set his flash powder, Liam imagined himself through that other eye, the one floating four feet above the stage, and in whose long glance he would become monochrome, rendered on paper and distributed on handbills and programs. Out in the city there were some young ladies who would keep those handbills and programs; some might even tuck them into the frames of their mirrors, to look at while they brushed their hair. Many of them would come to hear him sing.

The proofs arrived in the evening mail, which would impress Mrs. Kilgour, Liam thought, and good for Lyon; she would be a useful patron. Anyway, the man did fine work, especially these close studies where his eyes were so deeply shadowed they seemed kohl-darkened, and his hair so black against his white brow, and his hands wrought finely in soft grey and black. He was almost ashamed of his unruly happiness when he found himself on paper, looking as he did in his own heart. Lyon had seen him as he really was, had seen him as he could be, too, as an artist and a gentleman in charcoal broadcloth, leaning on the music rack. Liam propped his favourites up on the little lamp table, and took off his shoes so he could stretch out on the bed and look at the proofs.

That evening he went to the Castle for dinner, and together they picked out the suitable pictures. Mrs. Kilgour looked at him dewily and said, "You remind me so much of Clive!" And though Liam knew nothing about Clive, he smiled bashfully and said he was flattered by the comparison.

MARA O'MARIO

He was not prepared for her myopic generosity. After the initial flood of gifts and cheques, he tried to spend little and lay up a store against the days she forgot his dependence, though his name linked with hers meant unlimited credit and obliging shopkeepers who nodded and knew of course sir that they need not press, he was a gentleman. And did he wish a dozen pairs of socks or two—and had sir considered driving gloves, very useful in this climate. Once he had his cards (*Liam Manley, Tenor* they read) he went out each day and bought something, and when all the parcels arrived in his hotel, he set them on the desk in the bay window and looked at them in their brown paper, his name inked on their labels so nicely. Each afternoon he unwrapped shoes and books and socks, a wallet, a monocle, cologne, monogrammed writing paper, a fountain pen with three gold nibs, a traveller's writing desk, a valise of mahogany leather and burgundy silk. He unwrapped cigarettes and imported chocolates; he unwrapped cigar clips, ties, handkerchiefs. He bought charms for the bracelets of ladies he had not yet met, and scent for women he had not yet seduced.

He unwrapped them and put them carefully away, but found his eyes ran over these possessions—so handsome, that writing desk!—and he took comfort in them when he was meant to be reading a new book or *allowing the cavities of his head free play.* Sometimes he did not even like to use the things, but just admired them stacked in their drawers and cupboards and thought how well they witnessed his discernment. Other men faced with such new wealth would spend like the newly wealthy, but his long attention to good taste had saved him, and he was satisfied that his selections were indistinguishable from those a young man of quality might make.

Once, though, a week went by without the nearly-anonymous arrival of a cheque (folded into a sheet of writing paper with no message but her name and address engraved at the top), and the panic rose again, and he resented their unofficial relationship. He never mentioned this to her, saying to himself that he did not like to embarrass her with the reminder that he was a professional, and she merely an interested amateur. Or perhaps he did not wish to offend her delicacy.

Or he must not be disloyal: she was generous. He returned one morning to his suite to see that her generosity had reached a new pitch. The phonograph, its huge horn like a dark morning glory, stood in the centre of the room, on a cabinet of deep red wood. Beside it a box of brown envelopes.

He dropped his coat to the floor and knelt. He knew who had sent it, though there was no letter. It was afterward he considered that she did not need to identify herself because her hand on the machine was unmistakeable: Mrs. Kilgour hardly needed a name. She was the nexus of his life and the hotel knew it.

But there was the phonograph. He touched the case and left a faint smudge when he drew back his hand. He wiped his fingers on his handkerchief and polished away the mark, then lifted the lid and touched the black rubber of the disk, as supple and cool as skin, with a faint burr that grabbed his fingertips. The machine's scent was better than *eau de cologne*: beeswax, varnish, rubber, Bakelite, metal.

He turned to the boxes on the floor, fumbling through the closest; it didn't matter what or which record, just so he would hear it. Then he slowed himself, running his fingers over the loose corners of the brown paper sleeves, so they fluttered in his ears like cards. He pulled out one to read the label. Not Nash's gentrified Puccini, no nasal *La bohème* in the accents of the south. He flipped through the Caruso, the McCormack (he would listen to McCormack after he had found what he wanted, to determine what the man could possibly have. Liam had never heard anything compelling from McCormack) past de Reszke, Cortis, Gigli. Then he found the inestimable Mara O'Mario.

As he touched it he returned, in memory, to a night more than six years before at Covent Garden, when he had heard O'Mario in *Le Cid*, and been so transfixed by the man's voice that he had felt something in his bosom he could only call "surrender." He did not exactly know what he had surrendered, only that he had wept, and as he walked home across the city he had pledged himself to O'Mario, and to Rodrigo, and to the King and Judge and Father, and the life to which O'Mario seemed to call him. The exhilaration had lasted weeks, and for a time he had been sure (so sure!) that such a surrender must be accepted, and that a response was imminent.

Sometimes when he sang, Liam thought of the man's voice and wondered if a little of it might live on in his own: he might still contain a rolling echo of that evening, in the pulse he felt that was more than memory; it was like a standing wave that reverberated in his own thorax, through his throat and his skull. If he had any gift, it was that memory inside him, which might one day change the quality of sound he produced.

Liam selected O'Mario's "Ô Souverain, ô juge, ô père." He slid it from brown paper textured like fallen leaves, and set it gently on the smooth disk of rubber. He dropped the needle, then rocked back onto his heels, then lay on the carpet with no regard for his shirt or his trousers. He shut his eyes. From the hiss the piano sounded, then the first whisper of the voice, beneath it the substructure of a breath not heard but felt. Liam placed his fingers beneath each ear and dropped his jaw, imagined Mara O'Mario's breath underlying the lyric line, imagined his own open throat like a hollow reed.

He replayed the aria fifteen times, each time listening for O'Mario's breath, so that it would become his own, and for a moment he held it. More than a memory, it seemed to him a change in his carriage, the angle of his jaw along his throat, the lift of his diaphragm and shoulders. Listening that way he could recognize (without doubt! without question!) the distance between his work and Mara O'Mario's. Again he felt the flutter of doors opening and saw stretching before him the path he would take through them, and where it would lead, and the sound that, in the end, would issue from his lips.

THE KILGOURS OF THE WEST: TEMPLE THEATRE INSTALLATION TEXT (DRAFT ONE)

Having secured her position as the city's Foremost Hostess, Leticia Kilgour turned her not insubstantial talents toward her first love: music. She determined that all the energies and resources of her extensive patronage would go to creating and supporting a community of musicians in this thriving outpost of Empire. Thus, Leticia Kilgour is responsible for the hybrid of frontier vigour and Old World sensibility that so marked the city in the early twentieth century.

Under the tutelage of her charming, musical father, Mrs. Kilgour had learned the best of the Highland tradition, and especially Robbie Burns' fine ballads. Often she described this charming scene to her children and grandchildren, and each of them remembered, late in life, the power music held over their otherwise tranquil matriarch. Mrs. Kilgour continued her father's country custom of musical evenings in a more refined and sophisticated manner, as she organized a series of concert parties during her first seasons as the city's foremost hostess. But even these rather splendid affairs invariably ended when Mrs. Kilgour, coaxed by her admiring guests, consented to sing one of the sad, sweet songs of that fine poet. One can imagine this noble, serene woman taking the floor with a quiet strength and lifting her lyrical, untrained voice—the voice of the country girl she always was—in one of those old favourites, "My Luve is Like a Red, Red Rose."

The photographs taken the night of Leticia Kilgour's Gala Performance show a woman at ease before an audience. A woman who, in the high summer of her middle age, has the serenity and strength earned from many trials overcome. Her carefully chosen partner is a charming counterpoint in all his masculine vitality. He is Liam Manley, an aristocratic Irish tenor trained in Europe, his career tragically curtailed by service during The Great War [INSERT BIOGRAPHICAL DETAILS: MANLEY]. Together they are poised at the watershed of Canadian history: the youthful vigour of the twentieth century—wounded, but ascendant—beside the wisdom and security of the nineteenth. United in song these two allow us a glimpse of the components that make up our nation, existing in mutual respect and admiration at the dawn of Canada's New Age: a century that will belong to Our Lady of the Snows, this great, northern nation.

On the evening of [INSERT DATE], 1920 the Temple Theatre and Opera House waited in hushed anticipation for eight o'clock. Mrs. Kilgour sat before the mirror in her dressing room at Craiglockhart Castle, and contemplated the face of a woman content, one who has laboured long and whose goal is in sight, one who need now only take the final leisurely steps to the summit, from which point she may survey the world she has created.

Elsewhere in the city at an equally elegant, though more masculine dressing table, Mr. Liam Manley ties the immaculate black silk tie for which he is deservedly famous. If it was not for the natural asceticism of the aristocratic face, one would almost call his attention to such details "foppish." But given the fine, aquiline nose, and the ache in his war-assaulted eyes, the word is inappropriate. Mr. Liam Manley turns the precise attention of the artist to all things. His perfect tie is an expression of his aesthetic nature, not his surrender to fashion.

As these two figures—so different, yet so closely bound to one another by their mutual aspirations and the burdens of their genius—make their way to the theatre, the final adjustments take place within the theatre. All over the city the elite make their way to the Opera House, unaware of the spectacle that awaits: the glorious return of Society after the long privations of War.

It is hard to imagine today the impact the six-storey Opera House would have had in a low city of wood and brick, still revealing its frontier roots in false fronts and transient hotels. One cannot remain unmoved by the thought of their arrival in the three-storey lobby of the Temple Theatre and Opera House, decorated out of Leticia Kilgour's purse, but for the pleasure and civic pride of every citizen in that youthful, thriving Metropolis. Mrs. Kilgour had given them a gift that betrayed her generous spirit: spectacle, genius, a whisper of elegance and grace at the end of the empire.

Never a woman of pretense, Mrs. Kilgour had arranged for the simplest of floral tributes, and to that end garlands of 10,000 pink roses, shipped in from California, decorated the pink pillars and oriental flourishes of the new lobby, bringing with them the summer scent of cottage gardens. The stage too was shrouded in pink velvet curtains and roses, these temporarily replacing the wine-red hangings that matched the Temple seats. Further, she had clad the ushers and ticket-takers in Highland dress, a new, blood-red tartan she had designed for her family. In their daggers and sporrans and eagle-feathered bonnets, the Temple's serving men struck a warlike note among the pink velvet and flowers, a whisper of the ferocious pioneering Scottish spirit that had so characterized the Kilgour success and still identifies its legacy.

As the glittering audience—as sumptuously attired as any Old World gathering!—rustled to its seats and held its breath, the houselights dropped and the stage leapt into glorious illumination. As the pink curtains parted, the true magnitude of Leticia Kilgour's achievement was apparent to all. The banks of pink and red roses—the choicest of those shipped up the coast—swirled in starbursts and spirals. Before the audience could even grasp the elegancies of the stage, the musicians, immaculate in black and white, each with a pink rose in his lapel, took the stage, followed by the first violin, by Mr. Manley, and finally Mrs. Kilgour, resplendent in the pink and red spangled costume of the prima donna.

One cannot hope to evoke the joy this great-hearted woman felt as she took the stage, one can only imagine her pleasure in arrival, and defer to the unimpeachable taste of her recital program, reproduced here:

[INSERT PROGRAM?]

TERTIARY ARCANA

Brynn only worked for the institute while she completed some manuscript. Brynn, who was ambitious, theoretical, going-places, and applying-for-things, had asked about her area over beer one afternoon. Anthea had explained about the cookbooks, and how she liked to read about old-time food, and other than that she didn't really mind. Brynn had said, "Anthea, are you really that clueless? No one can be that clueless except if they try. It's got to be for something."

"I'm not that clueless!" she'd answered first. Then after thinking and getting a bit pissy she'd said, "Maybe. I probably am. I totally don't care." Then she just took another big drink of her beer and asked Brynn what she did. It was military commemorative practices and performance in the Canadian post-colony. After that she didn't have to say much, except "hmm" and "really?"

When she delivered a box of photographs to Blake's office, she considered pointing out that Brynn would be a better choice for this sort of work, but Blake was on the phone and he waved his hand as she left the pictures on the floor beside his desk.

That was just as well: she had preferred not to think about the implications of her research. Instead she remembered the recipe she had read for a terrine saturated in goose fat and studded with pistachios, or the 1921 recording of "Ô Souverain, ô juge, ô père," or Liam Manley's kissable, kohl-darkened eyes. She also preferred not to think about how the Institute got its money, because Mrs. Kilgour exploited Anthea's coal-mining ancestors in the long-ago, or how it was rumoured that the Kilgours sent imported Pinkertons after labour leaders. That probably wasn't what Blake wanted for an installation in a recovery project designed to promote the performing arts on the poverty-stricken east side of the city. The east side, where Jasmine's Prophet was operating again, lost among his faithful, laying hands on nubile blondes, initiating them into the mysteries of Parach.

That afternoon Anthea walked home from the Institute with fifteen pictures of Liam Manley in her backpack. She had written 1,108 words in the double-wide office all the R.A.s shared, but she'd deleted them shortly afterward, because they sounded stupid. She was thinking about *Liam Manley, Tenor* when she saw a woman on a park bench beside a small sign that offered "Tarot Card Readings By Donation." Anthea sat down opposite her.

"I can give you one question," the woman said. Anthea nodded and set a toonie down on a silk-covered board that lay between them on the bench. The woman did not touch the coin, but neither did she reach for the cards. She had white skin and hair, and wore a black crocheted tam. Her lips were painted a hot, dark pink, faded in the middle and bleeding into the creases around her mouth.

"Do I need to cross your palm," Anthea asked, "with silver?"

The woman shook her head.

"Okay, do you want a question out loud?"

The woman made "um, yeah?" eyebrows.

"Right. Yeah. No. Should I just go for it?"

"Sweetie, we can't have a reading if you don't—" the woman stopped and lowered her eyebrows. She did not ask what it was. She shuffled elaborately, magician-style. Anthea liked the soft little claps the cards made, like a pigeon's wings. The woman set out three piles to the left with her left hand. Then repiled them. Then again. Then the three piles circled like a shell game.

"Sweetie, I want you to point. Not touch, 'kay? Point, at the pile that gives you the most heat."

Anthea held her left hand out over the first pile, then the second. She felt nothing she would call "heat," and when she tested the third it was only to make the Tarot Lady think she was actually considering the different energies presented to her. Then without thinking, she pointed at one, but pointed too quickly and touched the topmost card of the far left pile.

As she touched it, some blur shifted in the corner of her eye. A man she had not paid particular attention to leapt away from the fire hydrant against which he had been leaning. He slid in close beside her, talking hard and fast at the side of her head.

Everything he said smelled like cigarettes. "You want to let the devil in like that? You want to do that? You want to let him on your back? Hey?" He was a tightly wound man in a baseball cap and goatee. His eyes were tiny and brown, and they kept locking on hers, so it was an effort to look away.

The Tarot Lady didn't act like she noticed. She flipped the first card. It was the Queen of Swords, reversed to Anthea. It was her own card, but she didn't have time to think through the implications, because the two of them were talking at once and she wanted to hear what both of them said.

"You want to let him in? He's on your back now, woman."

"Right, the dark lady—she has dark hair, dark eyes like you got. Queen of Swords. Air behaving as water, think rain, mist, storm clouds," the Tarot Lady said. "The dark woman, intelligent, yeah, but cold. Infertility. Widowhood. Doom. That sort of thing. Also think Medea, Joan of Arc. Your basic martyrs." She looked away from Anthea and began scooping up the remaining cards, then passed them from hand to hand in an effortless bridge. *Doom*, Anthea thought, and the Tarot Lady made perfect fans out of her deck, then folded them and spread them again, and ran a wave along the silk-covered board.

All that time the Evangelist lectured them, though Anthea seemed to be his only audience. "Dark lady? You commend your soul to Christ, woman, before he eats you up—you want be swallowed by the devil?"

Anthea stood. He was still talking: "Yeah, you can run but you can't hide! I touch you." Here the man's hand shot out and held her wrist for a moment. His touch lingered like a hospital bracelet, so she tried to rub it away with her right hand, but found she could not. "And I cast him out, but that's not going to last—you can't lie today! I've touched you!" The Tarot Lady was staring in the opposite direction, as though she had just seen someone she went to high school with, and had to look twice to be sure.

As Anthea stood up, the Tarot Lady said, "Whatever it is, you be careful, girl."

The Evangelist had returned to his fire hydrant, but he was still shouting after her as she walked away: "You let him in, child! You're gonna need me to cast him out!"

If Jasmine were to make contact, it might be like that. But was she speaking through the cards or the tightly wound Evangelist? How was she supposed to tell the message from the surrounding static? Maybe the message was for someone who stood in the bus line on the other side of the street, who heard only a few words of the exchange— *dark.... soul... cast*— words that, to her, could mean something dreadful, or lovely. That was the problem with omens, she had once tried to explain to Jasmine when they were drunk, you never know when they stop or start, and once you accept the premise, the whole universe has suddenly become a message.

APOPHENIA

After the Tarot card reading, Anthea began to admit that something unusual was happening, but she still avoided the kind of explanations Jasmine would have liked. She did watch for signs, though, in dreams, or the way birds flew across the sky. She tried to remember the things Jasmine had told her about chance encounters, about the significant times of day, what it means when a knife falls on the kitchen floor.

"What you've got to *really get*," Jasmine said, "is that everything is a message, and everything is connected—what you did six months ago makes today, and what happened here a hundred years ago makes right now. So if you see red apples in a green bowl on a Tuesday, or if you wear gold, or smell sandalwood, or if there's a north wind—that all tells you what's really going on. We're distracted by the material" —here she gestured at the things around them, beach, fire, moon, streetlights—"we have to focus in order to perceive what's real."

So for the sake of argument, Anthea said to herself as she descended to Rm 023 at nine one morning a few days after the Tarot encounter, for the sake of argument, say someone was trying to tell you something. Unlocking the door, she heard Jasmine saying, "Alchemy!" —the voice from some night when they were still in their teens, with Jasmine all drunk and pompous on the beach with a paper-bagged bottle of the Butter Ripple Schnapps she loved so much at the time. "Mrs. Layton says that Alchemy is also known as terrestrial astronomy."

"If you spent as much time on school stuff like you put into this stuff you'd be, like, really smart."

"I *am* really smart! But it's terrestrial astrology. Astronomy. Like, you look at the earth and it tells you things. And when you know enough, you can control it and turn base metals into gold, man, and homunculi. You know they sell Cinnamon Schnapps where there are little flakes of gold in it? It's not as good as the Butter Ripple, except over ice cream. I really like it with vanilla ice cream. Gold is good for you. It's just too expensive. You need to come with me to the Aquarian Centre! You would love Mrs. Layton!"

Anthea hadn't asked any more questions. She wasn't feeling nice by that point, with the schnapps swooshing unpleasantly around her stomach.

Sitting on the floor of Rm 023, she wondered how she'd ever learn to translate for the Other World of Jasmine's drunken lectures, and if she did, how she'd ask it relevant questions about Jas's whereabouts. The regular way of looking for her had not been particularly effective, not since the Prophet had come back. Anthea took circular routes through the city on her way to and from the Institute, leaving early to stalk past the squeegee kids, the corner boys, past the missions. She hung around those corner stores where coffee was still seventy-five cents a cup. Often strange women followed her; sometimes they shouted. While she wandered, she held his image in her mind: dark blond hair, parted in the middle and winging his forehead. His eyes were beer-bottle brown. He was tan, barefoot, an army backpack over one shoulder. The Bible in his back pocket wore a white rectangle in the denim that covered his lovely ass.

All around her there were half-rifled boxes she had opened and shut again, and the room still contained the sounds of research, whispers and dry-newsprint susurrations that never entirely subsided, even when she sat very still, as she often did. The air was clammy, like it would be in a postnuclear bunker deep underground. She turned back to the box of 78s and put her hand in at random, pulling out a "The Sun Whose Rays," B-sided with "Poor Wand'ring One" by Leticia Kilgour, Soprano. The second disk was Liam again, this time "Ô Souverain, ô juge, ô père" B-sided with "Celeste Aida."

She set the turntable on one of the boxes. It had been hers since she was ten and her Grandpa Max had found it at a garage sale. He had included with it a box of records from the same sale: Bobby Darin, The Platters, Al Jolson, Carl Perkins, Harry Belafonte, Elvis. She had listened to them all on her little portable, sitting cross-legged on the floor of her bedroom, and she had really enjoyed them, to her sorrow. All the way from seventh grade she could hear herself talking about her record collection without a flicker of self-consciousness. *Oh I like music*, she had said to the cool twelve-year-old who asked if she had *Total Rock Megahits 7* on cassette, *especially Bobby Darin. He's neat.* That was the day she ought to have given up on high school.

The machine was blue canvas and white plastic, mono, tinny, with a regular twick-twick where the edging on the turntable had come up and bumped the corner, 33.3, 45, or 78 times a minute. She unsheathed Liam's "Ô Souverain, ô juge, ô père," and looked across it, admiring grooves and ridges as they caught and lost light from the fluorescent ceiling. She touched the disk, its textures an untranslatable burr against the fine skin on the inside of her wrist. She opened the portable and smelled the summer-scent of rubber and dust, as potent as incense to invoke some hazy day when she was eleven and listening to "Beyond the Sea." She blew on the needle, then dropped it on the record's edge.

The sound of the room in which they all sat, clustered around the recording horn. Then the thin sound of a piano, an arpeggio stretched by the seventy-five years between her ears and the fingers on the keys, the hammers on the strings.

Then him. She didn't mind him at first. It was the second line where he lost his way, running at the peaks and tumbling into the valleys as though afraid he would lose his breath before he finished the phrase. Before he'd gone on very long, she had to stop him, unsure if it was his voice or just the opera in general that was so unpleasant, or made the muscles down either side of her spine shut tight around her ribs, a sympathetic spasm at the obvious effort the poor man put into each phrase.

Next she picked out Mrs. Kilgour's "The Sun Whose Rays," and dropped it on top of the terrible Massenet. Which was wrong, Colm always said when he saw her doing that, very wrong, because the records always had some dust on them and it would get ground into scratches between the disks. She dropped the needle and this time heard:

pray make no mistake we are not shy we're very wide awake the moon and i

Anthea thought it was pretty, which was nice because she hadn't expected Mrs. Kilgour's voice to be up to much. At four that afternoon she left Rm 023 with five brown-papered 78s in the portable turntable's side pocket.

THE AQUARIAN CENTRE

Anthea didn't know where Jasmine found the Aquarians, but they very quickly gained on the Wiccans, whose passion for sisterhood and material reality only held her interest for a few months. From Anthea's point of view, the nice thing about the Centre was that it tended to hold events like barbecues, and firesides with tea and cookies. Anthea had even gone to a potluck for the autumnal equinox, and a Samhain party that ended with s'mores. These gatherings reminded her a little of the United Church basement potlucks her parents had taken her to as a child, for the NDP riding association or the Voice of Women. The politics were exactly reversed—the Aquarians were traditionalists, and talked a lot about government as an unnatural intervention in the subtle forces that guide real human life—but the earnestness felt familiar, though the Aquarians valued orthodoxy even more than feminists and socialists.

The Centre stood on a brick-paved, west-side street lined with heritage plaques and chestnut trees lit by white LEDs. It was a large bungalow with a deep porch, a stone foundation and granite plinths. According to the blue and gold plaque on the front gate, it was built in 1922 by a lawyer named J. Somers. Anthea knew this because she always stopped to read heritage plaques.

"But, like," Anthea said when she first saw the beautiful house, "how do they pay for it?"

"Oh, money," Jasmine said. "You're way too obsessed with money. If you're aligned with the universe, money happens." Anthea said nothing. Money did not *happen* to her, at least not yet. "Seriously. Mrs. Layton doesn't even cast money spells—I do that, you know, before I apply for loans, and they always give me more than I need—it's just *there*."

"But it has to come from somewhere."

"Money is energy, and energy is fluid, like water: when you're aligned with the universe's will, it will flow toward you. You just have to arrange your life so you're in the right place to catch it."

The bungalow was Mrs. Layton's home, temple, and place of business. Like the building, she was elegant, with hair that had once been dark blonde, but had faded to platinum with the help of a little peroxide, or so Anthea guessed: the strands of silver at her temples were so perfect she could not believe they were natural. She accentuated her cheekbones and pale eyes with Cleopatra eyeliner in dark grey. She preferred silver to gold and amethysts to diamonds. Anthea first saw her at one of the Aquarian Centre's firesides, to which Jasmine had invited her, promising, "They're doing really cool and important work and I can feel how much it's changing me. They think long term, like *seriously* long term, about human evolution, and that's awesome. It's not like the goddamn witches, or the Synchronites or anything."

Their topic that first night was the Akashic Texts, a name that made Jasmine nod and Anthea roll her eyes. They arrived early in the large front room, and sat on cushions at Mrs. Layton's feet, in the circle around the fire, with their artisanal mugs and a shared plate of macaroons on the floor between them. When Mrs. Layton finished speaking with the man to her right, she turned to Jasmine and held both her hands, and said, "It's very good to see you here again. I had hoped you'd come back."

According to Mrs. Layton, the Akashic Texts were written in the structures and patterns of nature itself; the oldest words in the world were hidden in the world, and to access them was to access the secret history of the universe. "Mankind was brought into being," Mrs. Layton said, "to read those texts. We have no purpose but that, to apprehend the subtle language of the cosmos, and to find our name in God's manuscript."

Anthea looked at her socks, and the sliver of toenail showing through on the left. Beside her, Jasmine nodded vigourously and glanced across the room at other listeners, the whole group telegraphing understanding and interest among themselves as Mrs. Layton spoke. Anthea wondered how many times she had made this address, and how often she had called on men and women to study the Book of Their Own Lives, which they would find was one with the Book of Nature, and the Book of the Sky. When Mrs. Layton opened up the floor for discussion, the conversation was a lot like an undergraduate seminar, but with new keywords beyond "akashic": flow, energy, consciousness, transcendence, the uttermost west, the subtle body, the universal principle. Once someone mentioned the theory of general relativity as a proof for the existence of the ghosts. Another recounted a long and complex dream about learning to fly.

Colm had impressed upon her that one should never look at the time in an intimate group, or at least not to do it conspicuously, so as she listened she did a forward fold across her outstretched legs and glanced at her watch as she held her feet: she decided that manners required at least another hour of thoughtful attention.

After that she just looked around. There were very old books on the shelves with titles she had never heard, and on a dedicated side table an elegant orrery under glass. All the heavenly bodies orbited the sun in clockwork, but pieces were missing, as though it had been roughly handled at some earlier date. It included comets among its wheels, passing in wide ellipses around the cluster of planets. It looked antique, made of bronze and enamel, glass and green Bakelite. For the first time she wondered how old The Aquarian Centre was, and how long it had stood on this genteel side street, quietly devoted to the transformation of human consciousness and the rising Aquarian Age.

After they were released from general discussion, Jasmine turned to Mrs. Layton and engaged her on specific points of interpretation, until there was a gap, and Anthea said, "Your earrings are really pretty."

Mrs. Layton nodded. "They belonged to my mother. A gift from my father." Anthea looked at the pattern—moonstones in stylized papyrus settings—and wondered if the Centre's economic equilibrium originated with her father: not a gift from the universe, but a trust.

"This is a beautiful, beautiful house," Anthea said.

"Yes."

"It must be expensive. I mean. I mean for a non-profit to maintain this sort of place."

"It is worth the expense if one is sensitive to one's environment."

"Oh yes. Yes. Of course."

"But, since that seems to be your question, I'll tell you that it belonged to my mother and before that my grandparents. My mother started The Aquarian Centre."

Knowing what she was about to ask, but unable to stop herself, Anthea said, "With your father?"

Mrs. Layton excused herself, saying, "Why don't you talk to our other members? They can tell you more about the sort of work we do."

Anthea wandered away from the party and the fire, into the dining room where it was cool, and then the kitchen where two women were laying out cheese and bread on large plates and making more tea. From there to a small porch that faced the back garden. It was raining. The heat and noise of the house fell behind her, and it was good to be in the dark where the air smelled sweetly of leaves and wet grass.

Almost a year later, she wondered if he had been at the fireside, too, unrecognizable in shoes and a regular shirt, no drum, no attendant blonde. She didn't know what he'd been before that, if he'd been clean-cut, or suburban, if he'd been an art school dropout, a barista, an engineer, a cab driver before some cerebral incident so disordered his brain that he was no longer quite like the rest of them, his mind a moving detonation that unsettled the world as he moved through it. Perhaps Mrs. Layton had recognized something malleable in Jasmine and overseen their meeting. Perhaps, in wandering away from the heat and conversation of the house, Anthea had missed the moment of contact, the bright flash of recognition between them, illuminating the crowd and the sky above their heads, while she stood in the garden, her face averted from the flash. Of course they might not have met under Mrs. Layton's influence at all, but by accident, only later discovering their mutual affinity for the Aquarians. On the street, maybe, when he volunteered to correct her aura and she submitted to his caresses, and they communed on the plane of spirit, a half-storey above the pavement.

Sometimes she imagined that she had seen him in a far corner of the room, out of the firelight's reach, watching Jasmine with predatory eyes. He was waiting to slip in beside her, and draw her away to the dark highway and the woods north of the city, and then beyond the woods where all things lead, eventually.

THE PLACE OF THE STONES

Panther knew that you had to climb around the second point, not the one with the cliff and the stone that jutted out toward the low-tide line, like a wall, but the other way toward the Taberners' if you wanted to see the little house. Later, Dad would tell her it was the Place of the Stones, which some people called the House of Mystery. She was climbing over the rocks to see around into the next beach over when she looked up and saw the little house standing in the undergrowth and the trees, between the Taberners' garden and the high tide line. It had two little windows boarded up and a little door. The whole thing was covered in ivy, like it hadn't been built but had just grown there. She wished it was hers, because Max had forts and one time last week he didn't let her play in them because he had friends over and then Dad told her to leave him alone so he could play with his friends and she felt sad.

Later she was back on the beach, when it was time for pink lemonade and Max was building a driftwood lean-to with Grandpa. She should have thought about the rocks, but she was excited about the little house. "Dad I climbed around the point there was a little house with a door and two windows and it was covered with ivy."

"Around the point?" Dad sat up in the gravel. "Did you climb around the point?" Panther looked down, wondering what to say that wouldn't be wrong. She had not been told not to climb around the point, not the one on the Taberners' side, at least. She had been careful not to ask. But now it seemed to be another inexplicable naughtiness, like standing in front of an open fridge door or not saying hellohowareyou to visitors. "You shouldn't climb around the point. Do you know what happens when you trip and fall on the rocks?"

Panther shook her head, her eyes still fixed on the gravel, shrinking under her skin in the way she did when his voice worried.

"Panther."

She wriggled.

"Panther, look at me."

She didn't want to look at him.

"Panther, do you know what could happen if you fell? If you climbed up too high and fell down, you could break your leg, or you could fall into the water. Sweetheart?" Panther looked up. His eyebrows were close together and his forehead was all bumpy. "You shouldn't climb around the point by yourself. Do you understand?"

"I understand," she said. She had liked the little house. He lay back on the gravel, settling in again, the bad feeling easing slightly—never gone—but still wound up tight in the back of Panther's neck and in her legs, so she wriggled again.

"Was the little house on the Taberners'?" Dad asked. She shrugged. "If it was the one I think, I know that house."

For a bit they were both quiet, but then Panther knew that it had to be okay again. "I want that house, one just like it only it would be right down on the beach and I would keep stuff in it."

"What sort of stuff?"

"Like my red cape. And Bennycat would live there, too."

"That sounds nice. You know, I hear the house was built by a prophet."

Panther didn't know what a prophet was.

"A strange man built that house a long time ago. He thought he had messages from God about what he should do. I hear he used to sit in that house and listen to them."

Panther looked at the water, pretending she understood but she didn't really. Max and Grandpa were having trouble with the roof, the pieces were too short and kept falling in, and she heard Grandpa explain something about crossbeams. Panther's mother wasn't there yet, she was bringing down deviled eggs and sandwiches and pink lemonade from the kitchen. Grandma Hazel was writing and *couldn't be disturbed*. Dad kept talking anyway, though Panther stared at the opposite shore and the mountain that rose above all the other mountains and islands. It was blue and white, pretty now but prettiest at sunset. It was a volcano, they said, and used to smoke a long, long time before.

She hadn't ever seen the mountain smoke. If she had the little house, she would paint it red.

"So, Panther, back in the thirties, or maybe it was the twenties—when Grandma and Grandpa were little kids like you—he got a lot of people together and convinced them that something awful was going to happen to them if they didn't live the way he told them to."

There was a fly. Panther batted it away. Dad was stretched out on the gravel staring at the water and he hadn't even taken off his tie; his arms were crossed behind his head. He hadn't even taken his work shoes off. He was tired, Mom said again and again when Panther or Max asked. He was tired.

He was still talking. "So he got all the people together and promised he'd keep them safe."

The house would be right out beside the water, and she would keep a bucket in there for a sink and a box for food and a little hibachi she would cook on, and she would fish right out the window and at night she would sleep right next to the water.

"And when they were all gathered, he said that the world was going to end."

Panther looked at her dad sideways. His eyes were closed. The sunlight and shadow flickered over his lids and he put up a hand to shade them. "The end of the world?" she asked, and an unpleasant shiver spread over her, and she felt chilly like her feet were in cold water even though she sat in the sun. She started digging in the gravel beside her. It slid away with each scoopful so she dug faster and faster. You couldn't dig in gravel properly, and the waves were up over the sandy parts of the beach, which was the only place you could do castles. Down the beach Grandpa and Max had found a long stick they could use as a crossbeam.

"The end of the world," Dad said. "He told them it was coming very soon. He'd say 'Any day now! The world will end!' and they believed him."

In her little house she would be all alone when the world ended, because there wasn't room for anyone else. She would have her bucket and the fishhooks and the hibachi. She would have a bunk bed. She would sleep right by the water. She would always wear her red cape and Bennycat would always get to sleep on her bed because no one would ever tell her she was allergic.

"So they got everything together they would need if the world ended—horses and goats and ploughs and food and clothes and seed, and they waited. They waited for a long time."

She would wait in the house. She would wait and a great wave would come up all around her and flood the world, all but her in the little house she would paint red, she would be all on her own with nothing in sight but the waves around her rising and falling. Nothing but the little house and around her the water going down down down to the bottom she could not see.

Panther stopped digging. She looked at her dad.

"The world didn't end, though, so they all packed up and went home. He left. He left everything behind, even the little house. No one knows what happened to him."

Panther nodded, pretending she knew what he was talking about. His eyes were still closed. "When's supper, anyway?"

"Mom said soon."

"You shouldn't climb around the point by yourself, Panther. You could get hurt. There are some big rocks and some places you could get stuck."

She nodded.

"We worry about you."

She nodded. And because she also knew, though not in words, that he wanted everything to be alright with her, she did not talk about how much fun it was to climb around the rocks and find starfish and spider crabs all by herself, but instead said, "I like the little house. What was his name?"

"Simon Reid."

Anthea repeated the name. It felt familiar, like the name of someone she could've known once. A teacher she maybe had in pre-school. Mr. Reid.

Max came up the beach then. Behind him the lean-to looked very nice and tidy. Dad kept his eyes closed, stretched out in his work clothes on the gravel and Max fell down beside him.

"You ever hear about Simon Reid, Max?" Grandpa was there and looking across the water.

"Who's Simon Reid?" Max asked, and Dad started in again.

Panther was going to tell him to stop, but felt ashamed that she didn't want to hear it because it would remind her of how it felt to think about the little house and the water all around it and her alone with her cat and her red cape. If they kept on she would go down to the edge of the water and splash and blot out the sound of their voices. She wished she had before, but too late the rising water and the little house were something Panther knew and Simon Reid, whose name was so familiar. She looked at Grandpa, who was squinting at the water.

"Oh, they don't want to hear about that," he said, and Panther was happy.

WAKE THE DEAD

Okay, so she had been a Searcher, too, in the capital "S" sense of the word that's so common in esoteric bookshops and meditation centres. Way back, on a night that probably involved Butter Ripple Schnapps, Anthea told Jasmine the story of The Place of the Stones to gain a little occult credibility. They hadn't known one another very long, but already felt like deep-time sisters, permanent threads in one another's lives. Jasmine even pointed to the line on her palm that was like Anthea's, evidence of other lives spent in one another's company, at Delphi or Machu Picchu.

"So yeah," Anthea said, "apparently there was this guy who lived on my Grandma's place like a million years ago? And he was a kind of a prophet."

"What kind of a prophet?"

"Like, an end-of-the-world prophet?"

"But which world? And which end?"

Jasmine shrugged, but Anthea thought hard and said, "Like. How many are there?"

"Oh, the world ends in lots of different ways. I bet he was a spiritualist."

"Okay?"

"There was a lot of that around. There was also this one Theosophist woman from Russia who liked the Rockies. She said there was a secret lamasery there, and Those Who Are were all in hiding and guarding the secret knowledge of the ancients. It sort of trickles down to the coast. But that's Blavatsky. You're saying he came to Duncan's Crossing?"

"Yeah, right, so he built this community and told a bunch of people the world was going to end, then he got them to come and build houses? And he took their money and no one knows what happened to him?"

"That's not unusual," was all Jasmine said for a moment. Anthea assumed that she had lost any occult credibility the story might have gained her, had she told it correctly. Even at the time, however, she was beginning to suspect that she did not wish to be occult; it involved too many arbitrary rules, like not lending your nice Tarot cards to people, so they had to use the ones with all the tea stains and cigarette burns, that smelled kind of skunky like they'd spent a long time in someone's stash.

After her long, dramatic pause, Jas started again. "I think we should look for him. Where's the house?"

"The little house is next door to Grandma's. But the big house—the manor I think she called it?—was on the point."

"He had a *manor.* Classy. We should definitely go there and try to look him up."

"But it was a while ago—like, the twenties—"

"We should go to the house site. We should call him up." She said this with a ten-year-old's *Ya scared?* look.

Anthea chewed her bottom lip and imagined going to Hazel's house and saying she wanted to raise the dead. Hazel's atheistic derision at self-deluding spirituality would elegantly balance Jasmine's contempt for Anthea's—*wilful,* she implied—clumsiness with all things esoteric.

"No. But. Like, my Grandma?"

"Oh don't worry," Jasmine shook her head, "we wouldn't *tell.* You shouldn't let the uninitiated know too much. Tell her we're visiting."

"Okay. But."

"We're visiting 'cause you miss her. They like that sort of thing. Say I'm interested in local history. Which is totally not a lie."

Anthea imagined the phone conversation, realizing that Hazel *would* like it. It would be awful, but Jasmine was still staring at her. "Okay?" was all she said.

Just before they left in the late afternoon, Jasmine sat on the floor of Anthea's dorm room showing her all the things she'd packed. "The idea is," she said as she brought out myrrh in a small alabaster box, "the idea is that all things have associations. Correspondences. And if you assemble all the things—like actual objects, I mean, but also colours and smells and flavours—that correspond to a force or idea you can attract that force. And each force or idea is attached to a deity who acts as a kind of handle, so you call on that deity and if you do it right and raise the right powers you can direct the force too. So gods' names—or saints, even—are just the handles that allow us to invoke natural forces."

"But. Like. This guy isn't an idea. He's a guy."

"Yes, but he's dead and he has associations—the occult and leadership and priesthood and that sort of thing. So I've decided that we invoke Hermes Trismegistus, called Hermes-Thoth, thrice great. He's associated with occult secrets, magic, mysteries. And our guy is dead, so we put down myrrh. We light white candles, we go to a place that mattered to him. It's like if you bring together enough pieces of him and invoke the forces that he was bound to in his life, he can't help it, he's got to show up. You're just opening the right door." Jasmine paused, and then said in the low, important voice, "Remember, doors want to open. They're not walls."

By now Anthea's bed was covered with bits of magic. She picked up a book about correspondences and flipped through it. So many elements: plants, stones, times of day and year, days of the week, numbers, letters, metals, colours, scents, flavours. She wondered what a complete list would look like, like a dictionary of objects, or a concordance for the entire world. As she wondered, Jasmine wound white ribbon around the tapers and put them back in her knapsack with a large piece of silk to hide the more peculiar objects: the bundle of twigs, the vial that held something red and viscous.

In the car she asked, "Are those all the correspondences? I mean, every single one you need?"

"Oh no. There are lots more. I guess there are as many as there are things in the world. Everything corresponds."

"So does that mean that everything you do, like every time you get dressed or make supper or pack a bag you're casting a spell?"

Jasmine stared out the windshield. "I guess by your kind of thinking," she said vaguely. "But that doesn't sound right. Spells are big. They don't just happen by themselves."

But it meant, Anthea thought to herself, there was—what would it be? A web, she thought, of some subtle element that linked everything to everything else. And to deploy the web one would need a language Anthea did not know, organized in a dictionary as large and varied as the universe that contained it, and containing among its entries the universe itself. It meant that any moment of contact was not only about the intersection of skin and dashboard, but all the forces associated with Anthea colliding with all the associations of a 1986 Colt, its olive-green vinyl dashboard mended with grubby duct tape. So each action was a spell, invoking unknown powers and redirecting them, all the ripples from those moments travelling outward, and their interference patterns were called fate. It meant that the impressions of a moment—say, the shade of red generated by the flicker of sunlight over eyelids, the smell of cold coffee at the bottom of her cup, the fact of its being a Saturday, the fact of its being the full moon, the flutter the wind made when it blew up the sleeve of her dark red Indian-cotton blouse where it rested in the open car window, the taste of the lemon drop melting on her tongue—these impressions were actions in themselves, invoking acetic acid and ethical coffee beans and sunlight and cotton and Saturdays and road trips. Invoking the gods and goddesses associated with these things and sending Anthea wheeling down a path toward further actions and associations she could not control, but had brought into the world by observing the taste of lemons and the sunlight on her lids.

It was two hours of highway to get to Duncan's Crossing. She knew she was in the valley when she smelled, through the window, the first crop of hay lying in the fields.

Just north of town there was a place called the Glass Castle Resort, an RV park where the main office was built of old beer and pop bottles, a homemade attraction some local entrepreneur built in the early sixties. It was a permanent source of irritation to Hazel, though she had stopped writing letters to the editors of local papers and was resigned to saying "Tacky, tacky!" every time she passed it. They turned right at the Castle, down the narrow lanes away from the cars and the suburban developments. The houses there were older and larger, properties that had served as country places before the wars, with tennis courts and gates at the head of the drive. Pioneers and early gentry had been driven out by new money, people who demolished the post-war A-frames and earlier, faux-Tudor manors and brought in steel and plate glass and swimming pools.

Hazel did not have a stone gate, nor a tennis court. Anthea's grandfather had been a mechanic and in his retirement he had filled the property with machinery, much of it overgrown now: the bush reclaimed anything left unattended for more than a season. The most remarkable of all the things he had left behind was the grader that stood in a thicket of alders where Grandpa Max had parked it the day he finished grading the driveway, and though Hazel had called it an eyesore, he had refused to move it. Caterpillar yellow still showed through the lichen and the moss, and the trunks of the alders had grown up through the blades and locked it in place: it would never move again. Anthea thought it was beautiful.

When she pointed it out, Jas shook her head. "It's so masculine," she said. "You can't leave the woods alone. You've got to put a grader in there and mark your territory."

Down at the house Hazel came out to meet them. She hugged Anthea, quick and hot, then kissed her, then held Jasmine's hand and smiled up at her. "You must be Jasmine!" she said, and pulled them into the house and out onto the deck above the beach. She watched for Jasmine's reaction, and Jas complied: exclaiming over the water that stretched south toward the islands, and beyond them, out of sight, to America. Hazel made tea. They chatted until Anthea felt brave enough to bring it up.

"Oh! Of course, darling," Hazel was saying. "Of course I remember that story. Mr. Sweeney was one of them. I tried to talk to him about it when I was doing research, you know, for My Book—darling, would you like cream or milk?—I tried to talk to him about it. He was always such a nice man, but that time he got so angry he told me to go to hell before I'd finished my tea."

Jasmine looked at Anthea. It was obviously important to hear about Mr. Sweeney, but Anthea wasn't sure how to ask questions without arousing Hazel's hot and uncomfortable interest.

It was Jas who asked, outright, "Why didn't he want to talk about it?"

"It's quite mysterious, I know from my Research. The things that went on there—" Hazel set down her cup and turned to Anthea. "You remember Mr. Sweeney, darling, he lived on the other side of the Taberners and kept his boat on the old dock. He wanted to take you out once but you were too scared to go with him."

Jasmine looked at Anthea and laughed. "You were scared!" she said. Hazel laughed too.

Anthea wanted to say, *You weren't the one in the boat.* She remembered Mr. Sweeney: walking up and down his garden with a wheelbarrow; hauling seaweed up from the beach when it was thick. He didn't pay much attention to property lines and used the Brookes's beach path, but no one ever told him off. He smelled strongly of unwashed skin, or maybe it was from under his skin, an antique inside-of-the-body smell Panther couldn't properly name. He always wore a shirt and tie, and brown polyester slacks, and a flat cap that was spotty with black grease around the brim and darkened by hair oil inside; she saw when he took it off to come in the house. He used to smoke with Grandpa Max and they sometimes built things together. Sheds. Fences. If Anthea hung around she'd listen to them hammer nails and roll cigarettes and drink coffee from a tartan thermos. They didn't say much.

No, but there was one time, when he wanted to take her out fishing and she was too scared and said *no no* right after they'd put the horrible orange canvas life preserver on her, tied too tight under her ribs and smelling like garages. She had said she was too scared of the waves, and he had laughed and called her cowardy custard and tried to put her in the boat and said the waves wouldn't bite. She had clung to Grandma, and he'd gone out alone, and brought a fish in to show them. She remembered it flopping on the bottom of the boat. Flop. Flop. Stillness. Flopflop. He'd picked up a two-by-four and clubbed it over the head with a heavy, off-hand flick and it had stopped flopping. Then he'd asked if she wanted to help him clean it. She had reached out a hand and touched the cold body that glinted like wet pebbles did when the waves unrolled from them. It was dense under her finger, and she thought it was too heavy and solid to swim like it must have done ten minutes before. She withdrew the hand and looked at her shoes not knowing what was expected of her, and Mr. Sweeney had cut in under the gills and severed the head, then there was the thick smell of blood and salt. Hazel had taken her back to the house and made cocoa in the blender, that was extra foamy.

"Mr. Sweeney? He was such a regular old guy."

"It was a long time ago, dear. Anyway—I'm so glad you girls are taking an interest in Local History, it's such an Important Subject. We have to know where we're coming from to know where we're going. Those who do not remember the past are doomed to repeat it!"

There was a moment of quiet Anthea spotted for one of Hazel's fraught pauses, which meant she was about to ask Meaningful Questions. Hoping that they were for Jasmine, not her, Anthea sat as still as a rabbit in the undergrowth, hardly relaxing even when Hazel turned to Jasmine, smiling, squinting slightly as though in fascination.

"Now, dear, tell me. Are you the historian?"

After Jasmine had spoken, at length, about her interest in Local History, she and Anthea went down to the house site alone. By then Anthea almost believed that they really *were* doing a case-study for Jasmine's paper about coastal architecture. Hazel had been flattered by all the questions about the bungalow and how she and Max had milled the lumber from drift logs on the beach, and how she had built its stone walls herself, and showed Jasmine where there were still barnacles clinging to the rock.

Jas forgot it all. "Why did she call you Panther?"

"When I was little? It was my nickname."

"Why?"

"'Cause Anthea rhymes with it, if you say it with an English accent. I guess. That's what they said."

"Does anyone in your family *have* an English accent?"

"Well, *no*, but I guess they *did*. At some point. Maybe a long time ago?"

They were in the old garden by then, where the ornamental cherry trees had grown up in watershoot thickets. There were carp ponds full of dead leaves; there were rambler roses and English ivy. Anthea led Jasmine through the woods to the rocky clearing that had been the manor, right on the point, where the earth gave way to granite that rimmed the whole inlet, showed at the tideline on the opposite shore and on the mountains above them.

"It must've been huge."

"He had a lot of money, I guess," Anthea said. "Where do we go? The Place of the Stones is on the other side. But that's the Taberners'."

Jasmine closed her eyes and Anthea tried not to watch her, though she admired the sharp cut of her cheekbones, the yellow hair blowing across her throat, her long arms and legs in repose. Jasmine never failed to costume herself thoughtfully for whichever role she had chosen. Under her lids her eyes darted back and forth as though she were dreaming. "Only we have to wait for a declining sun," was all she said for a minute. "He liked sunset. There." And she pointed at the corner that faced the water. "He wanted to look to the east."

Anthea looked past the pointed finger to the airport, still in sunlight on the other side of the inlet, and did not tell Jas that it was more northeast than east. She took off the backpack and sat on a corner of the foundation. "We have to wait for sunset?"

"It'll be in the right quadrant in a bit," Jasmine said. "And we have to prepare."

They sat together on the manor's foundation and arranged their things. First the four white candles on the outside, marking the directions, then the central ring of nine white tapers between the two of them, then the largest candle in the middle. Anthea had gotten them all at the dollar store the day before. The wicks were all clean and white and Anthea picked ivy to put around them, to complete the circle, and added Rose of Sharon and periwinkle, then hemlock because it smelled nice. She liked that part. Jasmine sat with her eyes closed and the central candle held between her palms, until they were in shadow, and the sun only tipped the other side of the inlet, and the islands beyond.

"Now," she said, and put the last white candle in the centre of the circle.

Anthea sat down opposite Jasmine. They had decided that she would call North and East, while Jasmine called West and South. Once they'd lit all the candles, except for the centre, Jasmine began to hum. Anthea almost recognized the melody, something bittersweet and familiar like "Auld Lang Syne" or "Cheek to Cheek." As Jasmine's eyes fluttered in her sockets, she reached out and lit the middle candle.

"We call the Prophet, Simon Reid. We call you back to the place you knew and bid you speak with us. By your Master Hermes Trismegistus, thrice great, we call you! By the Simonian Heresiarchs! By the Emerald Tablet! By the King in Yellow! And by his Yellow Sign!" Jas's eyes still rolled under her lids. Anthea tried rolling her eyes in the same way, but it hurt her temples so she stopped.

But then she began to shiver.

It wasn't that she was cold, but something made her skin shudder like a sleeping cat's. Looking east Anthea saw the wrinkle of wavelets, the sea gone dark grey as the last fringe of sunset dropped away, the sky above not opaque but a luminous black with its new stars, and in the moonlight the islands, the trees around them, the jumbled foundations of the old house were sentient and articulate, though she did not know what they said. Now her skin gathered into goosebumps down her back, and the muscles in her chest constricted around her heart, and it stumbled, then caught, then stumbled as Jas finished her call.

"Simon, are you present? Do you hear us? We have called you to this place, we hold your key and command your answer!" She intoned like a priestess, then looked at Anthea, as though she expected something.

Anthea's lips were cracked from mouth breathing. "Simon!" she said. When she didn't continue, Jasmine made little "spit it out!" gestures with her upheld hands. Anthea raised her arms, too. "By these objects we call you!" She reached behind her and grabbed a bit of brick from one of the chimneys and flung it into the centre of the circle. "We bid you come to us!" Jasmine added a flower she had taken from one of the rambler roses that still grew under the trees. Then they both lowered their arms.

The wind freshened.

Jasmine's eyes focused on some point in the woods, above Anthea's head.

The candles fluttered. South went out, then North. Jasmine said "Shit!" and went to relight them, but she stopped herself. Instead she murmured, "As above so below."

The leaves around them unsettled as though by fingers, and the same hands ruffled the waters below them and snuffed their candles. Up far above them the arbutus trunks groaned that familiar, atonal moan in the new breeze.

"Anthea," said the trees, the first and last part only *ahhhh*, and the consonants only a whisper, but she was sure, oh she was sure she'd heard her own name hidden in the ambient groan of arbutus trunks.

She stood up. The sea before her still wrinkled in the moonlight, and the islands were like the backs of animals that might turn and see her at any moment, harbingers of a change now horribly imminent. And then the flood of panic gave her the stuttering, adrenalized run of a frightened lady in a silent film. The groaning was drowned by her own heartbeat as she knocked over the candles and fled the circle, up the bank tripping over foundation stones, the roots of trees, tangling in the curtains of ivy that hung around the old garden, cut by rose wands that dragged at her hands as she tore overland, ignoring her usual deer path for the straightest line to light, even when she stumbled into an uninhabited carp pond and slithered onto the bank. And then she was out, with Hazel's porch lights burning in a lovely, steady incandescence.

She stopped and looked down at the bloodlines drawn across her palms, up her arms, welts on her legs where she'd struggled through nettle and blackberries. There was a bruise and a deep scratch on her left shoulder where some branch had torn right through her red cotton blouse.

Ten minutes later Jasmine picked her way up the path, *not* tearing through the woods like a maenad. She carried Anthea's backpack, and had obviously taken the time to pack candles, myrrh, and silk. She smiled. She was very kind. She told Hazel she'd had a lovely time. Hazel wished her luck on the paper and asked for a copy of it when she was finished.

Hazel drew Anthea aside before they left and held her hands. "I had a lovely time too," she said. "I haven't had such a good talk in a week! It's so nice to talk to you girls about what's really important!" She gave Anthea one of her short, tight hugs. Once in the car under cover of darkness, Anthea rubbed her hands again and again over her jeans, wiping them clean.

During the drive, Anthea kept her eyes away from the hollow darkness under the trees and the patches of moonlight, instead watching the headlights flick over the road in front. She willed Jasmine to speak first.

"Well, that was wild," Jas said, finally.

"Wild."

"What did you see, anyway?"

Anthea hesitated. "I heard. I heard something. Did you hear anything?"

"I mean, in your heart, did you see anything with your heart?"

"No."

"No?" The car filled with the scent of Jasmine's irritation, something like burning plastic. "You know Anthea, I don't mean to be mean, but if you weren't so resistant, it wouldn't be so scary, you wouldn't go all freaky. I'm open to it, so it's just natural to me. That was just a really intense place, but intensity isn't bad if you know how to *handle* it."

Anthea nodded but volunteered nothing. Jas hadn't heard the arbutus groan.

"Are you afraid of death?"

"What?"

"Death. Dying. Because it's nothing to be scared of. It's just a doorway. You don't have to be scared of it. I'm not scared. I'm not scared of anyone I know dying, because I know they'll be okay. It's just going through a door. It's only if you're all repressed that dying is scary."

Anthea thought, *Yes I'm fucking well scared of death. It's* death, *you stupid fuck.*

She couldn't bring herself to say that or anything else, so they didn't speak for a while, but then they did and it was okay. Except that Jasmine hassled her to go back and look around some more. She mentioned research, and archives and interviewing anyone who might remember. "There's something there," she said, "there's something in that old house that needs to be put to rest."

Anthea nodded every time and said, "Oh yeah, definitely that was weird."

It was much more than just *weird*, and while Jasmine declared often that she would find out what, she never did, and Anthea did not volunteer her skills, though they would have been useful. Jasmine never asked for help, presuming that Anthea would read old books, and she would invoke absent gods, and they'd Watson-and-Holmes around the city until it was time for something else.

AUGURIES

What had come after their investigation into Simon Reid, Prophet? After that they tried ornithomancy, though they had preferred "auguries," once Anthea got to that part of Intro to Classical Studies. Sometimes if they were out walking, they'd stop, close their eyes and ask a question, then watch for crows. Then one day in November of Anthea's fourth year, they were walking across campus in the rain, and Jasmine stopped and shut her eyes and muttered something:

One for sorrow, two for joy,
Three for girls, four for boys,
Five for silver, six for gold,
Seven for a secret not to be told
Eight for heaven, nine for hell,
And ten for the devil's own self.

They didn't see a crow until they were nearly at the SUB, where a shiny little black one ate spilled chips. Anthea saw it first and said so, but then Jasmine said "Hah!" and pointed to the second crow, that had dropped from the tree opposite them and was gunning for the first crow's snack.

"That's two. Joy! He *so* wants to fuck me!"

"But did you see one first? Doesn't that mean it's one?"

"No, there's two. That's Joy! Joy is the eternal yes!"

"But it took a second for the other one to get there, so maybe the answer is one."

"Seriously, Anthea! Two crows!"

After that, Anthea had trouble counting crows. If you saw one crow and another joined it, was that two or one? How long was the time unit for each answer, anyway? And for that matter, how did one define "murder"? If, for instance, there were three murders each made up of two crows, did that mean six crows—gold—or three sets of two crows—joy joy joy? Or did one actually see two, one, and three crows—joy sorrow girls? Or sorrow restated six times? And what if you saw one crow twice? Or three crows in sequence? And how, really, did you ever know that the crow you saw was meant for you at all, and wasn't someone else's sorrow or joy you had only happened upon?

At first Jasmine patiently explained that if you saw an omen, it was your own and that was all that mattered. But then, was every crow an omen? Was the act of seeing it what made it an omen, Anthea asked, or were crows out in the woods, unseen, still omens? And Jasmine rolled her eyes and said "fucking *pedantic*," which was a conspicuous new word she had picked up that year.

The line of argument opened unsettling possibilities regarding the relationship between the crows and the world, and whether it was not one of augury, but of influence. What if in saying, "the next crows I see will tell me if I will die young," you were surrendering choice to the wild card arrival of black birds? In which case, three or seven or thirteen crows appearing did not predict your future, but determined it. She did not like that thought, but it followed too irresistibly on the belief that crows might predict the future, or that the association of objects and sensations might redirect the events of one's life. She felt she could not reject the second if she accepted the first. After that, she stopped counting crows.

A GENTLEMAN AND A PROPHET

Three weeks after the Pink Rose Gala, Liam detrained in a small town three hours north of the city. It was a leisurely tour, with two recitals each week over the month, and a long rest at the Kilgour Hunting Lodge midway through. He travelled ahead of Mrs. Kilgour's party, which had expanded to include her maid, her secretary Nora, youngest daughter Euphemia, Euphemia's maid, a footman, a nurse and her manager, Goshawk. Mrs. Kilgour had organized a valet for Liam, but he declined to travel in the same coach. The valet—silent, austere, bowler-hatted—was intimidating, and Liam was disconcerted to find he did not know how to behave around a gentleman's gentleman. Still, it was a fine thing to have his suits properly looked after, and for his own comfort, Mr. Hickey could remain with the footman who tended to the luggage in second class.

Liam travelled lightly, stepping out of the train at another of the familiar rust-red stations, this one with "Duncan's Crossing" written on it in white paint. He enjoyed, as he never did before, the tidy little plot where flowers had bloomed the previous autumn. He had dreaded towns like this when he'd travelled on the small-time circuits. The dressing rooms were grotty and cold, and the boarding houses he could afford always smelled of congealed gravy. He was not prepared for the new charm of the place as seen from a first-class berth.

He checked into the town's best hotel and had his dinner there (mushroom soup, veal, winter vegetables, apple pie, cheese, coffee and he didn't even *look* at the price). He was finishing his cheese and considering a walk to settle his stomach, when he noticed another man watching him. The man had finished his meal and was making coffee with a Turkish set. He wore a fine grey suit. He had long, thin fingers, and Liam admired how easily he managed the high-necked pot over the chafing light. He had a small, neatly clipped beard, grey-brown only a shade darker than his skin, which was yellowish, as though he had been ill. The bones of his skull stood out sharply under his close-cut hair, his crown was wide and well-shaped, his forehead high and finely domed. An *ascetic aesthete*, Liam thought, exercising his vocabulary.

The man in the grey suit caught the waiter's eye so adroitly that Liam was entranced. The waiter obviously attended to what he said, too, because in a minute he had approached Liam with Mr. Reid's invitation to join him for coffee.

As he paused a moment, Liam rehearsed in his head what he would say, then folded his napkin and dropped it beside his plate. *That's very kind*, perhaps, or simply *Thank you*.

He did not have a chance to say anything, because the gentleman stood up as he approached and spoke first: "My name is Reid." The man inclined his head and shook Liam's hand. The fingers were thin and dry and very strong. "You're kind to join me."

"Well, Mr. Reid. My name is Manley."

The coffee in the little white cup was bitterly strong and black and sweet with an unpleasant sludge that lingered at the bottom, so Liam took the tablet of chocolate Mr. Reid also offered. "Delicious," he said, then, "Well, Mr. Reid, what brings you to this town?"

"I live not far from here, but I found myself fatigued after travelling from the city, and unprepared to meet the challenges of my estate, so I thought to break my journey here rather than pressing on. And it is one of my small indulgences to travel with this equipage." He gestured at the little pot and the flame. "I am particular about my coffee."

"Yes," Liam said, and forced himself to sip again from the sludgy little cup. "I am as well. You have a large home place then? Where is it located?"

"To the south, some miles. It's small, only three hundred acres at present. I hope to add more, though the negotiations are interminable. And you? What has brought you to this town? I ask because you don't look quite rough-hewn enough to be a native."

"Well, no, I'm travelling through here on my own business—music. It is a pretty spot, though, I can see the appeal," he said, generously. He meant it, too.

Mr. Reid leaned back in his chair and steepled his fingers. "Music? I thought you were an artist, Mr. Manley. Are you part of the Kilgour party?"

"Yes—and how did you know?"

"Advertising, but I would have guessed anyway. You have the look of genius about you."

"That's quite flattering, Mr. Reid."

"Only honest."

Liam sipped again. He caught the waiter's eye and called for brandy in a low, effortless voice, quite impressing himself, for he sounded so natural, and the man listened so attentively. They talked about the weather and Mr. Reid referred again to his estate, to the redesign of the dock that had been on the larger of his beaches when he first arrived. He discussed his plans to extend the orchard and put in more cottages, once he had purchased a quarter section to the north.

After another brandy, they retired to the lounge and sat by the fire. It was ten o'clock, and there was a cloud before Liam's eyes as he sipped away at his glass and Mr. Reid went on about the importance of building for the future. Liam nodded occasionally, found himself agreeing—yes, one should think of the future, build foundations for one's children, or improve on the foundations given one by one's parents (if one's parents had the wherewithal to give one anything). While Mr. Reid spoke, he could see his own children, their mother bright-faced but indistinct. His daughter would sing like Melba or Tetrazzini in family groups, but never venture onto the stage. His son would play Chopin like a master, but it would be a private passion. While Mr. Reid spoke, he imagined not only his children, but theirs. A kind of dynasty, built on his sacrifices to Mrs. Kilgour.

"Do you ever think of why this is such an instinct for us—for men, I mean, particularly European, or if I may be direct, northern European men? We know instinctively to fight the modern curses of trade unionism and the perversion of race."

Liam found that his mouth hung open a little. He closed it. "Northern Europe?" he thought. *Swedes?*

"In general, the European Man is superior to others because he shares his essence with the great races who passed this way before us—the Hyperboreans, as they have been known, the devotees of Apollo, but also the Beringians and Atlanteans and the ancient people of Carcosa. The Northern European Man more totally embodies that eternal substance than the southern races, which are a degraded offshoot, a failed experiment. The eastern races... well." Simon smiled.

Liam's mind was still half occupied by the great house he would have, the estate, somewhere in the country. Horses, he had been thinking. One ought to learn to ride, and now here was Apollo. He thought Apollo had something to do with music, or perhaps only singers. Once he had read a pamphlet called *Classical Mythology in Today's World*, but he had forgotten the details.

"Yes, yes, I suppose that's it," he said quickly.

"I knew you would agree, Mr. Manley. It's why I chose to speak to you of it. When I saw you come in the room, I recognized you as a gentleman with great faculties of understanding."

"Thank you. Yes, of course," he said. The brandy-fug had been pleasant before, but now it so obscured his understanding that he wanted to bat it from his eyes, to look back and see where the conversation had turned toward Hyperboreans and Apollo and trade unions. And then he realized that Reid was watching him, and Liam did not like it. For a moment Reid's stillness did not seem to be natural, but a self-contained quiet that put Liam in mind of a yellow marble statue he had once seen in Italy, and how the guidebook said that they did not know the god's name, but the statue was thousands of years old. Liam felt that he had been staring and looked at his glass again.

"My estate is more than simply a bit of land, Mr. Manley, it is a bulwark." Here Mr. Reid stood. "You will be in town another day?"

Happy to have a simple question to answer, Liam nodded and said, "Another three days." Mr. Reid seemed so affable, just a gentleman again, and he wondered if he had imagined the words "evil" and "Hyperboreans." He hoped he had. Mr. Reid looked exhausted with worry, certainly in ill health, but not so fantastical as to discuss these strange histories with a coffee companion he hardly knew. It must have been a moment's lapse, and it would be better manners to behave as though Mr. Reid had done nothing out of the ordinary. Illness did strange things to men, he knew.

"I would like it very much if you would visit me tomorrow and see the estate. I would benefit from the company, so you may think of it as a favour."

Recognizing an invitation even through his brandy haze, Liam stood and responded with something automatic and juvenile. "Of course, it sounds awfully fun," he said.

"Good. After breakfast my car will take us home. And tonight—Parach, Mr. Manley."

Mr. Reid held his hands in prayer and bowed. Liam nodded and stood until he had left the room. More doors swinging open, Liam thought, and at speed. Of course Reid was a bit odd, but what else would he be, here at the end of the world? He ordered another brandy and crawled into his bed a little after midnight.

The next day Liam woke with a sour taste in his mouth and clammy pyjamas. It was not until after his tea that he remembered that man Reid. He had said some peculiar things about being Northern, but Liam remembered Reid's discussion of his estate quite clearly. He rolled out of bed to the bathroom, congratulating himself on being in a position to take a room with private facilities.

Down in the hall, Mr. Reid waited with his newspaper. He wore pale grey flannel. With his hands behind his back, Liam surreptitiously caressed the cuffs of his dark blue tweed and slid the silk lining against his wrist.

"I'm glad you have joined me, Mr. Manley. It will be a pleasure to show you around the estate."

The car outside was a new grey Lagonda, driven by a man in a black suit, not a uniform. It took them forty-five minutes to reach Reid's gates. They were disappointingly simple, to Liam, who had expected wrought iron and brick, at least, though ideally stone. Reid nodded to the man who emerged from the little house beside the drive's entrance. On either side, the property's boundary was marked by barbed wire on high wooden fences, which Liam did not like. Such fences were ugly. The grounds on the other side were impenetrable bush. It all looked very raw.

Reid seemed to read Liam's mind. "It isn't necessary to tell other people what one is working on, is it, Mr. Manley? Particularly when one isn't impressed with one's neighbours. I've planted lilacs and English ivy, though, to soften things a little. And periwinkle, which is sometimes called joy-of-the-ground."

Liam nodded. Of course, a man like Reid didn't need to advertise, and suddenly the plain steel gate compared favourably to Mrs. Kilgour's granite and rose gardens.

"I think I'll bring in blackberries, as well. Very fine fruit from the Siberian blackberry. And Scotch broom, too, for hedging."

The drive wound through woods at first, but soon clearings emerged—filled with stumps and gravel—that were even uglier, to Liam, than the barbed wire. Still Reid gestured to one clearing and said, "I want to expand the orchard there, I think there's room for another row along the back." And of another, indistinguishable from the "orchard," he said, "Goats, I think. Very efficient animals." He mentioned pigs, sheep, an apple barn, cottages for weavers, a dairy.

"You seem to be looking for self-sufficiency, Mr. Reid," Liam said as they passed through the village, planned prettily around a little green, Simon said, though all Liam could see was stumpy ground full of turned-up stones and mud, mud everywhere. The cottages were coarse and new, the unpainted cedar shakes still red-gold and the air that crept in the window smelled of sawdust. Once out of the village they approached the house, and Liam saw a garden, though it too was embryonic. There were ponds, but the stones that paved their edges looked freshly broken, and the ornamental cherry trees were still spindly.

"Yes," Reid said as they passed between the low stone walls to the private garden that surrounded his house. It was yellow granite and half-timbering, with warm gold plaster between the artificially blackened beams that crossed the gables. There were many gables. "Yes, you have great insight. I do plan for self-sufficiency."

After touring the house and garden, they went into the dining room for lunch laid on a table that faced the water. This at least was as it should be, Liam thought, admiring the view down the cliffside, and agreeing about the dock Simon meant to modernize. After lunch they went into the library and sat as they had done in the hotel lounge.

"With your permission, Mr. Manley," Reid began, "I would like to continue our discussion. Last night my exhaustion prevented further explanations regarding this estate."

Liam glanced out the window rather than looking too obviously at the clock over the mantel. Still, it had been such a nice pork roast with baked apples and pear pie afterward. He liked pear pie. He should listen, and even ask questions. "I am eager to hear more, Mr. Reid," he said.

"Well then, I gave you to understand that this place is more than a refuge on the earth. It extends into other, subtler realms, ones that are not as widely known to the common sort of human. We are a community of believers, small but determined and—if I may say it—blessed."

Liam checked the clock as Reid closed his eyes and steepled his fingers once again. It was ten past two. He leaned back and took refuge in the texture of the Egyptian cotton he wore beneath his jacket, and the warmth of the fire on the hand that hung over the leather arm of his chair. It was pleasant, except for the sweet, lambish smell of the leather as it warmed.

"Believers?" It seemed polite to ask after all the custard he had poured on his pie and the cigar that he had slipped into his pocket when Simon pressed him to take another. It was a very nice room, with so many impressive-looking books under glass. He noticed something called *The Necronomicon* and another called *A First Encyclopedia of Tlön*. On the top shelf there were black and silver spines bigger than church Bibles. Some were attached to the cabinet with fine bronze-coloured chains.

"Yes, Mr. Manley—no, it is important that we speak honestly, and I call you by your first name. And you must call me Simon. I realize this disturbs your sense of decorum, but I hope you will allow me."

"Of course, Simon, you may call me Liam."

"Liam, I said last night that I knew you to be a gentleman, but it was more than that. I saw in you one who has fought with me in the past, though he may be blind to that history. I have known you before, Liam, and you have known me."

Liam was alarmed. He wondered how alarmed one had to be before one abandoned one's good manners. "Mr. Reid, I'm not sure—"

"Yes, you are right to resist such naked declarations, but please listen. You are a musician because you were drawn to your ancient tools. Long ago you had the gift to work magic by the sound of your voice. I knew that last night, when I saw you, but then I dreamed further of those days when we were together at Delphi, and even farther back, when I knew you on the island of Lesbos, and lost Carcosa before that! In those ancient days you were a high priest, and you have returned to us, though your eyes have been darkened in this incarnation. I know that you doubt what I say, though I am warmed by the flame that still burns within you. Think on it, Liam, and when you have thought on it, consider joining our great work here."

In the silence that followed this extraordinary statement, Simon produced a small handbill. Liam recognized it as an advertisement for the next day's concert, including a program and two photographs, one taken by that man Lyon some weeks before, on the stage of the Temple Theatre. Looking at himself—his dark eyes, his hair falling forward across his brow, his long fingers on the piano keys—Liam thought he recognized something of what Reid had said.

Looking at his host, he saw, again, the stillness that had so arrested him the night before: the face immobile and the eyes gleaming in the firelight, the long yellow fingers at rest in his lap. He did not even seem to breathe, as though all his attention were fixed on Liam, as though what Liam said, what he was, mattered beyond all things.

Simon said softly, "Liam, my friend, do you remember setting sail, a thousand ships on the tide?"

He felt the little leap inside at each word—ships, sail, tide. Looking out the window, he didn't see the grey water; he saw the wide stone terrace above the sea, the linen robe over his shoulder, and in his hands a lyre; below him the boats full of fighting men smiting the furrows, his song rising in their sails.

Liam knew that Simon's yellowish eyes were still fixed on his face, but he did not look. He caressed his cuff, and felt against one knuckle its silk and cashmere. "Simon, I think you have mistaken me for someone else."

"We live in a suspicious age, and I do not ask for an immediate commitment, only that you consider the memories that are—I can see it, Liam, in your eyes—rising to consciousness. We have long known one another, and I trust you. I only ask that you give yourself the opportunity to remember."

"Of course—"

There was a knock on the door. Simon turned to face it. "Excuse me, Liam—yes, come."

Another man joined them, a roughish man with dirt under his nails and worn brown trousers. "Simon? Betty in the kitchen said you were back and I thought you might like to go over the new arrivals. I also need to talk to you about the orchard." He looked at Liam and nodded.

"Thank you Michael, I will be there in a moment. Liam, this is our very capable manager, Michael Sweeney. Now, Liam," Simon said as he rose, "I hope you will take your time, and allow any memories to surface, if they will, and remember that this place is safe for you. It is good to have you back with us, friend. I've been waiting for you." And then Simon was gone.

Liam stretched out his feet to the fire and closed his eyes.

He did not know how much later he woke. He was half out of his chair when it happened, finding himself in action before he was conscious. A nightmare, it must have been, though he could not remember what. He wondered as he dropped back to the chair whether he had shouted aloud, or if he had only stood. The room seemed the same, the shadows unchanged, the fire still burning. His watch said it was only twenty minutes since he had last looked, but for a moment he felt he had slept through a whole day and night.

He stood at the window for a moment, then went to the door which opened into a long, still corridor. Far away someone sang, badly, so he only recognized the song when he heard the words of the chorus: *the west a nest and you dear.* Very far away, footsteps ran and stopped and ran again. He hesitated in the doorway, wondering what was expected of him—should he find Simon? Or did he have the run of the place? He decided that he was free to explore and cheered himself up by remembering that Reid was obviously a nutter and one could not assume the civilities would be observed in all detail. Besides, he did not like to stay in the room where he had dreamed.

It was more than the dream that had disoriented him, though, because the hallway felt different as well, its corners no longer true. He could not name the new strangeness, felt only the fretfulness of a sick child, ran his fingers through his hair and rubbed at his face. His heart—startled by the dream—still thumped painfully in his eyes and ears.
At the end of the hallway, he found a door that let onto a porch, then a dismal greenish courtyard filled with the twigs and stumps of a young perennial border. Outside he took deep, slow breaths and began to feel square again.
Simon was waiting for him when Liam returned.

"I went for a walk. I went outside. But it was raining," Liam said. "Did you—" he began, and could not remember why it was Simon had left. "Did you finish?"

"You dream—yes?"

Unaccountably, Liam's mouth was dry. He couldn't think of what to say, but he did not like silence, just then, and did not want to hear what Simon would say next if Liam allowed him the opportunity.

"Yes, you dream. You should sit."

Liam sat in the chair he'd taken before.

"Do you fear sleep?"

Liam shook his head.

Simon's voice pressed on in a monotone. He did not wait for responses; he did not require them. "You fear sleep. You should not. I, who am shown scenes of unimaginable horror, do not fear sleep. All that fear—Liam, you must meet my eyes when I speak or I can impart no true knowledge to you—all that fear is only a measure of His Greatness. To know Him is to know pain, yes, but He judges us by what we endure for Him. Suffering is only a measure of our exile from His subtle realm, prisoned as we are in this corporeal hallucination, this unsubtle flesh. When you feel dread, remember that it is His light, refracted through the prism of your body and be content with that little knowledge. We are not given to know Him. Even when I am in His presence, He hides from me behind a yellow silk mask."

Here Simon stood quickly, and as he moved his body looked suddenly counterfeit. His yellow-ivory eyes conducted the heat of his words, and Liam wanted to look away but felt himself hooked on that gaze. Simon saw, he thought, the texture of his skin, heard the new wheeze that dogged his deep breaths, saw a new grey hair surfacing at his temple.

Simon stood as awkwardly as a masterless marionette. Then one hand raised by the wrist gestured to the fire, and he dropped to the hearth, marring the knees of his pale suit with coal dust.

"We must feel things for what they are, feel the destruction of the body for joy, feel its pleasures for ash, feel the institutions of the earth for monuments to dust."

Here he turned back to the large, green-tiled fireplace. He stretched his right arm toward the coals, the knotted string and dry sticks that composed his wrist visible through his skin as his cuff fell back. He reached into the fire and picked up a dull orange coal with his right hand. He set it in the palm of his left hand. Before Liam could close his eyes he saw first the reddening, then the blackening skin around the coal, and the smoke rising from his fingers.

Then Liam closed his eyes, but he could not escape the smell—first bitter coal smoke and burning hair, then burning flesh. Though he tried to hide his face, he knew Simon still gripped the bit of fire and that the man's hands followed his evasion, so no matter how he turned, the coal was before him. He could hear its hiss, could smell, he could smell the burning—

"Open your eyes, Liam."

The man was used to command.

"Open your eyes," he said.

And Liam did, though he did not wish it. Simon held a lump of red coal on his outstretched palm. He dropped it back into the fire, and then showed Liam his skin, which was whole and yellow, not red and weeping.

"You see the lesson. We burn only if we accept the premises of flesh and fire. I do not accept. I do not burn."

Liam looked away, and noticed the line of fine white cotton against his blue cuff, his fingertips pressed into the green leather arms of his chair until the skin around his nails turned yellow-white and dead-looking. Carefully he released his fingers, thinking he could not let them go into fists, and never unknot for days. He stretched them out, but as he did, they trembled. He glanced up to see Simon was still staring at him. He wet his lips. He tasted blood.

"You do not burn," he said.

"No, Liam."

Still the quiet voice, and Liam again saw the tremor in his own fingers and felt how clammy the leather was, where his hands rested. Sweat, thick and rank, gathered under his arms, down his spine, soaking the waistband of his trousers and his underclothes.

Still the man's voice: "Do you remember? Do you remember, Liam?" Though he swallowed to clear his throat, he felt the familiar constriction, like the nightly return of a bad dream daily forgotten, and he could not breathe as one by one the alveoli in his lungs shut tight like the fingers in his own fist. He might have the next breath and if he was lucky the one after that, and if he stood, he would feel the prickle of white sparks in his eyes, and the black snow slowly filled the field of his vision.

All the same, he stood. After a moment he made his way to the door, then out to the huge entrance hall where the stairs and gallery of the upper story seemed filled with people watching him. *I do not burn*, Simon said again and again in his head, or perhaps out loud, whispering in his ear, *I do not burn*. He flickered in and out of Liam's peripheral vision, then ahead of him, around a corner, out the double doors and into the grey light of January. In the moments before the car arrived to take Liam away, they stood in the hall and that man Michael joined them, saying nothing, but watching Liam as though they knew one another. Finally he turned to the man and asked if there was anything he wanted.

"No, sir," Michael said and looked down.

Mr. Reid smiled. "Michael confessed that he remembered you, and hoped you would feel the same familiarity. Do not trouble yourself, Liam, it is never easy to wake up."

In retrospect Liam wished he'd said something cutting like "quite." But he had only nodded as though saying, of course, one always has trouble awakening to the true, terrifying nature of reality.

Then the car pulled up and Mr. Reid shook his hand and then drew Liam close to him and clasped his head, pulling it down so his dry lips touched the skin beneath Liam's ear. He spoke quickly, sharply, and his breath smelled old: "Prepare for the worst, for the chaos that is rising in the East will not recede without a great battle on both our parts. I have in my possession the plans for an Engine that can protect us, and the means to build it. If you have need of shelter, you will remember us?"

Liam, wheezing, said nothing.

"You will remember? And remember us to Mrs. Kilgour?"

The lie came easily to him: "I will."

"Parach," Simon said, and kissed him. The long fingers of his left hand unwound from Liam's throat and jaw.

Standing before the mirror two days later, Liam could still feel the kiss on his mouth, and he found himself rubbing at it, as though to wipe away the sensation of dry lips and beard-bristles, the barest hint of saliva. When he reached his hotel in the late afternoon he was not well, and he called for basins of hot water and extra towels. After many hours sitting up, he managed to sleep in the armchair beside his bed. The next day he took no risks, and by late morning the attack had passed and he was ready to join Mrs. Kilgour for lunch, though there were dark, purplish circles under his eyes, and Mrs. Kilgour remarked that he looked delicate, as Clive had been.

As Liam left his room before dinner that evening, he glanced once more in the mirror over the dressing table and found himself arrested by the face he saw. In the lamplight it was the face he had seen in the handbill Simon had showed him. He thought suddenly of a novel he had found on a train and begun but never finished. Maria Corelli? L. Adams

Beck? It was set in some ancient Mediterranean place full of gold-tinted gods and olive groves and cypresses, stony hillsides dropping down to waters of cerulean or aquamarine or (at sunset) wine-dark magenta. In general he preferred magazine articles detailing modern travel or developments in recording technology, but it was a very long train trip, and he had exhausted the two back issues of *The Etude* he carried. What he remembered just then was the hero, some musician with dark, tousled hair and fevered eyes (epithets repeated every chapter). The man was insipid, constantly thwarted in his pursuit of a shepherdess who was, secretly, a princess, and composing songs for birds and trees and things, neglecting to commit enough time to daily exercises.

But there had been ships on the tide below a gold-hued sky, driven to Asia Minor on the breath of a song. In the mirror—for a moment—he had seen a face like that described in the novel, the face of a bardic magus in linen and purple, illuminated as though by sunset or stage lights, so his mouth was cast in shadow and his dark hair shadowed his brow.

The next day Liam dressed for the evening concert in a suit carefully tended by his valet, whose careful and impressive work had so improved his toilet. Liam felt, finally, that he had learned to the handle the man.

Downstairs Mrs. Kilgour was waiting in the great room (hired for their private use), already dressed in the long spangled gown of the Edwardian prima donna. Her hair was done up in feathers of some kind, very expensive feathers, he guessed. He stood patiently near her, waiting for the final adjustments to her headdress, and thinking of what her money and her will achieved: an eternal 1905 that rendered all her attendants children in a pre-war idyll.

At least his suit was fashionably cut. That night's recital was held in a Girl Guide Hall hired by Mrs. Kilgour's agents under the name "The Orphic Society," though it was a silly fiction: Mrs. Kilgour was the Orphic Society. Even knowing that, and knowing the power his employer had in Duncan's Crossing, Liam still swelled a little when he saw that the house was filled with 350 souls seated and another fifty, at least, standing at the back. The quintet was in position when the lights went down. Then Liam made his way slowly to his place and bowed sharply. The crowd clapped. There were a few inappropriate whistles from the back of the room, but he greeted them with a formal little bow. Finally Mrs. Kilgour made her way across the floor and the applause trailed off as she reached centre stage. She raised her hands for silence and curtsied deeply.

"Friends!" she said. "Children! It is a great privilege you do me coming here tonight to share with me the most innocent pleasure of song. But still, I must remind you that all true pleasures are of God, and lead to Him. So as you listen tonight, allow your hearts to open to the mystery and the beauty and the goodness of music." There were a few tentative claps. "First I shall sing," she turned to the music stand, "first I shall sing 'Ye Banks and Braes o' Bonnie Doon,' a song of our own homeland, so far far away."

The quintet began its wet arpeggios. For a moment Liam relaxed. The pressure of an audience sometimes made a difference, she might—

No. He tried not to fidget. He watched the crowd for a distraction. There was a suspicious silence out there, a rapt, confused quiet that he felt sure would crack at any moment. Then what would happen?

The song ended, followed by sparse applause.

She launched into Bellini's "Ah! non giunge uman pensiero" from *La sonambula*, whose flourishes, properly executed, ought to have had the texture of a meringue. Mrs. Kilgour, however, attacked them with a lugubrious sincerity that rendered them almost suetty. Liam watched a bearded man smile, and thought he must be deaf. A young woman held her husband's hand, both their faces transfigured by horror. A girl cowered in her chair, as though someone had been just about to hit her. Three boys in Sunday suits laughed silently and slid low in their seats. Liam wondered if Mrs. Kilgour could see them, but when he looked, her eyes were closed.

She was turning to him then, and he stood and took his place beside her for a duet from *Werther*. He did his job manfully.

He endured. He sang "A Wandr'ing Minstrel I" when she surrendered the stage. He had just reached the last line about his rags and patches when he noticed a familiar face near the exit. Simon Reid in another pale suit, far too pale for January, Liam thought critically when he had discharged his duty to *The Mikado*; he can't really be a gentleman with a suit like that. All the same, when he left the stage, he felt a blush creep up his throat, as he wondered what Reid thought of the whole business. But no—he would not care.

Reid met him on the steps as they left the hall.

Liam nodded. "Mr. Simon Reid," he said.

"Mr. Manley, our visiting Orpheus. I very much enjoyed the performance. Perhaps you could introduce me to Mrs. Kilgour? Her voice is impressive. Divine, one could almost say."

"Perhaps. I will consider it," he said, and slid into the car waiting to take them four blocks to their hotel. He hoped he wouldn't see Reid again. He would warn Leticia against the man, if Reid ever pursued her.

In his room the next morning Liam opened a heavy white envelope with the Castle Dunsinane souvenir letter opener and pen knife Mrs. Kilgour had given him at Christmas. The letter was written in an elegant black hand, leaning hard right as though subject to some irresistible westward momentum. Liam's eye ran past the greeting and date, straight into the body of the letter:

> *What you must understand, Mr. Manley, is that humanity is not divided by sex or wealth or religion. Humanity is divided by consciousness. This consciousness is inherent; it cannot be learned, but was earned many millions of years ago, among the Hyperboreans, the Beringians and the Atlanteans. Those who survive—Those Who Are—chose to take up the burden and evolve, sacrificing themselves out of love for Man, and desire for his continued evolution. Now, we are in the Age of Cronos, in the realm of the Kali Yuga, Mr. Manley, and only the strong and brave recognize the cost of survival.*
>
> *Of course, for them it is no cost, it is only the obliteration of flesh, and what is flesh? The unsubtle body to which we were chained at birth, inveigled into possessing, a prison house shut down around our souls. You and I, a handful of others, we will pass on to the west, and there occupy the subtle realm where time and death shall be no more. If anything the accelerating destruction of the material world is the final grasp at transformation—in destruction is freedom from material.*

I know I shock you with the starkness of my words, but the hour is late. I have a message concerning your eminent Patrona, Mrs Leticia Kilgour. It is imperative that I deliver it at once. I ask that you arrange a meeting. There is one—a young man—from the Other Side who would contact her, and who thinks she is in grave danger. I am compelled by the knowledge I have of her fate to help her. Parach!

Liam shredded the letter carefully, then disordered the scraps and scattered them in the wastepaper basket beneath his desk.

CLIVE

During ten recitals up the coast, Liam heard three variations on Mrs. Kilgour's speech regarding the Virtue of Music, and saw ten evening gowns in shades of pink, mauve, and red. During her performances, he grew used to the rapt and/or horrified audience, just as he had grown used to the unquestioned truth that Mrs. Kilgour was an exceptional woman. He simply complied (perhaps it was inevitable when one was in her orbit), and by the end of the tour, he contented his mind with thoughts of the recordings that would follow in the first week of February. February, he thought, when the weather would be brighter, and he would begin his real work. He amused himself in train carriages and in Mrs. Kilgour's Rolls-Royce (which travelled with them, like an enormous lap cat, even when the rain-gutted streets were too rough for city tires and it stuck axle-deep in the mud of a northern coal town), imagining and re-imagining his eight sides, and ignoring the duets. He had begun ignoring them when Mrs. Kilgour decided to expand the duets to a quarter of the catalogue, the other quarter being Liam's solo work.

Though duets horrified him, they were preferable to really thinking about the ten recitals or the little towns through which they had travelled. The largest and pleasantest had also been the first: Duncan's Crossing, where much of the audience hadn't belonged to the Kilgour Industries. After that the towns were smaller and grimmer, the audiences in the tiny halls and churches silent, and whether mistrustful or horrified, Liam did not know. Once, as they picked their way through the mud toward the manager's house where they stayed, a rock flicked past Mrs.

Kilgour's head, and Liam had looked sharply around at the loafers and children and housewives on the street. None of them looked any guiltier than the others, but they all looked interested. She might be an old harpy, incapable of carrying a tune in a bucket, and intent on punishing everyone with her voice, but surely she did not deserve rocks.

Mrs. Kilgour had scheduled a long weekend midway through their tour, to give the artists and their party the opportunity to recover from the exhausting demands of the stage. They stopped at the Kilgour Country Estate, the Hunting Lodge, she called it, in the mountains north of Duncan's Crossing. Mrs. Kilgour retired to her rooms with Nora and Euphemia, and left Liam and Goshawk to their own devices: they spent their days reading or smoking outside.

Occasionally Liam thought about writing letters at the desk in the drawing room, or sat at the piano, or wondered how difficult it was to ride a horse (he hadn't brought the clothes, so he did not try). It would be a nice country place in summer, he guessed, but the rain and the hills foreshortened the views, and it was awkward to demand entertainment when he was meant to be resting.

It was on the third and second-to-last night that Mrs. Kilgour called Liam to her upstairs parlour. It had been raining for three days, and Liam entered the room on a gust of fresh, damp air from outside, though when the door closed behind him, he felt the close atmosphere of her fireside overtake him. Mrs. Kilgour sat at the window, with a bit of gauzy stitchery in her lap. He never saw her work on any of these projects, only saw her lay them aside when company arrived. Once he wondered if Nora was instructed to begin embroidering scarves and tea-cloths so that Mrs. Kilgour might look as though she were in progress on some delicate bit of work. His mother had never been without sewing at hand, but when she was expecting friends on some ladylike occasion, she made a point to Ella about the kind of fancy work that should lie around the front room, or beside her rocking chair on the porch. He had not understood at the time, but looking at Mrs. Kilgour, he wondered if she had learned the same esoteric principles.

Mrs. Kilgour set the bit of white aside and smiled at him. "My dear Liam. I have something about which I must speak to you."

She gestured to a low chair set conveniently at her side, and Liam sat, knees above elbows until he rearranged himself. "What is it, Mrs. Kilgour?" he asked, looking up at her. The angle was not kind to his neck, but he knew better than to find another seat.

"I haven't told you much of my son Clive, have I?"

Liam had heard of Clive. Mrs. Kilgour had spoken of him quite early in their relationship, and initially Liam had thought he was just away, and had not asked further. The Kilgours were clannish, and their family consisted of a huge extended network, so large Liam was not bothered with remembering all their names. He knew that Clive had seen service and that he did not live in the city; beyond that he did not care.

"Very little, Mrs. Kilgour." Without thinking, he added, "But I have often wondered."

"I'm not surprised. You remind me of him. He volunteered and went overseas at the beginning of the war. He was such a handsome, brave laddie."

Liam smiled, but sadly and sweetly now.

"We don't know what became of him. He fought bravely for two years, and he fell in early 1918. Three years gone now, I know, but sometimes I can't find it in me to believe he won't come back. Perhaps he will return, when time and death shall be no more."

Liam's smile remained fixed on his face, in a way he hoped was still sad and sweet, because he found he did not feel sad nor sweet. He would prefer not to think about Clive, and about what might have happened to him. He imagined Mrs. Kilgour at home, waiting for letters from him. Clive was a young man; he wouldn't write often. He would be too busy. He was a rich man, too, and there were many distractions for young, rich men in England and France. In light of all those entertainments and diversions, he would neglect his letters.

Mrs. Kilgour was still speaking: "I intended to join him over there. He was such a brave, headstrong laddie, he needed someone to look after him and see that his officers appreciated him. He was too gallant, often, for the Canadians. He told me often how much better he would have suited one of the Highland regiments. But he was a Canadian laddie, and he saw his duty. It was only that he needed his mother to see to his career."

Liam said nothing. His smile was gone. He turned his face to the fire.

"But he was gone before I reached England. It is one of my great sorrows that I did not join him sooner. I was distracted by my responsibilities here."

Liam thought he should say something, but had to think a moment. "I'm sure, Mrs. Kilgour, I'm sure it was important work you did here, raising spirits at home and doing good work with the poor and deserving and—" But he could not think what else Mrs. Kilgour did, with her unending parade of garden parties and concerts and meetings and teas. Did she raise money? Had she headed a chapter of the IODE? He remembered his mother's knitting, and something about bandages. She had filled whole letters enumerating the quantity of socks and bandages produced in their little front room during Thursday night IODE meetings. Did Mrs. Kilgour knit in addition to working those gauzy bits of white?

She said, "Yes, Liam, but I am a mother first, and Clive is gone."

Liam framed sentences in his mind, about how she had obligations to her nation, or to the family she still had at home, and how the home fires were a woman's sacred duty, and how every man on the front line had an army of women with him, in spirit. How she was just as brave as her son was, and how she must live on with his memory, and how she had taken the torch from Clive's failing hands and would remember him at the going down of the sun, and in the morning. Though he collected a good little store of useful phrases and sentiments, he found them difficult to utter with the other thing that was now swelling in his breast, the tightness behind his ribs that grew and strained toward his throat, his tongue and lips. He was not sure whether it was some hard lump of scar tissue he would disgorge onto the front-room carpet, or something he would shout, or both. While the strangulation was familiar from other bad days, like that evening in Duncan's Crossing, it took him a moment to recognize what he felt was not the usual expression of his bad lungs, but anger.

The truth was, he hated hearing about socks and scarves and bandages. Further, he hated hearing about teas, and nice ladies who met up on the second Wednesday of the month to plan concerts. He hated, as well, the bits of patriotic verse they half-remembered from their school readers, the ugly, lumpy platitudes so enjoyed by women like

Mrs. Kilgour. Like his mother. Like Ella, even, though she was so young he did not mind as much. She might learn and know better, sometime, and would understand what he meant when he did not answer the letters, and sent only the pre-printed postcards from the commissary, his signature across the bottom, and everything but "I am well" crossed out with black ink. His mother, however, would always be what she was: a foolish, limited woman living on a cornfield outside of London. And not the right London, even, but the other one.

But he should reassure his Patrona. "I'm sure you did right, Mrs. Kilgour," he said. It didn't seem very reassuring.

"Yes, I am content that I have always done my duty, though it is so hard. But still, I wonder what would have become of Clive if I had been there to look after him."

Liam wondered what she wanted, and how quickly he could end their tête-à-tête. He could do what he knew best, and go to the piano, and provoke her to pleasurable tears with "Flowers of the Forest." He worried though, that if he did sit down he would sing something less suited to Mrs. Kilgour's mood: at best, "Never Mind the Food Controller, We'll Live on Love." At worst, he might walk over to the piano and play the bittersweet opening bars of "Auld Lang Syne," and then he might choose a song he had often heard in 1915, beginning in his best manner, clear and deceptively tender: *we're here because we're here because we're here because we're here we're here because we're here—*

It would not do to offend Mrs. Kilgour just then: she might forget his dependence. Instead of taking those five steps to the piano and singing "Keep the Home Fires Burning," or "If You Want to Find the Sergeant Major," Liam sat and smiled sadly, with the mechanical gestures and painted lips of the ventriloquist's dummy. Mrs. Kilgour smiled in a melancholy way as well, and together they sat in the darkening parlour, and Liam did not know at all what she felt, looking at him with such soft eyes, and he did not care.

As the afternoon advanced, she finally explained why any of this should matter to him: "What I want you to know, Liam, is that I feel Clive with me, even now. He is guiding our work. I think you should know that we are doing more than just good work for the poor Indians and coal miners. It's for Clive as well!"

"Yes, for Clive," he said.

"And not only for Clive, but for all the poor laddies. So we must do our best, Liam, not only for the living, but for the dead."

A STROH VIOLIN FOR MRS. KILGOUR

The night before he met with his accompanist for the recording, Liam dreamed that he and Reid stood on the beach, watching a fleet of cedar long ships with high prows, carved and painted to look like forest creatures and birds and fish. They sailed under green and yellow and brick-coloured sheets. It was evening and there were no lights on the opposite shore.

The next morning he rose early and drank tea with lemon in it. He sat a long time at the open window, breathing deeply and carefully, sometimes hissing, then trilling arpeggios and moaning until he felt himself ready. He climbed two flights to the suite Goshawk had booked for the recordings. It was a damp day. He was out of breath when he arrived, but ten minutes standing in the hallway put him right.

He knocked and entered. The hotel furniture had been removed, and it was warm and dark with shut windows and blankets on the walls and extra carpet underfoot. There were two men, one attending to the machine at the far end of the long room, the other sitting at the piano, reading a six-months-old copy of *The Illustrated London News.*

"You're early," said the one managing the equipment, before he disappeared through another door.

"My name is Manley," he said to the remaining man, "Liam Manley."

The man at the piano glanced up at him and nodded. Then he said, "Drysdale. The other one is Penney."

Liam waited. When Drysdale didn't speak again, he said, "We'll begin with 'Auld Lang Syne.' I think that was first on the list."

"Alright, then," the man said through his pipe. He turned on the piano stool and dropped the *Illustrated News* to the floor.

He began at a brisk tempo, and Liam stumbled to catch up, all the while examining the huge fabric horn. By the second refrain he had reached his stride, but then the other man rejoined them, this time carrying a chamois. For a moment he listened, and Liam flattered himself that the man had a sensitive ear, that he knew good music when he heard it, that he might even discern something Parisian in Liam's manner and voice, from his six months with M. Girard. It would be a relief to them, dealing with a professional. For all Drysdale's bad manners and lazy posture, they were building a fine crescendo in the third chorus. He thought of how a thousand copies of that crescendo would soon be all over the city, and the country even, and how after dinner a woman might say, "Oh, play Manley's 'Auld Lang Syne' again! I like it best!"

"You might reconsider the C, Mr. Manley," said Penney.

Drysdale stopped. "Yes, I think he might," he said.

Mr. Penney explained: "There's something, Mr. Manley, we call blasting. Often a note like your C, there in the fifth bar, overwhelms the diaphragm, and the mechanism that cuts the groove in our master disk. The effect is quite unpleasant on playback, though it is a common mistake. Perhaps we could pitch you a little lower? Then the song will lie in the best part of your voice."

Liam knew the C lay at the very margins of his talent, but he had always fancied that his audience felt a certain gallantry in his approach to that particular mountain. Gallantry was a fine thing in a performer, he always thought, especially when they faced the C. Drysdale played the opening bars again, at a lower pitch, and Liam joined him, self-conscious to find that a thing like "blasting" existed, and that he might be guilty of it. He concentrated, but despite his care, one by one the muscles down either side of his spine clamped tight, though he knew he must be a hollow reed, and let his breath build from his belly.

"Yes, I think that's better," said Drysdale. "I think we may be able to use that."

"But, I was expecting a rehearsal—"

"I wouldn't worry much, Mr. Manley. This isn't Berliner Phonograph."

Drysdale nodded as well. "Not Berliner Phonograph," he said.

Penney said, "I should add, you were quite right about the new spring," and flipped some switch in the wooden base of his pet Morning Glory. Then, his voice suddenly sonorous and his accent more refined, Penney said, "Mr. Liam Manley, tenor, singing 'Auld Lang Syne.'"

Drysdale thumped through the opening bars and when the moment was right, Liam began to sing.

That afternoon Mrs. Kilgour sang her "Ave Maria." Her eyes were closed. Liam had withdrawn to the windows at the opposite end of the room, only sparing the barest thought to what Mrs. Kilgour or Mr. Goshawk might think of his inattention as he watched the street through a crack in the curtains. Behind him, Drysdale thumped away at his accompaniment, and Penney managed his machine, eyebrows beetled as he watched the needle carve a thin thread of wax from the recording disk. When she finished, Mrs. Kilgour stood a moment longer than necessary before the electric Morning Glory that topped Mr. Penney's recording device.

"Well," began Mr. Goshawk. "Well, I think we may call that finished. Mr. Manley, what do you think? Do you think our Euterpe has completed her task?"

Liam did not answer.

"Our Euterpe, Mr. Manley," Goshawk said again. "But perhaps you remain entranced? You should break the spell, Mrs. Kilgour! You should break the spell you have cast on your poor, trapped Orpheus!" Here Goshawk laughed his horrible false laugh. But it was too late, for now Mrs. Kilgour covered her mouth and looked up at him through her lashes.

"Have I done, Mr. Manley?" she asked.

"Yes. I believe you have," Liam said, keeping his eyes on the street outside.

"Then we must celebrate! Goshawk—send a message that we will have late dinner for eight. Tell Nora to pick my good November family menu! Only I want hollandaise for the sauce. Mr. Manley likes hollandaise!"

Liam could not stand to think that he was a man who liked hollandaise. After an afternoon of six songs, each recorded once—so perfect was the first performance we need not trouble you for a second! Goshawk had told her, and neither Penney nor Drysdale argued—Liam could not face dinner at the Castle. There would be buckets of hollandaise, and Mrs. Kilgour would describe her afternoon, turning to Goshawk for confirmation, and to Liam. And she would talk of their mission in her low, serious voice, and Euphemia would say, oh yes, especially after her triumphs on the stage, such work could only contribute to the moral improvement of the whole province!

Defeated far in advance, Liam said, "Oh, Mrs. Kilgour, I don't think I'll join you tonight. I think I should take an early night, and rest." He smiled while he said it, but he thought that if he saw his own smile he would not like it much. He thought it would remind him too much of Goshawk.

Goshawk gave him a look that made Liam wonder what the man was like with Mrs. Kilgour's chauffeurs and skivvies and upstairs maids, and how he might treat his dog. But then Mrs. Kilgour spoke again: "Oh, my dear, go back to your room and order bread and milk—no, you must! I think I'll order it for you. Goshawk—see that bread and milk is sent to Mr. Manley's room. And honey, send honey, too!"

Then they were gone, and he was alone in the room with Penney, who stood over the machine, rubbing it with a soft cloth, while Drysdale looked at his watch. Liam searched their faces for smiles, but Penney was intent on his machinery and Drysdale picked up his *Illustrated London News*.

A month later it was mid-March, and he was again at Craiglockhart (a blue-grey suit, a new green silk tie, and indigo socks). He was standing before the wide windows that overlooked the rose garden, but now there were leaves covering the ugly, thorny stems. Behind him Goshawk did something with the phonograph.

"I think the 'Ave Maria' will be our finale. Yes. The zenith of her art, she called it. She will like to hear it last. What do you think we should begin with, Mr. Manley? I think we should begin with the pretty one about the little sleepwalker. Mrs. Kilgour likes singing that one a great deal, and she will like to hear it first, to set her mood for all the others, don't you think Mr. Manley? You will, I think, have to wait to hear your own work." Mr. Goshawk did not pause for breath or conversation until Mrs. Kilgour joined them, accompanied by Nora, her current niece-secretary and Euphemia—all the older children being away with husbands and wives, or attending to Kilgour interests in California and Toronto.

Alive to the occasion's gravity, Mrs. Kilgour had prepared a little speech. "I will take this moment," she began, "before we hear the fruit of our labours, to say thank you, thank you Goshawk, and Liam, and dear Nora and Euphemia!"

Goshawk led the applause, followed by Liam and Nora, and finally Euphemia."What can a simple man say? No, I think it best to let your own voice speak for me, and ask you to listen to this first printing, which will carry the work of your voice farther than you can imagine!" He was about to speak again, but Euphemia had already set the phonograph going, and Liam's fingernails dug into his palms.

Drysdale was not as he remembered. In person the man had a lazy left hand and a heavy foot on the pedals that was more sentiment than sensibility. In the large horn of the phonograph he was much cleaner. While he noticed that initial discrepancy, he doubted his ear and it wasn't until the vocalist embarked upon those first coquettish notes of "Ah! non giunge uman pensiero," that he realized that it was not the suetty coloratura of his rehearsals with Mrs. Kilgour. The woman whose voice floated from the large, elaborate horn—though she sang Mrs. Kilgour's song, and though the label bore Mrs. Kilgour's name—was not the dog-eared, red-faced lady. The woman was talented, disciplined, a prima donna, though not one he recognized.

Liam looked at Goshawk. Goshawk did not return his look. Nora listened as though she heard nothing, her face as always so plain and virtuous that Liam ignored her on principle. Euphemia listened as though she had taken a slug from some ancient bottle of medicinal laudanum, and only the occasional roll of her eyes betrayed the daughterly contempt Liam had often seen in her face. She did not care. Goshawk, however. Goshawk. Liam looked again to the man, but he had turned away to the windows. His hands were knotted behind him. He beat time inaccurately on the small of his back.

After "Non giunge" it was "By Yon Bonnie Banks." Here the anonymous prima donna seemed utterly fresh, with none of the insipidity he found so repulsive in Mrs. Kilgour's interpretations. This woman executed the ballad with a grief Liam thought of as *refined*—another *mot juste* that made him proud. He would have liked to discuss it with her, whoever she was. Perhaps she was tall and aristocratic and blonde, with grey eyes. After that it was her "Queen of the Night," in English, and even in English it was lovely.

The first four sides having been considered, Mrs. Kilgour rose again, and Goshawk stopped fussing by the phonograph. Euphemia crossed her arms tightly over her chest, pushing her breasts forward and up against the fine white fabric of her afternoon dress. Liam looked, then looked away.

"Mrs. Kilgour," Goshawk began, "Mrs. Kilgour, I hope you are not disappointed! This machine cannot hope to capture your voice in truth, but you must not be downhearted, and expect that it—"

"Yes, Goshawk. It is not my voice—there is a delicacy but also a vibrancy missing in the recording. You had told me that it would not be quite as I had done it. It does very well, though."

Late that evening, after family dinner (with hollandaise) and a short program of hymns from Mrs. Kilgour, Liam saw Goshawk slip out through the French doors and stand smoking on the terrace above the roses. Seeing the red spark of Goshawk's cigarette he, too, slipped out the door and stood beside the man, among the splashes of yellow light from Craiglockhart's windows. They looked into the gloomy park, past the roses to the trees and the shrubbery, and through their branches, city lights below them to the north.

Well, he began in his head, *these devices transform their subjects more than I had imagined!* He thought he would say it with a delicately nuanced irony, perhaps when Goshawk had finished that cigarette and then Liam could offer him another from his new silver case, which would be both generous and worldly enough to show Goshawk he was not taken in, only amused. Then he thought he might be blunt and say, *Who was it you recorded?*

As he weighed the different approaches, Goshawk spoke first. "The woman was not, of course, our Mrs. Kilgour. In the most rigourous sense, at least."

"Oh—yes?"

"No. She is an Englishwoman, a singer of popular opera and ballads with a quality of voice not unlike our Patrona, though hardly known to Canada. I heard her once in Toronto when I was travelling there on Kilgour business."

Liam said nothing, but then Goshawk had finished his cigarette. He squatted and carefully stubbed it out in a planter, digging a little hole with his right forefinger and pushing the remains under the earth. Liam wondered if it was some holdover from another house, where one was not allowed to smoke and must hide one's evidence. Perhaps his mother took a hard line on smoking. As the man rose, Liam opened his silver cigarette case and held it out. Goshawk took two.

"When I heard the recordings for the first time, I knew that Mrs. Kilgour would not find them an accurate representation of her own voice—you saw how she reacted this afternoon. Which left me to wonder how I could satisfy my employer's need for veracity with a technology that so changes the things it purports to reproduce. It was then that I remembered something the technician told me—you remember the young man named Drysdale?—he told me that often they must replace familiar instruments in recording because the process so distorts sound. For instance, he told me of something called a Stroh Violin. It sounds quite vulgar in life, but its vulgarity is softened by the process of recording into something like the sound of a true violin. And thinking on what that young man had told me, I considered that I should find the equivalent of a Stroh Violin for our Mrs. Kilgour. That is, a voice which sounds—in recording—like what Mrs. Kilgour hears within her own head. And then it was only a matter of engaging this woman to record the same compositions. It was very simple. Well, once I had exchanged a few telegrams with our Toronto Office."

Liam threw away his cigarette, which had burned close to his fingers while he listened. He found Goshawk looking at him, though his face was nearly lost in the gloom.

"Of course, but it wasn't her."

"You will find, Liam, that men in our line of work must learn to read not only our Patrona's stated wishes, but her unspoken desires. It is not wise to expose them to ridicule, Liam."

Our line of work? Liam wondered. Then he asked, "But have you thought about the next tour? About her plans for distributing these recordings—have you thought about the duets?"

Goshawk sighed. He seemed to shrink, as though at his margins he had given in, a little, to the darkness of the evening, and of Craiglockhart Castle.

"I trust that Mrs. Kilgour's fascination with music will be short-lived—"

"She has extensive plans for the spring."

"All the same, I trust that it will be short-lived."

"But the duets—"

"Then we will find a way to direct her from such plans. And I suggest that you, also, find ways beyond music to keep yourself in Mrs. Kilgour's thoughts. I trust her fascination will be short-lived." This last time when he spoke, he intoned the words as though they were the terminal phrase of some incantation, and Liam did not press. Behind them the doors opened and the curtains parted, spilling light on both their faces—Nora calling them back into the close, hot room.

When they were inside again, Goshawk looked at his watch and said to Liam, "Would you like to hear your own work? I think we have time for one little song." Before Liam could speak, Goshawk had selected "Auld Lang Syne" and set it on the disk.

There was the soft whirr of the machine, then what had been an aggressive accompaniment rendered almost subtle by the recording process. The first time Liam heard his own voice detached from his body he wondered who the man was, and for a moment he supposed that some amateur's work had been sent in place of his own. How else could he account for the hissed sibilants, the flubbed K and G? The stranger's voice filled the room with an uncomfortable urgency, as though he was running away from something and singing over his shoulder, so that the sustains faltered and fell a fraction sooner than the notation required. As instructed, he had avoided the C, but now he heard his own throat strangle the A. He had always felt his A was adequate.

"I am surprised," said Mrs. Kilgour when the last, flannel-tongued sustain had faded away. Liam hoped she was about to say it was not Liam's voice at all, coming from the shellac disk, but some imposter. But instead she went on, "that your recording is so accurate. Perhaps your voice is better suited to reproduction than mine."

“I think it’s lovely,” said Euphemia.“It is so much like him! It is magical to think that his voice will exist long after we are dust!”

It was only one day, Liam reminded himself, one wet afternoon in a stuffy room, with an accompanist he’d never met and whom he disliked. It was less than a single day, it was four minutes, and had nothing to do with all the other good afternoons before it or to come.

Mrs. Kilgour’s fascination with music was short-lived. Not through any work of Liam’s or Goshawk’s, but by the sort of chance event Goshawk depended upon. The event so redirected Mrs. Kilgour’s life that, when Anthea came to write about it, she put it like this, and then deleted it: *Mrs. Kilgour’s musical ambitions were short-lived.* The day she was to enter the recording room again, she received a telegram from the Imperial War Graves Commission informing her that they had found her son’s body, and that it had been interred in a small cemetery outside Reims. She left that day in a private railcar with Nora, Euphemia, and Goshawk, and sailed for France a week later. (68)

MRS. LAYTON AT HOME

In the afternoon of the fourth day of her haunting, Anthea left work early to visit the Aquarian Centre. At two o’clock she opened the door on the entrance hall, and stood alone among the Arts and Crafts furniture and green Turkish carpets. Visiting for the first time in daylight, without a crowd, she had time to examine the walls, covered with lithographs of ancient monuments, and rites observed by nineteenth-century occult travellers. Curious apparatus—shamanic, alchemical, mesmeric—lay on shelves among books: Beck, Blavatsky, Burgess, *The Great God Pan*. The room was cool though it was warm outside, and quiet under the hypnotic tick of the clock on the mantel.

“Hello?”

No one answered. Mrs. Layton had said two o’clock would suit, and just let herself in the front door when she arrived. She sat down on a club chair and smelled the lamb stink of the leather. It was hard to sit still, so she turned to the locked bookshelf beside her. She made out titles under glass: *The Necronomicon*, and *A First Encyclopedia of Tlön*. She craned her neck to see the black and silver spines on the top shelf, bigger than church Bibles. Some were attached to the cabinet with fine, bronze-coloured chains.

Then the sliding doors opened and when she turned toward the sound, she again faced Mrs. Layton's original and surprising loveliness. She was as she always had been: cashmered, moonstoned, her hair up-swept in gray waves, her expression benign but uninviting. Anthea stood up. As she did she felt a sudden, vertiginous self-consciousness, and knew that Mrs. Layton saw the missing button on her blouse, the place where her elbow poked through her cardigan, her shaggy, untrimmed hair, the roll where her stomach spilled over the waistband of her jeans. Her eyebrows ungroomed, her fingernails clean but ragged. She had looked in the mirror once when she brushed her teeth, but could not remember if she had also brushed her hair.

But unbrushed hair hadn't ever stopped her talking. "I just sat down the door was open so I just came in and I sat down."

"Please, sit down again."

"You said two o'clock," she said, then returned to the club chair and the lamb-scented leather.

"And it is two o'clock."

Anthea pulled a notebook and a pen out of her bag, scattering three candy wrappers on the carpet. "Okay, like," she said and picked up the wrappers, trying to remember what she had planned to say next.

The first thing she noticed when she looked up from the wrappers was that Mrs. Layton didn't seem to blink as often as other people. She fixed her pale eyes on Anthea's face for a long time before she spoke. Anthea remained very quiet during the staring, though it provoked her to compose, in her head, a long list of questions that ended with *what are you looking at, anyway?*

"Anthea," Mrs. Layton asked, "why are you here?"

"Because of Jasmine."

"Why now, though? Why today?"

"Because I want to know."

This seemed to temporarily satisfy Mrs. Layton, and she returned to her contemplation, now with her eyes closed. When she spoke again her voice was warmer. "Often the things I see are indistinct, but this is quite clear. I don't understand it, though, so you will have to help me. I see a strange place. I see a building, and I see a payphone. If you wanted to help me, you could tell me what these things mean to you."

"Okay, but. I don't know."

"A payphone. Let the answer rise in your mind."

Anthea found that her mouth was open and her lips were dry. She licked them. There was only one payphone that came to mind as Mrs. Layton spoke.

"There's. What kind of building is it?"

"It's large. It's unusual in some way I can't see. The walls are crooked."

"There's the Glass Castle. It's made of beer bottles. It's on the highway outside of Duncan's Crossing. There's a payphone out front, by the main office where you buy tickets for minigolf."

Mrs. Layton closed her eyes and nodded. "Yes, Anthea, that's right. When I think of the Glass Castle, it's dark. I sense that Jasmine is nearby. I sense that she wants something from us, something urgent."

"She was seen there. One of the last times anyone saw her. It came up on a missing persons site, where people collect articles and police reports."

"Yes, that's right. But does the Glass Castle mean anything else?"

"We passed by there, too. On our way to somewhere else."

Mrs. Layton sat back in her chair, and while she didn't make a sound, there was a feeling in the room like a sigh. Anthea shifted as well, just enough to see out the window and into the deep, green garden that surrounded the Aquarian Centre. "I don't know."

When Mrs. Layton opened her eyes again, her look was urgent and she said, quickly, "Anthea, it is not given to me to know the future, but I do sometimes see the past, and the present, and in our few encounters I have recognized you as a woman marked." She reached for Anthea's hand and held it in her hard fingers. "You and Jasmine did something, something you should not have done, and something you cannot escape. I think if you want to know more, you might return there."

With the suggestion, Anthea felt the now-familiar sensation of portent, as though the subtle currents of Jasmine's reality were about to reveal themselves. She felt a new pressure in her eyes that seemed to say revelation is imminent. It left a mark in her peripheral vision, a sunspot, a retinal burn.

"We can't always know the consequences of our actions. Where did you go after the Glass Castle?"

"We were going to visit someone."

"Yes, Anthea. I can see it. Amends must be made when you disturb the dead, or the living. You have already noticed the signs. You are often attended by black birds in the sky. You have bad dreams."

When Anthea shook her head the sunspots followed her glance. "Maybe. Maybe that's true."

"I'm going to ask you to do something that will sound strange, something you might not like to do. But I want you to promise me that you will think about the Glass Castle, and what happened there, and then you will come back to see me again next week."

"Okay. But."

"And when you have done this, I want you to bring me an egg."

Anthea peered through the glittering field of her vision, about to say, *What?* when Mrs. Layton continued, "An egg from your kitchen. Do you have any?"

"I don't think so."

"Buy some today. Let them sit in your refrigerator, and then bring one of them with you, the same time next week."

"I don't know—"

"There's no need for you to know, just do as I ask, as a favour. Bring me the egg."

"Alright. Maybe. But I want you to tell me something in return. I want you to tell me his name."

Mrs. Layton made a face Anthea had seen before, a look of confusion that suggested Anthea's very nature was incompatible with the rising Aquarian Age. Then she said, "I don't know his name, but we called him Menander."

Menander, Anthea thought. She stood. She decided, suddenly, that she would go north to Duncan's Crossing and visit a castle made of beer bottles that stood, shabby and out-of-time, on the edge of the highway. What would happen after that, she wasn't sure. It would involve an egg.

"I know you do not trust us, but we only want to help. And think, Anthea, where are you going? And what are you looking for?" *An egg* was all she could think to answer, so she said nothing.

On the sidewalk outside, she willed the shadows and flickers that lit her left periphery to coalesce into vision, but by the time she was home, her eyes were full of scintillating architectures that meant nothing but the onset of headache.

PART TWO
THE
PARADISE
ENGINE
PART TWO

THE CROSSING

If they were lucky hitchhikers, they could have reached Duncan's Crossing in a few hours. She thought they would be lucky on the road north, before plunging off the highway into the unmarked places. Taking the same road, Anthea left just after eight on Friday morning, suddenly believing that Mrs. Layton's vision meant she was on a path, that there would be a real sign, not the wilfully obscure messages of the dead.

She would stay with her parents on the way. Though she had hated the Crossing while she was growing up—it was Hicktown, Nowheresville—she liked the country, the hills around the valley, the coast, the rivers and farms. In the years since she had left, it had become more and more fashionable, a destination for outdoorsmen and foodies. Now there were biodynamic vineyards, unusual organic vegetables, herds of Italian water buffalo specially imported for mozzarella. Though old families still survived—mining families, farming, logging, fishing families, tuned-in drop-out blended families, second generation polyamorists, the children of remittance men and pioneers—the newcomers tended to be wealthier, with exacting tastes regarding food, wine, and real estate. They were often retired baby boomers from Toronto or Alberta. Anthea liked that she could get really excellent bread—made with local wheat and organic hazelnuts from a farm down the road—at a bakery in the fishing village near her parents' place, but sometimes she was sad that it was so hard to find a bad cup of coffee, and an old guy to talk to while she drank it.

While the neighbourhood grew more refined, the Glass Castle Minigolf and RV Park grew smaller and shabbier every year, until Anthea no longer even noticed it. When she was little, it had seemed exciting—a castle made of glass!—but her grandfather Max had taken her into the parking lot to look at it, and she had seen the cement that joined the beer bottles together, trowelled right over the glass in many places. You couldn't see through it, and it didn't have a proper tower or transparent battlements or pennants: it was a crooked wall of brown and green, crenellated with stubbies. When Max asked if she wanted him to pay the dollar for a tour, she had shaken her head in disappointment.

Getting out of her car, Anthea wondered what she'd do now that she was there. She started along the old-timey boardwalk that ran from main office to minigolf to general store to hotdog stand. As she walked, she imagined Jasmine and her hollow-eyed prophet. She imagined the two of them walking in off the highway, their jeans grubby from hem to thigh. Their long hair parted in the middle, falling down their shoulders in symmetrical wings. They were barefoot on the cool, wooden floors of the general store. After all the fasting, and walking late at night along the bone-dry highway, they were as lovely and attenuated as figures in an Arthurian Burne-Jones tableau.

Tourist season bewildered them, and anyway Jas always hated tourists. She'd hate the minigolf on sight, if she could still comprehend it, and the opaque blue paint on the bottom of the swimming pool and the ludicrous folk-art Mounties riding wooden horses outside the beer bottle wall, the one punctuated in no clear pattern by the green of Canada Dry and 7 Up. The two of them descending from their quest along the heat-glassy highway, just long enough to beg for food before they left again.

Her parents knew enough not to ask her about work. That made her snappish. Since she had taken the job at the Institute—which had rescued her from the more obvious opportunities in coffee shops or retail—she had gone out of her way to discourage her father's interest, mostly by accentuating the dull and pointless aspects of her research. It was unfortunate that he wanted to be interested in what she did, because that meant it had taken a long monograph on Mrs. Kilgour's handkerchief inspection ledgers to dissuade him.

This time, though, she arrived in a better mood than usual. When her mother asked about the handkerchiefs, Anthea said something about new theories regarding hygiene and cotton production, and then talked about a burlesque show she'd gone to the week before, how she'd watched a man swallow a neon sword that made his throat glow blue, and how she'd had a cold so she thought it was time for a long weekend. It was important that they not suspect anything unusual, as they tended to ask probing questions about how she *felt* regarding her "career," her ambitions, Jasmine's disappearance, provincial politics, gentrification, globalization, their retirement plans. She wasn't even sure how to explain why it mattered that she go to Jas's last known whereabouts, at least, not without relying on esoteric language. Words like "haunting" and "ill-advised séance" would disturb them far more than her aimlessness.

For some reason, the four-day weekend worried Colm and he asked carefully, "But, yeah, Panther, how does that work with the Institute?"

"It's cool," she said brightly, "I brought some with me." She reached into her backpack and yanked out the wad of papers she'd screwed up and shoved in on top of her socks and underpants. "See!" She unpeeled one of her lists—"Mrs. Kilgour's 'fashionable ensembles,' as witnessed by the social pages of the city's papers"—which was grubby from living in her bag for the last couple of days. In her mother's kitchen, it smelled strongly of Rm 023. She dropped the papers onto the table, and then added a few proofs of Liam Manley looking hot, and one of Mrs. Kilgour's ledgers. If they asked, she could show them a new part about the handkerchiefs and call it "evidence," and make them read it until they gave up.

"So you're working at home a lot now? I bet that's nice."

"Oh yeah, totally. And even if I was totally slacking off, like, what are they going to do? Fire me?" She laughed. It wasn't as though they paid a living wage, and she was pretty undemanding. Besides, it was just the 2,000 words that mattered, and if they did try to fire her, they'd find she was the only one who could untangle the filing system she had established in Rm 023, or find the bits of the Kilgour Legacy that she'd removed to other locations. Eventually that kind of knowledge would pay off.

Anthea's mother picked up one of the fallen photographs.

"Who's this one?"

"This guy? Okay. Mrs. Kilgour liked to sing. This guy was, like, a tenor? You know. Yeah. You know. Vaudeville." Teresa looked at Anthea with an expression half-amused, half-anxious. Anthea remembered how once people had thought she was clever. She would win prizes, they said. She picked up another picture of Liam, one where his left arm draped over the piano's rack, his fingers brushing the keys. "He's pretty hot," she said. "I bet he looked superhot on stage." She didn't want to talk about anything important, like akashic texts or correspondences. Jasmine's voice said, *it does not do to let the uninitiated know too much*. Then her mother's eyes flicked downward and she said, "Anthea, you've got got your cardigan buttoned wrong."

As she re-buttoned, she turned to Colm and asked, "How's the other place going anyway?"

That was a quick way to redirect the conversation. "Yeah. It's pretty steady. Your Mom's working on the house, and I'm just trying to figure out what's what in the woods."

Colm and Teresa had inherited Hazel's house and property, but since her death it had remained empty. Only recently, they had taken on the huge task of cleaning it up: Anthea's grandparents had collected compulsively, so the waterfront property was a wooded junkyard, overgrown with invader species: English ivy, Siberian blackberry, Scotch broom, sometimes mint or lemon balm in the woods left over from the old gardens and cottages. Inside, the house was not the problem it had been, as Hazel had spent weeks before her death burning letters, photographs, clothes, and books. From Anthea's point of view, she had left an archive so carefully edited it was useless. At the time of the fires, Colm had asked gently, in his circumspect way, and Hazel had explained that she was dealing with it now because no one should have to do it for her, she wasn't the sort of woman who left a mess for other people to clean up. There had been a week of fires in the barrel by the woodshed as Hazel burned a whole career of negatives, a whole lifetime on paper.

Anthea had been in her second year, writing the last of her December finals. She was nineteen. When Colm called to tell her, to ask if there was anything she might like that he could save, she had snapped and said no, she didn't care about that sort of thing. She said *Hazel can burn it all. It's all her stuff.* She had believed what she said.

"I kind of want to go down on the beach. And do you guys want some help?"

Colm looked brighter as he answered. "Yeah? You want to help? I could use some help sorting through things. If you have time. Only if you have time." A sudden spasm of regret distracted her from her mission. She should have asked sooner, seeing him so happy. "But only if you have time," he said again, and looked at the stack of grubby papers on the kitchen table, the photographs, the ledger, the notes in Anthea's tiny cursive, the lists.

Again Anthea smelled Rm 023 in those objects, on her skin and in her hair. She turned to her father and her eyes were very bright and very dark. "I have time this weekend," she said. "I have lots and lots of time."

INVENTORIES AND ASSESSMENTS

The next morning was the first Saturday of Anthea's haunting, with 3,634 words written, and 3,153 deleted. They left early for Hazel's house. Colm smiled in that way Anthea remembered from being a kid, though it had been a rare, holiday thing when he was working full time. Even though it was better than his work-week frown, it had still annoyed her as an adolescent, the way he looked when he ate a bowl of ice cream or watched a hockey game or kissed his wife. At a time when Anthea strove desperately for the cool, the copacetic—when she still thought those words might describe her—his uncomplicated enjoyment of ice cream and hockey and kisses had seemed like a curse, a spectre of the adult she would one day become. The evening before she left for her parents' place she had been out walking and stopped at La Casa Gelato. Carrying her cone out the door, she caught her own eye in La Casa's plate glass window and spotted that familiar smile as she took the first lick. It was one scoop of Grand Marnier chocolate and one of durian, selected after ten minutes contemplating more than two hundred flavours. She really did like gelato that much.

In the truck she wondered if she had looked as happy as Colm did.

She waited until they were on one of the narrow lanes, driving between the woods and the hayfield that lay just beyond their property line. The last crop smelled nice through the open windows, and after Colm told her it had been a good year—three crops from that field, and maybe a fourth. All that rain in July did it. She asked, "Do you remember that guy? That guy Mr. Sweeney? He lived in one of the old cottages. He used to fish. And he wore brown pants."

"Brown pants?" Colm thought a minute. "Old Sweeney. Right. Yeah."

"What do you remember about him?"

"Oh, I don't know. He didn't talk much. He and Dad used to fish together sometimes, but mostly I remember old Sweeney going on about raw milk. He didn't believe in pasteurizing. Which is an *E. coli* risk, of course. But he called it dead food. I wonder what he'd think of irradiation?" Colm went on a little longer about the consequences of untreated milk, finishing up, "I'd say pasteurization is a good idea."

Anthea tried hard to listen and be patient. "But about Mr. Sweeney. He lived in a cottage."

"From the old estate, yeah, but it's gone now. He only had a couple of acres, though the way he acted, you'd think he owned the whole point and both beaches. He went everywhere; they had a sort of a system where Dad would say don't trespass and he just would anyway. I know he used to pick the yellow plums and Dad was always telling him not to but then old Sweeney said, *well I planted that tree, I guess I'm entitled to a few dozen* and they sort of left it there. That tree had the best plums." Colm looked reverent for a moment, thinking of yellow plums. "It's way past bearing. We should plant another one this winter."

Anthea gave up. "I like yellow plums," she said. "What are we doing today anyway?"

"Yeah. Right. So. The plan. The plan is that we're going to start sorting for the recycler. There's a lot of stuff. There's the scrap metal. And the things in the buildings, and the things that are buried."

Anthea shivered. "Buried?"

"Oh yeah, buried. With the backhoe. Some of them by hand, I guess." Colm's fingers tightened around the steering wheel. "Fridges. Stoves. Iron. Galvanized steel."

"Teflon frying pans?" she suggested.

"Frying pans? Where? I haven't seen any frying pans. Are there a lot?"

"Well," Anthea began, "I kind of remember a pile under that big bunch of blackberries to the left of the shop doors. But what do I know?" He looked overwhelmed so she added, "I could be wrong." On her last visit she had recognized the orange and green diamond pattern on the lid of an electric frying pan, and remembered Sunday dinners: pot roasts, potatoes, mahogany gravy. She guessed Hazel was bad with Teflon and had to replace it often, dumping the old pans in the woods. When Anthea looked down, she found her fingers wrapped tight around her travel mug. She forced herself to relax and they flicked out.

She had tried, but there was Colm triggered: "Teflon. Nails. PCB. Creosote. Aluminium. Old cars." He trailed off and then began again. "Refrigerators. Air conditioning units. Galvanized scrap metal. Paint thinner. Acetylene. Licence plates. Cinderblocks. And then there are the things from before."

They passed the gate as he made his list, and despite what he said Anthea could almost believe the woods were pristine. Undergrowth grew fast and thick in the clearings, and though some things were visible—the cars, the grader, some burn piles—the more serious problems were beneath ten years of blackberry canes. Down at the house, Colm parked near the front door and Anthea followed him onto the porch. "Things from before?" she repeated as they walked through the sliding glass doors to the kitchen. She didn't think he heard.

He sat at the kitchen table and looked through the open dining room to the deck and the water beyond. Then he said, "There are stones up in the woods, from the old gardens. Got to think about those, and the old shacks, lots of the boards just fell, all those nails. Nails in the trees, too. Which makes you worry about chainsaws, even though we need to cull the woods." He stopped. She set thermos and cup on the table between them and poured his coffee, black with one sugar. She passed it to him, and for a moment when he took it they held the cup together, their right hands touching. She noticed, as she often had, the sameness of their hands, something her father had pointed out to her many years before when he had held her hand in the car; she had liked that about her hands, that they were his.

They weren't only his, however. Though Colm and Anthea were both dark, with none of Hazel's freckles or pale brown hair, they had both inherited her hands, slim and tapered and strong. With those fingers she had left them both her temperament: all three were tenterhooked and nervy. Sitting across the table from Colm while he drank his coffee, she could feel his mind turning because it turned like hers did: he was imagining all the variations on Teflon frying pans and cinderblocks that could be buried in twenty acres. The years of work, the cost of recycling, the consequences of dumped chemicals, broken environmental laws.

Then she picked up her cup as well, and for half an hour they sat together, remarking on the weather, the colours in the water, and whether the bird that flew overhead was a raven or a very large crow. Colm thought she was being optimistic calling it a raven. Anthea talked about listening to Patsy Cline while she sorted things in Rm 023, and Colm told the story of the guy who worked for his father, back in the fifties, who could sing just like Patsy Cline. They liked talking about the guy singing "Walkin' After Midnight" as loud as he could, in his truck with the windows open.

After that they walked halfway up the drive to the old boat house Max had used for extra storage. Colm didn't think there was a key, so they jimmied the padlock; dry wood came away with the nails, flakes of paint and dead bugs on the ground as they each swung one of the protesting doors. The shed was dark except for the light that speared in at the cracks, each beam so shot with dust it seemed solid. On the floor there were leggy, white-blind spears of grass that had wound up through the old Massey-Harris. Dead flies, paper wasps, desiccated rags.

Colm swung his arms, the crowbar in his right hand grazing the earth. Anthea looked down at her own spindly wrists in their giant leather work gloves. She held a crowbar, too. "So?" she asked. "What you think?"

"Ehhhh."

He took a step into the darkness, picking his way through the greasy cardboard boxes that formed the outermost layer of junk. There were neat shelves down each wall, which he could not reach, good solid shelves of two-by-sixes, the unplaned, slivery kind Max used for workbenches, back when he still had the little sawmill and milled his lumber from the drift logs. Those shelves were full of small wooden boxes with finger holes, like drawers. He'd labelled them with black Jiffy Marker on little cards stapled to the wood: "rusty nails all sizes," "cable clamps," "washers."

And that was just the walls. Looking at the floor full of auction boxes, she wondered out loud: "Why don't we just—" she knew it was wrong while she said it—"why don't we just take it all out? Burn what we can? Take the rest to the dump?"

"No!" he said with the sound of a tight spring released. Then in a calmer voice: "That's not the plan."

Anthea had never been sure about the plan. She knew parts of it, had the barest idea of the stages through which it would progress, and its intended results. Colm alone carried the intricate mechanism in his head, designed to separate the useful from the useless in his father's rust-hoard, to turn the junkyard property back to wild, and on to a garden. It would take years.

"No," he said again, only quietly this time, as he seemed to regret the loosed spring and was now carefully recoiling it. "No—there's too much to just burn, and look—" He gestured toward a loose pile of black piping. "You can't burn that. If you did it would gas us both. What we'll do," he said, brightening, "what we'll do is, yeah, at least we'll drag stuff out and rebox what we can. Then fix the roof maybe. No. Yeah—we'll see what we can do about all the rain."

With her hands dust-dry in her giant gloves, Anthea did not believe in rain. Overhead arbutus bark peeled away from the trunks in red curls like sunburned skin. Somewhere nearby broom pods burst, scattered seeds with the sound of falling pebbles. One day soon, broom would cover every open metre of their twenty acres, and beneath it nothing would grow, and only the barest outline of a garden and a drive visible under the branches. Broom died where it stood, turned the colour of old iron but remained upright. Even dead it didn't give way to other plants.

Anthea dropped her gloves from her wrists and knelt beside Colm as he turned over the objects in a box. "No," he said, "yeah, get your gloves. Start carrying them out."

"But. If we just take them out and put them back, what good is that?"

"If we don't weatherproof, we won't have any choice in a couple of years. It'll all be shot. But if we sort it all out—well, there isn't time to make, what, ten-twenty thousand decisions for everything in there, for every single box. And if we just burn, well there might be PCBs in there. That's a carcinogen. Neurological damage, too. And PVC? Those pipes? If you burned them, you'd release carbonyl chloride. That's a chemical weapon. They used it in the First World War. There's R11 and R12 from old A/Cs and fridges. They're toxic. We have to make sure they don't leak until we know what we can do with them." He glanced up. "Old paint cans," he said. "And thinner. Creosote. Shellac. Engine oil."

"But it's old so wouldn't the thing—the coolant—already be gone?"

Colm didn't answer. He had half-uncovered an old fridge that stood next to the wall. As he moved boxes, he revealed a rusty wound in its almond-coloured side. "See—this is why you don't leave fridges out in the woods." His finely pointed fingertips touched the corroded metal of the pipes. "See there?"

Anthea saw. She breathed deeply in the dusty air, wondering what else had escaped in the years her grandpa had left the slowly exhaling fridges hidden in outbuildings or half-buried in his earth. It was a lovely day. Even now sylphy particles of dichlorodifluoromethane were winging up to congregate at the poles.

Ehhh, she thought.

"Ehhhh," said Colm.

Picking up her giant gloves, Anthea turned to another box.

"Don't spill anything," he said "and get away quick if you drop something. I saw some fluorescent tubes. Mercury."

Anthea returned to the shed for another armload. She was already bored, and she couldn't see after the brightness: the interior seemed to go back beyond the Massey-Harris, beyond the shelves, the shed much larger on the inside than on the outside. When she returned outside with yet another armload, Colm was standing a little distance from the doors. He was looking up the hill into the undergrowth, and around them at the disgorged contents of the shed. She joined him, and put one hand on his and squeezed. They stood together, graceless, beset among the salal, with the flicker of the fir canopy, and the glitter of the inlet below.

"Break time," Colm said, finally. "Hit her hard this afternoon."

In the house they took sandwiches and orange juice from the fridge; it hummed gently, devoid of postcards and the artwork of children, unfilmed by dust, its coolant secure in a closed system, an apocalypse temporarily suspended.

After lunch Colm sat in his father's chair beside the window, Anthea across from him. They watched the beach and the islands. A kingfisher hung in the air above the water.

"Do you remember," he said. She waited. The kingfisher dove. Colm didn't speak. She couldn't tell if the bird caught anything.

"Do I remember what?" she asked.

"Do you remember how scared you used to be of that story, the guy who had the place before Hazel and Max?"

"I wasn't scared!" she protested. "Jesus! I was just a sensitive kid."

He laughed at that. "Sweetheart, you were terrified. You were never very good at hiding it. I mean, you weren't a brave kid. Anyway. Sometimes I think about him, how he lived here. Do you suppose he's still out there?"

"Sensitive!" she said. "Not a coward. Not *terrified*. I guess he's dead now. It was a long time ago."

"I suppose so. Suppose so. But I think about all the people who lived here."

Anthea held her breath. She didn't want to disrupt the current of his memories or his conversation, so she waited and looked where he looked: across the water where the kingfisher had flown. After another moment of his silence, she asked gently, "What sort of things did they leave behind?"

"Those new people tore down Old Sweeney's place. You should see what they built. All glass, for the view. Solar panels. Geothermal."

"Green."

"Yeah, and earthquake safe. No beach where they are. You know they asked for an easement? Through our place? Actually, right where Old Sweeney used to walk, now I think about it. Anyway, I told them no. They'll probably have waterfront in a few years, anyway, when the sea levels go up."

Anthea nodded. Colm thought a lot about the sea levels as well as erosion and tsunamis; it came of living on a high bank above salt water right near a fault line. Colm went on, "We used to find things here, you know. We'd find buried things. I think." Here he stopped again and pointed at a seal who surfaced for a moment and seemed to look up at them. Irritation then, that he would be so vague when she had such particular questions. She was about to ask again when he said, "I think it wasn't a very good place. You know. I think he was sort of..."

She waited, then started him back with, "You mean, when he took their money—?"

"Not just that."

"Not just what?"

"Oh. I don't know. Did you ever hear the story about his plans? What he wanted to do?

"Old Sweeney told me a bit, once. He didn't like it if you asked, but once he said that they were working on an Engine."

Anthea held her breath, then she asked carefully, "What kind of Engine?"

"I don't know. That was all Sweeney said." He stopped again. "You heard anything about Jasmine?"

"Nothing."

"That's another sad story."

"I wasn't scared, you know. And Jasmine might be okay. She might."

"You used to love the little house," he said. "Looking at it, I mean. You stopped me talking about it when I told you stories."

"Did I?" She didn't remember anything like that, though she remembered how much she had wondered about the little house, thinking it was just the right size for her, but how its name—"The Place of the Stones"—had been so strange and full of some quality she couldn't understand. "It made me sad. What was the plan, Dad?"

"Plan?"

"The guy here. The prophet. You said they were building an Engine."

"Yeah. I don't know. Old Sweeney never told me."

While her father had an after-lunch sleep on the floral chesterfield in the front room, Anthea went down to the beach. That day the path was overhung with maples and a Sleeping Beauty wall of blackberry vines, what had once been wide enough for a car now reduced to a narrow passage between the trees, gouged by winter runoff from the top of the hill, like a dry creekbed.

The water was calm and high. She sat on one of the logs up past the tide line and thought about how the points that enclosed the beach were as they had been when she and Jasmine cast their circle, before that when she and her brother made rafts as little kids, when Colm learned to swim, when Hazel and Max built their house. In Simon's day, they had stretched out on either side of the beach in just those angles. Long before that, since January 26, 1700, when the last megathrust earthquake had shaken the earth to its modern configuration. Every season rearranged logs and gravel, but in three hundred years the tide had only managed to soften the corners of the megaliths on the point. Looking up toward Simon's foundations, she saw that salt-poisoned trees withdrew from the encroaching shore. The arbutus might not last as the climate changed; like Garry Oak, they had a narrow range. The coast would look different *then*.

She climbed the second trail, the steep, sliding trail that wound up over the rock face where all the soil had been worn away, and beyond that to the point. It too was undercut, and what had once been a staircase was now only a slight interruption of the high bank's incline. Watching earth and pebbles dislodged by her feet, Anthea wondered why they even tried to save the topsoil. A cliff didn't want to be a cliff, after all; it wanted to be flat, riding winter rain down to the bottom. Stone hangs on longer, but earth slides further with every storm. When the arbutus die, the whole hillside, unsupported, will follow.

Emerging at the top some distance from Hazel's house, she stood at the entrance to the old garden, near the place Jasmine had selected to raise the dead. On the other side of the high garden wall, fir trees were sunk like triffids in the old carp ponds. She thought of Craiglockhart and the estate wall that still survived along front lawns and back alleys in the neighbourhood around Mrs. Kilgour's Castle. She wondered if Simon, like Mrs. Kilgour, had planned for the long term, a dynasty to lead the coast through a thousand dark years in the Kali Yuga. His manor had not lasted the generation. It had burned down, its masonry cannibalized for other houses on what was left of the estate, for the summer cottages built after the war, for Hazel's house, a stone bungalow on the site of some acolyte's cedar shack.

She found the place where they had cast the circle and sat for a moment, remembering the evening sunlight, then the first yellow moonlight. She waited an extra moment for the fear to rise again, watching the airport as she had done that night and wondering what it was Jasmine had wanted her to see, and what Mrs. Layton thought they had done wrong. The trunks of arbutus groaned in the breeze, speaking their own language, and though she listened she did not understand. It was strange to find that she was not afraid.

Back at the house again, she noticed a two-year-old buck standing on the drive beside Colm's truck. It watched her, flicked its ears, and then picked its way across the grassless clearing of the drive and back into the woods. Grassless now, but green leaves and white roots squirmed up through the seams in the pavement. It didn't take long.

Through the window Anthea saw her father sleeping. She wanted to say that he should join her in the woods, and they should release the house, let the leaves blow through the doors, let the water run, clear the topsoil, undercut the foundations until the house tumbled down the high bank to the beach. There would be a new point on the coast, indistinguishable from the others, unless someone stripped the rockweed and the purple mussels, revealing the original machined surfaces, unchanged beneath the water.

Anthea followed the buck away from the house, along the old pathway that led from Simon's manor and through the village. Much of it was gone—interrupted by Hazel's flowers and the driveway—but short passages survived, leading toward the Taberners' and past their woods to Old Sweeney's place that was no longer his, but a new glass mansion up the hill. She followed the path to the barbed wire fence on the edge of the property and looked through the narrow belt of trees and across the Taberners' lawn in the direction of a small wooden house she could not see: The Place of the Stones. The Taberners used it for storage, though it also made a good story to tell when they had people in for drinks. Old Sweeney had always disapproved of the way they kept broken oars in there, and life preservers and gardening tools. He said it was too important for that. Once when the Taberners had invited him around, they had prodded him for stories, but he had shot his rye and told them all to go to hell and that had been that.

After his rest Colm was in a better mood, and suggested they go for a bit of a walk before they returned to the shed. As they followed Max's tractor trails through the bush, they found things that had been collected with obvious intention, though Anthea could not always tell what had fallen into relation by chance and what had been set just so, the rusted rebar placed opposite the boiler by one of her grandfather's plans, the scribbled papers he liked to fold up tight and keep in his trouser pockets, or in that shortbread tin beside his recliner, the one with the Scots laddie on it, done up in a kilt. Grandpa used to tap the tin's lid and talk about building a better mousetrap, about how any man could get ahead with a little ingenuity.

It was good that they went for the walk, because some of the projects made Colm remember nice things. He rested one foot on the lip of a boiler and pointed at the cannibalized tractor opposite. "Yeah," he said, "this's one of his projects."

Anthea knelt and brushed away the moss and found three glass dials with smashed faces above the boiler. Black characters on white, concealed by the seep of greenish water, the scum of previous rain marks.

"Once he tried to make hydrogen, electrolyzing water. I think it was in *Popular Mechanics*."

"For blowing things up?" she asked, and Colm shrugged *maybe*. The gauges of her grandfather's experiment were marked in hieroglyphics when she looked again. It was funny what smashed glass did.

"Sometimes I think—" Colm said.

Anthea was going to prod him to a complete sentence with the tiny, imperious gestures of irritation that made her hands look so much like Hazel's. Instead she crouched, careful and listening, above the three hieroglyphic gauges.

He only said, "You shouldn't be too hard on yourself, you know. About Jasmine. And about the money. We're all just doing the best we can."

She began to laugh: "Don't worry, Dad. Besides, there's no way I could afford to work at the Kilgour Institute if I didn't have extra money. Like, they should give me a tax credit or something. I'm really okay with being a remittance girl."

He made a face. "Don't call yourself that, Panther." She didn't know what to say, and she just crouched a little longer, looking at the dials. But then Colm spotted some blackberries, and together they stood over the hanging bunches for a quarter hour, eating what they could reach.

ABOUT THE HOUSE ON THE POINT

Jasmine had said that Simon liked to face the water, so she thought his rooms would be on that side of the house. From those windows, he looked down the rocks toward the east and south. He might contemplate grey mist, or the veiled shore opposite; the winking lights of fishing boats or bootleggers.

Though the war was long past, he still thought like a soldier. Even before the house was finished, he cross-hatched the beaches with intersecting lines of fire. He planned cement gun mounts above each point and pillboxes in the woods. In the meadow at the top of the drive where Hazel grew potatoes, they unearthed a roll of barbed wire rusted solid. They found two army-issue entrenching tools and the tin spoon of a mess kit. At the edge of the potato field, a shallow groove zigged once before it disappeared under one of the new roads. You had to be told by someone who knew—someone like her grandfather, or old Sweeney, or Colm—to recognize those distortions as the remains of a forward fire trench.

The precise dimensions of Simon's earthworks were gone, the regulation two-foot step, the revetment all lost to the collapsing walls. They had been present at some time, Anthea was sure; she thought that Simon would enjoy such precision. She could imagine the breastwork in the curve that remained of the forward face. She imagined men in khaki, dusty handkerchiefs knotted on their heads. They wrestled stones from the ground, listened to the ring-and-chop of their blades cutting clay. They stopped to swig cold tea from a milk pail. Each man ate a slice of grey-white bread and seedy blackberry jam for lunch; each man took an hour at two o'clock to lie in the shade.

Touching the crusted remains of one of His Majesty's entrenching tools, she thought she saw them: they worked slowly; they didn't rest. They woke to nightmares triggered by the scent of freshly turned earth and the balance of an entrenching tool held in the right hand, blistering the base of the palm. Colm told stories from when he was a kid, when they uncovered food caches while digging the footings for his father's workshop. Hard tack. Bully beef. In the years after Simon buried them, the cans swelled, so rusted they resembled clods of earth. The contents separated: salted meat at the bottom, yellow fat at the top. Colm remembered finding one hoard that had gone off, and how he and his sister Ada had spent a stinky afternoon breaking open the cans so the pressurized contents shot out in a rotten geyser.

Simon's boxes rotted. Iron hinges oxidized and crusted over, their nails rusted deep and brittle in the wood. Three generations hardly seemed to account for the scent of deep time that drifted up from each opened cache, and each time one was unearthed, Colm thought of the grave goods of some distant Chieftain. Each barrow might contain a warrior in a seagoing canoe, arrayed in mother-of-pearl and hammered gold with a cedar death mask marking the place where his skull lay. The Enfields decayed in their oilcloth, and the bayonets—unfixed, now unfixable—turned to rust.

There were caches Colm didn't know about.

In the course of Anthea's long weekend, they did not finish sorting the shed, but she convinced Colm to start another burn pile at least, and she added a few things he hadn't okayed; she hid a half-rotten valise under some rope and reduced a chest of drawers to kindling. The piles still worried Colm because the local CarbonNinjas chapter was cracking down on burning—not only the off-season kind that started forest fires, but the general kind that caused climate change. "They're sending people around with cameras," he told her, "to document burn piles." He shook his head. "I don't know if we want to cross them. They get pretty mad."

Uncaring, profligate with carbon, Anthea threw greasy rags onto the heap, and at the end of the day tarped the two new burn piles so they'd still be dry when the season changed. "What are the chances they'll be able to see this far in? Just tell Mom to avoid them."

He looked doubtful. Earlier in the summer some disapproving neighbour had reported the old cars that Grandpa Max had left in the woods, and which Colm had not yet removed. "People around here are getting kind of fancy," was all Colm said about that, but she knew what he meant.

She stopped at the house again on her way home Monday evening, but didn't tell her parents. With her feet on Simon's old highway—from his manor house through his village to his spiritual refuge at The Place of the Stones—she walked the route the buck had taken, past the overgrown green of Hazel's once-garden, past the grader, the rust-hoards, the old cars still in the woods and the new burn piles she and Colm had built, until she reached the belt of trees and fence posts that marked the property line. She slipped through the loose wire to the Taberners' side. The house was dark as she crept into their perennial border, and then onto the open lawn between the garden and the edge of the bank.

The Place of the Stones should have stood opposite the long perennial bed, under the trees. She was halfway across the grass when she realized that it wasn't there. "Son of a bitch," she said.

Where it had been there was a heap of loose boards and ivy trunks as thick as her wrist, and underneath them the yellow granite foundation piles. A sledgehammer and an axe still leaned against the wheelbarrow nearby. She looked through the plywood and two-by-fours, where little green fingers of ivy seemed to dig themselves out, and when she had cleared some light and worm-holed floorboards she saw the crawlspace. She picked up more wood, stacking it neatly near the wheelbarrow and when she had cleared a little bit of the floor, she crouched to look through to the ground below.

Among the fir needles and pebbles she saw a conspicuously flat spot. She felt around its corners, then brushed it clear: a panel of wood like a trapdoor let into the earth. She thought of Simon Reid, and how he had been this way and set the door into the earth, and she wondered if he had left it for her, and willed the prickle of vision to fill her eyes—Simon Reid, nearby, his gray suit a blur in her periphery. Then she worried her strong, pointed fingertips into the corner nearest her and pried it open.

The scene was set for a revelation: a chamber lined with brick; a buried box; the declining sun above the woods illuminating the opposite shore like a painted backdrop. In the last light she set the sheet of plywood back in place and recovered it with old needles, carefully pushing them into the cracks. Then she carried the box over the rubble toward the fence, though it was heavy and had bruised her hipbones by the time she reached the car. It was deep twilight when she left, and as she drove she kept her eyes on the road in front of her headlights, and averted from the dark under the trees. In the two hours it took her to reach the city, the box's scents filled her car, and as she inhaled spores and grains, she imagined the things she could find inside, from a beating heart to a cache of jewels to the Emerald Tablet to an alchemical formula for the philosopher's stone.

At home with the door locked, she cleared a space in the papers on the floor of her front room, and set the box down with a halo of clay dust and fir needles already settling around it. She knelt before it, and slipped the claw of her hammer under the metal flap on the box's lid where it was secured with a rusted padlock. When it didn't give, she knelt carefully on the lid and leaned back until the nails slid out of the wood. She opened it.

The box was full of books. When she split the first spine, fine dust leapt into the air and hung in the candlelight. The pages were tea-coloured like the parchment she and Max used to make for pretend ransom notes. The edge of each book was charcoal and spotty where it had been exposed to the narrow airspace at the top of the box. In the first book, there was the date, a wriggle of ink and entries in a spiky Victorian hand. She flipped to the centre of the book. It was blank. She flipped back. Only the first dozen pages were filled, the rest were empty. The last in a series she thought. The dates were from the late twenties, just four entries written over an entire season. A not very devoted diary keeper; she thought of Mrs. Kilgour's extensive records and disapproved.

She opened the next book. It had a few more entries, then more blank, these from the early thirties. The next had even fewer. She worked through the entire box, hauling out journal after journal. All of them were scribbled in the opening pages, and then empty. The entries she could decipher were either boring or cryptic.

December 17, 1933

It is impossible to work under these circumstances. I will return to the city.

December 31, 1933

In the event of my death I would like to come back as a stone on the floor of the sea. I will tell Mr. Sweeney this.

January 22, 1934

Annie was a better housekeeper than the one we have now. She ruined my best grey suit.

At the bottom of the box there was a sealed envelope. Anthea put on her gloves and opened it carefully on the kitchen table, her eyes scratchy and her nose running. Only a few of the sheets inside were whole, the others were odds and ends, grubby bits of envelopes and lunch receipts with diner grease on them. These were pencilled with words, a few numbers and the signs of the zodiac. Calculations, admonitions underlined and exclamation-pointed. There were names parsed by number and element and hieroglyph. MICHAEL SWEENEY. ANNIE SWEENEY. ALICE SOMERS.

She sorted the papers into acid-free plastic and carried the box downstairs and outside to shake its dust onto the grass in front of her building. Her hands were dirty and dry. Inside again, the room smelled of mildew. When she turned the lights on, everything around her seemed hot and brightly coloured, and she couldn't tell if the dead smell rose from Simon Reid's books or her own skin. She sneezed. Mold. Mycosis. Librarian's lung. Standing under the shower, she looked up to see that mildew had begun to spread over the white ceiling of her bathroom in interlocking circles: negative halos, little grey fingerprints.

In the end, there were only three useful things in the whole box. The first was all the lovely blank paper in the leather journals and ledgers, which witnessed Simon Reid's fine taste in office gear. The paper took ink beautifully, and she found herself writing in long, slanting cursive because it was such a pleasure. Another was a clipping from the magazine called *The Messenger*, a publication of the Canadian Order of the Yellow King, in assc. with the American Theosophical Society, dated 1932. The final object of value was a plan made in black ink on stiff white cardstock about one metre square. It was a detail from some larger plan, a drawing full of gears, a governor, a series of levers and dials.

At first *The Messenger* and the blank paper preoccupied her. Later she found the plan again in its acid-free plastic and unfolded it, laying it out on the floor beside her portable record player while she listened to Patsy Cline on LP. She never grasped its significance, or what the engine was supposed to do, but she liked it, and many years later framed it and hung it on the wall, and when people asked about it, she liked to tell them the story, as far as she knew it.

FROM THE ARCHIVE OF SIMON REID, PROPHET

The Messenger, A Publication of the Canadian Order of the Yellow King. 14.4: 1932.

I would like to take this opportunity to respond to Mr. Burgess's last letter in the Autumnal Number of this Publication, as he seems to have misunderstood my attempts to correct his rather anthro-centric approach to magic. I will attempt also to counter his charges of anti-humanism by presenting my points as simply as this complex matter allows.

Of greatest importance in any casting—and this is the point where Mr. Burgess and I reach our disagreement—is the hidden space left in which the G-d may act. Beyond all things—if we value our lives—we must avert our eyes when the G-d deigns to glance our way. We are not their equals; we are their supplicants. They do not respond to commands; they cannot be bound—we appeal to them at our peril and to our glory. For these reasons, each ceremony must be designed around a hidden space, an element of the random or the wild, in which the G-d might choose to dwell and act in secrecy. It may be achieved any number of ways. The participants may be blindfolded, or stripped naked; their consciousnesses may be altered by special preparations. They may, at the last moment, change their incantations and speak spontaneously. The conduit may break the circle when he is drawn to do so. He may change the sacrifice at his whim. All this is a deferral to the inaccessible order of the eternal, which may appear to us disorder, for our tiny ceremonies cannot hope to contain it, and must be smashed by any real manifestation of the G-d.

I thank you for the opportunity to clarify my position in this delicate and critical issue. This publication is, for many, an introduction to our world. We have a responsibility to such chelas as seek our path to reveal both the benefits and the consequences of the magus's life.

WORDCOUNTS

Nine days into her haunting. Two days to her deadline. 5,671 words written, 4,889 erased. That left a title, her name and the date, and a few dusty sentences about the Temple Theatre. No help from the photographs propped up on the mantel of the boarded-up fireplace in her tiny front room, or the shrivelled rosebud she kept in a saucer on her coffee table. Anthea asked Blake for a copy of the biography to date, or at least what was available in .docx format. "To get a feel for the voice," she put in the email, though she hoped to avoid that voice. Blake sent her the first draft of the opening chapters of *The Kilgours of the West, Volume III: Arrival, 1914-1918.* It didn't help much.

In 1920 Mrs. Leticia Kilgour embarked on a new adventure when she (12)

Mrs. Leticia Kilgour's artistic ambitions did not limit themselves to patronage. Rather, she was a Renaissance woman of unusual capacity and sensitivity who (23)

Mrs. Leticia Kilgour's ambitions extended to performance as well as patronage, and in [1912ish?] she began searching out and succouring promising young aritsts (23)

With her unusual capacity and sensitivity it was inevitable that Mrs. Leticia Kilgour should become the city's first patroness (19)

Determined as she was to (5)

Liam Manley granted Mrs. Kilgour the opportunity to expand her (10)

Liam Manley was born [somewhere in Ireland?] in [1897ish] he was a formidable man [and kind of hot—can I put that?] who recognized in Mrs. Kilgour the (27)

Liam Manley was (3)

Mrs. Kilgour was a woman of old-testament repressions, one whose regime extended from her devotions to her husband's stomach to her maidservants' fingernails. She was a woman so tightly corseted that her spine collapsed on that fateful day in 1933 when she attempted to remove her stays, a transgression of womanly boundaries she had long avoided, but made necessary by the suppurating blisters that had formed where one rib of her corset had torn loose.

She inspired in her attendants only a deep, slow dread, disrupted occasionally by weeks of adrenalized activity. After the crash of '29 she often walked the long corridors of Craiglockhart alone, and smelled the faint, haunting stink of despair at some confluence of hallways. One such miasma marked the place her niece-secretary Nora had stood, pre-dawn, and wondered where in the rising November Sunday she would find the daisies Mrs. Kilgour had demanded for Euphemia—her youngest daughter's—hair. Knowing her task to be Sisyphean, Nora had felt the cold, black terror of Castle Craiglockhart creep into her heart, and in a long sigh left the air forever perfumed by her desolation. In later years it was hard to know whether Mrs. Kilgour reflected the Castle—massive, crenellated, many-corridored—or the Castle was the Kilgour soul rendered in stone.

In light of her incipient madness, how did she maintain her influence over western Canadian society? Mrs. Kilgour's fascinations are documented in journals and private memoirs of the colonial city she ruled. Such journals might accurately have described her as "undiscerning, wealthy and irresistibly insecure" those qualities most admired by her legion of sycophants. Known throughout the city for her low, black Rolls-Royce—a concession to modernity that, in 1905, replaced the barouche of her adolescent dreams—Mrs. Kilgour was both guardian and avenging angel. At Christmas she bestowed gilded Fortnum & Mason gingerbread on dirty-faced white children. In summer she held garden parties at the Castle for the city's unfortunate—also white, preferably from the British Isles, though not Irish—serving syllabub, strawberries and oatcakes at long trestle tables beside the vegetable gardens. She sponsored gifted musicians and artists to study abroad. All year round she condemned socialists, actresses, suffragettes, unwed mothers and union organizers at the public lectures she also sponsored. Her husband's employees—her serfs purchased, some thought, to complement her castle with their coal-blacked faces—did not pity so much as hate, nor hate so much as fear.

Liam Manley arrived in Mrs. Kilgour's life already deliciously wounded, with the face of a dying subaltern poet. In the autumn of 1920 he stood at her front door, with hidden scars and tremulous hands, his eyes darkened with fever as though with kohl. (438)

TIME PASSES FOR LIAM

Liam's haunting, the one that dominated the final decade of his life, began very much as Anthea's did, in the early hours on the day of his return to the city a little more than a decade after he ended his creative partnership with Mrs. Kilgour. It was November. He had taken a cheap room with Mrs. Qualey, a matron who did for theatre people in a boarding house on the eastside. Like Anthea, he was asleep for this first manifestation, and also like Anthea he found, on waking, no way to answer the call that disturbed his rest. When he awoke, the initial urgency melted into the more general dread that had brought him back to the city and, perhaps, to Mrs. Kilgour.

When he described his time in Mrs. Kilgour's keep, he suggested that he had dissolved the partnership, but it would be more accurate to say that she had gone first: he only bought the ticket for San Francisco when he found himself alone in the city again, and discovered that in her absence she did not remember his dependence. He liked to think there was generosity in his withdrawal, that he did not pester her for the funds which—according to implied agreements and gentleman's contracts—she still owed him. Not while she grieved anew for her lost laddie, and wrangled with the War Graves Commission regarding the repatriation of Clive's remains. She should not think of money at such a time; she should think about grief and sacrifice and things of that nature. All vulgar thoughts of money and performance flew from her mind: the last cheque was more the work of Goshawk than of Mrs. Kilgour, Liam guessed, and it was not her signature that sealed it, but a lawyer's. He cashed it quietly and paid his bills and packed his new suits in his new luggage and wondered about goodbyes, and whether he should call or write notes. He left much behind, things he had not thought to use that winter, but had bought for some future season. For the summer perhaps, when he would learn to play tennis, and meet young women, and would need white flannel trousers with cuffs. (Slightly worn and a little out of date, so they did not look as though he had bought them just that season. He had been wearing them around his rooms to the right degree of shabbiness).

Goshawk saw him to the station in the very early morning, and waited with him half an hour longer than Liam thought was entirely necessary. He had been trying to work out a means of getting away from Goshawk, and had just decided to be manly and direct when Goshawk tried again to say the thing he had been trying to say for twenty minutes already.

"Between you and I, Manley—" Goshawk began but did not finish. Liam was pleased to recognize the little grammatical slip. He had learned that it was incorrect quite recently, and was extra careful to feel its vulgarity. "Men like you and I. It's a kind of a brotherhood, don't you see. I will miss you." At first Liam didn't know what to do, but then he clapped Goshawk on the shoulder and they both nodded.

"She may call me back, still," Liam said, but did not believe it. Neither did Goshawk, he thought, but the man agreed anyway: "She may, that's true. Though I think she will have something else by the time she comes home again. I don't know what. She has been talking about Scotch history. It started with the ballads, you see. I wish you would stay, and we would find a way to fit you in. She likes you. She likes you a great deal. Do you know much about the ballads?"

"I do like it here, Goshawk, but I don't think I could endure another season as her protégé. I have other plans, you know. I always have."

Goshawk looked unreasonably sad for a moment, and then he smiled in that bright way he usually kept for Kilgours. Liam very nearly told him to cut it out, that sort of smile. It wasn't necessary.

"Of course, Liam. I know it is a great thing you are doing. I will expect to hear from you soon, from San Francisco, and Montreal, and Buenos Aires." Liam only smiled at the narrowness of Goshawk's ambition, thinking of Covent Garden and La Scala.

And then they were walking toward his car, and Goshawk stopped again just as Liam was beginning to check his wristwatch and make "goodbye" noises. "But if you should pass through again on your way to Montreal, you will come and see me?"

Liam reassured Goshawk, feeling at once sad to be going from the bosom of such a friend—for so Goshawk suddenly seemed, this early in the morning—and also embarrassed. He was ready to be on the train again and on his way somewhere else, reading the morning newspaper and watching the city fall behind him, and the border rise in front. Travelling south into warmer weather, accelerating through spring along the coast, arriving at summer in San Francisco only a few days away. Caruso had loved San Francisco, for a time, and Tetrazzini had as well. It would be brightly coloured and wild and American, with money and beautiful women and a proper opera house, and palm trees here and there, or orange groves. And he had a little money this time, squirrelled away in his luggage, and in his inside pocket the monogrammed clip with the bills he needed handy— enough to smooth his arrival in the city, and make it amusing, and anyway he would not mind a return to the popular stage. Perhaps this time he would approach the Sullivan-Considine offices.

For Liam, the years after that morning, but before his return to the city, and his haunted room in Mrs. Qualey's Boarding House, passed like a montage in an old movie, cut against the fluttering pages of a calendar. He stood in the midst of it, the ceilings above him vaulted or domed, square, ovoid, eight-sided, inset with plaster rosettes or arches evoking Spain, New Spain, India, Etruria, Egypt. Carpet swirled under his feet, or spread out in geometric lattice, and over his head, the indigo night sky and silhouetted towers of a continental chateau. Above the castle walls were stars—Orion—rising over the green fringe of sunset and the tips of a pinewood. The stages were hung with the red plush curtains of a bordello, and the aisles lined with gold eagles, like the standards of some abandoned legion. The fretted screens of the Alhambra. Onion domes tiled in red and green. Gold-painted plaster draperies in the lobby, caryatids supporting the proscenium, and the dome frescoed with blue-skinned goddesses in flimsy nighties. Or Isis in sheer cotton, lolling under peacock fans above a border of geometric papyrus fronds. Outside, ibis-headed Thoth greeted all who walked through the double doors.

All so extravagant, these new theatres, that still smelled of plaster dust and the workmen's cigarettes. Soon, though, they were not so clean and new, and then they began to show frayed velour, and grubby fingerprints appeared on the doors to the dressing rooms and on the walls, and in Liam's eye they did not gain the picturesque of the antique. They were just worn, after appearing so splendid a few years earlier, and in them Liam withered, and around him his profession withered, too, and the vaudeville circuits that had employed him died away like the etiolated tendrils of grass that grow up under and around old cars abandoned in the woods, the blades that rise and fall back again, whitened by the dark.

Sometimes he climbed from the dressing rooms at the bottom, up past the projection booth—if it were that kind of theatre—to a heavy door that stood at the very top. If there were such a door, it took him past the fans and the great metal ducts of the ventilation system and into the dark above the false ceiling, where cables as thick as his little finger supported the plaster dome that capped the auditorium. When he could find his way to that place, he looked down at the wrong side of the fresco, the side that was just grey and dusty plaster oozing up through wire mesh. Sometimes if he were lucky, the ceiling had holes in it, little bits of blackness cut into the painting so that what seemed to be a deeper shadow behind Thoth's head or under his arm was really nothing at all, a dark gap through which someone hiding above the ceiling could watch. If there were such gaps, he would kneel on the catwalk, and resting one hand on the plaster, he would look down, down to the upper balcony, the dress circle, to the proscenium. He thought of stepping onto the mesh, of how it would support him a moment, then break and let him through the egyptien figures—perhaps right through Thoth himself—so he'd fall like a star to the stage.

CLEOPATRA'S NIGHTMARE

Liam's haunting began more than ten years after that morning of optimism when Goshawk waited with him at the station, after hundreds of "I'll Take You Home Again, Kathleen"s in hundreds of theatres. Long after the disaster that was San Francisco and the Sullivan-Considine offices, and those years on the declining circuits in the east, and big little-time in the south, and the dustbowl circuits of the southwest, to arrive finally back on the north Pacific coast of the continent, and the little

little-time, where he could find it, and a patchwork of small-town engagements where he could not.

It began on the morning he returned to the city of his only known triumph. His train was again delayed, and again he made his way to his lodging after midnight on the first day of his engagement at the Temple Theatre. This time it was a boarding house, not even a hotel, and he had no money for a cab. As he walked through the wet air to Mrs. Qualey's, he hoped that she might see how ill and tired he was and make him a cup of tea, and he could add a few drops from the flask in his inside pocket, and then carry it up to bed with him. Her hospitality might even extend to toast, or a sandwich.

He stood a long time knocking at 456 E. Cordova before her face materialized in the window, sudden and baleful in the light of an unshaded bulb. She wore curlers and a grey robe tied under her low, blousy breasts. She rattled the lock conspicuously and opened the door.

"The train was late," he said by way of apology, but she only led him to his room, without offering even sardine sandwiches or a mug of tea.

It was a room like all the others he'd ever occupied, in crowded houses that smelled of lemon oil and old suppers. Mrs. Qualey was any of an army of respectable women, reciting the menu: stew, corned beef, hash in perpetual rotation. The next night's supper, she informed him, was corned beef. He should keep in mind that first served was best fed, and she didn't hold with keeping plates warm in the oven if folks happened to be late. Then she left him to it, and though it was quiet, his ears still rang with the noise of the train and the street outside and his own exhaustion. He sat a long while before he tried to sleep in the cold room with yellow curtains the colour of smoke stains.

He had not bought the papers at the station, because he did not want to see her name or picture so early on his return, and not know what to do about it or how to feel. He had encountered her name occasionally and avoided her, though sometimes he thought of the money she still owed him—not legally at all, but on principle—and drafted imaginary letters. But the fine suits were gone, and he did not like to think of how it would feel to walk up the long drive to the door of her house, unknown to the maid who would open it. He hadn't any cards. All the same, his name still meant something—a very little something—here, and he had decided, finally, to accept the invitation for a one-week engagement at the Temple. He had always declined before. Occasionally he encountered people who remembered him, and they were always from the city, always women, and they always mentioned the Temple and the pink roses and how he had stood in his black suit and sung "Ô Souverain, ô juge, ô père."

Forty-five minutes after he fell asleep, Liam awoke to the sound of his own fingernails as they raked the wall beside the bed's headboard. The knuckles of his right hand were bloody, though he did not know when he had grazed them. He was half out of bed, with a feeling behind his ribs like broken glass, as though something unknown to him had smashed in the moment before he came to consciousness. He looked up to see if the window was broken, but it was not.

Once he remembered where he was, he dropped the rest of the way to the floor and knelt, inhaling the draft from the badly-fit window. For a lurching moment he smelled the incongruous scent of hay, lying in the fields. It was the smell of home in July, the oppressive heat of southern Ontario, and the scent of crushed dandelions and slow water in a creek.

After a few more breaths, reason asserted itself and the scent was gone. He hoped he hadn't shouted. He was wet, too, his pyjamas limp as dead petals and stuck to his back, a trickle of sweat under his arm and one at the base of his spine. He mopped his face with a sleeve. He was cold. But then there were footsteps in the hall. They approached. They paused. He wondered again if he had shouted, or wailed, perhaps, like a child. He held his breath. The hall light streaked across the floor through the crack under the door, illuminating his knees and the white sheet he'd torn from its hospital corners. His face was hot and fierce with shame. Then the light under the door went out. The footsteps retreated, and when they had gone Liam got to his feet. His heart slowed to a deep, steady rhythm that pulsed in his eardrums and behind his eyes. He returned to bed, and drew the heavy grey blanket over his head.

Much later, when he was dying, Liam would still be unable to recall the particulars of the dream which announced the arrival of his ghost, though he would remember clearly the day from which the dream had come. He would remember a nine-minute dance act before the intermission that had seemed strange and portentous, as though some epoch had ended, and something new and unnamed had begun.

He was in a small, grotty, northeastern city, sitting near the back of a theatre, part of a circuit that had declined to employ him the previous month. He was waiting to hear the tenor they had employed. It was between acts. He read his newspaper until the discordant arabesques of the dancers' accompaniment interrupted him. When he looked up, there were two men on stage dressed in gym strip, heavy black boots, fezzes on their heads. Over their football shorts they wore robes of draped white cotton with little skirts slashed at either hip. Their faces were made up with white paint and kohl around the eyes, heavy moustaches and thick, black eyebrows also darkened with something dense and greasy. Their limbs were long and white and made Liam think of medical dissection and anatomical drawings, the way each muscle corded the stretch of thigh and calf and throat, and all their joints stood out like knots tied in coarse string. Thick, black hair grew under their arms and in their white cotton décolleté, and crept down their thighs under their short, white skirts.

After an initial *egyptien tableau vivant*, they began to dance—but it was not, exactly, a dance, rather a quick progression through more *tableaux*, hieroglyph after hieroglyph to the minor-key discord of some Oriental jazz band. Their faces were identically hangdog, unmarred by sweat, with eyes fixed on some point on the theatre's back wall, high above Liam's head. Behind them the backdrop—pyramids, a flat blue sky, two palms—swayed in a draft.

It was then that a third figure appeared, this one a girl in diaphanous white rayon and paste diamonds, her long, blonde hair drifting down her shoulders, and her long, pale legs slipping in and out of her slit draperies. She stood on a platform that rolled across the stage on invisible machinery. She did not move, and her skill was only to remain standing during her progression, to raise her arms over her head and accept the fealty of her ugly, dancing slaves.

Even when they'd left the stage and in their place a jet-beaded woman managed a dozen black rats in frilled collars, Liam still saw the two men, their slow dance of elbows and knees to the nervous disharmony of the invisible band, their synchronized precision which must, he knew from his experience, have cost years. He imagined them repeating the act a thousand times, ten shows a week. He imagined that if he saw them in Brighton or London, Kiev or Hong Kong or Saskatoon, he would find no variation in the order or design of the hieroglyphs, the greasepaint, the folds of Cleopatra's gown.

Those nine minutes seemed, to Liam, as though they contained some significant message he should remember and apply to his own life. The tenor he had come to hear—emerging from the darkness after the beaded lady fled with her basket of rats and cream of wheat—was as insubstantial as an echo. The man, Stephan Greco, had sung before the war in a room that smelled of conservatory roses, and Liam had loved him that evening. In this new room—gritty with coal smoke, the scent of newsprint, cold coffee, wet wool, the imprint of the sand-dancers still in Liam's eyes—in this room he was unreal. What would it mean to be real as the sand-dancers had been? They would smell of basements and newspapers and cold coffee, meetings underground where dingy foreign men plotted sabotage, or workmen with dirty boots arranged irritating general strikes. As Liam contemplated them, and the future they represented, he imagined himself as dour as they, his pale, scarred legs turned outward as he clumped arrhythmically across the stage, his face a grotesque with kohl and white powder, a greasy Stalinist moustache on his upper lip. For the rest of that afternoon and evening he tried to think of other things, but found the vision inescapable, unlike the man singing in a beam of gold-coloured stage-light, who dirged through "Macushla" and "Come Into The Garden, Maud."

Still on stage, Stephan Greco clasped his hands then opened his mouth for another dreamy Victorian ballad. His voice travelled across the auditorium as though he stood miles away, in another time, and people in the audience saw him the way they saw the figures in a snow globe, behind the distorting curve of glass and water and glittering flakes of false snow.

When he woke again just after noon, Liam unrolled his shaving kit beside the basin and examined his face in the greenish mirror. He looked away from the pale, smudge-eyed man and unfolded his straight razor. The two halves—monogrammed ivory and blade—opened like wings in his hands. It was steel stropped to an almost painless edge. He knew how sharp and how nearly painless because he'd cut himself with it in the first week when he traced the blade unthinkingly with his right thumb. He'd seen the red drops in the basin before the cut properly registered, having noticed only the barest parting of flesh. His thumb bled fast, spattering the taps and the mirror, then the drops fell into the basin, hanging together for a moment before they dissipated, reddening his shaving water. He fumbled for gauze, and wrapped it around his thumb, though the blood broke through the fabric and he left prints on everything he touched.

It was a fine razor. It even pre-dated his time with Mrs. Kilgour. Though he had bought many elegant things during those months, he had not needed a razor: the one he owned was already suitable for his station, though it was only for a little while that his condition in life matched the quality of the blade. It was an artefact of his own early history, before the war, bought when he thought he was becoming the sort of man who needed a fine razor. He still remembered that it was fifteen shillings of the pound he earned from that first performance. He hadn't paid his tailor or his landlady, but when he saw the creamy ivory and felt its weight, he knew he must have it, and have "LM" engraved on the handle in clean Roman capitals. Twenty years later the blade still shone, though he'd had it reset and reground more than once, and though it had been through France with him. Amazing that it hadn't been blown out of his hand that first morning and taken flight—a bit of particularly dangerous and expensive shrapnel.

He had resolved to be the sort of man who shaved every day. He would carry on as he was, an artist, a civilized man forced by his own sense of duty to act against his fastidious instincts. *A mot juste*, he thought at the time, and proudly called himself "fastidious." In the morning, when the dust of his first bombardment still hung in the air, he squatted near the dugout and unrolled his kit across his knee, beside him a mug of hot water requisitioned from the teakettle. He opened the razor and saw how dull the metal had grown, already, and that he had left fingerprints on the handle. Rooting in the bag, he dragged out the little silk mirror case and felt it give under his fingers. When he opened it, the pieces fell out into his palm, no shard bigger than his thumb. He stared at them, confused, the razor open and useless in his right hand, the water cooling beside him.

Glancing up, he saw his captain leave the dugout and prop a bit of highly polished metal against the dirty sandbags of the lintel. He opened a common sort of black-handled razor. As Liam watched, he lathered, then crossed each cheek without incident, his chin, his upper lip even. Each pass was measured, followed by a critical glance in the mirror. He checked his throat against the back of his hand, relathered, the blade bright against his sunburn as it cleared the jugular. As though nothing could jolt him from above and knock him forward against his own razor. He might have been at home, in an enamelled bathroom, with a cup of coffee beside him.

Liam shut his monogrammed, ivory-handled razor, and dropped it carefully into its leather case. He dumped the mirror fragments into their little silk bag and dropped it to the mud. Above him the sky was blue. Around him were the shredded remains of a wood. He ran the back of one hand across his stubbled cheeks and thought he felt the bare rumour of a vibration, as though his hand contained the rolling echo of each shell that had fallen the night before. After that he preferred the French barbers. And anyway, they were cheap.

Dispelling such tedious memories, he finished shaving, and went to Mrs. Qualey's front room to read the paper. Then he went looking for the theatre, having only a vague memory of where the Temple had stood. All around it were brick apartment buildings; the ones that had seemed respectable on his last visit now were dingy and soot-stained. The streets were full of young men who always had their hands in their pockets, and stood in great crowds on the corners, so Liam either chose to walk in the gutter or found himself shoved there by a casual shoulder, and his shoes got wet. These young men were not the sort that moved aside for a gentleman, and Liam was still a gentleman, despite the wear on his good suit and the state of his cuffs.

He found the Temple much changed as well. He had only known it for a few months under Mrs. Kilgour's patronage, but it had been very clean and modern then, if not in particularly good taste. A year or more after the crash, it had been dropped from the circuit, he had heard, and now it hosted occasional performers and films, the new management having upgraded the projector and installed speakers. Already it seemed hopelessly out-of-date, a remnant of the age of flappers and bootleg gin, and that age was centuries past, leaving behind those awful flourishes in the baloney-pink ceiling, the plaster rosettes, the pink pillars of granite, the gilt-edged portraits of Egyptian gods with the heads of jackals and long-beaked birds. He wondered how he had ever thought it was a nice theatre, and been for a moment proud to sing in it. Now it was rented out two mornings a week to a bunch of dull men in work clothes, who paid for the manager's non-interference as much as for space in the lobby, or occasionally the stage if they had a large group. These groups of men often carried stacks of leaflets, he was told, and had threatened to distribute them to the theatre's patrons—people, the manager told Liam, who only wanted to see *Cavalcade*, or the latest Joan Crawford film, and did not want leaflets. Men like that were fools if they thought anyone cared for leaflets in this day and age, and the manager had told them so and that had been that, they knew where their bread was buttered. Men like that only needed to be told what for, and they usually slunk away. The manager was a short, thick man like a sea lion, who smiled an unpleasantly knowing smile whenever he talked about his customers or the leaflet-men.

Liam saw the pamphlet-men that afternoon when they had the lobby. He looked in from the theatre itself, where he had been meaning to practice, but had fallen, instead, to smoking and contemplating the dreadful pink and gold plasters. They sat in a circle, the dingy men in shirtsleeves. One of them was standing; he wore overalls and heavy boots that badly needed a cleaning. He was mid-sentence when he noticed Liam.

"I know you," he said.

Liam nodded. "My name is Manley, but I think you have the advantage." He had heard that line in a film, *you have the advantage* from some dinner-jacketed trans-Atlantean. He found, more and more, that he drew his habitual dialogue not from short stories in good magazines, but from films. He wondered if this showed. Often he didn't care.

"I remember you, Mr. Manley. I saw you sing."

"Yes?" Liam said. He did not want to cross the floor toward the group of shirtsleeved men with their pamphlets, but they had grown silent and were staring at him.

"Yes," said another one. "Mr. Liam Manley. Sweet Singer of Sweet Songs," and laughed. "You sang with that old capitalist, Kilgour. I remember when she came to entertain us. We called that insult to injury. But I liked your songs—you sang my father's old songs, from Scotland."

"Yes," Liam said.

"I saw your name on the marquee, but didn't think until I saw you. You sang with her, though, I remember that."

Liam nodded, smiled, then said the little speech he had thought up as he entered the foyer and wondered what to do about the little cluster of fellows. "I'm sorry, gentlemen, but I am currently at work, as I see you are. Please do not be disturbed—but I must do a little further preparation for tonight."

"Yes, of course, but you should join us, before you leave," the first man said, and now he stretched out his hand toward Liam, holding one of the leaflets. "And why not take this? It's a great thing we do, Mr. Manley." For a moment Liam did not think he was going to oblige; he thought instead he'd gently close the door then return to the stage and smoke another cigarette. Instead he found himself crossing the floor and taking the little folded sheet, and smiling, and nodding, and saying something slight about the dreadful state of the world. He glanced at the paper, then stuffed it into his inside pocket. The leaflet was about the Kilgour interests in the mining industry, full of acronyms: IWW, AFL, CIO, BCFL, RCWU. The man who had given him the sheet smiled a hard, grim smile that had filled Liam with an obscure fear.

That night at the Temple, at the ten minute call, with the houselights still burning, Liam looked out from shadowy stage left to watch the audience, their white faces and empty seats like the dots and dashes in a line of Morse code. He glanced down at his cuffs, noticing again that they were frayed, though the wear was so slight he was probably the only one who'd see it.

Someone behind him shuffled. "Mr Manley?" It was the stage manager, a little man with pale blue sleeve garters. He held a poppy in his left hand. "Thought you might like one," he said, then continued with the inevitable story. They all did it, Liam thought; he had for a while some years before, though no longer.

Liam hesitated, but took the thing that was in the stage manager's palm and said, "Thank you, sir. Where was it you mentioned?" He pinned the flower over his heart. It would look well—black, white and red—he thought critically, and be a reminder. He should have arranged to sing "The Minstrel Boy" or "Wi' A Hundred Pipers." The man went on about some moment somewhere with the 29th. Liam watched him, wondered how many times he'd told this story with pride. His wife would know the details intimately, would exclaim at the right times. His children, too. Stupid little man.

Liam fixed his eyes again on the audience. Yes, the red spot repeated, more expressive than just the white faces. It was like a sacred heart, as though each flower were swollen with blood. *In the end my immaculate heart will triumph.* The line emerged mechanically, like a *glory be.* He distracted himself with an *Ave* and wondered why the stage manager dwelt in the past, and why he had singled Liam out like that. He would have to be avoided.

The stage manager had finished. He reached up and clapped Liam on the shoulder and left. That was a relief. *Five minutes to curtain.*

Liam watched the audience from his dark corner. They were as nearly quiet as a half-filled room could be. He ran eyes up and down the rows, forward and backward, his hands quietly at his sides, hanging, not even in fists. He began to look closely at their faces, at their eyes like the glass eyes of dolls, and their good navy satin dresses stiff and shining, their white hands knotted in their laps. Cheap stones around their necks.

Two minutes. Liam waited, and then when the houselights faded he thought, it's time. He stood very straight with his hands behind his back, and pinched the cuffs' frayed hems between his fingers. He stepped into the darkness of the stage and felt himself illuminated. There was applause. The man who accompanied him was already sitting at the piano. They had agreed on an a cappella opening for "Believe Me If All Those Endearing Young Charms." The man sat mouse-quiet, with light for his music from a silver-coloured candelabra. Nothing that could distract from Liam, who would stand in the full gold lights of the stage's apron. Under his feet the black boards were solid, but for a moment he could not believe they persisted beyond the edge of his own lighted circle. Out there he heard coughs, the nearly-quiet rustling darkness full of stiff navy satin and doll's eyes fixed dead on him, shut mouths with painted lips. Men leaning back in their seats resigned to an evening's nap and women watching, their necks taut and their fingers knotted.

Liam reminded himself that he was here to do a job, and thought of "Believe Me If All Those Endearing Young Charms." But the longer he stood silent—three seconds, then five—the more dreadful it seemed that he should sing at all. And then ten seconds, then fifteen, and he heard a cough. One cough always brought others, he would have to do something soon. The gentleman at the piano glanced at him. But though the bad moment continued through the whole performance, Liam stepped away from it, clasped his hands before taking a breath and began:

believe me if all those endearing young charms that i gaze on so fondly today were to fade by tomorrow and wilt in my

SWEET SINGER OF SWEET SONGS

Liam didn't return to Mrs. Qualey's directly after the first performance. He walked to the park on the other side of town and back again. The rain slackened. He smoked. Occasionally his hand reached for the poppy on his lapel. After an hour of touching it in the dark between streetlights, he pulled it off and let it fall into the gutter, didn't look back to see it glow on the wet pavement.

When he'd found his way back to Mrs. Qualey's, it was at least one-thirty and he'd nearly walked himself numb. He might sleep through, tonight, dreamlessly, and wake in the morning refreshed. He lay awake, though, clammy with the damp air, until his hands and feet warmed in the unheated bedroom. He heard, distantly—the sound tiny and precise like a miniature—the train couplings locking and unlocking in the station yard.

On the third afternoon of his seven-day engagement, he recognized the girl outside the theatre. He wasn't quite sure she'd been in the audience, certainly he would have spotted a pretty one in that mutton-as-lamb crowd of the first and second nights, but he thought he might have seen her. She stood with her arms crossed over her chest and her head bowed, the nape of her neck exposed beneath the short curls at her hairline.

He continued past the theatre on the opposite side of the street, dropped his cigar and crossed, watching her from the corner of his eye. She shifted her weight from one foot to the other. Her eyes didn't scan the pavement. She seemed to be waiting but she didn't wait. No powder compact out with hair patting, or checking of teeth, no little smiles, as though in her head she choreographed a conversation. She only stood.

Liam ran one hand through his hair and dishevelled his pompadour. He dropped his hand again and held it behind his back, surreptitiously wiped the Brylcreem on his shirt, beneath his jacket. He ran one finger along the hem of his cuff. He slowed to give her time to notice. She shifted from her left to her right foot, her hips swinging in a tick-tock. Or just a tick. She raised her head and her hair fell back and obscured her neck. Her coat was light for November, water-darkened about the shoulders. She'd walked a long way in the rain. She wore oxfords and socks. Her long bare legs would be rough to the touch from cold. The hem of a tweed skirt brushed the backs of her knees.

She tocked, weight left, right leg bent.

He was near the overhang now. She hadn't turned around. No one else waited outside. Well—doors didn't open for a few hour yet, though there had been a time when there had been a real little crowd waiting for him, and he would watch them from the windows of Mrs. Kilgour's slow, black Rolls-Royce.

He was level with her, had just turned his head when she looked up.

"Oh," she said.

He smiled, kept walking, but slowly.

"Mr. Manley." He turned and nodded. "Mr. Manley," she said again, and then, "I saw you sing—the opening night. I wanted to say—" this fast, as though it was a message someone had entrusted to her. She stopped again.

He stepped toward her. "Yes?"

"How much I liked it. How much I liked it when you sang."

"Thank you. It's very kind. Are you coming again tonight?" That might be too much. A bit desperate, asking her that.

"Oh. No." But sad. Sad-ish.

Ahah, he thought. "Unfortunate," he said.

"I'd like to hear you again—"

"You're fond of the old ballads of Ireland?" he asked, slight emphasis on "Ireland," and it came out "Oir-land." He tried not to listen to himself, so that he would not hear how tired his little speeches were, the little inflections that were not quite stage-Irish, but were close enough that he recognized their shabbiness.

"I like them. And Robbie Burns. And all the sad songs." She was blushing right up to her hairline. Her freckles were nut brown all over the bridge of her nose, her skin very white under the blush. She'd be that pale naked, smooth and slender, unfreckled where the sun never reached.

"I do like the classics, myself, but I find not much demand for them now—and Miss, what are you doing listening to tenors? You should be dancing. Is it Bing Crosby?"

"I don't like the music now," she said. "I hate it. I like things from before."

Before, he thought, *from before*. He persevered. "You're an old fashioned girl."

"I guess I might be. I don't like things now. They seemed to be better then," she said and squinted as though looking for *then*. "When people lived in villages, and had horses. And," she paused, trying to bring what she saw into focus, "went haying."

Haying. Good Christ. He thought of the damp heat on the horrible, uninterrupted fields of his father's farm. He thought of the smell of new-mown hay. He laughed, "And a romantic too."

She blushed.

Too far, too far. He should be solicitous, avuncular. Not tease her until she was used to him.

"You don't have the money for the ticket," he said gently. "Is that right?"

Her freckles were nearly gone in the blush. She looked away, but she nodded.

"But you love the music, do you?" She nodded again. "Right. What's your name, love?"

"Hazel," she said. "Hazel Lyon."

"Well, Miss Lyon, I'll put your name down for a ticket when the box office opens."

Her eyes flew open. She looked at him steadily, without squirming. For a moment he doubted himself, wondering if this had been her plan all along, and he only obeying. She had pale brown eyes, almost the colour of her hair and her freckles. Then she blushed again and he thought no, no, she would not know how to play like that. "I can't," she said. "I shouldn't."

"You can, my dear, and you have. Now—" He pulled some coins from his pocket, thankful he had any money on him. "Buy yourself a cup of tea. See you back here at seven-thirty, and on time, Miss!"

He pushed the money into her hand and quite naturally she took it, and then he left her, smiling.

He saw her from backstage. She sat in the tenth row, a good seat. She was to his left, her face uplifted, examining the faded red brocade of the curtain, the worn gold woodwork. He thought of men he'd known in hospital, young men with permanently wet, bemused smiles on their faces.

The set went well, or at least better than the previous night. He glanced at her occasionally and during "She Moved Through The Fair" he permitted himself one prolonged look during the last sustain. She didn't smile in return, but watched intently, as though reading him, and he was hard to parse. He thought of the rest of the evening, after the recital. He thought about the rest of the engagement. He wondered where she lived. She was a nice girl, he thought. She folded her hands like a nice girl, and pinned her hair away from her forehead, and her downward glances were modest.

He hadn't asked, but she was waiting for him, not outside the stage door, but across the street in an archway out of the rain. She was staring at her feet. He was halfway across the street before she looked up and took one involuntary step backward. He smiled and held out his hand.

"Come and have tea," he said. "Did you before?"

She nodded. She didn't take his hand. She looked cold, and when she stepped out of the doorway, he took her arm and slipped it through the crook of his elbow.

"I liked it better tonight," she said as they walked. "The song. I liked it best tonight."

"The song?"

"She Moved Through the Fair." She phrased the title as though she were singing it—she *mooooved* thro' the *faair.*

"I'm glad." Then they reached the corner and she stopped suddenly and he squeezed her wrist tight. Her arm fluttered under his, like a bird, and he did not let go. "What is it?" he asked, knowing the answer.

"Where? Where are we going?"

"There's a café around the corner," he said. "You look cold." He affected a deadly serious concern, as though her comfort were his single goal. He had discovered that too much smiling, or possibly incorrect smiling, made young women self-conscious. They sometimes accused one of mocking them if one smiled too readily. They hated the suggestion that this—this *thing*—might be absurd, arbitrary, amusing.

"A café?"

"Yes. Ah—we haven't been properly introduced, have we? My name is Liam Manley." He turned to her and held out his hand. "And you are Miss Hazel Lyon." He shook her hand solemnly. "May I buy you a cup of tea?"

This time, she let him thread her arm through his elbow and lead her two slow blocks to the café. When she stopped resisting, there was something limp and abstract about her, as though she'd only just been struck deaf by some explosion.

He was meditating on conversation topics—they must be appropriate but suggestive, so she might feel important, even desired—when she seemed to rouse from her rag doll state. Her arm alive again under his as she dragged a bit, made him stop and face her.

"We met," she said, "ages ago. A long, long time, before. When I was little. Just after the war. We heard you sing. We came to the theatre in the morning to take your picture, and we heard you sing. Then we heard you again, later, and there were pink roses." She said it firmly, as though it was a very particular message trusted to her. "We heard you in the theatre, and Dad took your picture."

It would have been the Kilgour business. It would have been 1920 or '21. He tried to remember and thought there was something—a man, a child, the empty stage. But then he thought of going to the Castle again—

perhaps tomorrow or the next day—and speaking with Mrs. Kilgour, and how it would feel to do that in his old suit, with his hat held carefully in his hand so that he hid the place on the crown where the felt was discoloured. He could not think of that. Instead he allowed a light of memory to rise in his face, then he smiled though he found himself irritated with her, wanting something from him like that. He laughed. "You remind me of my age, my dear. I hadn't thought I was such an old man as that."

"You look just like you do in the picture. I brought it with me. To show you." She fumbled in the bagged pocket of her coat and pulled out a crumpled handkerchief and a white card. She pushed it at him. He dropped her arm and took it, fastidiously avoiding the handkerchief which she crammed back into her pocket.

It was him, though he didn't recognize the picture from among those they'd used in publicity. Quite a good one. He looked fragile but masculine, leaned forward slightly so that one lock of heavily Macassarred hair fell across his forehead. His eyes were dark without benefit of kohl.

He smiled again, but more seriously this time. "Thank you, Miss Lyon, for the reminder of what I once was." He looked deeply into her eyes for a moment, as though searching them, and when she looked away, he turned them again toward the café. He waited for her to speak first. She still held the photograph in her free hand.

"Do you remember?" At first he didn't say anything, just nodded, but she was watching him so closely. "Do you remember?"

He lied. "I remember."

"Good," she seemed satisfied. "I'm a bit hungry."

Again Liam wondered if he'd misread her, but dismissed the thought before they'd even opened the café's door.

"Of course," he heard himself say as he leaned across a table near the back of the café, "of course this is not what I think of as my real career—who could think of the recital platform in those terms? I have a few years left and I would like to spend that time with a real company. The allure of the road—" had it ever had this allure he spoke of?—"is certainly fading. A good company, a tour each year, through the west, or to South America, those I would enjoy, but not this constant travel. I have the itchy feet of my race certainly." He drank from his cup to cover his embarrassment. He was coming across quite Oirish he thought, which appealed to women for reasons he never quite understood. He was glad he'd learned a passable accent from his father, and picked up some phrases from vaudeville-Irish comics out of New York. She was still watching him. "But I've had my fill of wandering."

She nodded as though she knew what he was talking about. He did not imagine she did, but he meant her to feel that way. He'd been talking for half an hour by then, his voice floating down melodious and carefully modulated, drifting into a chuckle or dropping an octave to his serious baritone. He listened as though it weren't his own, to the way it chastised her, teased her, cajoling, friendly, flirtatious, desiring, all these shades of seduction. He saw the vision that voice built, describing offers he had not received, a life he did not lead, ambitions he did not have for a career he had lost fifteen years before.

She looked into her teacup and then back at him. She had lovely eyelashes; they curled at the tips. Her skin was fine under the eyes, like pale kid leather with a purplish shadow; it would be cool and soft under his fingertips. Skin like that would line her thighs, her breasts— translucent, shuddering over the ribcage with each heartbeat. He could feel it, imagine handfuls of it, imagine gripping her shoulders, throat, thigh, the tight curl of her ear.

If he had admitted to himself his anxiety regarding all kinds of performance, he would have recognized his relief when he felt the first, new pulse at the base of his cock and the familiar heaviness spreading down the whole shaft. He had been afraid—in a deep and secret place—that he had brought the girl along only to find he lacked real ambition. Now, though, he would not even mind if he found later in the evening that his pants were sticky with anticipation. It was rarer now, though when he was eighteen there had been a year of permanently damp underthings, the leak of fluids at the barest provocation: a woman in a low gown took a deep breath, a glance thrown backward over her white shoulder. He had not thought he would miss that, especially on cold nights in November.

Her voice clogged, so she had to clear her throat before she spoke. "Will you take one of the offers, do you think? From a company? Will you sing in operas then?"

Again he heard himself speaking. "Of course, I don't want to presume anything. I must remember I am not as young as I was." He looked to her then with a smile, waiting for the simper and the little shake of the head, a coy shrug. There was nothing, only that uncomfortably *appraising* blankness as she met his eyes again. "And the popular stage belongs to men younger than I am." She offered no disagreement—she even nodded.

He wanted, then, to stop, but didn't know how, and his voice continued, as though reading from a script: "So I don't know. I imagine I may join one of the companies—" (what companies? what companies do you speak of?) "But no—I spoke about how little I like the vaudeville life, but in fact it still has a hold over me," he went on. "The recital stage is a different animal entirely." He stopped talking. He suddenly wanted to apologize.

She said bluntly, "I liked what you did at the theatre. I don't know that I would like you in an opera. I don't know anything about opera, but I like the songs you sing."

"Yes, you would like those songs, wouldn't you?" he said, sharper than he intended. She knew nothing. She was a fool. She was looking down into her teacup then, her cheeks reddening. "There is no real art here, nothing pure or sublime, only this grovelling to the crowd."

She looked up at him quickly then away, and he saw for the first time a glimmer of fear in her eyes. He saw it in the way her hands shook, too. There was no judgement there, only her indiscriminate acceptance. She was only afraid of saying or doing the wrong thing. She hadn't any capacity to consider what he was doing at all.

He didn't even want to finish the speech. "Miss Lyon, you're out very late. Will your mother worry?"

"I don't know. I don't think she has time to worry."

"She'll worry, no doubt. I'll see about getting you home."

The next day she did not come, but he thought perhaps she would on the Friday. That afternoon he shaved carefully, and afterward stood in his underwear brushing his suit; his only other shirt lay on the high metal bed. It was a narrow bed and uncomfortable. She wouldn't want to stay, anyway. She would have to go home. But still, he wanted it to look nice. That afternoon he'd bought a white rose and set it in a glass by the lamp, and taken care that the empty hearth was swept, and the coarse grey blankets smoothed over nicely.

Putting on the last white shirt, he glanced at his face in the mirror, black-shadowed by the bare white bulb in the ceiling. Candles would have been nice, but possibly the half-darkness of streetlights was a more soothing choice. It did not do to look at these things in too a clear a light. All the same, he thought he *would* buy candles on the way to the theatre, just two for the empty sticks on the mantel.

He finished with his tie, carefully adjusted his pocket handkerchief, and looked once more into the glass over the sink. He didn't look bad, he thought carefully, a bit worn maybe, but not unattractively so. Leaving the boarding house, he felt buoyant for the first time he could remember, wondering where she was just then, if she was having supper, or sitting with her mother. In thinking of her and the evening ahead, he had forgotten his previous gloom, hardly concerned with the difficulties of performance. He felt, even, that he could face Mrs. Kilgour and that he would do so, perhaps even the next day. That he would knock on the door—yes, older, yes a little worn—and smile at her and find her receptive as she had always been. He would go there tomorrow, in the afternoon, and they would sit together in the huge, hideous drawing room that overlooked the garden, and he would let her talk about Clive all she liked.

And he only felt more certain when he saw Hazel. He hadn't asked her to wait, but there she was across the street from the stage door. Well, he thought, they had known one another for years. No one else was waiting for him, but that almost didn't matter this time. She crossed the street to join him, and he took her limp arm. She still had the trembly look of a rabbit, but she had done her hair prettily, he noticed, and her mouth was painted, and he liked the hard, clean line between red lip and white skin. She pushed a lock of hair behind one ear.

"Would you like a cup of tea?" he asked. "Where shall we go?"

"I'm not hungry. I ate already," she said. "Let's walk a bit and talk. Then." She said nothing else, but met his eyes unapologetically, defiant.

He swallowed. "Alright. We'll walk a bit." He led her toward Mrs. Qualey's respectable establishment, forcing himself to let her set the pace. No rush he thought, no rush at all. She hardly spoke, and he kept up a light patter, though he was never quite sure what he was saying. *Really, no rush.*

Two other guests were in the drawing room when they arrived, one sleeping under a handkerchief, the other reading close to the fire. Mrs. Qualey, thankfully, was not sitting up with them. Liam glanced around as he opened the door, holding Hazel back with one arm, not thinking as he threw it across her chest; he felt the pressure of one breast through the fabric of their coats. He dropped the arm.

"There's no one here," he said abruptly, then regretted it. The implications were too obvious.

"Good." She looked relieved and nodded, a real smile now.

He glanced at her again, unsettled by her pragmatism. "We should go in."

They climbed the stairs together, and she let him take the lead only when they got to the top and he opened his door. He took the two white candles from his pocket and lit them on the mantelpiece. He opened the small bottle of port wine he had in his other pocket, bought before the performance.

"Would you like some?"

She nodded, and sat down on the hard chair beside the hearth.

"I wish my rent extended to fires, but I'm afraid the lady of the house does not think they're necessary in bedrooms." He sat on the hearth itself, stretching his legs in front of him, then he laughed and added, "She thinks it's healthier, anyway, all this fresh air."

"Coal is expensive," she said, sipping the port. She made a face (and hid it quickly) at the little mouthful and set the glass down on the floor beside the bed. "Very expensive. I bet she worries about money. I mean. I mean. I expect she does. Do you always stay here?"

"Mrs. Qualey is well-known to those in my profession. She is a formidable woman, but I respect her. And given the state of the world at the moment, I am thankful to have a kind of home here," he said, and looked into the empty fireplace. Mrs. Qualey was a parsimonious old sinner. He hated this soggy city, and his "engagements" anywhere were fewer and fewer. Sometimes he thought it was only habit that kept him going round in circles, through these cities. Just as it was habit that kept his bookings intact and people showing up. But even that was fading, a broken habit. Would he keep arriving at stage doors for years after the last audience member had turned away and bought tickets to a Hollywood musical, or stayed home to listen to the radio? Probably, like a ghost in black serge, not dead, but forgotten. He looked up from the empty fireplace to find her staring at him. He was surprised again by the frankness—or the blankness?—of her gaze. He wondered what was on the other side of her eyes, or if there was nothing but what he saw in front of him. He did not permit that thought; it suggested too many things he did not like.

"Have you come here before? I mean, after the time I saw you?"

"No. Not since that first visit."

"I could have seen you if you did. Like I saw you when I was little. Dad would have known—he was at the Temple until this summer."

Liam paused. Perhaps that accounted for the impression she gave of one perpetually waiting. "No, but it's only just this time I'm back to the Temple. I played some other circuits in-between, you know. When did your father die?"

She jumped. "This summer. June."

"I'm sorry, my dear." He did not like how quickly and accurately he had recognized grief and abandonment.

"Yes."

There didn't seem to be anything else to say. He wondered if he had made some mistake, whether she was just the rag doll she seemed to be, but then she drained her glass and slid to the floor beside him. She did not touch him. When he held out a hand she didn't take it. He touched her wrist, picked up the hand and touched the cracked skin of the palm—a charlady's palm, a dishwasher's. He kissed it.

She was limp as he raised her head and kissed her, but he did not mind as he stood and helped her to stand. She fell against him, abruptly as though the strings that held her upright had been cut. She was a little thing, smaller than he had imagined as he felt her chin pressed into his chest before he turned her mouth to face his, and kissed her again. He let his hands drift to her hair, though they wanted (desperately) to wrap right around her breasts first. Instead he ran down her back to her waist, where he could feel the line of her underthings through the fabric of her skirt and blouse. None of the armour he was used to on nice girls, he realized, which was pleasant, if shocking. Getting a girl out of a corselet was awkward and unattractive, especially with someone as inexperienced as Hazel appeared to be. He was relieved again to feel that familiar heaviness in his cock as his hand brushed the tops of her thighs, his balls tightening and rising as he pushed his tongue between her lips.

He tried not to rush, but then his hands moved over her breasts—so small under her blouse—and slid down her back, and he paused at the base of her spine over the cleft between her buttocks. He breathed relief into her hair as he felt himself grow, straining against the fabric of his trousers. He wondered what she would think when she saw him fully erect, or if she would be the kind who didn't like to look. He worried that she—being inexperienced, having nothing with which to compare—would not be cognizant of his unusual size. He worried, equally, that she would be frightened. Once a woman had taken one look at what was between his legs and turned him down, saying "none of that, laddie!" And he had been both angry and pleased and lay beside her, throbbing even more painfully at the implications of her refusal.

Having successfully removed Hazel's clothes—an ungraceful and awkward procedure that made her blush and sweat under his hands—he hung above her on the bed, balanced on one elbow and his knees, his bare bum stuck up in the air from his arched back, his right hand on the base of his cock, which was stiff and wet and aching. He lifted his head from her neck and looked in her eyes. Her lips were wet all around from his kisses, though her mouth was dry and sticky, tasting faintly of peppermints and unbrushed teeth under the port. She did not smile, but watched him, heavy-lidded, as though through a thick pane of glass. He was breathing sharply now, and with his right hand he pushed his fingers between her legs and rubbed at the hooded little bump above her cunt. Her eyes flew open wider. He rubbed harder, but then she grimaced and made a pained noise. Sometimes he found it hard to tell which sounds were pain and which were pleasure, but often the two blended in his ear.

Then he was in between her thighs and pushing, pushing inside her. She was so tight that at first he could not move, and they clung together very still and awkward, and he felt that if he thrust and pulled out he would leave the skin of his cock inside her, like a discarded French letter.

They lay like that a long time, with Hazel whimpering with every pulse, her mouth small and wet against his throat. He turned his head and kissed her and slowly—slowly!—she relaxed around him, until he could not stop himself and he moved, and moved again.

LAST THINGS

Many years later, Jasmine said, "Not everyone is lucky enough to love like I do." Then she said, "If you can't figure it out, that's your breakdown." They were sitting on the floor of her empty apartment. By then she had given away or sold most of her possessions. They drank warmish water from plastic fast food cups. The cups weren't very clean.

As she put her lips to the cup's rim, Anthea's stomach shrivelled. She said, "Okay, maybe, but." She suspected that if she were standing, her knees would wobble. She didn't want to look at Jasmine, so she kept her hair in her face, and hid from view the pulse that fluttered at her throat. She swallowed. Dry mouth. She didn't want to drink from the plastic cup.

"There's no neutral here, Anthea. There's no moderation." Jasmine stood up then. She went to the window and lit a cigarette. "Do you want to know the truth?"

Anthea said nothing. She had never wanted to be different. Jasmine dribbled smoke out her mouth, into the room, out the window.

"I don't mean to be mean."

Anthea made a small noise. Sometime later she would remember that noise and she would be angry, and think how she should have laughed at Jasmine with her high school slanginess and said *you don't mean to be mean but you always were kind of a cunt.*

"I don't mean to be mean, but if you don't choose you'll be chosen. You can't play it both ways. We're all going to be terminal cases, so where do you want to be when that happens? Here?" Jasmine gestured toward the dirty window, the city outside, the crows flying overhead, the lights flickering.

Anthea's skin was clammy. The floor on which she sat was dirty, a coffee splash covered in lint beside her foot, beside that a bit of dark cursive that might be from a dropped mascara wand.

"He's coming here. He'll be here soon. You should talk to him. You should talk to him about where we're going. We're going to go north along the coast. We're going to get out before it's too late. We'll be back, but it won't be for long."

Anthea stood up. She thought about firestorms and EMPs. She thought about leaving the city on foot, through the suburbs and the nine-lane highways and the tunnels and the bridges. "The thing of it is. The thing of it is," Anthea said. "The thing of it is."

Jasmine looked up with a wrinkle on her forehead, like disgust. Anthea realized that she didn't know what the thing of it was, but she said again, "The thing of it is." The thing of it was that she had known this apartment in an earlier world. She had loved it. The place over there where she'd kissed Jasmine's downstairs neighbour at a New Year's party, his hand cradling her head as they lay on the floor. Over there was the place where she'd sat on the futon after she drank too much wine and wept about Hazel.

Jasmine exhaled. Then she said, "Parach, Anthea. Parach." Whatever it had been, it was over, and the real thing of it was *that*. Jasmine would leave the city, she would escape the endtimes, she would follow her prophet into the wilderness. She would unhitch herself from the world. She would be pure.

Anthea set her plastic cup down on the floor between the coffee splash and the mascara doodle. She stood up carefully, for the last time seeing the window, the crooked walls and crappy construction of the crappy little suites in the old house. She looked at Jasmine and Jasmine stretched her arm out in a gesture like blessing and said, once more, "Parach."

At the bottom of the stairs, before she left through the front door, she paused and thought, *this is the last time I will ever see this stairway*. She waited and listened, but Jasmine didn't follow, and then she turned the lock to go out.

Halfway across the threshold, she thought suddenly and vividly of a day from the year before when it was raining and they had sat on that same floor and played cards, and Jasmine had shown her a gift from a boy. He had cast his cock for her in purple silicon; she kept it on top of her fridge, with her loose change, a delicately veined and textured souvenir. They had played catch with it, and when they got bored, Anthea stuck it, head up, into a dying potted plant on the windowsill, like one of those ornaments that come with bouquets. It must be gone now, in a Smithrite, or wherever one donated second-hand marital aids.

She was about to close the door behind her, and resign herself to never knowing, never ever knowing what had become of that name-forgotten boy's cock, the one in the plant. That was when a brown-eyed man climbed the steps. He was barefoot, though it was evening on a rainy day in April. His hair was wet and his skin would be cool to the touch, she thought, if she touched it.

"Hold the door," he said in his slow, dark voice, "I want to see Jasmine."

When she held it for him he said "Parach!" and smiled with his mouth, until it crept into his beer-bottle eyes, and Anthea looked longer than she wanted to at his bottom lip, which was full, and the smooth collarbones at the base of his throat pressing against skin that made her think of honey.

As he passed, she smelled his patchouli and tobacco sweat, and under it a pervasive skunk. His feet were dirty and his jeans wet to mid-calf. He left high-arched footprints on the floor and up the stairs.

MRS. LAYTON AND THE EGG

At two o'clock in the afternoon, three days after her return from Duncan's Crossing, Anthea again found herself in the Aquarian bungalow's entrance hall. She held a white chicken's egg in her left hand and an old manila envelope in her right. She waited among triple goddesses and divine feminines, counterfeit papyrus depicting dancing, *egyptien* gentlemen in short, white robes. Mrs. Layton appeared, draped and cowled in pale grey cashmere like the abbess of a particularly sophisticated holy order.

When they were seated she asked, "What did you bring me, Anthea?" Anthea had not yet decided what she would say to Mrs. Layton regarding the contents of the paper hoard beneath The Place of the Stones. It would be easier if the box had contained a still-beating heart; she imagined Mrs. Layton would know what to do with a heart.

"I took your advice," she said.

"I gave you no advice," said Mrs. Layton. "Though I think I asked you to bring me something."

The egg was still cool from the fridge, and felt smooth like a beach-stone. She set it on the table beside the teapot.

Mrs. Layton picked it up and cupped it in the palm of her right hand. "Eggs, Anthea," she began, in her explaining voice, "are precious because of their potential." Now Mrs. Layton covered the egg over with her left hand and held it to her forehead. "But that also means they are vulnerable to the unconscious currents of a household. An egg reveals a great deal about the place from which it comes. Where do *you* come from?"

Though she wished to remain calm, heat rose at the centre of Anthea's cheeks and crept up her throat.

Mrs. Layton did not seem to expect an answer. "And where are you going?" She continued: "After our meeting last week I began to see more, and now I can tell you this. In the late spring of this year a man and a girl hitchhiked north along the highway. They passed through a town called Duncan's Crossing and on the edge of that town they came to a shabby little resort called the Glass Castle. They were begging. They went to the general store and the clerk took pity on them—they were dirty and very thin by then—and gave them a box of animal crackers."

For a long moment Anthea was preoccupied with the animal crackers. She tried to imagine Jasmine eating them on the highway beside the beer-bottle Castle, thought of them carrying the box to the very ends of the earth, first eating the elephants, and then camels. She wondered if they saved the lions for last, as Anthea had done when she was little.

When she had thought through the animal crackers she said, "What the fuck does that even mean?" Her palms were soft and sticky around her cup. "Did you know where she was going after the goddamn animal crackers?"

"Don't use language like that, Anthea. It's ugly. And, no, no one knew."

"She didn't even take water, I bet. I bet she didn't even take water with her."

"Anthea, the mundane events of our lives are chosen long ago. We manifest physically only what we have already decided after deep reflection and debate. You may call that fate, but it is a simple word for a complex mechanism."

The word "fate" triggered something unpleasant in Anthea, something for which she was not prepared: a red surge, and her skin gathered into hard, painful goosebumps all down her arms and legs. If she were a braver woman, she would have hit Mrs. Layton with the soapstone reproduction of the Willendorf Venus on that side table. Hitting her would have been right and just, with the way she looked.

Mrs. Layton was still talking: "She was part of something much larger than you can imagine. For women like Jasmine, there are more important considerations than biological survival."

Something dry and sour stuck Anthea's tongue to her teeth. She would not hit Mrs. Layton, even if it seemed to be the only way to make it real to her, what might have happened to Jasmine, what happened all around them all the time, down here in the material where the rest of us live.

"Why are you here, Anthea?"

Anthea set down her cup, and the noise it made when it struck the table was very loud.

"I brought you the egg, but I found something else as well. The kind of thing Jasmine would have liked." She undid the string that held the envelope shut, and upended it on the table. Bits of paper fell on the floor, Depression-era diner recipes, envelopes and datebook pages covered in tiny, meticulous printing. It was often plain English, but felt like encryption, whether by code or the disordered mind that produced them. "I found it in a hole dug under a little house. It's called The Place of the Stones," Anthea said.

Mrs. Layton pulled one bit of paper toward her. Anthea recognized it as a bill for scrambled eggs, orange juice and two slices of toast, from some long-gone lunch counter in Duncan's Crossing. On the back, there were figures in long strings and multi-directional equations, an irrational mathematics that involved the alchemical sign for Sal Nitrum and the Hebrew character "aleph" and Fibonacci numbers and π. They seemed to mean something to Mrs. Layton, and she touched them in a way that made Anthea think of bones rendered holy by reliquaries and ossuaries. "How did you know?" Mrs. Layton asked her.

"I don't know anything," she said.

"Then I can do something for you, as well." Mrs. Layton slid to her knees, gray cashmere and raw silk puddling around her on the red carpet. Her eyes rolled back into her head and fluttered there, her rib cage lifted and her shoulders dropped as her arms fell behind her. Anthea crossed her arms over her chest, flung back in memory to the days when Jasmine tried to raise the dead or conjure jinn from Butter Ripple Schnapps and the evening air.

Before her, on the floor, Mrs. Layton's face took on the quality of yellow ivory, smooth and expressionless and very old. Anthea stood up and thought *I should go I should go*, but Mrs. Layton said, "Parach ach Aleph leukos meloch ach Parach."

Then she held her left hand above her head and brought it down hard on the egg that still sat beside the teapot. She smashed it flat, and before Anthea saw what was in it, she smelled a deep rot that filled the room, not sulphurous, but animal.

And Mrs. Layton stood as well. She said, "Do you doubt that this egg came from your own home? Whatever did this is with you now."

Anthea took a step back from the table and the mess beside the teapot. She saw shell fragments, and wet, but looked away before she could identify what had been inside the egg.

"I don't know. I don't know," was all she could say, and then as she made her way toward the door Mrs. Layton's hand shot out and her fingers wrapped around Anthea's wrist. She pulled the girl toward her and kissed her, a cool, dry kiss. And then Anthea was backing away with that ivory stare following after. When she reached the doorway, Mrs. Layton said, "You are afraid of what you have found, Anthea, I know, but I can help. There are things I can tell you, things you will want to know. But first, go to the bottle exchange, and then to the coffee shop across the street. Talk to Menander. And when you have finished, you will both come back to me and I will tell you the story of my father. After that, I think you should stay with me. Your house is not safe."

The last time Anthea had been properly out with Jasmine, with no mention of the Aquarian Centre or Akashic Texts or Sauces Chosen for Family Dinners 1901–1905, inc., they went to eat Ayurvedic food and watch the Thursday night flamenco dancers at a place on the west side. The woman they liked best had danced *el baile flamenco*, and as always they had loved her shoes and talked about how she was both hot and terrifying in her imperious perfection. At the end of her dance, she stood perfectly still, her smooth, corded arms stretched upward, like a caryatid or un-Winged Victory, and Anthea had seen a snag on the ankle of her taupe fishnets and that had made the long muscles on her calves seem even lovelier. After she danced and they held the required, respectful silence, the man with the guitar laughed and sang "A Mi Manera," and Anthea felt momentarily sentimental for high school and Sid Vicious. Around midnight they left the close, warm air of the Ayurvedic place to find something richer for dessert.

The dessert place on the east side was decorated in red-flocked velvet wallpaper, and the man who waited on them wore a black silk padded jacket with sleeves that covered his hands. Their coffee came in translucent demitasse; Jasmine ordered the lava cake and Anthea had a crème brûlée with raspberries in the bottom. Jasmine said it was a Victorian bordello in Shanghai, and scraped her fork across her plate for the last of the chocolate. Anthea ate her raspberries one by one. Outside on the street, three kids waited for a cab in front of a market, beneath an orange sign with black Arabic script.

After an hour over coffee Jasmine walked southwest and Anthea walked east. Almost home, she stopped at a street corner and listened to an old man at Bayani's on the corner karaoke "My Way" through the restaurant's terrible speakers. It began to rain. Inside the trickling windows they all laughed and clapped and the man bowed.

Now she was back home again from the Aquarian Centre, wondering if all the eggs in her refrigerator were rotten. Anthea stood at her kitchen window and watched the rain collect on the sill and drip down the wall where it distorted the floorboards. If the rain kept up, she thought, the water would reach halfway to the kitchen counters by morning, and then it would run down the walls to the apartment below. Above her head, something scratched at the attic floor. She thought it would be damp up there as well, but they were furry and it was probably better than a tree. Above her head there was a whole colony, and now the scratching came from the walls as well as the ceiling, and sometimes it seemed to be under the floorboards. She often thought of the dark, and all the climbers and hiders and nesters running through the hollow places behind the walls, over the beams in the ceiling. If her landlady didn't do something, they would unmake the house, squirrels down from the attic, rats up from the basement. Chewing through the electrical, shredding the insulation, working as one with the mold in the plaster and the rot in the step.

INHERITORS

Though he had planned to knock on her door and arrive, prodigal, in Mrs. Kilgour's enormous drawing room, Liam put it off another day, then a third. Hazel was a far more interesting and demanding project, and he quickly decided to stay in the city after he finished his week at the Temple Theatre. He spent hours walking with her, sometimes they stopped at cheap cafés, or the tea rooms that Hazel initially considered superior and more genteel. Without asking, he saw her most mornings at the White Lunch, a restaurant just a few blocks from the boarding house. He had not expected her the first time, but then he had seen her on the sidewalk, and he had stood and waved his newspaper at her and they had spent the day together.

She took him places he would not otherwise go, for rituals he did not understand, and he enjoyed, vicariously, modern adolescence: once he trailed after her through Woodward's while she selected one handkerchief and a pair of cotton gloves, and made him hold her pocketbook while she paid and then carry her bag afterward; they shared a milkshake at Adele's Café and listened to some boy crooner on the radio, while the girls lined up at the counter looked at him over their shoulders and whispered; they walked through the large urban park along wooded trails that seemed entirely wild and private. She took him through the heavy fir wood and out the other side, where they looked away from the city and toward the invisible islands and past those to the Pacific, and then the far western reaches of the sea. It was late afternoon in November, with a few bare lights winking on across the inlet, overlooking a huge stone that knelt in the water, a little Douglas fir growing out of its top. Hazel told him the story of the stone, how it had once been a man who so loved his unborn son that he and his wife and child were immortalized while purifying themselves in the waters of the inlet. He smiled at the little story and thought about how kissable she was when she was talking, and then he kissed her. And he thought of how dark and cold were the fir trees and the lowering sky, but where they touched, his skin was warm.

On these days he sometimes heard news regarding Mrs. Kilgour while he pushed Mrs. Qualey's hash around his plate. He read the social columns of the local newspaper and learned that she was so unwell she had cancelled two parties and would not leave Craiglockhart. Each morning, he imagined approaching her, but then there was another afternoon to spend with Hazel and then it was evening and too late. There was the saltwater swimming pool on the beach—abandoned for the season now—where she learned to swim, and there were long, damp walks along the shore, and the view across the inlet to the mountains: those two were called the Lions; those others were the Sleeping Beauty, the huge figure of a reclining woman sketched into the horizon. After a few days looking for private places in parks, they were more reckless, and she came to see him at Mrs. Qualey's. That respectable landlady compressed her thin, crusty lips and made unkind comments. They liked kissing on a tiny landing halfway up to Liam's room. Hazel laughed and talked about convention, and after Liam used the word and explained it to her, she often called things "bourgeois," and talked about escaping the city and its colonial respectability. She would get away, she said, and travel. She would be original. She would resist the genteel. She would not be polite.

By then he had resolved to send Mrs. Kilgour flowers. As he read his morning newspaper at the White Lunch and waited for Hazel, he wondered where he could find Lilies of the Valley. Appropriately Victorian, he thought, and stored up the phrase to tell Hazel when she arrived. She laughed when he said it to her, and rolled her eyes and repeated in a delicately sarcastic way Liam took credit for, "*appropriately Victorian.*" Together they went to a flower shop that Hazel knew—*so few in the city,* she said, recognizing that it was something to disdain—and he wrote a short note and Hazel asked the florist to add some *appropriately Victorian* ferns to the arrangement, and they had it all sent to the Castle. Liam felt good afterward, and though it was far more expensive than he liked, he still treated Hazel to lunch at a little café called Moderne. She was a good girl, anyway, and he could rely on her to order from the cheapest part of the menu. He did not like that he was thankful to her for that little economy. He wanted to be generous. He would have liked to treat her to other things, buy her the little presents that one should give a mistress.

Initially he had not known how to refer to her. He had carefully avoided the issue as too awkward to discuss, but then one evening he had picked up the bill at the Commodore Ballroom for Hazel's whiskey sour and she had offered him money and he had smiled and said, "I must surrender something for the pleasure of your company. A man must keep his mistress happy, and money is such a little thing." He had bitten his tongue then, and there had been a moment of silence that could have been awkward, but then Hazel had fluttered in a way that reminded him of a dreadful film he had seen, once, about debutantes. After that, she had regularly referred to herself as his mistress. When he first heard her repeat it, he thought she liked the little frisson of bohemia, but later he worried that she saw some affectation in the word and teased him with it. He was not sure, though, because just when he suspected her of subtle derision, she'd change so quickly, wilt in his arms and smile a dewy, girlish smile, and he could not believe her capable of such sharp wit.

Having sent Mrs. Kilgour the Lilies of the Valley and the note, he did not think any further about her. That evening he and Hazel were caught in the rain and found a chop suey place east of Main Street. Every time Hazel went east of Main she made the same joke: "*Really*, Liam," she said, "east of Main? Nice girls aren't allowed over there. That's where the White Slavers work!" She'd say it and then she'd take his arm and walk east as though flouting a particularly bourgeois convention, an *appropriately Victorian* anxiety regarding the virtue of unaccompanied white women. After they'd eaten, Hazel brought out her little pack of Sweet Caporals—the same one she'd had last week, he guessed, it did not look depleted—and held one to her lips, waiting conspicuously for him to light it. She'd probably been to the movies again, he thought, as he brought out his lighter and watched her dribble smoke out her mouth. In other circumstances, he would find this sort of behaviour irritating, and tell her to cut out the little games, but watching the cigarette burn down to her fingertips, he felt something else in his breast, something warm and sticky that made him look on her with nothing but affection.

The next morning, he had asked Hazel to meet him at the little pastry shop, Bon Ton, for breakfast. He was badly overspending on the girl, but economy, he thought, required a certain narrowness of spirit. While he knew in a vague way that he would soon regret the coins that slid out of his pockets, he could not stand the smallness, the pettiness of those thoughts. The girl was hungry for fine things, as he had been, and he felt charity in his heart when he watched her smoke her cigarettes, and feel her way around words like *bourgeois* and *convention*, and learn to deride the city that had quite recently seemed adequate to her adolescent desires. He cultivated her natural good taste, and taught her to be embarrassed that her mother liked to sing "With My Little Ukulele in My Hand" around the house, and listen to Gracie Fields on the radio, and repeat antique witticisms familiar to Liam's own mother: *My face I don't mind it because I'm behind it it's those in the front that I jar.* He suggested Caruso's more accessible recordings, and bought her a selected Keats. All this was absorbing work, but expensive. He would approach Mrs. Kilgour when she had recovered, and then there would be a little more money. He decided that he would make Hazel known to the old woman. Mrs Kilgour liked protégés. Perhaps she needed a secretary. Hazel would make such a pretty secretary.

He walked six blocks to Bon Ton and arrived early, taking a morning paper on the way. It was one of those unusual November mornings that felt spring-like, rather than autumnal: the air was soft, and the sun shone on the remaining leaves, yellow rather than green, but still bright. His lungs were clear. He had slept well. Soon he would see Hazel, then kiss her, then lead her back to Mrs. Qualey's, where they would slip upstairs for an hour or two. He sat down at one of the little tables, and turned to the social column.

Mrs. Kilgour was dead. If he had known she was so ill, he would have gone to see her sooner—braved the dark eaves of Craiglockhart and knelt at her bedside. He could have sung her a song, one of the Scottish ballads she always liked, "Will Ye No Come Back Again" perhaps, and held her hand, and she would have been happy to see him, if she could not see Clive. He thought he would have done those things, and more, if he had known her illness was so final. There would have been more flowers, too.

He did not permit himself to think about the change this would make to his plans. At least, not until he had properly lamented the lonely old woman locked up in the Castle. He thought he had seen her at a kind of peak, before the Edwardian idyll of Craiglockhart faded along, with everything else bright and hopeful, aging centuries in a year or two. Mrs. Kilgour shipwrecked in the present with her prima donna gowns and her ostrich feathers and her benevolent societies, her Great House, her *nouveau riche noblesse oblige.*

Then Hazel arrived, walking smartly into the patisserie and removing her hat, shaking out her hair in a gesture that looked familiar. Perhaps this one was Bette Davis. Hazel often talked about how much she loved Bette Davis, and held her up as a model for unconventional elegance.

Liam pulled out a cigarette. "I'm afraid there's some rather bad news," he said.

The funeral service was at a largish stone cathedral downtown, one of the older C of E churches in the city, though to Liam, Mrs. Kilgour had always seemed oppressively Kirkish. Liam had timed his arrival so the pews would be full, and with the latecomers he found a place at the back, near one of the stone pillars. He found he did not mind sitting far from the centre of things; her whole clan was present, including a much older, fatter Goshawk.

After the service, he lingered for a while on the steps outside, standing in the thin sunshine and watching all the dowdy-genteel families trickle out of the cathedral. He meant to speak with Goshawk, but then Euphemia and Nora were there, Euphemia dressed like an American, Nora still virtuously plain. They did not look in his direction, though at one time he'd flirted with Euphemia and she had liked it. Well, he had changed. They wouldn't know what to do with him.

Goshawk was hurrying people into cars, and Liam watched him walk up and down the pavement in the thinning crowd, pointing, directing, fussing. He thought about how Goshawk had made such a peculiar but comfortable life for himself here at the end of the world. It was good to be without ambition, Liam thought, and resigned to the small tasks that suited one's talents. Goshawk was a success in a way he had not previously recognized, even with his thickening waist and his thinning hair.

He was so preoccupied with this line of thought, he failed to notice that Goshawk had tidied his charges into their cars and now stood on the pavement nearly alone. The man stopped for a moment, and had just taken a cigarette case out of his pocket when he raised his eyes and stared straight at Liam.

Inadvertently, Liam held his breath, wondering if Goshawk would know him, and thinking he couldn't possibly. But then he was on the steps, holding the case out toward him, and Liam was nodding and had taken a cigarette, and they were smoking together in the pale sunshine of Mrs. Kilgour's funeral afternoon.

"She was touched by the flowers, you'll like to know. She regretted that she was unable to issue an invitation, but visits were exhausting in that last week."

"I wanted to send something."

"It is good to see you, Liam. I always thought you would have done well here if you had stayed. We would have seen you to a place somewhere. A school perhaps."

"Yes."

"I saw your engagement advertised. I meant to attend, but with Mrs. Kilgour in the state she was in … Would you come to the house today? I'm sure Nora would like to see you again."

"Oh, I didn't mean to impose at all."

"It is a good time to share our grief. You'd be welcome. You could sing her a song."

That was just the wrong thing to say. Liam dropped the cigarette and said no as he ground it into the pavement. "I only wanted to say goodbye in the service," and as he turned to leave, Goshawk asked him where he was staying. Before he could think, Liam mentioned Mrs. Qualey's. Perhaps Goshawk knew the place, with the corned beef and the damp walls. As he walked away, he wished he'd lied.

THE TEMPLE

A few days later, he was glad he hadn't lied, because a large buff envelope arrived for him at Mrs. Qualey's. Liam had already outstayed his engagement at the Temple by nearly two weeks when Mrs. Kilgour died. Distracted by Hazel, then by the change to his plans, he was unsure what to do next. His only other commitment that season was a week's worth of evenings in Alberta where he had an ongoing relationship with the ladies who organized Palm Court recitals each Christmas in Edmonton and Calgary. Until then he was a free, albeit poor man.

He thought about Hazel and the future as he sat by the stove in Mrs. Qualey's front room. He opened the large envelope to see a copy of Mrs. Kilgour's will and a letter in Goshawk's fussy blue hand: *It is in confidence that I send you both this letter and the document. I only hope that they reach you before you leave the city again. You will see that Mrs. Kilgour remembered you even at the end of her life. While her estate is still a little tangled in the lawyer's probate, it is my feeling that we may be able to do something about your particular bequest.* There was an address as well, and the hours he kept, and a suggestion that the following afternoon would be suitable.

The next morning Liam did not see Hazel. She stayed dutifully at home with her mother and sister writing letters to possible employers. It was just as well. At noon Liam cleaned his shoes, and at half past he dressed carefully in his best. He left at one for Goshawk's office, so early that he sat for half an hour on a park bench. He tried not to think about how quickly the will would be executed. Whether he would have the money within a month. Whether it would be next year. How much longer he could stand to wait.

When he thought the hour was no longer too eager, he left the park bench and climbed the stairs to Goshawk's office and knocked. The door opened. He was shown through to another office, where Goshawk nodded and said, "Please sit down, Liam. It's good to see you again."

When he walked home late that afternoon, he hardly felt the pavement beneath his feet, or the thin place in his coat where the damp penetrated to his skin. It was fifteen blocks from the lawyers' offices to Mrs.

Qualey's, and the meeting had finished at three that afternoon. Including a profligate stop at a department store—not the cheap place Hazel liked, but one a little superior, right downtown—for things he had previously economized on, like socks and underwear, he walked slowly toward the Temple Theatre on his way home. There were no matinees that day, and the evening shows hadn't begun, so the scruffy men in work boots still used the auditorium for one of their very large meetings. On his last day there, the stage manager told Liam they were having more meetings every week, and that more shabby men were attending, and he did not like the crowds, as they didn't tend to stay for matinees, to but to slink off somewhere, most likely to other meetings. If that kept up, he wouldn't allow it anymore.

Liam was so distracted by the thought of his annuity, he didn't notice the unusual crowd: the men in heavy boots and caps had spilled out of the lobby and into the street so he had to shoulder through them. As he did so, he thought of the next weeks: no more begging for work, or writing hat-in-hand letters to his Toronto agent. He needn't worry, now, not when he had that annuity. That had been the sound of respectability to him, as a young man. He remembered looking at the advertisements in an Officer's Field Service pocketbook, and reading the list of banking services as though it were a psalm: club subscriptions paid, periodicals attended to; allowances credited (and customer advised); half-pay and pensions of every description collected and credited to customers' accounts. To be advised that one's allowance had been received and one's club subscription(s) had been attended to—it had the quality of a fairy tale.

Now, thanks to his gentlemanly instincts and his way with the ladies, he was pretty near a *real* gentleman. There was justice in that, as well as a generosity he had not expected from the universe, as though someone had, all along, been watching him, and on weighing his sacrifices had determined his reward, then written a cheque for services rendered.

He must have been smiling, because as he wound through the crowd, the men in work boots smiled back at him, and some shook their heads, but he did not care because their elbows were not akimbo and they did not make him walk in the gutter. It was when he realized how crowded the street had become that he stopped for a moment under the Temple's sign. He was standing beside one man he knew—the man he had spoken to on his first afternoon, before that evening performance when he had seen Hazel.

"Liam Manley, Sweet Singer of Sweet Songs!" the man said. "Have you come to join us?"

"Join you?" he asked.

"We could use your voice." The man smiled at Liam, "They'll hear us pretty near across the whole country!"

"Where are you marching?" Liam asked. "What should I sing?"

The man was laughing. He said, "Whatever you want, Mr. Manley, but I've always liked that old song 'The World Is Waiting for the Sunrise.' Do you know it?"

Liam nodded and hummed in his best, clearest voice, *dear one the world is waiting for the sunrise ev'ry rose is covered with dew.* The other man was about to say more, Liam thought, or perhaps he would join in and they would sing the whole song right there on the pavement, and then begin marching to it (though it was a bad song for marching; they would have to foxtrot to city hall, or wherever it was the man wanted to go) and Liam's voice above them all.

It was just five o'clock in the afternoon when Liam looked over his new friend's right shoulder toward the Temple's front doors—thick crystal with copper vine patterns and pointed arches like the Alhambra—and watched the glass leap out of the door frame and into the street. The glass on either side of the doors erupted as well, and as Liam watched, it hung in the air for a moment in a perfect half-circle around the frames, blown outward like a bubble. The men who stood directly before the doors dropped to the ground, their hands thrown across their heads, and a white glitter settled over their coats and the wet pavement.

Liam knew there was shouting around him, but did not know what was said. He was aware only of the oppressive noise and the pain in his head that was not the sharp pain of flying glass but the dull kind, and of the weight in his guts and the sweat that ran down his spine and under his arms. Then he was walking quickly away toward Mrs. Qualey's Boarding House, brushing at his sleeves and shoulders, for there might be glass in his coat. The noise followed him: a deep, tuneless ringing that reverberated through his skull but did not dissipate. He had heard ringing like that before, many times before.

The foyer was blessedly empty, and he climbed the stairs to his room and sat in the hard little chair beside the fireplace. After an hour, he remembered that Hazel was to join him in celebrations that evening and stay the whole night. She had already arranged an alibi, having shown an unnerving aptitude for deception: she liked to talk about how dull and trustful her mother was, and how bourgeois expectations made her too easy to deceive. He was to meet her at eight at the library, and they were to go to the movies until between nine-thirty and ten, when they would slip back to Mrs. Qualey's house, their arrival coinciding with Mrs. Qualey's favourite radio program and glass of port and ginger ale. Hazel enjoyed planning their assignation, especially when she learned that Mrs. Qualey forbade overnight guests, and doubly forbade unmarried overnight guests. Mrs. Qualey was, therefore, both bourgeois and Victorian, and ought to be deceived just as Hazel's mother was.

When it was suppertime, he preferred not to join the other guests at Mrs. Qualey's table. Instead he took the time to bathe in the bathroom off the kitchen. That made him feel he could face the rest of the evening, even if the ringing in his ears did not subside. He should not pay any attention to the ringing. Instead he should think about the annuity, and Hazel and the night ahead.

He put his mind to shaving, taking time to strop his razor and turning his whole attention to the careful negotiation of his lip and nose, the fine skin of his throat. When he had finished, he felt better, and turned that single-minded attention to his hair, then his tie. By the time he was respectable—he did not look at all like the kind of man who would be at those sorts of meetings in the lobby of the Temple Theatre, he hoped—he was prepared to enjoy Hazel's company.

He left the bathroom, passing close by the dining room and smelling corned beef, onions and cabbage, and the gluey custard Mrs. Qualey favoured for her horrible Ritz cracker pies. He had almost escaped, when he thought he heard someone mention a theatre, and an explosion. He was not sure, but he thought he heard "Temple" and "bomb" and "a dozen or so killed." He did not think anyone had been killed. They were all fools if they thought someone had been killed. He did not like the men and women at Mrs. Qualey's. They were of low calibre and unpleasant.

He had intended to leave directly he had finished his toilette, but instead he found he must return to his room. He took the hard little chair again and sat very still for twenty-five minutes beside the little fireplace that never held a flame. He set a hand on either knee and stared at the green pattern on the pink carpet. He stared at it with such attention that finally he could, again, look forward to seeing Hazel.

He was half an hour late at the library, where she was waiting. Waiting conspicuously, he thought, with her arms crossed, and her foot tapping occasionally. Before he had even reached her, he heard her sigh.

"Liam!" she said. "Liam, *darling*, what time is it?"

"I don't know. I think it's about half past eight."

"Oh, half past? Is it? But I thought we were supposed to meet at eight. But it's half past now?"

"Yes," he said. "Yes, half past. I was detained."

"By what?"

"Business."

"At the lawyer's?"

"No."

They walked on in silence.

"If it was the lawyer's I would understand."

He said nothing. He wished she would be silent.

"I heard some bad news today. I heard that there was some business at the Temple. Those men you were talking about, I guess. They were trying to hold some meeting. Probably something horrible—men like that always get so excited about things, and make so much noise it's hard to take them seriously."

As she spoke, Liam recognized the sentiment because it was his own. He had said that to her one evening when he had wished to entertain her with his sophisticated commentary on world events: about how those revolutionaries would never be taken seriously with their loud voices and their constant complaint, because sensible people would only listen if they'd calm down. Hazel was still talking, though, and he should listen, but he would prefer not to listen, and so he was silent, and as they walked he concentrated on the people they passed and the lighted windows that lined the sidewalk.

She was still talking. "Can we walk past it? I've never seen a bomb site!"

"I would prefer not," Liam said.

"Darling! Don't make me coax!" she said.

Definitely a Bette Davis day, he thought. He should forbid her from seeing Bette Davis films; they made her insufferable. Liam did not respond to her last little comment. They were nearly at the theatre, and Liam knew he should change the subject and turn her derisive little laughs in some safe direction, away from the glitter of broken glass. He should turn her attention to the people they were passing, or the film they might choose to see. Or the annuity. "We had the meeting. With the lawyers," he said, hoping to distract her.

"But why can't we walk past the Temple?" she asked again, and tugged his arm in that direction, where he did not wish to look, the street down which he did not wish to walk.

"We had the meeting," he said.

She nodded sulkily, her bottom lip pushed out in a parody of Hollywood petulance. Shirley Temple?

"About an annuity."

"An annuity? What's that?"

"A yearly stipend. A regular income from the Kilgour estate."

"Oh! Liam!" Hazel said, clinging to his arm and forgetting her outthrust bottom lip. "Oh, how tremendous! How really, really lovely!"

Having turned her attention from the carnage at the Temple, Liam relaxed as well.

Liam's second visit to Duncan's Crossing was at Mrs. Kilgour's request; he was to perform a concert in partial fulfilment of the will's stipulations. Liam didn't recognize the town's name at first. He was reading his newspaper and imagining his trip south to dry air and heat, first California then Mexico, when they called his stop. It was only another of those red-painted stations, and they all looked alike. Out on the street, he again felt a familiarity: there was the hall where they had sung, and where he would sing again tomorrow night.

It was too fine a joke to keep to himself. He wished he knew someone in town, someone he could take to dinner, and make a story of his strange relationship with Mrs. Kilgour, and reveal the amusing circumstances of his return to this little town. He would enjoy being generous. He could afford to be. They would eat roast beef, and he would stand the man cigars, if he knew someone, the best the town offered.

There had been someone: Simon Reid. He had a kind of estate in the country, but he had been unusual in ways Liam had not liked. Reid was still stuck on the war, though in 1921 it was understandable that some people still should be. They had talked about survival. And being European. He would enquire in town, see if he could surprise the old man, treat him to a dinner, repaying the lunch with interest all these years later. He would even put it like that, when he phoned Reid; he would speak as though they had only parted last week. It was the sort of thing that would make a good story for the old man to tell, so dramatic and unexpected.

The Tzhouhalem Inn had changed in the years since he had last been through. Though the heavy fir-wood staircase still ran four-square up the walls of the foyer, now the carpet was worn and the newel post was dusty. A man slept in a hard wooden armchair beside the front desk. A huge moose head hung over the pocket doors to the hotel's drawing room. The manager—for the man could only be a manager—wore grubby tweeds, drenched in November sunlight so late it seemed almost amber.

"Hello?" Liam called. He did not like to ring the bell. "Hello," he said again, softly.

The man in the tweeds woke and blinked. His eyes were pale and lashless in baggy-skinned sockets. "Yes?" he asked. "Yes?"

"Hello, my name is Manley. I've got a reservation."

"Yes? Yes?" The old man hauled himself from his chair and to the desk, where he stood over the ledger. His mouth hung open with a white crust at one corner. "Yes," he said. "Manley, did you say? Yes."

"Manley," Liam said again, "Liam Manley."

The man fumbled over the pages of the ledger and Liam wished to reach out and turn them himself, run one finger down the column and help himself to a key. He did not. He kept his eyes on the bell, his hands behind his back while the man continued, "Yes, yes. Manley did you say?"

He found the key, and there was the trouble of his bag. "I will ring for the boy," he said and rang the bell. Then he rang it again. Now the man was close enough that Liam could smell him—greasy soup and elderly sweat and tobacco. They did not speak until the old man made a move to take Liam's valise.

"No sir," Liam said, "I need the exercise. I will carry it myself."

"Oh no! Oh no, you will not! You will not carry it—"

But Liam already gripped the dark handle of his valise, and together they climbed the dusty stairs. Liam matched his pace to the old man's, who dropped the key into his waistcoat pocket and patted it, and checked the number, once, twice. At the door there was a moment of panic as he felt through his pockets; then he had it in his hand, but the lock stuck. Then, at last, they were in the room, and the old man opened the blinds and rattled the pipes for heat.

When he was finally alone, Liam sat on the bed and listened to the hotel, the whole town, that sounded like it would always be five o'clock on Sunday. The November afternoon ticked away with the quality of the dreams one has when one sleeps during the day, so still, so long each moment.

He would go down and ask about Reid. He would put in a telephone call and invite Reid to lunch and share the good news. It would be a fine joke. He would toast Mrs. Kilgour in whiskey and water, the old teetotaller, the old harpy. He would share this unexpected bounty as he had done with Hazel two nights before, their last night when he had been very kind and taken her to dinner in the city's CPR hotel, a huge and appropriately Victorian edifice..

For a moment he had a pain behind his ribs. He wondered if he ought to sit down. It was like the pain he felt when he could not breathe, and he hoped it was not the first sign of an episode. What was Hazel doing, just then? Was she working at the café, wiping tables with a dirty rag, or sitting with her mother, or had she gone for one of her walks along the beach to watch her own lights from across the bay? The question had hung there for a moment, between them, but when it came properly to the surface he had stopped, shocked by his own inclination to ask, not because he felt he ought to, but that he *wanted* to. For once, no Bette Davis affectations, her eyes were rabbity and pale and so still.

She had found a job, she told him, at a café. A waitress. And she had said, "I don't know if I will take it," and looked at him. She had looked so intently at him, he wondered if she felt the question, too, but he did not think she did. He had been holding her hands on the table, and then the waiter had come with wine and his eyes broke with hers and then he had slid his hands away. She had a tiny glass like a thimble and ordered chicken. He had steak au poivre. Afterward they each had *crème brûlée* and he showed her to break it and that had made her smile.

"So I shall be going to warmer places, south of here," he said, lighting his cigarette, "when I have fulfilled Mrs. Kilgour's wishes."

And he did not wish to remember further. The pain behind his ribs seemed a sympathetic ache, delivered in her remembered glance. So while he had forgotten her quite quickly in his journey north, she returned to him, not in mind but in body. Something in him remembered her, and held embedded within some hook and long slim line that followed all the distance he had travelled, yet only now made itself known by the little tear it left.

He had been particularly careful to seem calm, because the last weeks had been full of such agitation: the meetings with the lawyers, the letters to and from ladies' arts clubs along the coast. He had rushed to fulfill the will's requirements and claim his annuity, which meant the recitals would be badly attended and poorly advertised, he was sure. He did not mind that. He was in a state of feverish energy that would not let him rest, and filled what sleep he did have with dreams he did not like. He wanted to be away from the city, southbound and feeling everything that had been fall away behind him, beyond the curve of the earth. The will had not stipulated a performance at the Temple, and though he would not have minded performing there if it had been necessary, he was glad he did not need to. He went so far as to tell Hazel he hated the theatre, and he did not think he could stand to set foot there again. Once on his way back from the post office he had accidentally glanced down the street and saw that the doors and windows were boarded up and the pavement swept clean. He wondered where the radicals met now. He hoped the theatre would be properly condemned, then demolished and replaced with something useful: an apartment block, a department store, a movie theatre.

He found his health improved slightly and he could sleep when he limited his attention to three points: four recitals; the annuity; south. And now there was Reid and dinner and it would be such a good joke. He changed his shirt and walked down the stairs, but quietly because he saw that the old man was asleep again under the moose head.

He walked through the sliding doors to the lounge where other guests spoke quietly, and a dog lay in front of the low wood fire.

"Good evening," he said.

Three men and three women looked up at him.

"Hello," one man said. "A new guest?"

"Yes," he said. "My name is Manley. I wanted to introduce myself and ask after an acquaintance who lived in this neighbourhood."

They relaxed. The women returned to three-handed bridge. The man who spoke nodded and said, "Of course, sir. You should sit down. And about whom did you wish to enquire," asked one of the other men, who sat on a low chair close to the coals, a heavy shawl around his shoulders and the dog—grey whiskered, hollow-eyed—sleeping on his feet.

"His name was Reid," Liam said. "He kept a kind of home place not far from here."

He heard a noise like fluttering leaves and the cooing of distant pigeons. A soft, anxious murmur above the snap of cards played, drawn, cast and swept over felt.

The man who had spoken first addressed him: "Reid, eh? Simon Reid? Did you know Reid quite well?" There was a slight stress on "quite," and no title. *Reid*, he was *Reid* here.

"No. Not at all," Liam said. "I hardly knew him."

"Yes. My name is Henry, by the way." He reached out his knuckly right hand. The bones closed hard and dry around Liam's fingers.

"Pleased to meet you, Mr. Henry." Liam did not ask further. "Pleased," he said again.

"Yes, well, if you're a friend of Reid's, I'm not sure."

"I only met him once. He wanted me to join a kind of village. A model village he was building. This was ages and ages ago."

"Just after the war?"

"I suppose."

"Yes, well. Not quite a *model village*."

"Not at all," whistled the man with the dog at his feet.

The third man said nothing.

Liam looked up to see the women watching him as they passed their cards. One stared at him with the shiny black eyes of a crow. She looked down after a moment, addressing her hand. Her expression did not change. He thought she would bluff well.

"Not a model village, then? He talked about, about Apollo," Liam finished confusedly. So much trouble for one silly plan, what had he thought? To show up one man, to make a good story, to be for a moment original, and now this wheezing tea party sat about him, ruffling and settling their feathers, and he did not know where to look or what it meant.

"If you wish to hear about your great friend Reid, you had better sit down, Mr. Manley." Mr. Henry looked to the card players. "Alright there, ladies?"

"Yes, of course, Archie. I, at least, am not so sensitive after a month."

Liam could not imagine that crow-eyed woman was ever particularly sensitive.

Mr. Henry continued, "Reid has built a village, though there won't be much left of it now. It's quite empty now, I imagine."

"There's Mickey Sweeney. The American."

"Michael was hardly one of them. I imagine he'll stay on. I imagine it's empty otherwise."

"Yes, quite empty. And until recently there'd been a veritable exodus," the card dealer said. "The roads *awash* in refugees."

"But what *happened*?" Liam asked, feeling again that he would like to take the conversation from them and shake it straight.

"They've been leaving, don't you see, his *model village*." So beautifully enunciated, those last two words, such quiet, killing irony. Liam remembered when that sort of voice always brought a blush to his skin, though he had never been able to say why.

"The first was Alice, and her child, Archie, in September."

"Yes, my love, I remember. Her name was Alice Somers. She carried the child until she found a house with lights on. It was cold that night. Very wet."

"I heard she was barefoot. I heard her feet bled."

"The Borgersons took her in. They had seen many odd things and were not, I think, entirely surprised. They called a doctor, but the girl and the child were both remarkably healthy. She would not speak until her parents arrived."

"Alice wasn't more than eighteen. Can you imagine? Eighteen!"

"But by the time they had come for her, others were on the roads, only a few that first day. Then there were more than I could count, all throwing themselves on the mercy of the Tzhouhalem. Can you imagine?"

"They're gone now. Some of them had to be collected."

"But what *happened*?" Liam asked.

"That is a matter for the courts, Mr Manley. We know only that Simon Reid's model village is no more. His house is in ruins and his flock is fled. He did something wicked, though we aren't sure of its nature. Common sorts of problems, embezzling from his own charitable organization. The sort of libertine-isms that attract men of Reid's type. But more than that, some stories of the nature of his experiment, of his ambitions to—" Henry's patter had been easy. Now he stopped and looked away, as though brought up short by what he was about to say.

The third man spoke, his voice like an Anglo-Canadian bishop's: sonorous, liquid, ambiguously accented. "It seems," he said, "that your Mr. Reid had ambitions to bring about the end of the world."

No one spoke. Liam swallowed and wondered how he had come to be in this room, listening to words that made so little sense.

The man went on, "I have it on good authority—the two Greenwood brothers were fishing near the model village on the night the girl and her child appeared at the Borgersons. And they heard sounds. Remarkable sounds."

Henry made a noise, sub-lingual, delicate.

"The Greenwoods are quite reliable. They called it keening. The sort of sound that makes men remember a darker age. We may attribute it to banshee, boggarts, or jinn, if we must give them names. It is the sort of sound that makes one feel a chill that rises from the soles of one's feet and look for fire and company."

"Yes, well, one doesn't like to encourage—" Mr. Henry began.

"That was only what they *heard*, Archie, there's also what they saw." Now all three men were quiet. But too late Liam had the girl in his eye, the barefoot walking girl, carrying her child.

"What they saw, young man"—this to Liam alone, as though the Bishop saw the girl, too, and knew that only he and Liam shared the vision—"what they saw was Reid's house, the Manor he called it. I never saw the point of such huge places. If one wants to return to some bucolic, pre-industrial state, one ought not be quite so married to one's architectural history. Cob houses, perhaps, if one must. But really longhouses are the only appropriate alternative for this coast. They are the autochthonous architecture of the place, after all, and worked for many generations before the smallpox. After we follow the original citizens into the west, a return to longhouses seems quite poetic.

"But, young man, you wish to *know*. On the day before the girl walked out with her child, the Greenwood boys saw a fire on the point, around Reid's house. This was in the late afternoon. Not, they said, a common sort of fire, for this one rolled slowly with a cap like a mushroom's. It was yellow and high—higher than the roof. Its smoke was dark and it smelled bitter.

"Well, being curious. And possibly drunk—I would not put it past the Greenwoods to be drunk—they tacked around the point to a place where they could see more clearly."

"The Greenwoods didn't think to shout *fire*?"

"Well, I do think Reid made himself clear regarding interference—after the incident with Mrs. Sweeney—when was that? Five years ago now? Well, the Greenwood boys sailed around the point until they saw that the fire was indeed moving, and from their deck they could just make out the figures about this mechanical flame, though they seemed... well, shrunk was what Matthew said, but I will say stunted, and they did not move as men move. They seemed a mass, a knot of people and above them, this device—this engine with its flames spreading over the house itself."

"It being dark, and them being drunk, I can't think what conclusion Mr. Manley is to draw."

"No conclusions, though he might nod and say, "How strange." Well, a whole wing of the house is burnt. That's been confirmed."

"Hideous building. Bogus Tudor!"

"It is the thing itself that makes me wonder—the engine. What do you suppose it did, Mr. Manley?"

"I don't. I don't know."

"Well then, how strange," and the Bishop turned away to fill his pipe.

Liam stood.

"Not going I hope, Mr. Manley," said the card dealer. "I hope you will stay, have a drink before dinner." The invitation was so perfectly phrased, so perfectly meaningless. "And perhaps after dinner you will give us a song?"

"Yes, a song." This time Archie said it. "I understand you have a series of concerts here and in some of the other Kilgour villages. I seem to remember some of your work, with Mrs. Kilgour, poor lady."

"Perhaps it will tire his voice," said the Bishop.

He had endeavoured to remain calm, but finally he found himself blushing. "Thank you," Liam said to the card dealer, "but I must go to the hall first."

He left the room. He badly wanted a cigarette. He passed the sleeping man without stopping, walked out the door and to the street and did not care which direction he took, because wherever he looked, he saw the girl, walking, and the engine creeping sideways toward the house. The man had gone and done something horrible and destroyed it all, ruined the manor, the garden that was only just laid out, the cottages—which would be comfortable now, nearly fifteen years on, with real gardens and grass growing. The man had gone and wrecked it all and while, really, Liam didn't care, there was something shameful in it, in the smashed windows and the whole wing burnt down and the barefoot girl limping along the roads. *Shame shame*, he thought, and said aloud as he walked and swung his arms sharply. *Shame.*

He knotted his hands behind his back so they would not shake. As he imagined the girl and her child, she was like other girls he had seen in high summer, the long road heat-smeared so he could not see her feet, but could just make out the silhouette of a girl with a bundle in her arms. Around him the buzz of flies, the glittering blue air, and somewhere, far away, the hay lying in swaths across the fields.

That evening he walked from the inn to the train station, down the wooden sidewalks to the block they called "China Town," to the inn and back to the train station, and down the wooden sidewalks toward the river, and then back to the inn and on to the train station, and then north along the tracks, and then back along the street that ran parallel to the tracks until he reached the river, and then back along a dirt road until he reached a wooden sidewalk. When he was too tired to walk, he lay smoking in bed until he slept, with that vision playing through his sleep. The engine itself was shadowy, but he could guess its size. He saw black enamel dials marked with white degrees of declination, then the crosshairs and the click-k-k-k-k of calculated trajectories and angles set, and all around it the believers keening, fallen to their knees and raising their hands to worship it, until they bruised on the black metal, their eyes rolling in the ecstasy of comprehension. It would fall on them and crush them, he thought, it would fall soon. It would detonate, and the detonation would ripple outward through their bodies, the house, the village, the water and land all around them. Passing through them, it would break bones and rupture organs and toss them high into the air, then drop them down, and something wet spreading over the earth beneath their bodies. What was the range of an engine like that? How far would it reach?

When he closed his eyes he saw fallen men in the street by the Temple Theatre, the bare skin of their faces turning red. The man he liked, the man who had asked him to sing, held one hand up at his forehead, and when he pulled it away there was red on the fingertips, a red trickle down the side of his face, then another and another. When Liam looked at his own skin, there was no blood, no pain. All around him there was shouting, and men running under the still-falling glass, and sound reduced to smog, oppressive and indecipherable. It would not do to remember the explosion itself, and how the windows had blown outward like soap bubbles from a wire loop, and think that if he had stood a foot farther from the wall, he would have been in the path of all that glass and shrapnel, the disrupted material world inside the theatre. He would have lain on the pavement before the advancing engine, his blood staining the fabric of his coat, spilled from some unseen wound onto the splinters and glass-dust that covered the street.

The next morning he slept late. He avoided the hotel's restaurant and went instead to the lunch counter in a five and dime, and drank coffee and read the local sheet. There wasn't any mention of refugees in the paper, no neurasthenic stragglers with pushcarts, no exhausted mother with child slung over her shoulder, walking barefoot out of the model village behind the gates of Reid's estate. Outside his window, he saw no obvious emigrants from Reid's kingdom, nothing but the cenotaph with the pale granite cross and the black names, the wooded hills rising around the town and the tidy, bloomless geraniums of the station flower-beds.

He would leave soon. He would go south. He would go to Mexico where the air was better for him, far from the damp that shortened his days. He would be well away from the northern raincoast. In Mexico it would be hot and dry and still, and he would drink tequila beside the beach, just a few steps from a warm blue ocean, or in the mountains.

But don't think about the girl. Think of the dry inland, and tequila. Think about the *annuity.* He would be able to make plans, and think what he would do next, and he would do it as he sat somewhere in the black afternoon shade, watching women walk through the ruthless light outside his café.

PART THREE

THE CITY OF THE END OF THINGS

PART THREE

NO PLACE FOR SISSIES

Anthea's grandfather Max died when she was eighteen. Shortly after that, Hazel began telling her about the injustice. "You get old," she said, "and everyone leaves you. And you can't do all the things you thought you'd do, because you put them off to look after people. And it's not fair." Her voice was emphatic but quiet. Hazel didn't like raising her voice. Instead, she throttled a sob in her breast, and Anthea glanced away, pretending not to notice because Hazel didn't like to be seen in a state.

"Old age is no place for sissies," she said. "It's *not* for sissies. You have to be tough, but even if you're tough—don't we deserve dignity?"

"Of course. Yeah, totally," Anthea said—always said. "Dignity."

"You don't understand." That was what Hazel said when anyone tried to agree with her.

Even before she was properly old, Hazel had hated the habit of some elderly women who took cups of hot water in the evening. She hated them, because if one couldn't taste the difference between hot water and tea, it seemed like one should take a hard look at one's life. Anthea wanted to remind Hazel that there was more to her than her faculties, and that probably hot water was nice when you were ninety; she didn't dare, though, because once she'd said something like that, and it had ended badly. She didn't like it when Hazel yelled at her. Besides, the hot water ladies—deaf, drifting in time and the wheelchair-friendly corridors of some old folks' home—were no longer alive by Hazel's definition. They were no longer themselves; they weren't anyone anymore. Hazel wouldn't be like that, she insisted when she still showed her characteristic defiance of circumstance. *She* wouldn't be one of the others. *She* wouldn't be a burden—mean and suspicious, turning on their children like ugly toddlers who pull books from the shelves, driving even after they failed their eye exams, buying high-tech stocks over the phone.

Hazel glared a hot glare, as though to defy Anthea, with her four limbs and her appetite and her *faculties*.

Their visits were regular and frequent, whenever Hazel expressed a desire to see her granddaughter, and made her wishes known through Colm. Though Anthea complied, she dreaded these meetings after her grandfather's death. After each one, she thought that next time she might arrange to be busy. She never did, because Colm was the one who told her what Hazel wanted, and he always did it in such an understanding way, she knew it wasn't really his fault. Anthea would submit to an afternoon spent discussing the last novel she had borrowed and read dutifully, though with little pleasure: Doris Lessing or D.H. Lawrence or Virginia Woolf. After Max died, Hazel began offering Anthea grown-up cocktails, usually gin and tonic with a fat wedge of lime, served in real crystal, not the red plastic glasses kept for kids' pink lemonade.

The first time she offered, Anthea said, "But. Can I have ginger ale?" though she was afraid it would be wrong. Hazel filled a red plastic glass with warm, flat ginger ale from a can that stood open on the kitchen table. No ice.

After that little ceremony, Hazel led the way outside, and sat in close on the porch swing and held Anthea's hand. They'd talk about *Briefing for a Descent into Hell* or *To the Lighthouse* as Hazel sipped her first and second G&T. By the third, she was finished with books; she grew sharp and bright and talked about atheism and the existential absence that was death, and how you'd have to be a deluded sentimentalist to think there was anything beyond the material world. Anthea, quieter and more agreeable as Hazel poured her fourth, tried to remember the earlier woman, the one from olden days who took photographs with an undoubting eye and no wasted film. She'd given up the camera after her husband died, as silently and conspicuously as she had abandoned writing local history or gardening.

In her last years she did little, though her energy did not seem to abate. As her friends declined and died, she began a stack of obituaries in her birthday book, hoarding her dead and accounting for each with an "x" over their name in the original entry. Sometimes when Hazel was outside on the beach at family parties and Anthea had a minute alone in the house, she picked up the little book and shuffled through the pages, reading bits of newsprint that reminded her of invitations for a party, or a girl's scrapbook from an earlier generation, recording the adventures of the local social pages. Hazel didn't mention the collection, just kept it on top of her desk beside the phone.

Having read and clipped all those obituaries, Hazel declared that she would not emulate the conventional dead, recounting her decline in the assembled thankyous to doctors and nurses and critical care wards and hospice units. Hazel particularly disliked the obituaries that read like yearbook entries, listing names, in-jokes and helpless clichés. No. Hazel read obituaries aloud the way Jas read personal ads, seeking out and stressing the flabbiest platitudes: "Look, darling!" Hazel said, "this one was a toastmaster, well known for his rousing songs on long bus trips, those who knew him knew him well, dear. And he's got an unattached grandson!"

Anthea laughed. She laughed every single time Hazel made that joke, though it grew steadily grimmer. She stopped laughing a moment later when Hazel grew serious and reminded her—as she had done many times—about her own preferences: no obituary, no funeral, no stone. Sometimes she asked for Auden's "Lullaby" in a tasteful corner of the weekend edition, and her name, no dates. Sometimes she wanted her initials and the years. She discussed that often with Anthea, repeating the arguments pro and con the inclusion of dates, whether the whole poem, or select lines from the last stanza, and the lineage "Hazel Brooke, *née* Lyon."

O SUPERMAN

It was Liam's shame that when he first encountered the places whose names had formed his earliest litany of arrival—Covent Garden, Thames, Piccadilly, Oxford Street and Pall Mall—he felt no joy in their radiant Englishness, but found himself inexplicably homesick. Until then, he had only known those places in cheaply tinted postcards he kept in a cigar box under his bed, sealed with a tiny padlock so Ella couldn't get at them. He bought them penny-by-penny, pored over them as he read the English news that filtered down through the local paper, thought about how it would be to stand on that bridge, stare across that river, be among those crowds.

When he finally arrived at that moment, he wasn't awed by the real width of the river with all its boats and barges, but thought instead of the narrow, root-choked trickle of another Thames, another Oxford and Piccadilly and Pall Mall. He had thought of a little cigar box, and a tiny, ugly bedroom in the attic. He was ashamed of this unaccountable nostalgia as he looked on the wet grey pavement outside his boarding house, which was so English and should be so completely satisfying. He did not like to find himself thinking instead of dull yellow brick houses on wide streets. That was not the London to be sentimental about, and with this arrival he should feel not homesickness but homecoming.

Because he hated Other London as much as he hated the farm he grew up on and the village. As much as he hated the summer air like a sweaty blanket, and the evenings after dinner when his father—stinking though he was so careful about washing the dust from his neck and hands before they sat down in the tiny, close dining room—his father played dominoes on the front porch with Ella. Across the wide road, another family sat on another front porch, in front of an equally respectable yellow brick house and waved over their lemonade. Liam hated them, too.

He hated his own London, and knew himself to be only temporarily exiled, and soon returned to the English city, where there were no yellow brick houses, no fathers who stunk, no mothers who suppressed their summer odour with Florida water and talcum powder. There were no expectations that he would walk nice girls home, nor that he would get a job in a bank—his mother admitted her unlimited ambition for him the day she said she thought he'd do very nicely in a bank! Once he was in London—the real one—they would see that there was only one possible trajectory, and it concluded with leading tenor at Covent Garden, La Scala or the Paris Opera House, places he had seen in postcards and loved.

Shortly after his arrival in Proper London, Liam saw O'Mario sing. For years afterwards, he counted the man as his true, his *spiritual* father. Often in the confidential darkness, late at night with men or women, he described the theatre, the illuminated figure on the stage below, the voice. It was like evening sunlight in summer, he said, or like amber water in a creek, or whitecaps. Once he had explained elaborately to a woman (she seemed enraptured at the time) that Mara O'Mario's voice had just the quality of the icicles that form near a stream on hanging roots or blades of grass, the smooth, round kind that seem to hold drops of light.

It was five o'clock in the afternoon. It was June at Covent Garden. It was *Le Cid*. He had begun the tedious round of private recitals that paid his room and board but was (he knew he knew) only the beginning. Liam, half an hour early, read and reread his program (he would do without coffee the next two weeks to make up the money for a real program, with pictures), and when he dropped it to his lap, he saw that his damp fingers had buckled the paper. His knees pressed up against the seat in front of him, so he sat twisted, his wrists spindly and white out of his cuffs, his hands at rest in his lap. He had intended to wear gloves, but none of his were nice enough. No one in his row had them, which made him feel even more ashamed: he knew better, after all, and did not like to be mistaken for the sort who didn't. The men down below in the dress circle or across, in the boxes, would wear gloves. They would arrive late, after the overture. He would not be so shallow as that, arriving late, even if he did have white gloves and a satin-lined opera cloak.

He had been there when it was empty—the very moment they opened the doors, he had found his seat and looked down into the stage below and imagined what he was about to hear: rings of fire and vigil lights, sounds like sunbursts, and others as dangerous and enticing as black water running under ice. He had the score behind his eyelids, the love triangle, and the Moorish threat, and the gleam of Rodrigo's sword. His initial devotion to Saint James and his third act celebration of the veiled father and judge.

The seats filled, the chocolate-eaters up top with him, down below the girls in dancing frocks trailing after their mothers, getting settled early, the young couples engrossed in conversation in the boxes below him, the ladies-of-an-age sharp-eyed as crows. And when the lights went down, finally, his heart wound up tight inside his breast, so it might break or burst, that only from the pleasure of waiting for the orchestra and then for the light to leap up from the stage. He imagined himself fifty years on, long retired and telling the story of his first vision of Mara O'Mario. How would he tell it? He would tell about breathing with Rodrigo's first aria, and how he felt a deep tremor in his belly as though it were his voice, his throat, the reverberations his own as they travelled through his lungs, trachea, larynx, pharynx, palate, nasal cavity, skull. It could have been him channelling O'Mario's voice, that voice rolling like an echo through his own body.

But then there were other things: the first rustle of chocolate papers, then a shuffle. He heard a whisper behind him. He seethed, tried to refocus his mind because there was the steep climb into Rodrigo's sword pledge and *listen to what he does here*, Liam thought, listen—

"Who's that?"

"I wonder if he's the one, the one they all talk about."

"Him? He's so fat!"

"Opera singers are fat, didn't you know? Tetrazzini is quite fat. I saw her once on the street years ago and thought, how could she be so wicked with the gentlemen with a figure like that?"

"Is she really?"

"She was three feet across the hips!"

The delicate edifice tumbled. He sat in the too-short theatre seat in the dusty back of things, and all around him rustled papers, shuffled feet, coughs. Down below him on a lighted platform, distant figures with painted faces made unusual gestures.

Someone behind him sucked like a nursing baby. There was a cough and a gust of peppermint on his neck. Sounds floated up from the tiny figurines on the stage, from their painted mouths. He heard nothing but the noise of the proles with their naive questions, their blank eyes and open mouths. He hated them, hated their scents of peppermint and Yardley Lily of the Valley toilette water and *Quelques Fleurs*. He hated the women with their lorgnettes. He hated the lolling girls in dance frocks littering the floor of the theatre, and he hated every last white-gloved swell sliding into a seat forty-five minutes late.

Far, far below him the curtains swept across the stage, and the house lights went up.

Around him the audience shuffled to its feet, relieved and exuberant, like children let out from church. Liam remained where he was. They excused themselves over his knees, and he would not move and thought *let them climb over me, if they'd rather be in the lobby.* For fifteen minutes he was left to himself, except for an old man down his row bent over at the waist and snoring into his knees.

There was of course Act Three to come, and "Ô Souverain, ô juge, ô père." He remembered the moment when the noises around him fell away again, and he heard only Rodrigo's submission to the Lord of Hosts. And Liam thought afterward that he had submitted, too, and made an incoherent pledge that matched not the words of Rodrigo's song, but the shape of the thing itself, with all its constriction and release, its slow climb to the top of the tenor's range and the final sustain that rippled outward from O'Mario's breast.

It was a call, he thought. He was sure it was a call. He left the theatre half yanked from his own body, so he felt he was walking through the crowds, but also somewhere above with the voice. He had a fancy that he travelled with the leading edge of a great concentric wave, all O'Mario's peaks and furrows carrying him forward irresistibly to the far reaches of the world. He stalked among the people as they scuttled after taxis, toward tea rooms. He heard them speak, and felt he did not understand them, so altered was he.

"Oh my dear, the beading on the Infanta's gown, I can't imagine what—"

"—can't expect La Scala, but one does assume they'll at least—"

"—evening entertainment should be more wholesome? I do think culture is as important as hygiene for—"

"Massenet, always so terribly lyrical when he—"

He thought, *They must recognize it, somehow I must look different than they do.*

"—could get us a taxi?"

Liam made his way through the crowd toward his boarding house. He passed young men in gangs. One dark blue evening coat among them—faceless beneath a silk top hat—shouldered him into the gutter. He walked faster, then, through the crowd, looking to see if any had noticed, but even the silk hat ignored him. One block, then two from the opera house, and behind him as he walked, he heard a warbling soprano with a voice like a wet-winged baby bird struggling from its shell. It might have been Chimène's first love song.

That night Liam lay awake in his narrow nursery bed in his hall room. *Yes,* he said in response to the unspecified question put to him in Rodrigo's sword aria. *Yes.*

It was a pity—no, a comedy, no a travesty—that he hadn't known the thing to which he pledged. Because now he recognized that evening for what it was—the lurid creation of the overheated romantic imagination of an eighteen-year-old boy (and very boyish even for eighteen), already disoriented by the brilliance of the city around him, and the effect his rather remarkable face had on the people he met, not yet aware that it was not his voice that had one woman or another watching him with such rapt attention, her hands clasped at her breast. If he had been older, or wiser, or had better guidance, he would have returned then to Paris, taken a job as a dishwasher and thrown himself on the mercy of M. Girard, who had been his master. But instead, he had mistaken a commonplace performance for a call. Instead he smoked slim black cigarettes and had found a tailor and knew, now, to be ashamed of the ready-made suit that had so impressed him in Toronto. Having pledged himself to that call, he thought the rest must be automatic. Surely it was rare to feel this way. Surely he was original.

He had hated the audience on that particular June evening; such hatred was familiar to him, and he had hated many audiences since then, in detail, and with the educated loathing of the failed artist. But twenty years on, he found the object of hatred had shifted until he felt only a mild irritation at the peppermint and the girls in dancing frocks and the men in fine white gloves. Instead he hated the imposter—who had not been evening sunlight, or black water, or ice, but marsh fire in the unhappy darkness. From the perspective of a washed-up thirty-eight, Liam saw through the pink and gold bloom, and recognized the real devil in all that, and hated what he still remembered from that night. O'Mario was a charlatan, a song-and-dance man, a white-gloved magician, no better than two men clomping through a sand-dance in ugly black boots and kohled eyes.

He saved his bitterest hatred for the voice itself, for that outward-rippling force that lifted him and cut him loose again and again and again each time he remembered *Le Cid*. He remembered it in camps, in boarding-house beds, in hospitals, in the wings of theatres. Liam was a gifted hater, and knew the dimensions of his own disgust: the misdirecting right hand that had beckoned him, the left that had hooked him so he wriggled inescapably against each twitch on the thread snagged under his skin.

AWAKE

What he remembered of 1918 was awakening. Sometimes it was those past-midnights when everyone else slept, and the windows down at the end of the ward were pearled with steam and illuminated by streetlights. On those nights, he lay marooned in fever, trying to remember what it had been to stand under streetlights with civilian shoes on his feet, and a cigarette, and a beautiful woman. Sometimes during the interminable half-dreams he couldn't tell the difference between waking and sleeping, and morphine turned the light through the long windows as thick as yellow mud. In those dreams he said, I will now sing the B natural, by way of demonstration.

They were nearby, waiting for him and the B natural.

The window at the end of the long corridor of beds filled half the wall. It was topped with a fanlight. Sometime, in a few days perhaps, he would walk the length of the room and stand at the window, and he would look down into the street where men in civilian shoes walked with beautiful women.

They sat close by his bed, or walked up and down the room. Some of them stopped when he spoke, but more often they ignored him.

He said, I will now sing the B natural, by way of demonstration. He had been trying to get through this note for such a long time. He rested his hands on his diaphragm as his lungs filled. The action was sticky, so he thought maybe the mechanism was clogged with oil or mud. Mud was a bastard to get at, you had to take the whole thing apart and ram a rod down the barrel. He would have to see about that. He allowed his throat to relax; he dropped his jaw.

I will now sing, he said.

The window at the end of the long ward rattled. Sometimes he thought that the note—this demonstrative B natural—would never come. Through the glass he saw a patch of sky darker than the inside of the ward. It was hard to see past the steam and the bit of reflected ceiling that obscured his view. It was twilight, perhaps. It was night.

The B natural, he said.

They rustled and settled again like crows. He saw them stand and fall again, passing close by him, pausing and going on as though on a mission of importance, though he could not see what or where. They were insubstantial, but careful listeners; they had been appointed to this duty a very long time ago, before he was born, or his father, or farther back than that. The B natural came first, but it was part of his progression to the C, which was his objective. They listened for it. They stood over him, and pressed his wrist with cool, thin fingers and then went on again. Sometimes he felt the air move across his face and that was them, too. Sometimes he heard singing; the melody was "Auld Lang Syne" and he thought of joining in with it, but when he listened he realized that the words were new, and he did not know them.

Someone sang *we're here because we're here because we're here*
I will now sing, Liam interrupted.
because we're here we're here because we're here
The B natural
because we're here because we're here

"Auld Lang Syne" was important because it had accompanied a moment of almost-revelation regarding the real nature of his talents. Or, regarding what the world made of those talents, and the use to which it would put him. Liam met with an agent in July, not long before the declaration, to talk about possible engagements. Some lady's musical evening, he thought, a party or picnic—just to feed him until more permanent work could be found. Liam walked into the Mercury Company's office with a wonderful sense of acceleration, as though all the doors in the world had blown open simultaneously and he walked through them forever, and would never put a foot wrong again.

Then he had to wait in the outer office for twenty minutes before the gentleman from the Mercury Company called him in and introduced himself as Mr. Jack Strain. He'd stood, stared at the man and nodded, remembering the swagger of the La Scala tenors in Milan, how easy their manners were, and how debonair. Sitting down in the hard chair opposite Mr. Strain, Liam steepled his fingers, his elbows resting on the arms, and a good three inches of pale blue sock showing above his shoes. He had chosen those socks with care, to complement (but not match) his blue silk tie.

"I thought to start with the 'Celeste Aida,'" he said, then nodded as though confirming his own choice. "I thought a little Puccini for the popular audience—possibly the 'Nessun dorma.' Something from *La boheme* if you must. I am at my strongest with Massenet or Verdi, of course, but I'd like to explore the German catalogue."

For a moment Mr. Strain did not respond.

"Your name is Liam Manley, is it not?"

"Yes."

"The Irishman." Liam nodded. "Well then, I have a request for music at a young lady's birthday." Liam nodded again.

"But as to the program, I think the 'Celeste—'"

"The young lady has already selected a number of songs. In particular she wishes to hear 'Auld Lang Syne,' at the end of the evening, so you must be prepared to stay late. She also wishes to hear 'She Moved Through The Fair,' 'The Last Rose of Summer'—"

"You seem to have misunderstood. I'm not a music hall entertainer. I am not suited to such flimsy, sentimental..." He stopped and began again: "Mr. Strain, my voice is of a more..." Liam looked for a word, paused, then said it bluntly, "aristocratic quality. Hadn't you better find an Irish tenor if you're interested in disseminating songs such as the disgusting 'When Irish Eyes Are Smiling'? I was trained to *Verdi!*"

"Sir, in your current situation—you are without a master, I believe? And lack the funds to return to Paris?—I would suggest you endeavour to be happy with the two pounds you will earn and sing the songs your employer selects."

Liam looked at Mr. Strain's boots. They were nicely blacked, but unfashionable.

"Mr. Strain—"

"If you do not wish to take the job, there is nothing I can do to stop you. If, however, you agree to the terms I have set—in spite of your aristocratic gifts—then sign the contract and go to this address next Wednesday at two o'clock in the afternoon. The accompanist will meet you there. The hostess has also allowed you dinner, as part of your fee."

Mr. Strain pushed a few sheets of paper toward Liam. "Not with the party, of course." Liam felt for a pen in his pocket, but there were only pennies and a handkerchief; he looked at Mr. Strain, who took his own pen from his inside pocket and dropped it on top of the sheets.

His morphine dreams: sometime long ago he's standing at a balcony. He's pretty sure it's before the war. There's the low wall, fat marble columns squatting under a wide marble rail. It's only knee height. For sitting, he guesses, but he has come to believe he's too tall to lounge gracefully, and so he stands and does not know what to do with his hands, and keeps them behind his back, sweaty fingers knotted about one another. There's the soft glitter of the sea below, light from a spotty yellow moon on the horizon.

There is a rose in the lapel of his cheap, cream-coloured suit. The suit bags badly at the pockets and has been imperfectly sponged. Sometimes he stands with his arms crossed to cover the marks, but he thinks that looks awkward. He suspects it is always less awkward to wear one's marks unselfconsciously than it is to hide them, but he still finds himself trying.

He looks down toward the wrinkled grey sea. The roar of water on pea gravel—each wave falls; another builds, rises thoughtfully and falls. He listens particularly for the quiet between breakers, and each time it seems too long, and he thinks this wave will be the last, it will not fall, but rise forever. Each time it falls. Each time the glitter of pebbles striking pebbles.

He has in his pocket a letter from his mother. It told him about a fowl supper she had organized, about his father's new thresher, and his younger sister's confirmation and his older brother's wedding. She signed it "With all my love for my own dear laddie," and nothing but "Mother" in place of her name. She had been very careful and recopied the letter at least once. More than once, he guesses, as she'd had trouble with the capital in the "Dearest" of the salutation. He had always disliked her capital Ds, being tippy, and he had tried to teach her better (the elegant, copperplate D he copied out of *The Books of Knowledge* he found at school—the set missing volumes, so he never learned numbers properly, or the lowercase "f"). Though he was the one who insisted on showing her the correct construction of the capital D, he had still been embarrassed by the way she pressed her lips together and knit her brows, determined to be a model student. How she had dipped and wiped her pen so quickly—to impress him with her efficiency—that she scattered drops on the paper.

This D was done quite sharply angled and particular.

Beyond the news and the affected little phrases like "such fun" and "quite genteel" and "estimable party of young people," there was the question of how much longer he would stay there, when he would come home and sing in Toronto, perhaps, or London, because it was close enough that Father could come and hear him. Or Montreal, or Salterton, or Elgin. She listed several towns and cities he might like for singing, as though he would not know their names, having been abroad nearly six months.

He's at a young lady's birthday party. The program of interminable Irish balladry approaches but never reaches its end. He has sung "The Bard of Armagh" (twice) and "She Moved Thro' The Fair" (three times) and "The Rose of Tralee" (twice) and "The Last Rose of Summer" (five times), and he has sung "The Harp That Once Thro' Tara's Halls" so many times he cannot remember a moment when it seemed fresh or original. The young lady to whom he is addressing his song sits with rapt, glazed eyes and parted lips that shine where she has wet them. She rests her head on her hands, in an attitude he has seen in advertisements for Cashmere Bouquet and Peek Freans. She beats time with one finger and sighs and says "Again! Sing it again!" and he repeats "The Bard of Armagh."

He has reached the last song on the list, the very very long list lengthened by every little gasp the young lady makes, and every soft glance she casts on him, and with every dreamy command "Again!" Finally he has arrived at "Auld Lang Syne." He hopes there'll be only one. From the back of the room, the hostess watches her guests with sharp, crow-black eyes, and—because it is a dream—Mrs. Kilgour is also there, humming, though he does not yet know that she waits for him.

Should auld acquaintance be forgot and never brought to mind should auld acquaintance be, he begins, *forgot in the days of auld lang syne*

But the audience has begun to trail after him in the song, not large enough to sound grand, nor gifted enough to sound elegant, and above it all, Mrs. Kilgour's croon, and the quivering little voice of the girl whose eyes are tear-swollen.

But as he continues, *We'll take a cup o' kindness yet in the days of auld lang syne*, he realizes that they are not singing what he is singing. He listens carefully and hears from all their lips these other words. Ugly words.

For auld lang syne my dears we're here because we're here we'll take a cup o' kindness yet we're here because we're here.

M. Girard stood at the foot of his bed. Though his face was in shadow, Liam recognized the man by his distinctive fawn-coloured spats. M. Girard told him he should not leave Paris. Liam began to tell M. Girard that he did intend to return when he was able, but then he could not remember the French for "convalescent home." *Maison d'Infirme?* M. Girard was not patient. He told Liam that if he left now, whatever slight talent he had would be lost to lazy habits and bad taste. Liam tried to explain that he had not the money, having lost his patron after their contracted year, but M. Girard said that money should not be an object, and himself, he would work as a dishwasher before he sacrificed whatever small gifts he had to bourgeois pretension.

Great artists are never so middle class, he said that last day. They are better than that.

"There is a letter from your mother, Corporal Manley, would you like to hear it?"

Liam looked past the VAD in her winged cap for M. Girard, who had gone.

They were always singing. On the troop train from Étaples it was "If You Want the Sergeant Major" and the ubiquitous "Tipperary." They kept it up until they detrained just before midnight, and stood around with tin cups of tea that steamed in the yellow lamplight. He'd looked up from the gravel platform and seen a blistered red sky to the east, rising like a false dawn. It was April. A wet breeze smelled like daffodils. Leaving the station, he saw bunches of King Alfreds as big as his fist, behind a row of white painted stones. Then they were off, down the white road in the moonlight, and there were poplar trees like in the songs he sang about France.

Somewhere near the forward ranks they started, and his mob picked it up. At first he couldn't make out the words. The melody was "Auld Lang Syne." Liam was in full kit, among bulky figures in greatcoats, and their tramp tramp tramp steady as a metronome: *We're here because we're here because we're here because we're here*. They had joyful voices and shouted into the countryside. Some were pleasant, even, he thought, though he heard an awkward shift from chest to head tones. Awkwardness did not matter, he reminded himself: they are interested in being heard.

The farmyards dropped behind them. Now there were stumped trees, burnt churches, earthworks. Liam looked away, up to where the moon emerged from the clouds, almost blue. It dazzled him. As it always seemed in moonlight, the world was changed, the earth conscious beneath his feet, the trees about to speak. They groaned, he thought, those that still stood beside their broken companions, shifted in the earth as though to uproot themselves and make their escape. When he glanced to either side, he was sure there were bodies—or things like bodies, once bodies, about to stand up and lumber toward him—looming and fading as they passed, dark shapes in the larger darkness.

He has a letter in his pocket, from his mother. She is very proud of her own laddie. She and Ella will send him socks and chocolate.

The last rise, the long white roadway turning to mud under their tramp tramp tramp. As they reached the low summit, the first thing he saw was the dead thing, a fallen hobby horse with legs stiff as sticks, spilling grey wool guts onto the mud.

He stripped naked and dropped his tunic in the corner of his billet. He bathed. Once in bed he drifted nearly to sleep, but then perceived a smell, a disgusting mingling of sweat and shit and wet wool, and more than anything, dead things rotting. He could not sleep for the smell. He got up to search for the source, planning how delicately he would draw the housewife's attention to it—"Madam!" he would begin—but then he traced the scent to the tunic he dropped. He picked it up, and the smell was suddenly so terrible, he dropped it out the window, not liking that it was his own self he smelled.

He wished morphine did not make him smell things like the stink of that tunic. The smell, sometimes, of hay lying in the fields. They marched through hayfields in summer, French ones that should be picturesque, like in songs, but only filled him with fear. When he first arrived, he'd sing, in his mind, *Oh the moonlight's fair tonight along the Wabash through the fields there comes the breath of new mown hay*, but that had quickly ended.

Sometime after that, Liam was running. He was halfway down the ward before he woke up. As he ran, he came down hard on his left leg, which was bad. His lungs hurt, too, and he thought afterward, it was the pain that woke him more than his fear. At the time, he knew only that he had seen something in the darkness above his cot and it was behind him now, and that his escape lay someplace before: the huge window at the end of the ward and down into the street. He was nearly at the window, when he began to wonder if the plan was excessive. That was also when he heard his own voice shouting.

He thought he might also be tangled in his bedclothes, which made him stumble on the linoleum. That might have been what made the pain in his left leg so bad. It was hard to tell, what with the noise and the urge to run, find the window, break it and leap, hit the pavement and across the city in strides so long that the time suspended between footfalls felt like flight. At the end of the long ward, he leaned on the casement's sill, felt the pain in his throat and knew with his waking mind that he still shouted, though he could not yet find the mechanism that would stop it. He fumbled through the Venetians for the latch, but found none, and in his frustration he tangled his hands in the blinds and hauled. Something broke. His feet slid on the enamelled metal, and now he hurt in more places than before, his palms and his knuckles.

Before he put his fist through the window, as he had intended, and climbed onto the ledge to leap two storeys to the sidewalk, he paused and posed himself a small, cool question: *Are you sure this is real?* It was a question he had not thought to ask for some time. As he struck the glass with the base of his palm and then his fist, the thought resolved a little further and he managed to stop his fist from swinging. He turned to look down the ward and saw the others struggling up; they stared at him, unafraid, irritated.

In that first moment of full consciousness, he felt like an electrically resuscitated corpse.

"What?" he heard. "Goddamn Manley again." The blinds on the left side of the window hung from the frame by one nail. The others lay in his hands and around his feet. He still gripped them; when he forced his fingers to uncurl, the slats fell and rang on the linoleum.

"Just Manley! Everyone, it's only *Manley*, not the goddamn Hun," that from the man in the next cot. "Only Goddamn Manley!"

Goddamn Manley was the closest thing he had to a nickname in the hospital.

But there was still the far end of the ward, and his bed where the dark thing crouched. He should be brave and turn to look, knowing that if he stared at the thing long enough, he would find it was not a monster, but his blue silk dressing gown hanging on the back of his chair. The one he found out (too late) the lads hated for reasons he did not understand. But he could not look, and therefore could not make the dark thing resolve back into something ordinary. He leaned instead against the window and looked down to the street where the lamps were bright and yellow. People passed, couples arm in arm like they'd been out to a show. Not late then, maybe a little before midnight.

Then a surge of yellow light close by, and he saw that his right hand was covered in blood and there were bloody prints on the glass. One of the double doors down the end was open and there was a VAD; he didn't know her at first. She was silhouetted, the winged cap and skirt kicking out behind her as she ran toward him. In the new light he saw blood on the white blinds, too, and on his pyjamas.

He heard mumbled complaints and curses: "Sister, sister—get him out of here, would you? Some of us need to sleep."

"Sorry, everyone," he said, confusedly, "sorry." He kept his eyes away from the wall beside his bed. He kept his eyes away from those who were watching the VAD lead him from the ward. He leaned on her all the way to the little office where she sat up nights, waiting just for him, he sometimes thought, for just this nightly disaster.

Once he was fully conscious, there were the lungs to worry about, and the left leg that throbbed dully and incessantly. Often Sister reminded him of his improvement, but on these nights he forget everything but the wheeze, and the slime he disgorged hourly from some deep, wet place inside, and that spattered the sleeve of his tunic.

Because just that moment he wasn't better: each heartbeat felt like a detonation behind his ribs, that filled his vision with black, and sounded in his ears like the enemy's approaching bombardment. He sat at the table, hands on knees, his spine and ribs caved protectively around the mass of sodden, swollen tissue that had once been a set of working lungs. He could not quite believe that some time, long ago, he had breathed without thought or care, and his eyes had not pulsed.

The VAD (it was Annie, he realized, whom they called Sister Flynn to be correct, who was nice and sometimes went to the shows and told him what she heard) cut the white gauze bandage and tied it at his knuckles. Behind her, the kettle sang on its spirit lamp. They knew the routine well now, and she set the white enamel bowl in front of him and handed him a towel. She filled the bowl from her kettle, and added eucalyptus and he leaned forward into the steam, with the towel hooded over his head.

He counted one. Another breath ended short and that was two. In the half-light beneath the towel, he saw that his fingers were white and purple where they curled over the edges of the bowl, like a dead man's hands. Though he tried very hard to be good and calm and still, and count breaths the way they told him to, he thought very clearly and coolly in a voice like the one that had stopped him breaking the window, I'm going to die like this. And with that thought, black and gold sparks swarmed again in his eyes, clearer than anything real he could see in the dim light. He would die crouched over a white enamel bowl full of warm water, with a hard, immoveable thing in his chest like an unexploded shell. It was true. It was not the thing in the dark above his bed that he should run from, but the white enamel bowl and his own scarified lungs. He knew it so clearly that he drew another breath to say it aloud for the first time, and make Sister Flynn hear him when he said it, and admit that he was good as dead.

He felt a small hand on the back of his neck. Her palm was calloused and dry; her rough skin caught his hair as she stroked his head. She leaned over him and whispered through the towel, close enough that he felt her arm's slight weight on his shoulder. "Breathe, Corporal Manley," she said, her voice low and close, as though she'd just awakened, too. "We know you must be still." The scarred thing inside did not respond at first to the sound of her voice. Then he drew another breath. Out. In. She breathed with him: Out. In. He felt her chest rise against his arm, then fall again. She seemed to speak, and at the time he was sure she said, "If you panic, Liam, it will get worse. You'll strangle. We mustn't panic. We must remember to breathe." But afterward he didn't think so. She never called him Liam.

When the water cooled, he raised his head and looked again at his bloodless fingers pressed into the table on either side of the bowl. He dried his face on the towel. Sister had a fresh kettle in her hands and another one already over the lamp. She was watching him, her eyes dark and smudged all around with purple. There were tired lines between her nose and mouth.

"Where is Doctor Beach, Sister?" he asked.

"We'll call him if this doesn't work," she said. She pushed the fresh bowl toward him. He tried to smile at her, and she managed to smile back. She waited, sitting across the table, through the rest of the night, as she had done the week before, and the week before that. She sat with him until Doctor Beach arrived in the examining room, smelling of the cold air in the street and his morning cigar.

MORE TIME PASSES FOR LIAM

Despite a decade of relentless movement from little big-time to little little-time, the world continued to shrink. Sometimes when he was sick, Liam suspected that what was before him at that moment—the sink in the corner of the room, the narrow window, the narrow bed—comprised the whole universe, and that depths he had once thought illimitable were now bound by the thin walls of a hotel room outside Mexico City, in 1939. This new conviction reversed the feeling he had once known of doors flickering open before him. If they had opened, they only led to where he now stood with the ivory-handled razor in his right hand and the fingertips of his left hand brushing the sink, before the mirror into which he must stoop to look.

And when he was really ill, the world grew even smaller: margined by his own body, with no opened doors and only his unbreachable skin, and the sound of his lungs in decline as he drew each breath and released it, drew and released. On these sorts of days, the razor hung from his right hand for a long time, while he leaned on the edge of the sink with his left and meant to pick up the soap and begin lathering his cheeks. But there were stars in his eyes when he moved too quickly, and the scar tissue in his lungs held shut each little alveolus, just as the puckered skin of his left thigh pulled tight and shone when he bent his knee.

He had once thought that a song so called him from himself that he leapt up through the top of his skull. He might have thought pain cracked him open and that he had spilled out the crack, and when he ran in the grip of a dream, he might think he had outrun his ruined body, and found the way outside. Even when he came inside a woman in the dark and could not see her face, but spilled irresistibly into her, he had only, really, remained as he was, the size of his own expanded lungs at their greatest capacity, a shape circumscribed by scar tissue. It was not the shape he wished it to be. Sometimes he thought that if he could find Mario O'Mara's tailor's records, he could compare those numbers to his own measurements, and so know the precise distance—a quarter inch? an eighth?—between his voice and O'Mara's.

On evenings when he was well enough, he walked the streets as quickly as he was able and found reprieve in the illusion of movement. It was a relief he thought he had once found in music, before this late illness had weakened him. Standing before his sink, he could not properly remember those times, but thought they must once have been. They had long since been replaced by other things, like women, and the few short, scripted hours between chance meeting and assignation. He left quickly afterward, out of remembered fastidiousness and the red flush of shame. Once he had tried to ask forgiveness. He remembered a woman, a dark-haired, dark-eyed woman, her large, blue-white breasts spilling out of a cheap red silk wrap. How she had looked in the lamplight with deep lines etched by the shadows of her nose and her brow, one hand raised to pull at the ring in her ear. The other arm crossed over her stomach, holding shut the robe that shone wetly and quivered with each breath, the rolls on her stomach pressing against the silk. She had smiled at him.

He had opened his mouth. "I'm sorry," he had said, wondering how it was that a moment ago he had cried out and clung to her and kissed her. She seemed unkissable now. She had gone on smiling, one hand tugging the gold ring, the other holding shut the robe, as though she had not been naked in the lamplight ten minutes before.

"I'm sorry," he had said again. She had laughed and rolled her eyes, as though to say *I know you*. He wondered if it were a little bit like forgiveness, that dismissal, but still it was dreadful that he was one of the men—the many men? he did not like to guess—at whom she shook her head as though saying, *I know you*. He could not bear to think he was that kind, whatever it was, and he said again, "I'm sorry."

She dropped the gold earring, and reached toward him where he sat half-dressed on the bed. She caught the back of his neck and held him between her fingers. "You should at least say thank you. I would rather hear thank you any day." One leg slid behind him, so he could feel her warm inner thigh.

He did not speak.

"Thank you," she said, her other leg warming his chest, and he felt her through the fabric of robe. "Thank you."

The scene was not repeated. He left the room, in whichever city it had been. Somewhere south, in California; he could not remember. It shocked him that he could not remember the breadth of his travels or the names of towns, only that the girl in cheap red silk had shaken her head and smiled.

AND LET THE REST OF THE WORLD GO BY

Trump Davis and his Western Gentlemen were one of those shabby little dance bands who cluttered up the western provinces, playing holiday camps and hotels in summer, trailing through small towns in winter. Liam never knew who mentioned his name to Trump, but sometimes he suspected Goshawk. By whatever chance, a letter waited for him at General Delivery in Winnipeg whose blotted, badly formed sentences were signed by a man who identified himself as Trump's agent. The agent mentioned that he had heard Liam's work the previous year at the Palm Court Charity Tea in Calgary, and it had recently been suggested that he would make a classy addition to The Western Gentlemen. The letter-writer actually wrote "classy," and went on to suggest that Liam might join them in Nelson for a short tour of dancehalls in the province's interior, culminating in three nights at the Vimy Memorial Hall in Chilliwack.

The agent—Liam suspected it was Trump himself—had included a flier for an earlier performance. Their signature song was, unhappily, "And Let the Rest of the World Go By."

When Liam received the letter, he had been tired a long time, and now in a persistent way, with a weight that seemed new, though he could not quite remember a time when it had not accompanied him. His breath often faltered during long sustains, and he had re-ordered his repertoire to avoid moments that tested his limits, or required such concentration.

Once installed as a Western Gentleman, Liam was not surprised to discover that he was no crooner. It took only three weeks, long enough to get him into one of the western-style suits—lurid houndstooth top-stitched in white, with a string tie—abandoned by an earlier member of about his height, and to put him on stage before the largest audience he'd seen in years. He was introduced to and forgot the names of twelve other Western Gentlemen.

He did not know that his third night in Chilliwack was his last as a Western Gentleman until the end of the final set, when girls in short skirts and boys in uniform shuffled around the floor and he sang Trump's signature song. Or rather, he sang his own signature song: *We'll find perfect peace where joys never cease somewhere beneath the starry sky we'll build a sweet little nest somewhere in the west and let the rest of the world go by.*

And those words, so bitter as he crooned the last sustain, and the shufflers ceased shuffling and clung to one another under the lights of the Vimy Memorial Hall, those last words made him wish never to sing again. Of course, what he did was not singing, but what they had once called whispering, but he decided in that moment that neither would he whisper, even if it meant he would cease to be a Western Gentleman. He also had an accurate sense of his own performance: it would be better to anticipate his dismissal and resign quietly.

He did not know what would happen next. After the last shuffler had shuffled away, he ate his cold supper in a side room and listened to the men talk about baseball, rye whiskey, and women. He thought about his annuity. He spread mustard on a roll and thought about capital, and how he had none, had never had any capital but his face and—sometimes, when he was very lucky—his voice. He added roast beef to the mustard, then salt and black pepper. He thought about Mrs. Kilgour and her fortune, the villages and hunting lodges and mines. He thought about how much time he had left, and the state of his lungs. By the end of his pickles and cheese and the two matrimonial bars, he had decided that he would go to Mrs. Kilgour's lawyers. He would go there tomorrow and suggest that he take his capital and not bother them again. It would see him through a year or two in Mexico, and as he reckoned it, that was all he needed. Before dawn the next morning he woke in the room he shared with four other Western Gentlemen, quietly packed his things and walked a slow mile to the bus station, where he bought a ticket to the city, and Mrs. Kilgour's lawyers, and a little of his capital.

He arrived on one of those milky mornings he remembered from earlier Novembers in the city, the buildings and streets swamped in a pale, lukewarm fog that blunted noise as well as colour. By eleven he had a place in an ugly rooming house on the east side, half-full of loggers. At one o'clock he found Goshawk's address, which he had kept for years in his little book, but never used. He brushed his coat and changed his shirt and set out, feeling the cracks in the pavement through the soles of his old shoes, and thinking that they would be the first thing he'd correct when he had his capital.

An hour later he was on the familiar corner, but the building was gone and in its place a pit and a sign that read "The Future Home of the Kilgour Institute." He didn't know what the Kilgour Institute could be, but it sounded dreadful. By three he was drinking coffee (pale brown, tasting of chicory and toasted barley) in a café called Adele's, among the boys in khaki—lads, he thought they still called them, or laddies—who laughed over tables covered in cups and dirty plates. Having made his pilgrimage to a demolition site, he could not remember what came next.

The only thing he could think was that he did not wish to walk back to the rooming house, with the sidewalks so rough and wet. He now wished that he had remained a Western Gentleman long enough to replace his shoes. He'd had new soles just two years before, but they were expensive with shoe leather being (apparently) necessary for the War Effort.

In early 1940, he had decided that he would not make a War Effort. He wouldn't buy victory bonds (not that he had the money), or march, or sing, or anything. He meticulously shredded and discarded his cigarette foil so as to prevent its being recycled by those hoards of scrap-collecting children. "Mister!" he remembered a child saying to him—where? It might have been Regina, or Nelson—"Mister, you want to give us the foil for Victory?" Some scabby twelve-year-old with freckles and dirty knees. Liam had stared at the boy, feeling that old arrogance come over him. He lit a cigarette. The child shuffled foot to foot. "Mister?" he said again, wrinkling his brow as though he'd just looked back to see his own muddy footprints on his mother's clean floor. Liam had pulled out the last cigarette and stuffed it in a pocket, then separated the foil. He balled it up in his fist and dropped it down the grate at his feet. Then he gave the snot-nosed little berk the outer case. He would get very little for paper.

Despite the wet, he would have to get up soon, get back to his hotel where he could solve the problem of his shoes, and then face the Kilgour issue. He would cut some cardboard insoles to delay the inevitable, if he could find cardboard. The soldiers at the other table were laughing very loud now over some stage-whispered joke about the waitress's tits. The waitress's tits weren't particularly intriguing. Liam was more impressed by her pompadour, which added four inches to her height. Without it or her high white pumps, she'd be a tiny little thing, like a midget. Her brows had been plucked bald and replaced by ink-black lines like quotation marks around her eyes. Her mouth was the bright red of a flag.

Liam decided in favour of wet shoes, pavement and the possibility of cardboard insoles rather than another round of obnoxious military laughter. The lads in khaki were no better than they had been in 1915, and it did not surprise him, considering how young they were, and how afraid. Outside again, he looked down a street full of determined activity and shades of drab. A flat disk of sun failed to properly illuminate the chalk-coloured sky. It was late afternoon. He would return to the rooming house, though it was ten blocks away and his feet were already wet. He wished for trolley fare. In a few blocks he reached one of the big department stores, glancing in at polished wood and perfume bottles gleaming in the incandescent light, women statuesque among them in their sleek, black dresses.

For the first time that day, he realized that he saw everything with the excruciating clarity of fever, a precise and narrow glance that picked out all the shades of grey between white fog and shadow, that saw every luminous shape multiplied in the mirrors of the department store, and the polished glass doors, and marked in detail the motion of a woman's hands as she wrapped tissue paper around a box. Everything about him was distant and tiny and perfect, made of translucent amber, and mother-of-pearl. In his ears the sounds of the street became a slurry, no words he knew, though in it he heard, unexpected, a through-line, like a motif, like a message. He would not go back to his room to cut insoles out of old cardboard. He would push through the bright, ordered world of the department store instead, and stare like a desert nomad in from the wild, eyes swollen with vision. He would follow that motif and discover its source. He would go in. He would go.

As he opened the double doors, a woman came out, dragging a child after her. She passed him so closely the fabric of her unfastened coat brushed against his wrist. She was heavily pregnant, smocked in an ugly blue dress with a white collar, like a nun would wear out of habit. The touch of her coat clung to his skin, like a hand briefly holding his. He turned to watch her.

She was pale. She had honey-blonde hair and freckles, and under the distortion of her pregnancy she was slender, with narrow knees and ankles. Her small hand around the child's was hard and strong, and the bones that jutted through the skin were held in place by whipcords of tendon. All this he took in as he saw her, and with it came a surge of recognition, then relief. He did not even recognize the trick of his illness, that on this unfriendly street he should feel such familiarity. He knew the young woman and was sure she would know him, too, as though she was part of a life he had mislaid just this week, and the last years were only a temporary exile in which he had wandered, before he found his way back.

She led her child down the block to a streetcar stop. He took a step toward them. The child hung onto her hand, rocking back and forth. The woman ignored her, but never loosened her grip. The child hung her head, and Liam heard "no no no" faintly. *I know her*, he thought again. He looked carefully at the little girl (dark-haired, dark-eyed child with skin like white paper), and slipped his hands from his pockets to see that they were shaking. He had almost caught up with them when the trolley stopped, and the doors opened, the line moved forward, and the woman dragged the little girl after her onto the trolley. The child looked over her shoulder at Liam, still on the sidewalk. He felt in his pockets for carfare. She walked along the aisle and took a seat, her daughter by the window staring out at him, but the woman looking away, the tendons on her neck standing out like the bones of her hands.

Other people wanted on the car. Liam stepped back into someone, confused, and felt a lady's foot through the sole of his shoe. He apologized: *Sorry, I'm sorry, sorry.* One hand wandered up to his forehead, down his cheek and felt the tight, hot skin beneath his fingers.

The trolley departed. Not liking to watch, he walked in the opposite direction, past the café that still held the lads in khaki, then toward the park. He remembered the park. During his last visit to the city, he thought he had walked through it, and someone had told him stories about the woods. He would walk there until his head cleared, look at the specimen trees, and keep out of the rain in one of the little tea houses.

He made his way toward the dark green at the end of the street, above it the grey sky now bluing to black. It was like a theatre, he thought, one with the castle walls all around the auditorium, and pinewood showing above the battlements, and the stars coming out in the domed ceiling overhead. He had sung in a theatre like that, where the arches were Romanesque grey stone, and there were oak-hewn doors studded with bronze. Though he felt the earth and gravel through his soles, he still thought that it might be boards he walked over, trailing his long black coat toward the apron and the accompanist. What would he sing when he reached the lights?

In the woods he began to shiver. His wet coat made him feel like a man with stones in his pockets. He felt no rain, but somewhere it fell, high above in the crossed branches of fir trees. He wanted to lie down and let the fever burn through his skin, through his coat until it warmed the wet earth beneath him and he could sleep, with nothing but rye whiskey to keep out the night.

He did not lie down. He turned and started on the path back out, trying to find the old stride that had carried him through so many other, earlier night walks. Once out of the woods, the night was no brighter: the streets were empty, and the only light came from narrow-beamed blackout lanterns carried by men he could not see, who patrolled the dark. He wanted to go to them and ask for help. Each cough now filled his nose with a sour yellowish scent. Each cough tore at the thin membranes inside him, and the ominous bubbling he felt might be blood as well as phlegm. He thought that sometime soon he would disgorge his own lungs, and leave them steaming, half-rotted on the pavement and walk away, newly lightened, the fever gone.

His room was damp and filmed with coal smoke. Liam lay in bed and listened to the noises of the house, the creaks and rumbles and talk from the other rooms on the landing. He had gone so far as to take off his shoes, which were drying on the register beside him. He would have to go out again in the morning and find Goshawk. He did not wish to do it in wet shoes. When he closed his eyes, it seemed he was still walking, through the woods or through dark streets with blackout curtains over all the windows. He opened his eyes to confirm yes yes oh of course yes he was not on the street; he was in bed, though the room was cold and he too tired to take the wet clothes from his back.

But soon when he opened his eyes he could not confirm his location, and when he closed them he felt as though he was tumbling, circling downward, drawn into the deep by some irresistible weight.

He slipped into deeper sleep, but the weight was there too, and now the air he breathed had the viscous texture of a nightmare, and the light around him inexplicably dreadful, a shade of yellow he knew and feared, the colour of stage lights that both obscured and revealed, not by daytime law but by some other rule he could not comprehend. As he fell, his own hands seemed so far away he could hardly make out their details, his head resting on earth and his feet in some deep reach of the universe, and all this time the weight on him, so he sensed it with the hairs of his scalp, with his belly. His heart felt the weight most of all, and its beats slowed, then slowed again. Each breath thicker and more taxing. In the end all he thought was

dear god, please let me breathe let me breathe let me
breathe let me breathe
please let me

DEAD THINGS

It was pretty much inevitable that something would die up there. After squirrels breached the attic above Anthea's apartment, the inside of the house wasn't much different from the street or gardens in what the CarbonNinjas called the city's *Urban Forest*. The attic, the walls, the floors belonged to rodents now, and pigeons, and all the attendant parasites and nesting materials such creatures required.

So when she climbed the long stairs to her suite after her last visit to the Aquarian Centre and she smelled something, she wasn't surprised. They had been loud and territorial for weeks, as though engaged in a war of succession or a campaign of occupation. One morning she awoke to a large grey squirrel chittering on her kitchen counter, tearing into a box of Cheerios. It saw her and pissed down the cupboards, then ran through the paper on the floor, knocking over candles and coffee cups and tracking piss-prints over that portion of the Kilgour Archive she had stolen. That first morning she was too frightened to chase the squirrel out, and temporarily retreated from the front room. When she crept back, he was pacing below the sill of the open window, before he fled under her stove. She fled as well, back to her bedroom. She still didn't know when he left, and worried when she turned on the oven that screeches and an unpleasant smell would emanate from beneath it, and then there would be trouble.

But the smell began in the closet and spread, in the course of days, through the apartment. She worried that she now smelled to those she encountered not only of the paper and mildew of Rm 023, but of the dead thing in the attic. Anthea called her landlady and said, "I think something died." And when the woman didn't respond, she called again and said, "I'm pretty sure there's a dead thing in the attic." And then the next day, "Yeah, that's what dead things smell like." When the smell worked its way down to the other tenants, they began to call as well.

On the third day of the smell. Anthea, sleeping in a mask doused with lavender essential oil, like someone in a medieval, airborne epidemic, woke to find the scent had developed a new intensity during the warm night. Lying in bed, she thought about the potato field that Hazel kept, now overgrown. She remembered walking there one afternoon in the summer before, through the narrow band of trees and the trench that separated it from the public road.

She walked among Douglas fir, alder, cascara, west coast crabapple, Pacific yew, spirea, Saskatoon-berries-of-the-dead, salal, wild rose. Everything filled in with green: the trenches; the outline of Hazel's potato beds; the strip of lawn that Max and then Colm had cut with the mower every week, now in the long grass since Colm had been so busy elsewhere. He had told her that it was once a goat field, though she wasn't sure if that was in his time—one of Hazel's many experiments with small farming—or in Simon's. Now the deer grazed it, and the rabbits. In the evening she often saw an owl on the high branch of a Douglas fir.

As she walked she smelled something. Somewhere among the stems and trunks, some animal had crept away and died and brought an edge of decay to the air. It was not the sweet smell of rotten leaves, nor the vegetable stink of compost nor seaweed. Anthea knew that if she looked, she wouldn't necessarily see it. Once, walking in the same woods, she had looked down to find herself standing in the ribcage of a young deer, long dead. She had jumped and kicked the vertebrae out of alignment. She did not wish to see a dead thing.

NIGHTSHADE SOCIETY

One day in March of Anthea's fourth year, Hazel called her little dorm room. She was drunk. "Darling," she said. "Darling, when are your exams? You do have exams, don't you?"

"Yeah. I really do." Anthea looked at her calendar and the neat block capitals that indicated exams, now cross-hatched with red blue black exclamations about what she ought to know where and when. She didn't have to say anything more, though, because Hazel kept talking. "Did you know that the ancient Greeks—" Her voice was all gurgly and spitty on the sibilant when she said "ancient." Anthea thought she heard the little drops of saliva hitting the plastic. The last time she'd used Hazel's phone, she could not bear to let it touch her face, avoiding the bloom of fingers on the receiver and the dirty hairspray smeared on the earpiece. She did not look closely at the mouthpiece.

Hazel tried again: "Did you know the ancient Greeks believed in assisted suicide?" She would be sitting at her small rolltop desk where she kept the phone and wrote letters. She would be wearing polyester knit slacks and a sleeveless floral blouse. Near her there would be a glass of gin and a can of tonic that was flat for being open in the fridge from the night before. Hazel didn't like a lot of tonic, so one can did two nights. There would be a small bottle of prescription pills nearby: Librium, Ativan, Clonazepam. One pill with the drink, maybe one before bed. Hazel liked to joke about her libritonics, ginazepams, ativonics.

"The ancient Greeks?" Anthea began, because this was something she knew. "Actually it was—"

"Yes yes, or the Romans. I'm not a professional historian, you know. I didn't get the chance. But I know they believed in dignity, darling, for the old, and that you should get to pick when you were ready to go. Do you understand, darling, why that's so civilized?" Again the wet sibilants. There was a pause and the sound of a mouth opening. "Because it gives people their free will, and their right to die. I can't remember if it was the Greeks or the Romans. I always understand the philosophy just as well, I just don't always know the details, but that's because details aren't really important. And I know that they believed in assisted suicide. One of them, anyway. You know I joined the Nightshade Society."

"Okay. Right to die?"

"I joined and sent them a check for five hundred dollars. There's a court case. They need the money, for that nurse who killed all the people in the critical care ward. A big fat woman; I can't remember her name. There's a court case."

"Yes?"

"Do you understand?"

"Okay. There's a court case?"

"Yes, darling! You understand." Then Hazel tapped a number on her phone's keypad and said, "Oh, darling, that beep means I have another call. I have to go!" She dropped the phone abruptly, as Anthea said goodbye.

For a moment she sat in the dark, illuminated only by the greyish light of her screensaver and wondered why Hazel always ended phone conversations with a lie. Why also her conversations were so saturated with import and yet so opaque, so Anthea felt Hazel's urgency, but never understood what was going on. Was the court case the point? Or assisted suicide? Or something to do with history? For another, longer moment Anthea imagined Hazel at her dark, gin-smirched tea table.

On the thirtieth of April of that fourth year, having finished her exams, Anthea caught a bus north to Duncan's Crossing to see her parents. Colm met her in town and told her they were going to see Hazel that night or the next, though he did not elaborate. Anthea wilted a little, but she didn't argue, because Colm wore an expression she knew well, where he sucked on his teeth and his fingers made fists around the steering wheel.

Anthea watched Duncan's Crossing go by and hated it: the Glass Castle and the RVs, the car dealerships and the new prefab fast food spots adrift in huge parking lots, the highway that bisected the town with four lanes and a Lego-green meridian, the low slate-coloured clouds on the hills all around.

While she hated the town, Colm broke his anxious silence. He tried to prepare her. He said, "Yeah, no. Anthea. You need to be prepared."

"What?"

"Just, yeah, okay. No. Yeah." Colm said. "It's Hazel. She did something."

Anthea thought down the list: heart attack, a fall, pneumonia, the first symptoms of Alzheimer's, home invasion, stroke.

"See, she did something." Colm stopped again.

"What did she do?"

"No. Yeah. She."

"*What?*"

"Well, see, we didn't want to tell you before, while you were away. We thought we'd wait. Max doesn't know either. We'll tell him when he gets here next week."

It came out painfully, in Colm's nearly impenetrable syntax. Last week he had been worried about Hazel, and in the usual way he worried since Grandpa Max had died. On Thursday, in the early evening, he had worried enough, and went over to Hazel's house where he found her on the Naugahyde chesterfield in her front room, with a thin plastic bag over her head, tied at the neck with a black silk ribbon. On the table beside her, he saw a bottle of Gordon's gin, and around it the empty containers: Valium, Nembutal, Librium, Clonazepam. She was still breathing when he tore the plastic off her face.

"She's in the hospital now," was all he said, and then Anthea did not know what to say, and sat watching the edge of the ugly town pass them, until they were in the country again. She wondered how it would feel, a plastic bag over her mouth, and the alcohol leaching from her stomach to her blood, and the tranquilizers following, and how the world would seem tiny and far away on the other side of the plastic, and there would be panic at first, then the tyrannical calm of the tranqs and then nothing until Colm and the paramedics and the horrible smell of plastic from the mask on her face, and the paralysis, and the taste and scent and texture of vomit.

"Maybe you don't have to go see her, not right away," he said, finally. "Maybe we shouldn't go so soon. Someone has to be with her all the time, but I don't want you to have to. Your mother's there now. We're pretty busy."

"Did you tell Ada?"

"Your mom called her."

And when the mask was pulled away, the narrow, high bed and the steel bars on either side, the weight of the covers on her legs as heavy as paralysis, now that she couldn't move properly, and the horrible fluorescents of the nighttime hospital and the windowless room and the long, long descent.

Anthea didn't go see her right away. She stayed at home in her old bedroom, in front of her old computer while her parents and Hazel's niece Beatrice shuttled back and forth to the hospital, sitting with Hazel as she came down from three days of hallucinations. Anthea stayed in her room while Colm talked to his sister Ada, and explained about Hazel's condition. Ada did not join them, though she asked for regular updates, which was more than anyone expected. Anthea played solitaire, and sometimes talked to Jasmine, and avoided calls from high school friends who wanted a reunion party, which was silly because they'd only been out of school four years. She wrote long emails to the boy she'd met at the last party of the semester, without mentioning the most important part of her visit home: Hazel with the plastic bag and the thin, black ribbon around her throat.

When it was time, Colm took her to the hospital. On the way, he tried to explain things, starting out, "The way she speaks. It's not always easy to follow." Then he said, "And she's changed quite a bit."

"Okay," Anthea said.

They were on the highway where it brinked the spiny ridge of mountains. Anthea looked up the stone face toward the summit, then down to the inlet below, and over the peninsula toward the islands, and beyond those, the strait.

"It's hard for her. She can't say what she means, even though she tries really really hard. And she keeps trying hard, all day long, when you sit beside her. She doesn't seem to sleep much."

She looked up through the stones and down to the water as it narrowed to a mudflat, then a creek, and said, "In *On The Beach*, when they take the nuclear sub down to Bellingham and Seattle, they pass by a place sort of close to here, and they see there's like a whole bunch of forest burnt out, and they say that probably an airburst went off short of its target. I guess the target would be the base? Or maybe the test range at Nanoose?"

"Why are you reading about that? That's the stuff that scares you." Years later, when she remembered that afternoon, Anthea coiled her fingers into fists so tight that her nails bit the palms of her hands and left red crescents in the skin. Of all the events around Hazel's suicide, it was the afternoon ride with Colm that brought to her heart a regret so deep and tidal it might have been the Pacific that lay west beyond the mountains. An instant, when the pickup flashed between light and shadow on the highway, with the narrowing inlet below them and the flashblinding on the mountains above them, that moment mushroomed, and she felt it now, Colm's silence, her empty talk.

"Okay, that was like a million years ago? I'm not scared of it now. Now it's just interesting." Colm didn't get it, and how she was just trying to make conversation.

The truck was warm and Anthea yawned. She thought about the scar of an airburst and how they'd discussed the *nuclear singularity* in a cultural studies course, which she knew Colm would find strange. He'd shake his head and talk about the practical effects of compression waves, and use terms like *p.s.i.* and *kilopascals* and *shear stress.* He'd point out that a nuclear detonation wasn't singular, because it had happened at Hiroshima and Nagasaki and Bikini Atoll and Nevada and in the northern deserts of India and deep underground in places they'd never know. It couldn't be singular, because it started at one place in one moment and moved through matter at a speed measured in time, even if that speed was so great it seemed an instant to the human brain. The word "singularity," he said, should be preserved for things that are properly singular.

When they arrived she was not prepared to feel as sick as she did walking down the brown-tiled wing of the old hospital, down the windowless hall decorated with amateur oil paintings. Down the corridor lined with hampers full of sheets the colour of pee stains, or a faded green like the blades of grass that try to grow up through sheds and under old cars. She could not bear to look closely at remaindered meal trays, bloody Jell-O stains, the pools of sticky, ash-coloured gravy, and above it all the smell of piss and the sweetish-salty aroma of institutional chicken fat from old suppers unexorcised.

They went through a door to a four-bed room of old women, surrounded by wilting flowers and stainless steel spit trays and bedpans. There was Hazel with white hairs covering her chin, which Anthea had never before seen, long, thick ones like the spines of a cactus. Her eyes seemed to stare at something they couldn't see, something in the middle of the room, five feet from the floor. Anthea had not meant to, but she found herself standing in that place, the unintentional object of her grandmother's slack gaze. She felt Colm behind her, and heard the long, deep breaths he made when he was trying not to be upset. Then one of his hands wrapped around hers and squeezed, and she did not know if it was for her comfort or his. She was preoccupied with Hazel's pale, wet eyes that looked back at her without seeming to see, and with the way the muscles behind her skin seemed to free-fall from the left side of her cheek and jaw.

Anthea stepped back into Colm.

"It's alright, sweetheart, it's alright," he said. "It's alright."

She said, "I'm okay."

Hazel raised her right hand. It looked like Colm's, except that her fingers curled about one another like the petals of some heavy, fleshy flower, a lily or a camellia. Her fingernails were dirty. Colm led Anthea closer to her grandmother, and with his left hand picked Hazel's arm out of the air, where it hung as though she had forgotten about it.

"Hey there, Hazel, hey there. How are you doing?"

Hazel, her hand in Colm's, opened her mouth and closed it again.

"Pudding," she said. Only it came out like she was full of marbles, a spit-choked plosive trailing off. *Pu-in.*

"Oh yeah? You had pudding? Was it tasty? What kind?"

Hazel patted the tray with her left hand, and dabbed at the mush-room-coloured remains of her lunch pudding.

Anthea looked away.

Colm fumbled for a Kleenex, and inexpertly wiped his mother's hand. "You alright there, Panther?"

"Ann-ah," Hazel said. She stopped. "Nuh," she said. She reached away from Colm's ineffectual Kleenex, and when her fingers touched Anthea's skin they were cold. She could feel the smear of pudding spread irrevoca-bly over her own fingers.

"Fin-uh. Bay-hen. Boo-fu," Hazel said. She chuckled then, and patted Anthea's hand with the fist that was like the bud of a decaying flower.

A month later Hazel came home to her old bedroom. She had stated in her suicide note that she wanted to die on her own terms, without the indignities of the hospital, and when the doctors said the time was near, Colm and Tess and Bea arranged the move, informing Ada, who still did not join them.

They sat with her on shifts, with Colm sitting two hours for everyone else's one. Anthea didn't know how he stood it, hour after hour in there with Hazel, who spoke so urgently each time she crept to consciousness, though there was no way to understand or answer her garbled speech, or do anything but hold her hot, dry hands as they plucked at your arms and your face.

On the first morning, Colm sat at the dining room table, filling syringes with a liquid morphine derivate, the tiny vials in a box beside him. Opposite him, Anthea watched the methodical taptap on the side of the syringe, and watched the bubbles rise, and the growing cup of 4 mL doses to his right. They said nothing. It was a bright day, and Anthea blinked in the sunshine. It was hot on that side of the house, facing the water.

The longer Hazel lay in the bedroom, the more her bones seemed to show in her face, along her wrists, her skull newly apparent through her thin, grey skin. She took the morphine derivative from the syringe, absorbed it through the mucus membranes in her cheek. She took it every four hours. Anthea was not yet allowed to measure doses, but she and Max had each taken a shift at her bedside, while their parents and Hazel's niece Bea slept on couches and foamies around the house.

When her shift was over, Anthea went out onto the deck and looked across the inlet toward the airport. She looked down at the water under moonlight and thought how much deeper it seemed at night. When she slept, she dreamed about all the submerged geographies, and the creatures that lived among them, about whales and octopus, the jellyfish blooms they saw in summer, and phosphorescent algae, and the deeper, colder places they could not see, valleys and plains that stretched out beneath the water, and far away to the west whole mountain ranges sunk in the dark parts of the ocean.

The next afternoon she and Max followed the short path down to the beach for a few minutes of clean air, and sat together skipping shells on the water. Max beat her with six skips. She couldn't crack five. Above them, in her bedroom, Hazel's lungs rattled like a rusty pump through the long, bright afternoon, through the darkening blue of evening, and into her second night unconscious. Every four hours the drug seeped through her mucus membranes and into her blood, so she remained beneath the surface of things. Some time that evening—a moment none of them recognized—she passed from sleep into coma. Outside, Anthea felt the night sky press down upon her head, the stars in deep space seemed so close, and so heavy, she could reach up and touch them.

Colm was with Hazel when the end came before dawn on the third day. The house was silent and the birds had not yet begun to sing. As they waited together, the dark around them lifted, and a patch of sky above the trees—not light, but lighter than the woods—showed in the window. He knew his family slept just on the other side of the door, but that seemed very far away, while the room in which Hazel lay measured the whole world, as though a globe of some subtle element enclosed just the two of them.

The steady, rusty noise of her lungs had not altered since late afternoon, but now the first change had come upon them. In his exhaustion he did not realize it for some time, but when he noticed the new sound he leaned toward the bed. In the dim light of the window, her eyes seemed to flicker, and for a moment he thought she had surfaced from her coma and, for the first time in days, looked at him. She made a noise—a sound of surprise, as though she saw something she had not expected—and then her breathing changed again. Each breath was quieter and shallower. She drew one more, and he touched her throat and felt her slowing pulse against his fingertips.

The birds outside singing. The scrap of sky above the trees illuminated. He waited with her for an hour and then leaned across his mother's body and kissed her forehead. Her skin was cool against his lips. First he was surprised at the touch of her skin, but with it he knew she was dead, and this was his last sight of her on earth. He thought then of her brain, beneath the bone, already gone, and of the margins of her body as they lost to the invading world. The stilled blood pooled in her heart and then coagulated, the electrical impulses no longer travelled along her nerves to light the deep reaches of her mind.

She has flipped the switch and it is dark. She had locked the door behind her. Here on earth only the organs of memory in collapse, and with them gone sensations and flavours, voices, music. And returned to mud and ash those parts of her experience she did not speak, the last sparks rendered untranslatable as they fire, at random, in the closing moments of her life. There were questions he could not ask, there were answers he wished to possess, and secrets he would never know, and explanations. And all that receding from him, as he was carried forward alive and her body remained behind, her flesh going first, falling in on the bones that supported it in the absence of her soul, but soon the bones gone, and then the dust.

REMITTANCE GIRL

Anthea had never seen a will before she saw Hazel's, which was delivered to her residence on an afternoon late in September, a month after her grandmother's death. She signed a form and the courier handed over a large buff envelope. First she thought that it was Colm's way of including both her and Max in the business of inheritance. But then she unfolded the sheets and found her name listed after Colm's, who was the executor, and beside that an article detailing her inheritance. Ada's name did not appear.

She sat on the floor of her dorm room and looked at the number, and plans blossomed in her mind: a doctorate, travel, a warm thought between her and the world. It came, for no reason she could discern, from Hazel. She thought of her grandmother as she always did now, in a plastic bag with a narrow black ribbon at her throat, but now signing the papers. And though the will had transformed her life, it gave no reason for Hazel's decision.

She phoned Colm and said, "I got a thing in the mail."

For the first time she realized how much his voice had changed since Hazel died. "Yeah. No," he said. Then he said, "Panther," and finally, "I don't know about it. I guess you'll have to talk to the lawyer."

"But why would she do that?"

She heard him breathe in and out again. Finally he said, "I don't know."

Suddenly the will, which had felt a moment before like the explosion of opportunity, seemed shameful.

"I didn't mean it. I didn't do anything. I didn't, Dad."

"I know."

"She called me before she did it."

"Did she? It's okay if she called. It's okay."

"But I didn't do anything. I didn't mean it." She knew she shouldn't say it again, but she did, because Colm seemed to think she had done something wrong, that she had made it happen.

She wanted him to tell her it wasn't her fault—that Hazel's will was like her suicide, out of their hands and beyond their powers to understand.

"It's alright," was all Colm said. For a moment she felt better, then he said, "It's alright," and the second time it meant less, and then the third time it meant nothing at all.

When she picked up the envelope there seemed to be a faint scent of corruption about it, one that she worried would cling to her, even as it made her into a little-time gentlewoman, a remittance girl.

THE KILGOURS OF THE WEST: TEMPLE THEATRE INSTALLATION CAPTIONS. FINAL DRAFT

CAPTION ONE On a day in February of 1921, Mrs. Leticia Kilgour stepped out of her private car in a small town called Duncan's Crossing. In attendance on Mrs. Kilgour were her daughter, secretary, two maids, a nurse and a footman. She carried in one hand a dove-grey Dorothy bag of Italian leather, containing handkerchief, peppermints, lorgnette, and a prescribed soporific, tincture of opium, to be taken as required. Looking across the tidy station green toward the cenotaph, Mrs. Kilgour thought of her middle son, Clive, who had gone overseas in 1916. His two brothers had declined commissions because they were needed on the home front, but Clive had joined Princess Patricia's Canadian Light Infantry, and set out with the finest kit Mrs. Kilgour could secure in three months.

At the time she had enjoyed her tears, and thought about sacrifice and the wonder of motherhood and how handsome Clive was. She thought how, in pictures, there was nothing to pick between the portrait of Clive that Lyon had taken on the week before he left in a first class berth to Edmonton, and Herbert Asquith's that was in all the papers. Mrs. Kilgour liked to think of their visible equality because she knew objectively that Herbert Asquith was a gentleman: his father was Prime Minister and he had written a book of poetry. Mrs. Kilgour was a proud mother in 1916. She hosted the Red Cross ladies once a month.

CAPTION TWO Mrs. Kilgour performed at the Temple Theatre in 1921, and then in a series of concerts along the coast in Kilgour-owned coal towns. When Clive left in 1916, she imagined following him to Edmonton and then England. She would do it, and contribute a little to the Kilgour family military glory that was, she knew, imminent. She thought about it often, though her work for the Kilgour family legacy and for the working man's lot compelled her to stay. In 1917, she resolved to join Clive, and early in 1918 she prepared to go. But news met her in Toronto that he was missing and presumed dead. She returned to a long illness and convalescence at Craiglockhart Castle, where all the mirrors were covered. Wreaths of yew, California cypress, and black grosgrain ribbon hung on the doors.

CAPTION THREE Two things sped Mrs. Kilgour's recovery: her commitment to the betterment of the working man's lot, and her commitment to the muse. Happily, the two were related, and she was sure that the workingman's lot would be bettered by song as often as it was by lectures on hygiene and cookery. Of course, Mrs. Kilgour preferred to teach by example, which is why she hosted those bucolic parties in the vegetable garden at Craiglockhart, so wives and miners might see what clean linen and freshly-scrubbed tabletops were like, and want them for themselves.

In 1919, more than a year after Clive's death, she arranged a party, and told her guests to look on the garden as a temporarily public pleasure-ground, a respite from the ugliness of the city, a reminder of finer, greener things. Her guests disappointed her. They wore straw boaters and ready-made suits and dresses from Woodward's. She had hoped they would know better and not show up smelling of *Quelques Fleurs* and Florida water, but of good green things, and sun-dried linens. They sang and played on ukuleles, and some of the men got drunk from flasks they smuggled in and took a boat out on the ornamental lake.

CAPTION FOUR The thing of it is, I'm thinking Mrs. Kilgour really didn't care that much about the working man's lot or his wife's. This, for instance, is the plan for a model village built near one of their coalmines north of Duncan's Crossing. Despite all their benevolent language, it was a company town with company stores and a company church—Presbyterian—and when the IWW moved in, there were strikebreakers. You should think about the village now: Condos in the old Admin buildings and the re-fit cottages selling for millions. The church, however, didn't survive. It was bombed during one of the long strikes of the late teens.

CAPTION FIVE Clive disappeared in 1918 during a Phosgene gas attack on the Allied line at Bois de l'Abbé. Carbonyl Chloride—called Phosgene in its weaponized form—does not immediately kill its victims. Once inhaled, it hydrolyzes in the lungs, turning to carbon dioxide and hydrochloric acid when it encounters water. There's oedema, then death. Men drown on dry land, coughing up water and blood.

Those who have survived an encounter with Phosgene gas say that it smells like hay. It is hard not to think of Clive lying in his trench and breathing deeply the night air when *from the fields there comes a breath of new mown hay*. It would smell like home, like the fields around their country place outside Duncan's Crossing, where he spent his summers as a child. He thinks of those summers and the gas slips between his lips and down through his throat, his sinuses. It settles in his eyes and in his mouth, along his tongue and soft palate. A little later he begins to cough.

He was MIA-presumed-dead until the end of the war. It wasn't until early 1921 that representatives of the Imperial War Graves Commission identified his remains, whatever that means. They removed him to a nearby military cemetery and contacted his family. When she received the telegram, Mrs. Kilgour abandoned her musical ambitions and left for France to bring Clive home. She would bury him on the grounds of Craiglockhart, beside his father. The IWGC refused her permission and he remained in the battlefield cemetery, marked only by a white stone bearing his name and dates and a maple leaf. This was unacceptable to Mrs. Kilgour, with her new family graveyard that held, as yet, only four stones: the Kilgours needed to accumulate their beloved dead if they were to make a place for themselves in western Canada's aristocracy.

CAPTION SIX Springtime in Picardy. Roses. Poplars. Hay fields. Mrs. Kilgour has hired two farmers and their wagon and their big, slow horses. They meet her at the gravesite and together begin digging until they unearth the narrow box in which lie the earthly remains of Clive Kilgour, her brave laddie. It's nailed shut. She would like to open it, but she is content to hurry now. Later there will be ceremonies, and more wreaths and flowers and speeches. The night is still and safe until after they've loaded him onto the wagon and are making their way down the white road in the moonlight and Mrs. Kilgour sings *She is standing and watching and waiting where the long white roadway lies—*

That's when the horses bolt. Mrs. Kilgour, who is a remarkably strong woman for all her ladylike manner, hangs onto the sides of the wagon and is knocked from her seat to the floor. Clive in his box is not so lucky, and when they hit a hole in the roadbed the wagon jumps, and Clive jumps and then slides out the back, the plain box splitting as it hits the earth, still sliding with the momentum of the bolt. Clive leaps out of his box and scatters himself over the earth, and his mother sees the bare outline of his disintegration, her brave laddie now unidentified refuse on the long white roadway, receding into the moonlight as the horses drive her further and further from her son.

CAPTION SEVEN People notice. The bones in the road, the weeping woman, the farmers shy and doubtful. Mr. Goshawk is particularly useful under these circumstances, as Mrs. Kilgour retires into her hysterical grief and refuses to speak to the representatives of the IWGC. The graveyards must be left intact, they explain. Clive will remain in France, collected from the long white road, reassembled in another narrow box, re-interred beneath the white stone with the maple leaf upon it.

There will be no body for the Kilgour graveyard. Mrs. Kilgour will be the last buried there, and when, in later years, Craiglockhart Castle becomes a public building, the five family graves will be fenced and carefully tended, and people who come on them unexpectedly will stop to look at the elaborate headstones with their carved poppies and angels and Latin: the last, curious evidence of an obscure dynasty.

She emailed the document to Dr. Blake on Thursday, which was only one day past the deadline, so she thought she was doing pretty well. She was surprised when he arranged a meeting for the next morning.

The first thing she said to him was, "I know it's a bit short. I know that." She was excited. She was even proud.

"It's a bit short, yeah," he said. Dr. Blake rubbed his forehead, then his nose. Then he closed his eyes. "Sit down, okay? Brynn came to see me yesterday." His voice flat and neutral. "She's been doing some survey work on Mrs. Kilgour's musical ambitions, especially the recordings. She's thinking we should release them. Might generate some revenue for the Institute. You know." That last bit trailed into silence.

"Is everything okay?" she asked. He shrugged, opened his mouth as though to say more and then closed it again, so she went on by herself. "Okay. I know it's short, and we need a few more pictures, but that's not going to be difficult. I mean, now that we have a story."

When he spoke he stared at the little stack of papers rather than look at her. "Brynn says some stuff is missing."

"Missing?"

"She says it's hard to tell, considering the state of the room, but there are a couple of boxes on the manifest that she can't find. I've heard that things are pretty bad down there."

"Okay. But. Yeah, my process is a bit *chaotic*. But the captions—"

He spoke sharply: "Anthea, the captions aren't what we need. I have a hard time believing you don't know that. They're useless and they're inappropriate. We don't need grave robbers."

"It's relevant. It's an important—"

"We don't need chemical weapons."

"Yeah. But. I'd love to read that in a museum."

"It took you less than two weeks to destroy the filing system in Rm 023. And remove half the materials. And write this. This. Thing." He flicked the paper on his desk. "And it's late. You're not a student anymore. You're actually an employee, Anthea. This is a job."

It was a long time before she said anything, and when she did her words were directed at the desk, as she kept her hot face away from him. "It was," she said. "I had. There was. There was a plan. I had a plan. For things. To make the."

"At this point it's out of my hands," he said. "I mean. I mean. It's just *theft*. We'll give you an opportunity to return everything, though. Assuming you can?"

She nodded. Then she said again, "I had a plan."

Blake scrunched his face. "Anthea, why did you even *take* the job?"

"The thing with grave robbing. It's interesting. I don't know why you wouldn't want to know that about Mrs. Kilgour. It makes her so much less boring. It makes her *amazing*."

"Were you ever interested in what we do? Do you even know what we do?"

Anthea didn't know what to say. When she looked up at Blake, wordless, she hoped for a moment that the frustration on his face would resolve into understanding, or compassion. She wondered if she should make evident the real circumstances of her life. But then Blake was looking at her with the wrinkle of antipathy on his brow, and if he looked that way before she spoke, what would he think when she talked about suicide and curses, or dead things in the attic?

"I don't know what to do."

"I think you've already done it."

"I can fix them."

"I think," he began, then began again. "We'd recommend that you leave. If we keep this really simple, I might be able to do a reference. I guess. But not for anything archival."

When he said that last thing the future went suddenly blank. A month ago she had hated the future, which appeared to her as a dull, forty-year road that terminated in a gold watch and an encyclopedic knowledge of Mrs. Kilgour's domestic arrangements. But now the future contained nothing at all, and stretched no further than the hours it would take her to collect her things and return what she had borrowed.

There on the desk were four sheets of paper, the work of ten days and how many hours meditating on the detritus of Rm 023. Once those sheets had seemed important, but now they were devoid of meaning despite the black marks scattered over their surfaces. Once, in the world that had a future, bits of paper like that had been important.

She said, "Okay." She wondered if she would miss him, or Brynn with her matronly advice, or the half-buried room the R.A.s shared. She knew she would miss campus, and the clammy air of Rm 023.

She had liked Mrs. Kilgour. "Okay," she said again and this time he looked at her.

"I think you should head out, Anthea. I think that would best for everyone. I think that would be best for you, too. This was never a good fit."

She had always known the Institute was a bad fit for her. She had gone into it knowing, had thought of the job as expiation, a relic of a career *in memoriam* to Hazel's thwarted intellectual ambitions. Despite knowing that, she was shocked to find that she was an equally bad fit for the Institute. It was some kind of misunderstanding. She wasn't a thief, after all; she had only borrowed those things as part of her research, to find and make apparent the other order in Rm 023, to illuminate correspondences, to discover answers submerged in the room's flotsam. When she left, Dr. Blake would look at the captions again, and he would perceive that order and recognize the work she had done, and then there would be a phone call and then the future would come into being again. It was some kind of misunderstanding. He would.

NOBODY GETS OVER ANYTHING

Anthea was unemployed in an apartment made unbearable by both its squalor and its smell. In the last dry week of the year—the last of September—she followed Mrs. Layton's instructions, and filled whole days and nights with walking. She walked past the squeegee kids, the corner boys, past the missions. While she wandered, she held his image in her mind:

dark blond hair, parted in the middle and winging his brow and temples. Eyes beer-bottle brown. Tan, barefoot, carrying an army surplus kitbag on one shoulder, a drum over his hip, and the Bible in his back pocket wearing a white rectangle in the denim that covered his lovely ass.

The first afternoon of unemployment, she walked to the place with the greasy green net curtains where she and Jasmine once ate $3.99 breakfast specials, and down to the water again, and then across the throat of the peninsula to the inlet on the other side, and along the inlet to the park, and along the park's seawall as far as the giant stone that stood knee-deep in the water. She climbed over the barrier and down the rocks to the tide line. She thought of Hazel's story that the rock was a man who so loved his unborn son that he took his wife into the wilderness when she was nine months pregnant. Together they swam until they washed away their human scent, the salt water leaving them so pure they were no threat or disruption to the forest. The wild creatures approached them, deer and otters and squirrels. And then something huge and awful took notice, and for his piety the three were turned to stone. Hazel said the wife and son were smaller stones in the woods above the seawall, where Anthea couldn't see them. The man, though, who lit out into the wilderness in search of inhuman purity, he was before her.

Hazel was wrong, though, or she didn't want to tell Anthea the truth: the man still stood in the water, but the wife and child had been dynamited when they built the seawall around the park. They were underfoot, reconfigured into fill for a bike path.

Below her the tide was out. His feet were covered in mussels and rockweed and barnacles, with purple starfish at the water line. She picked up a rock and threw it at him. It made a flat sound when it struck. She threw another and another and another, and then climbed back onto the path and finished her circumnavigation.

For a week Anthea spent her mornings at the lunch counter Mrs. Layton had named, sitting in one of the orange melamine booths at the back, watching the door, drinking coffee and leaving large tips to pay for her three hour occupations. She didn't bring a book. She didn't order food.

She spent her afternoons walking. Sometimes she worried that this course of action would produce nothing but further pennilessness, no prospects, and Jasmine's prophet slipped away before the weather turned, gone to ground for the autumn, or south across the border to a more hospitable climate. He might not come back to the orange melamine. She might have missed him entirely, and would wait the winter out at one of the tables, hoping for his return. She imagined there were women all over the city hoping for his return, though she guessed she was the only brunette.

She was luckier than that. Afterward, she could not say which of those days it was, but when she had been sitting in her booth for an hour she looked up to see him the doorway. He was alone and barefoot.

She joined him at the counter. "Hi," was all she said at first.

He looked down at her. After a moment he said, "Hey."

"Mrs. Layton sent me," she said.

"I know." His weight shifted onto his forward foot, now so close that she looked up into his face. "Mrs. Layton is cool."

"She sent me because I wanted to know something. A friend of mine is missing. I think you knew her."

His weight shifted back again.

"Do you know where Jasmine is?"

The woman at the counter brought him coffee in a paper cup. He pulled change from his pocket, but she shook her head. Jasmine's prophet bowed and said, "Namaste. Parach al mech. Mech lanoch ech Simoni Deo Sancto leukos!" Then he turned to the door.

Anthea followed him. "Okay," she said, "the thing of it is. The thing of it is I haven't heard from her for a while. I haven't heard from her and I want to talk to her. I miss her. Her mom wants to know where she is."

He said nothing. He walked slowly eastward along the sidewalk, drinking his coffee. She walked beside him.

"Please," she said. "Mrs. Layton sent me."

He stopped and swivelled, watching her with bright eyes, set in a face that was darkly tanned under his light hair. He was so still he might have been carved from wood, some statue uncovered in a sanctuary devoted to a god whose name has been forgotten. He was beautiful.

"I knew Jasmine," he said.

"Will you tell me where she is?"

He said nothing, but he also didn't stop. She wanted some confirmation of his willingness to take her to Jas, or explain what had happened, but in the absence of a "no" she followed him.

They walked six blocks further east, leaving Chinatown behind, and the busy intersections where he usually worked. He didn't speak to her. When he met someone he knew, he bowed and sounded guttural syllables, and Greek, and liquids that reminded her of Tolkien, telling them things she didn't understand. One of them offered him money, a handful of sticky-looking coins fresh from the bottle exchange. Jasmine's prophet accepted the fealty and laid his hands on either side of the man's face, and they stood for a moment forehead to forehead.

"She never told me your name," Anthea said, when they had done. She hoped he would lie.

He nodded. "Yeah. Jasmine called me Menander."

"Okay."

"You can call me Menander."

"Okay."

They walked on. There were fewer people on the street when they turned off the main strip toward residential houses built on the slope down to the inlet. These streets were quiet and dirty. There were chesterfields on front porches and long grass full of garbage. She saw an old grocery cart. She saw a building with "condemned" spray-painted on the pressboard that covered the windows and doors.

Menander pointed at that building and said, "They went in there, you know, last month. The basement was full of KFC buckets. The buckets were full of shit. No water, right. Got shut off. They just bought KFC and then shit in the buckets."

They left the street and turned right down a broken cement walk, then up wooden steps that gave under her weight.

"Is Jasmine here?" she asked, but could not believe it. Jasmine, for all her bohemianism, did not like grubbiness. She would have swept the steps. She would have removed the fast food wrappers.

"No," said Menander.

"Then why are we here?" He opened the door for her, and she stepped through it into the close, dark air of the house.

When her eyes adjusted, she saw blankets and flags over all the windows. There was an old mattress on the floor, and sleeping bags. There were lumps that were probably people. There were the paper-bagged remains of fast food meals: KFC, McDs, DQ. Menander climbed the stairs to their left. She stepped over the fallen banister to follow him.

This had once been a nice place, she thought as she climbed. Once it was owned by a nice young couple, just starting out after the First World War. Once it had cost them four thousand dollars. They kept the grass short and the trim painted. They invited neighbours around for lemonade on the front porch, when it was hot in July and August.

Menander paused at the top of the stairs.

"I want to know where Jasmine is," she said. "I want to know." It would be nice again, these squats washed away as real estate prices rose in a slow, eastbound wave. Not for young couples starting out, though, or those with modest aspirations. They wouldn't be able to afford it.

He walked away from her into one of the rooms that faced the street. She saw incense ash on the windowsill. A crucifix, Tibetan prayer flags, a bunch of dead flowers, Ganesh, a pack of Tarot cards, a black-beaded rosary with a clasp like a necklace. Despite the incense, there was an animal edge to the air: the smell of squirrels in the attic, rats or mice. Pigeons moaning in the eaves. Unwashed bodies. There were books on the floor, too, an old futon stippled with damp, a sleeping bag, two backpacks spilling their contents.

He was very close to her. So close that she felt his breath on her forehead, a moist current of tobacco ash in the sweetish-sick smelling room. He turned away to light a stick of incense. Patchouli. They faced one another again.

Anthea looked at his bottom lip. He wet it with a tiny flicker of his tongue. She thought, *If he was another sort of man, and this was another sort of situation, I would think he was going to kiss me.*

"I don't know where Jasmine is," he said. "Not now."

"Okay. You were the last to see her."

"No. I wasn't. I don't know where she is. I just know that she's gone away." With his right thumb he traced a sigil in the air between them. "But there's more to it than that. We can tell you things."

Then he leaned into her and kissed her forehead. Then he kissed her cheek. Then he took her wrists in his hands and held them and kissed her mouth. She gently unwound his fingers and hit him across his left ear. It was a while since she'd hit anyone, and she was surprised how much it hurt, but then she hit him again. That time she struck his arm when he blocked her hand, but she shoved him away and lunged for the statue of Ganesh, which turned out to be plastic, but by then she didn't care. She threw it at his face. She followed that with the crucifix, then the rosary and the dead flowers, then the Tarot cards. After that she looked around for anything that would break his nose, or crush the perfect cheekbone beneath his left eye. It was not until she ran out of things to throw that she considered how profoundly stupid she had been. It was as stupid as following him to a squat when no one knew where she had gone.

Menander, however, did not seem much bothered. He rubbed his cheek and sat down on the futon, where the plastic Ganesh lay, upside down. He reached into one of the backpacks beside him for a pack of smokes and lit one.

"Your problem," he said, as he dragged on it and blew smoke toward her across the room, "is your shitty attitude. You don't even know what the fuck you're doing, and you go raise the dead and then think you can walk away from them. Jasmine knew you guys had to make amends."

He offered her the pack of cigarettes. Her hands were in fists, even though her right knuckles ached. She would hit him again if he came any closer.

"Parach lo leukma. Do you know what Parach means?"

She said nothing.

"If you don't know," he said, "you can't ever know. It's not the kind of thing you find in a dictionary. Some people hear it and they follow it because they remember the truth. We call them Those Who Are. But there are other people who won't ever understand."

"Those Who Aren't?" Anthea asked, and wanted to laugh. He didn't say anything for another moment.

"Funny shit. You're going to run away from here. That won't make any difference. But that's okay, it's all going to hit the fan pretty soon. Jas knew that. Teotwawki. If you are on the plains, head for the hills.

Let them which be in the city flee into the mountains. She knew it couldn't last."

He was right. Jas always knew.

"If you were as smart as you think you are, you'd come with me to Mrs. Layton's. Sell what you own. Hand over all that money you know you don't deserve. Make amends and hope you'll be forgiven before it all happens." Then he said "Parach" and she fled the room, down the broken stairs to the front door, and across the broken pavement to the sidewalk. From there, she ran along littered streets where grass grew in all the cracks, and dandelions, and Queen Anne's lace, and the rats and the squirrels nested and the pigeons in the attics and the leaves were not swept away from the pavement, and the roofs sagged and then fell in and they might as well spray-paint "condemned" across the whole city and walk out, into the mountains beyond.

At home she crouched on the floor with all her papers, her candle stubs, her teacups and wineglasses, and the dead thing in the attic. She cradled her right hand, with its swollen knuckles. After a long while, her knees on the hardwood ached, and then she lay down and felt the base of her spine against the floor as well, the bones of her skull, her shoulder blades, her elbows, her heels.

The phone rang three times. She didn't answer. All spring and summer her voicemail had filled up with calls she rarely answered: Colm, Brynn, Max, friends from out of town, from high school, cousins, the sound of a room full of cold callers. And someone else, who didn't seem to be in a room full of cold callers, but who left no messages. Different numbers on caller display: different payphones, but the same silence.

In the late spring and early summer she had been pretty sure it was Jasmine. Jasmine being difficult, requiring—as she had always done—that Anthea know without being told. She was tired of it. She wouldn't do it again, not even if Jasmine came back and got a proper job and finished her degree and cared about the things Anthea did, and dated a not-crazy not-gnostic-street-priest kind of guy.

Then, one evening in June, the phone rang six times in a row from the same number. Anthea resolved that the next time she would pick up. She thought about what she'd say, perhaps just *what*? Max said he answered the phone like that because it put people off immediately.

She sat on the floor beside the phone with a glass of wine. She watched it. After fifteen minutes it rang again. She let it go twice.

"What?"

One breath exhaled.

"*What?*" There was a sound like a mouth opening. Then all she heard was traffic, somewhere loud and open near a highway.

"Jasmine. Is that you?" She knew her voice had squeaked sharply on the name, but after that she couldn't remember what she said, only that she had been angry. Before she lifted the phone her head was full of all the awful things she felt: no words, only the intensity of her emotion. She was happy, now, for the chance to make Jasmine's head ring with all the things she had done wrong, all her vapid pursuit of fictional gnosis, all her little cruelties and pretensions.

In the end, that rage and pleasure was all Anthea could remember, and she hated the memory of her own anger more than she ever hated anything Jasmine had done wrong. Four months later and she accepted that her last living encounter with Jasmine witnessed her own small, venal heart.

When she finished saying whatever it was she said, she thought a truck passed close by the phone's mouthpiece. When it had faded, there was again a small noise like a mouth opening and closing, then the fumbled click of the receiver hung up and then a crackle and the line sounding empty. It was not enough, though; she wanted to say more, and she wanted Jasmine to answer, to explain herself, to say something that made sense, and that meant she was listening. She found the number on caller display, but when she dialled, it rang and rang, and no one answered. She dialled again, then again. She wrote down the number and waited half an hour, and rang again.

No one ever answered it. No one ever would. But because she was the sort of person who kept things, she tucked the Post-it into the back of a desk drawer, where it could be lost among other scraps of paper, but remain.

Lying on the floor with all her bones settled into the scarred hardwood, she thought of the drawer and of the bits of paper among which she had lost the number. She sat up and crawled over to the desk, and pulled the whole thing out, and emptied it onto the floor with everything else, and began sorting: there were phone numbers on napkins she had never called; the birthday card her grandfather Max gave her when she turned twelve; the letter confirming that she had a job at the Institute; messages from boys she no longer spoke to; Hazel's will and suicide note. At the bottom, under candy wrappers and recipes, there was a pink Post-it with one of her hairs stuck to the back. When she touched it she felt sure, and straightened the creases and turned it over.

She dialled the number, and as she did, something took shape in her mind, a vision of the Glass Castle with the payphone outside the main office. If there was a way to dial Jasmine's ghost, it might have been on that bit of pink paper with her hair stuck to the back. The line it opened would reach back to the Glass Castle on an evening in the spring before. She listened to the ring of the payphone, and imagined she heard its echo, across the parking lot and out to the highway, and then careening into the woods and fields until it was lost in the green.

Mrs. Layton was wrong when she told Anthea to make amends, feed the hungry ghosts and put them to rest. You can telephone the dead, she thought, and you can tell them how sorry you are, and how much you miss them, but they don't have to answer.

XHAAIDLAGHA GWAAYAAI

Max said Hazel should go, after supper one night. He was sitting by the stove. He was almost asleep. The boot he had been polishing hung in his hand for a moment, before he set it carefully on the newspapers he had spread in front of his chair. She hated watching him spread the newspapers, the old-lady way he did it, and thinking it pleased her because it saved the floor. She also hated watching him clean her shoes as he did twice a week, caking the polish all over, then carefully buffing it, always so slow and laborious. She told him that her father used to use a match and got them just as glossy and that was faster, but he shook his head. He sat in his undershirt, with his suspenders down. His huge, grease-stained hand picked up the next boot and turned it over and over as he spoke. He said, "Alright, Hazel, why don't you go and stay with your mother for a bit?" And she hadn't said anything either, though he said it as though it was part of a conversation they were having. She hadn't said anything, hadn't complained. She had been doing dishes, and when he spoke, she stopped with her hands wrist-deep in the cooling grey dishwater, not liking to look at him, or at his hands with each graze black-stained, though he scrubbed them before he came in the door, and the stubby nails he cut with his pocket knife. Or the callouses, though she liked them scratching her back at night.

It was hard to believe that the Gwaii was only a few days from home. She did not like the darkness of the islands; it made her uneasy. The little cottages around the base, all tarpaper shacks with no running water, looked like old cabbage lumps in the wet, and it was twilight all the time. The new baby was heavy on her, seven months along, and her daughter Ada pinched and silent in a way that Hazel hated, so she wished Ada would stamp her feet and shout for what she wanted. She worried that she did not like her own child and that she wouldn't be the mother her own mother had been. She did not tell Max these things.

She learned to cook for him when he came off shift, mostly from their ground beef ration and potatoes. In the first month she was lavish with the beef, and ran through their week's allotment in three days, so they lived on hash and the corned beef and sardines his mother sent them sometimes. Her mother sent useless things: once papery cambric handkerchiefs with a cursive "H" in large, machined stitches, another time leg makeup and a black pencil for the seam. Hazel had tins and tins of salmon but didn't know what to do with it, and when she joked about that with one of the girls on her road, the girl told her she had a good recipe and wrote it out:

Salmon & Corn a la Pesce
1 can corn, the medium sized one (not the big one)
1 can of salmon about the same size as the corn can
½ Onion chopped
some salt

Have your oven draft on for at least ten minutes before you cook it. Butter up your pirex dish and mix the corn and salmon up with the onion and salt. Stir stir stir! Put this is in the dish and put it in a hot oven AFTER you've turned off the draft. Bake for about half an hour but make sure onions are done because they will taste aweful! I just remembered that you should add milk if it isn't sloppy enough (at the beginning not when it's out of the oven silly) Yummy yum yum!

That was the first time that Max said she made a fine supper and sounded like he meant it. Her biscuits had been good that day, and he had banged on the table with his fist and said *that was a fine supper*, and she had laughed.

Hazel wrote cheery letters to her mother about life on the base, about how she felt like a gypsy, and how strong and kind and good Max was. And how she had heard stories from the local Indian women, and she was thinking of joining their tribe and writing about it, like Pauline Johnson, only more modern. How clever and quiet and good Ada was. Only the bit about Max was true, and while she knew objectively that he was a good man, sometimes she hated his forbearance. She wanted to fly at him, provoke him to slammed doors and strict orders, anything preferable to that flimsy kindness, which seemed like no asset against the steady rain and the damp, hunched little cabins.

She went visiting sometimes, so Ada could play with other children and she could drink someone else's tea. Ada—such a quiet, dark little girl!—did not resist these visits, but did not seem to enjoy them. She played politely with other children, though her eyes always seemed turned on Hazel. She went where she was sent, came when she was called, was vigilant to all her mother's wishes. She shared her rag doll when commanded to do so. Hazel hoped the next one would be different, would be sunny and get angry and stomp his feet with none of Ada's or Max's quiet, enduring consideration.

Other women's cabins could be almost pretty, though some of the girls were a bit tacky and wore overalls and men's blue jeans when they worked in their tiny gardens or chatted and smoked on the corner. Lots of them went out in curlers with scarves over their heads. None of them were from her neighbourhood. She supposed the girls she'd grown up with would be officers' wives anyway. Well, maybe Max would be an officer someday. Then she'd have bridge parties, and she'd have a girl in, maybe, to do the scrubbing so the floor would be nice when people came by. She hated scrubbing the floor, didn't think it was right when she was so big, and it was so hard to get down or get back up again.

Other women's cabins had red and white checked curtains and ragged bunches of daisies in chipped creamers. One woman—the one who gave her the salmon recipe—papered her kitchen in striped butcher paper. She bragged about how she got it for so cheap from the grocer in town, which of course was important, but it wasn't nice to *brag* about not having money for real paper. Hazel wrote home about it, making it funny, especially about her bragging. She didn't say that the kitchen looked pretty and warm and the paper covered all the raw boards. She didn't say that Mrs. Pesce's house was neat as a pin and there were always sweet-smelling leaves of yarrow or tansy, or bright rosehips from the wasteland in November, on the kitchen table beside the lamp.

She learned to wash clothes in lukewarm water and hard soap that cracked her hands. She learned to bake bread, though for the first months it was spongy and fallen in the middle and hard around the edges. She learned to mend Ada's clothes with coarse white stitches and sew buttons on Max's uniform. She learned to depend on his kindness, and remember how shocking it had been, when they first met, that reservoir of stillness she had found, and how she had longed to sit with him for hours, just him and his quiet. She had not, however, learned to acknowledge it.

"Why don't you go stay with your mother for a bit, do you good, so Ada could see her grandma and her aunt. Be good for you, too, in the city again."

"And how are we going to manage that, Max? Can I just get on a transport from the Gwaii? Can I just go?" She heard in her voice the sarcasm she had hated so much in Claire.

Max said nothing, returned to the steady back-and-forth of his boot brush. The caked polish gave way under his hands first to a dull shine, then a hard parade brightness. Beside him sat two of her own little shoes, already caked with polish, the black leather pumps she wore to church on Sundays and when she visited for tea in the afternoons, that were otherwise useless on the dirt roads of the base.

Hazel was secretly happy that the Japs advanced along the Aleutian Islands, giving some RCAF wives an opportunity to leave the Gwaii. Max told her the Aleutians were a long way from them, and had sketched a map on the back of an envelope, but Hazel allowed herself to panic and talked very fast about rape and the special pain-enhancing wrist-knots she'd seen in a *Life* magazine pictorial about what would happen if the Japs attacked the Pacific coast. Max found a real map to show her, but then she cried harder and Ada began to whine, and he gave up. She wrote Mother the next instant, and used the word "evacuate" several times. The next day, she and Ada were on a transport, crying again, but this time because they were leaving Max to defend the coast against invading Japs armed with pain-enhancing wrist-knots.

After she had been home for a few weeks, she insisted on going downtown. Mother said no, she should rest in her condition and considering what she had been through, with the evacuation, but Hazel couldn't stand the house anymore. *It's too, too grim, darling*, she told an old high school friend on the second afternoon. Dreadful for a young wife and mother, who had endured such hardships and separations and needed cheering up. *Practically haunted*, she said to the same friend, a week later.

It was in the middle of Woodward's, looking at little cotton gloves, that her feet began to hurt, and by the time she was four blocks west of there, she felt one of the sudden, irresistible waves of melancholy and fear that marked late pregnancy for her. Her feet were so very sore and her bag so heavy, and Ada so demanding. She held tight to Ada's hand. For a moment she couldn't imagine what to do next, but the hard part lasted only minutes, and when she surfaced for a moment, she realized she was near the Hudson's Bay Company lunchroom, and she had five dimes and two quarters in her pocket. She would have a cup of tea. It would be good for Ada to see the HBC lunchroom, having spent so many months in those dark islands at the edge of the world. The very thought of the Gwaii gave her shivers, the thought of returning there filled her with dread: the little shack, the darkness, the rain.

In the lunchroom Ada began to whimper. Hazel ignored her at first, finishing her tea and leafing through a magazine, while Ada clutched her sugar cookie, her bottom lip wobbling and her nose snotty. The whimper became a whine.

"What a *mess* you are!" Hazel said to her, then took her to the ladies room, where Ada began to cry good and proper. "Good little girls carry a handkerchief, Ada. Do you have a hankie?"

Ada shook her head no.

"Well, I suppose we'll have to go home, then. I suppose we won't visit the toys, and you won't see the bears. I thought you wanted to see the bears."

"No!" Ada said, but it was not a command; it was long and whiny. "No-oo!" Ada said again.

"If you were a good little girl, darling, you would see the bears. There are bears in the park, too. Perhaps we'll see them one day."

"Bear?" Ada said. "Bear?"

Accepting that she had lost her afternoon out to a child's snotty nose and dirty hands and irrational demands, Hazel cleaned up her daughter in the lady's and took the escalator to the bottom floor, past the jewellery and the perfume, out the big golden oak doors to the street.

It was on the street that she had a curious experience, brushing through the crowds as she dragged Ada toward their stop. The streetcar was coming, and she would not miss it, though Ada hung on her arm and said "No, no" faintly, and, sometimes, "Bear?" She could not imagine where Ada had learned to love bears, real bears, too, not the fuzzy toys that seemed appropriate for a little girl. They often saw them on the Gwaii, when they went out to pick blackberries. The three had been out together at the end of August, before Hazel got too big, and they had seen a black bear squatting among the salal bushes eating constantly and intently. Max had held Ada up and pointed toward the woods, and they had all watched it, and Max had said he was just a young bear, not three years old, and out on his own for the first time. Hazel had been afraid, and made them go back to the jeep without filling their buckets.

On the street with Ada hanging on her arm and slowing her as she pushed toward the stop, Hazel brushed past a man who, for a moment, seemed to touch her wrist with warm fingers, a touch that lingered on her skin long after he was gone in the crowd. As she rushed away from that touch, a familiar shape emerged in her mind and in the corner of her eye, one she had not thought of for years, one so long gone he had seemed a fantasy from her overwrought adolescence and the stunted years of depression that followed on her father's death. They had hardly known each other; it was a few weeks that had bloomed, temporarily, into something enormous that consumed her waking hours and her dreams. But she had recovered, and six months later, it had died back into some lightless part of her mind and heart. She did not often think of him, but as she rushed toward the streetcar a memory—distant and precise—blossomed again in her mind.

At the time, she had thought it was like being splashed with very hot water. She didn't know what she felt, and it was a moment before she had even recognized pain in the reaction of her fast-beating heart, the constriction of her throat and stomach, the prickling skin, the sudden appearance of sweat. And then she had felt her knees go funny and wobbly, and she was glad she was sitting down. She had looked at the floor in front of her feet. The toes of her new shoes were still bright and uncreased. She had bought them because they were so adult—black patent with ankle straps like Joan Crawford—and perhaps Liam would like them. She had saved the money in a dozen tiny ways, skipping church collections, eating nothing. She thought that when they went away, she would need nice shoes.

He hadn't noticed the shoes. He was leaning on the horrible little mantelpiece that never had a fire under it. He stooped slightly to examine one of the stupid little prints on an easel. She thought it was called "The Blue Boy," and looking at it she realized that it hung—in one version or another—in every house she had ever visited as a child, in every front room and guest bedroom and entrance hall. She wondered how many copies of "The Blue Boy" hung in homes and hotels and tea rooms around the city, and wondered why it had been chosen, of all the pictures in the world, to scatter on every wall.

He stared for a long time at the horrible little picture.

"Mr. Manley," she started. He looked up at her, his eyebrows pushed together and his forehead squashed. His mouth was slack and shiny with spit, like he had just licked his lips, and she thought, suddenly, how ridiculous he was, with his jowls beginning to sag on his jaw, and how white and pasty the skin on his bum, and how long were the black hairs under his arms, around his navel. She thought of how his breath had smelled once when he kissed her after eating garlic, in itself a disgusting habit that nice people didn't countenance. She was suddenly revolted by the thought that she had ever touched him, his horrible body, bad-smelling and elderly and creaky, and the horrible purplish scar that ran down his right thigh and over the kneecap, and how slowly he moved in the morning, and how he blew his nose, right there in front of her, and looked into his handkerchief for a moment before folding it up in his pocket, then smiled and kissed her, as though he hadn't done anything disgusting at all.

And that was the whole of her memory, the sudden flood of it as Ada hung on her hand and the streetcar arrived and she pulled Ada forward and the child dragged her feet. They took their seats, Ada in the window, and Hazel looked down at the poor, dark, lost little girl for a moment, and suddenly she found that the ache in her heart turned soft, and she looked at her child without bitterness or anger. In a sharp, quick movement, she wrapped the girl up tightly in her arms, pressing Ada and the unborn child close together. She said, "Daddy will show you a bear, darling. He will show you the bears."

Her face buried in the girl's hair, which smelled like white soap, Hazel would not look out her window toward the man who had left the touch that still lingered on her skin.

THOSE WHO AREN'T

Three weeks haunted, one week fired. She brought in the things she'd taken from Rm 023 and, for the last time, turned her key in the stiff lock. It took two trips. Among the boxes she returned were a dozen notebooks that had not originally belonged to the Institute, but which were easily hidden in one of the other rooms, along with Mrs. Kilgour's private correspondence. They were journals. Very tedious journals written in a lovely, slanting cursive, driven hard west by some invisible momentum.

After that, she cleaned up her desk in the R.A. office. Brynn had cleared out because, she told a mutual friend, she didn't want to embarrass Anthea in a moment of such total humiliation. If Brynn had been there, Anthea would have pointed out that it really wasn't so bad, then Brynn would have imparted words of wisdom in her counsellor-voice, telling Anthea that it was hard to make a go as a real academic, and Anthea probably had other gifts, anyway.

She was done quickly with the desk because she mostly just tossed everything into the recycling, the common room or the garbage. She was almost finished when she looked up to see Dr. Blake standing in the doorway. He nodded to her, then walked out of view down the hallway. A moment later he returned to the open door, took a step into the room, waited, and then fetched up beside her desk. He held an envelope in his hand.

"This is for the thing down at the Temple Theatre." He opened the envelope and held the ticket toward her. "You might get a kick out of it."

"Is that okay?"

He still held the ticket out to her, so she took it. Then he said, "You might as well. You'll get to look around."

"I'd like to see the inside of the Temple."

"I thought. And I wanted to say before you left that I'm sorry it worked out this way. You did some good work for us, at the beginning." And then he was gone.

Three weeks later. The ravages of memory receded, and though the dead still cast their long shadows, Anthea felt convalescent for the first time in a year. She got to the Temple Theatre early and waited for half an hour before the doors opened. She wore a red dress and sunglasses and heels, and hoped it wouldn't be too chilly later on the October evening.

Soon Anthea stood in a little knot of well-dressed people waiting to slip through the doors. Above their heads, she could make out the T and the E, but the restorers had only just reached the leading edge of the M. From where she stood, she could see faint traces of what the doors had been early in the Temple's history: polished copper, vine-patterns and leaves that curled around Moorish arches, above them a pink granite archivolt framed the porch and the doors. Through clean patches in the glass, she could see the lobby, dirty grey carpeting and fat, pink pillars of granite, lit by white light from fluorescent squares in the low, false ceiling. Anthea knew that if she could see into the darkness past the fluorescent panels—part of renovations in the 1970s—there would be plasters, arabesques and mandalas and *fleur des lis*. Colm had walked among them on his way to *Easy Rider* in 1969, one of the last people to see the plasters before the false ceiling covered them. Long before that, Hazel had gone with her father to see John Barrymore perform soliloquies from Shakespeare's tragedies, and she had stretched out her little girl's hand and touched them as they walked past.

Outside, Anthea wanted to touch the broken faces that decorated the box office, the corners and the columns around the entrance. She could still make out ivory-coloured gods among the papyrus and acanthus leaves, though many were gouged from the wall, revealing the tracery of wire that supported the concrete ornaments. She wondered who had stood in front of the façade like that, and struck it again and again with a hammer or a stone, and how long it took to chip away a face.

After they unlocked the doors, she knew she had an hour to explore before the program began. She walked into the lobby among potential investors and future-possible-members, high muckety-mucks, artists and journalists, academics, performers, politicians. In one corner of the lobby, beside a pillar, there were white-linened tables covered in bioplastic goblets, bottles of cider, white and red wine from a biodynamic vineyard near Duncan's Crossing. The attendants were uniformly elegant in black trousers and shirts, like actors with day jobs. In the corner opposite the food and drink there were easels with large posters that told the story of the Temple, the city's theatre district and Mrs. Kilgour's contributions to both. Anthea avoided that side of the lobby. Brynn would probably be there, somewhere, networking, looking for people interested in the Institute, telling them clever anecdotes about vaudeville and burlesque. Dr. Blake might show up. She hoped she would not see them.

According to the narrow strip of paper Anthea held, there'd be a speech about the original theatre district, and there'd be representatives of the local arts community, a Q&A, a few words about plans for the renovation, and some performances. A note from the Orphic Voice Arts Society indicated that they were scrupulously aware of the dangers of gentrification and would endeavour to make a welcoming space for people of all backgrounds and from all neighbourhoods. Looking around, Anthea guessed it meant that some of the attendants—those who didn't handle food, at least—had been drawn from the city's poorest postal code. They held flashlights where the wiring was still in pieces, and warned people away from the doors to the structurally unstable backstage, and the dressing rooms below the orchestra pit. She recognized them because often their skin was darker than that of the other guests. The men wore jeans that bagged at the knee and the back pockets, and layers of matted polar fleece. One or two women had dressed up, and wore white high heels and little stretchy dresses under their fun-fur jackets. The theatre was cold, and Anthea worried about their thin, bare legs.

She found her way through the lobby to the stairs, hoping to see through holes in the floating ceiling to the original walls. She sensed what hung above them in the darkness: plaster rosettes in pink and robin's egg and pale green, up past the galleries that ringed the lobby, rising toward the invisible vault. She stopped at the bottom of the enormous staircase that led to the upper balconies, and looked up past visitors who stood in knots and condescended to Eastside men and women, then she climbed up through the crowd to the double doors.

The auditorium was lined with more ugly, grey wallboard, but where it had been torn away, Anthea saw chipped gilding and paintwork. She was alone beside one of the struts that supported the box at stage left, near a long slit through which breathed damp and cold, a smell like abandonment. She knelt, listened for rats, then reached one hand through the dark tear, and touched the blue and gold mandala on the other side. It was softer than she expected. It would give under her fingernails if she scratched it, and though she didn't, her hand still came away with grey dust and mildew. In the damp and dark above their heads, she knew there was a dome, painted on plaster supported by a wire net, in the manner of Parrish or Wyeth, a frieze of Isis, Hermes-Thoth with the head of an ibis, Anubis the Jackal, attended by papyri, palm fronds, sand-dancers in white muslin, and the distant, hazy blues of the Nile.

The ceremonies began as she climbed up to the balcony, and knelt and touched the old wall of the theatre. A man on stage spoke into a portable PA: "We at the Oh Vee Ai Ess," he said, then stopped. "But you know we've been calling ourselves Oh-vas, and I think that'll catch on. So we at OVAS. We're proud to be part of this amazing recovery project that will not only rescue a piece of our heritage, but also reinvigorate a neighbourhood that's been neglected—we're going to bring a whole lot of people to the Eastside with the place, just like in the old days when there were a half dozen theatres around here. And I think that alone deserves your support, and maybe a round of applause for our volunteers?"

After they'd all clapped he went on: "You know, it's funny the sort of things you learn doing this—we're finding out all sorts of crazy nuggets, just the thing for a bunch of history nuts! Did you know that this place was bombed in 1933? Apparently it was a hotbed for revolutionary types during the Depression. Crazy stuff like that I've been hearing since I got involved! Dr. Ojea over there will tell you more about that later when she takes you through some of the history. First off, though, we're lucky enough to have a couple of kids in from the university to give us a show, and maybe wake up some of those old theatre ghosts from the Twenties. I hear they've got a program that dates back to the Temple's first decade, and I can't think of a better way to welcome you all to the evening than listening to them. Thanks, I should add, to Brynn at the Kilgour Institute for helping us figure out what sort of music would be suitable. You should take a look at her work in the lobby, too! She put together quite a little exhibit out there."

The gentleman clapped again, then they all clapped and he left the stage. Two figures stepped forward to the apron; a tenor, and a soprano in black wool and boots, gold taffeta glimmering under the long skirt of her coat.

Anthea stood forward in the dress circle, where the centre aisle had been, though there were no longer seats, nor even a balustrade to mark the edge. Below her on the floor and before the stage, men stood with flashlights and caged work lights, casting shadows and gleams on the prima donna's taffeta. After the introductory bars the duo sang:

> *with someone like you a pal good and true i'd like to leave it all behind and go and find a place that's known to god alone just a spot to call our own we'd find perfect peace where joys never cease out there beneath the kindly sky we'd build a sweet little nest somewhere in the west and let the rest of the world go by*

There was talk of renovation. There were speeches and applause for each benefactor. An elderly board member from the Kilgour Institute accepted a bottle of wine on their behalf, but Anthea had never met her. When they were finished, the crowd was released into the cold, dark theatre, drinking their wine and dry cider while pineapple, chèvre from the islands, rye bread and salmon skin rolls circulated on trays and waited on the white tables in the lobby. Anthea refilled her glass and ate a B.C. roll, but she tasted nothing. She continued to avoid the posters, which were covered in photographs she had not selected, filled with texts she had not written.

On the other side of the lobby, the singers stood before a shifting half-circle of admirers. Anthea approached in a quiet moment, while around her the crowd spoke loudly about vaudeville revivals and regionalism and the local residents' association. An urban matron in expensive ceramic jewellery tried to do a buck-and-wing. Anthea averted her eyes, and joined the prima donna and her tenor. She made polite noises, first, about the theatre and the evening's speakers, then said, "So, have you heard of someone named Leticia Kilgour?"

The prima donna looked excited. "Of course! Are you with the Institute? I've been listening to her work."

"My God!" Anthea wasn't prepared for her sudden possessiveness. "How?"

"It's part of the project, isn't it? I was talking to a woman named Brynn at the Institute. She talked about our 'artistic foremothers' and there was this CD. I had no idea the province supported that sort of talent in the Twenties."

"Okay." Anthea then had to ask again, "Like, really?"

"Her phrasing is incredibly sophisticated. She's always been a bit of a joke—you know, one of those eccentrics people tell stories about. After listening to those arias, though, I'm kind of smitten."

There was one of those pauses that meant the conversation was going to change directions, or people would leave or arrive, and Anthea's opportunity would be lost. Before that could happen, she pressed on and asked, "Did you ever hear of a tenor named Liam Manley?"

The prima donna shook her head.

For another moment Anthea stood before them, then felt the change again and knew it was time to withdraw. She thanked them for singing, and then returned to the lobby and the poster display. She looked at the pictures of Mrs. Kilgour and Liam, the silk-tasselled program from their gala performance in this very theatre, the pink roses that wreathed the photographs from that night. There was a poster from Duncan's Crossing, and sheet music annotated in Mrs. Kilgour's hand. No mention of Clive, strikebreakers, grave-robbing, or Phosgene gas. That was probably a good choice.

On the last panel of the display, Brynn had written about their plans for the Kilgour Archive, not only the Biography—*The Kilgours of the West: Volume III* was due next year!—but a short monograph on the province's early music culture to accompany Mrs. Kilgour's discography. It would be a digital release, with liner notes by some musical historian from campus, pending funds. Brynn's slick little addendum smelled like a grant application. Well, it was a good idea, Anthea thought, and she deserved the good luck if she got it. She worked hard. She applied for things.

Anthea returned to the auditorium and found other cracks in the ugly grey wall, through which she saw more of the original plasters, and where they had been hidden by dirt, they were still bright. She was looking through a crack at a plaster figured with papyrus and a bird-headed man when she realized that someone was standing beside her.

"Anthea. So good to see you here. Really good. I was worried you wouldn't. Blake thought you were going to stay away."

"Yeah."

"I'm impressed that you're dealing with this so well. I was worried." Having got through her manners, Brynn went on to say what she really wanted. "Did you ever come across anything to do with a man named Simon Reid? When you were working in Rm 023?"

Anthea looked at the bird-headed man on the wall. "No," she lied.

"It's just there's a lot of stuff in there related to him, and I thought you might have an idea considering how much time you spend in there. It's interesting, whatever it is." Then Brynn gave her lots of advice, and they walked in opposite directions.

Anthea was the last guest to leave, after the staff and volunteers had begun collecting garbage and stripping the white-linened tables. As she left, she looked up once more toward the walls that rose above them, before she passed into the darkness outside.

THE END

On the last day of Anthea's haunting, she was standing on the Express as it stopped just outside a busy intersection. It was five o'clock in the afternoon, and it was raining. The bus was too crowded to sit or think, and ten minutes into her ride, all the noise around her collapsed into a shallow field from which she could distinguish no meaningful sounds. She was content to surrender to the noise of her commute when she heard, suddenly, a string of notes. First she ignored it, then she listened, and just as she had decided the phrase was some accidental convergence of talk and engines, she heard it again.

The melody was sweet and familiar, something operatic she might have found within Mrs. Kilgour's collection, though she could not name it. As she listened, the singer seemed to draw closer to her, and then she realized it wasn't a recording, but a real man singing an aria somewhere in the crowd on the sidewalk. She knew he was walking because she could hear his changing breath, and the song changed, too, bounced off the plate glass coffee shop by the bus stop, and the plaster rosettes that decorated the building, through the bodies of the people passing by and the glass doors where she stood.

She wanted to name the song. She wanted to find the man and tell him that she liked to hear him sing. In the end she could do neither, and when the bus pulled away from the singing man, she listened hard for his voice until it was gone.

AND I ONLY AM ESCAPED ALONE TO TELL THEE

Simon Reid, the prophet, resolved to end the material world ten days after the birth of his child who, being a girl and not the prince foreseen, had disappointed him so bitterly. This was midway through the September before an unusually early autumn, when the late golds of August had already begun to darken, and in the mornings fine rain spattered the gardens and the branches of Douglas firs that shadowed the village. Simon Reid spoke to Michael Sweeney, who was his aid in all things related to the material function of the Foundation, and told him to ready the engine for their final progress to the Uttermost West. The necessary fires must be lit that night, and no later, before the season turned, and the true, autumnal descent began. *We belong to the light*, he had told Michael many times, and winter darkness—even close as they were to the West—held subtle threats to their safety and organization.

They had been assembling the Engine since the vernal equinox, when Simon had revealed the true nature of his plans to the Foundation's council, and described the endgame he had foreseen at the founding in 1918: the Engine, the transformation of the material world, the coming of the West.

Though he had not known their purposes, Michael Sweeney had begun collecting the Engine's fittings years before, since many required long, alchemical processes. Others were simpler: he buried hollow cow horns full of ground quartz under the apple trees, and hung silver talismans in the waters off the point for 243 days. For years, they collected lumber for the Engine's frame, and firewood for its boiler: oak, crab apple, fir, cedar, maple, arbutus in the right quantities and from the right quadrants. Boxes had been arriving at the Foundation for more than a year: springs in tight silver whorl, finely milled gears with long teeth, each stamped with a figure in Greek or a hieroglyph. Slender bars of brass, wheels of copper wire as fine as baby hair. Other spools almost pink, soft and thick, easily dented with needle-nose pliers. Counter weights, pendulums in copper, governors with long insectoid legs. The Damascene steel, the Levantine hardwoods. Wooden crates of glass gauges, the small, heavy boxes from England and Germany that Michael Sweeney unpacked himself, and kept hidden. There was a disk under a glass dome, its needle fine and black measuring some quantity numbered in Greek, the central circle surrounded with figures of the zodiac and a ring of periodic elements. A brass toggle marked Alpha and Omega. A collapsible instrument of levers and arrows and weights, that seemed to measure the ascension of stars and planets, but fixed facing down, an astrolabe marking subtle oppositions in the earth below. There was a spyglass with lenses of impenetrable purple obsidian. There were calipers and slide rules marked not with Arabic numbers, but with Mayan glyphs. There were bars and insulators and resistors in gold, lead, steel, copper, bronze, and porcelain. There were glass vials and tubes and wide beakers of polished crystal. There were disks of quartz rimmed in gold. There were diamonds.

At five o'clock in the afternoon, Simon lit the fires, and the engine began its work. It was the first time Michael or anyone else had seen all these pieces in one together, and he was disappointed, thinking not of the coming transformation, but his own early history, before Simon. He thought, *It's like the shop floor, with a furnace and all that heat— in August, on those days that had the tar oozing on the pavement; if you were on the floor on a day like that, you'd feel the whole world was burning.* So Michael wondered if the new world—the return of the Hyperboreans in the western Beringia—was really so far from the old one he had known when he was just a kid, working nights in the foundry.

It was just one of those engines, he thought dully in the terrible heat, as he felt his eyebrows and eyelashes burn away. It wasn't a new sort of an engine at all, but just the old tired kind, come back in a different, more expensive form. It was true he could not trace the movement of force through all its gears and arms and governors, but by then he didn't need to, because he was too busy trying to get away.

Michael returned to the estate in June, just before the lawyers and RCMP and assessors could go through and determine what must be sold to make up the losses to the noisiest—and wealthiest—investors. Michael was not among them, of course: his two hundred and fifty-seven dollars were long gone. The time he had given Simon was unrecoverable.

He did own part of the land, however. His name was on the deed for the heart of Simon's little kingdom: the fifty-acre parcel that held the manor house, his own cottage, the gardens and the orchard. That was the land from which the Foundation's thousand acres grew, a confluence of angles and leys that Simon had recognized when they first set foot on the place.

He hitched to the familiar corner, and then walked the remaining two miles off the main road until he reached the stone plinths on either side of the gate. Someone had retracted the metal bridge that crossed the trenches. He slithered down eight feet to the bottom of the forward trench, and followed the duckboard around a zigzag to the exit.

As he did, he found himself making lists: the bridge was rusted, the windows broken in the gatehouse, the trenches had not been mended after the winter rain and had already begun to fall in. You still knew them for trenches, though, and he guessed people would come on them in the woods for a good long time, and animals would shelter in them, or boys from Duncan's Crossing would use them as blinds when they shot cougars in late summer, for the bounty. He walked down the drive, which was gutted with runoff. It would need grading before the next winter, if anyone was ever going to use it. He walked past the weed-grown orchard and the empty barns, glancing over the vegetable garden and then quickly away from the tangle of dandelions, beets that had been left in the ground the September before, scarlet runners in the strawberry beds. He looked for strawberries under the leaves, but there were only husks, the fruit taken by crows and raccoons and wasps. He wondered about the quart jars of jam they had put up in the kitchens, and the green beans and the pickled beets he had liked with his stews in the winter.

The chicken house came after the strawberries. He did not want to think what had happened to them, with Simon alone there. He looked once at the three little doors with their ramps, and saw that someone had nailed boards over them. The human-sized side-door was barred and nailed as well. He did not want to think. He had liked the chickens.

The day was beautiful. When he came to the bend above the village, he saw the water and felt surprise, somehow that it was still so bright and fine, with a fishing boat chugging by just off the point. It was different from the surprise he had felt on that first day, seeing the land fall away at his feet. This was the shock of homecoming, that he still found the familiar skyline on the opposite shore, that the enclosing points around the beach should still stretch out like arms, and not even the boulders changed. It ought to have changed, he thought, somehow. Hadn't change always been Simon's promise?

The village, as quiet as the hen house, the orchard and garden, had begun to show its abandonment. Already, just a season unchecked, the mint in the back gardens had withered; the stinging nettles spilled out from under the trees, and the blackberries crept out of their beds and over the verges. Miner's lettuce grew in close along the paths, and sorrel with tiny red blooms spread outward from the green strip in the middle of the drive. It would not be long, just a few years, and the whole thing would be swallowed up, only a few walls here and there, and unusual plants surviving under the trees, scented violets and daffodils springing weakly from the clearings.

More slowly now, Michael walked to the wall that separated the village from the garden. He followed it along to the little gate that came out in the field Simon had chosen for the hedge maze that was staked, but unplanted, with a few dead boxwoods still in burlap at the edge. Michael left it, avoiding the inevitable accounting he made whenever he looked at the village: those saplings had been very expensive. He walked through the garden, between the empty carp ponds to the house itself—herons, he guessed, had liked the carp, which had also been expensive—looping around to the side where the bonfire had been.

It was bad. The fire had not done much damage to the main house, but he thought there had been some later fire to account for the destruction in the garden and the east wing. New grass and nettles had come up to cover the blackened ornamental trees, and some of the hardier perennials had survived—periwinkle and English ivy and St. John's wort and Scotch broom. The plaster walls that faced the courtyard were smoke-stained, and the library wing windows were gone, the walls charred inside and out.

Michael walked around to the side door that had always been his particular entrance and pushed it open. It was whole but scarred with shallow gashes, the kind made by an awkwardly swung entrenching tool or a hatchet in a weak arm. He walked down the hallway to the library and saw all the windows broken that faced the water, and the wind and rain had blown in all winter, so the carpet smelled strongly of rot, and the books were stained and swollen where they hadn't been yanked from their shelves and scattered, now on their way to birds' nests or bedding for mice. Birds had sheltered here from the weather, and shit white and purple all down the fireplace, chair backs, shelves. He watched a pair of swallows sweep into a nest at the top of the bookshelf nearest the broken window.

Only the books on the glassed shelves were safe, though some of the doors were broken. It had taken Michael fifteen years to collect them, contacting obscure booksellers, creating false identities with which to purchase the more dangerous volumes, travelling to foreign cities to collect them. All the books Simon had demanded were still there: *The Necronomicon, A First Encyclopedia of Tlön, The Book of Eibon.*

Michael left the library again and walked around to the front entrance with the big double doors. They stood scarred and ajar. In the sunlight outside the portico, he heard the buzz of the garden. For a moment he turned his face to the warmth and smelled the thyme, blooming and bee-covered. Then a blue glitter in the air over the grass caught his eye; it joined another iridescent speck and another, and then there were half a dozen—no, more, he couldn't count how many, all near the broken windows that lit the entrance hall. They made half-circles and loops, retreats and advances and disappeared into the house by ones and twos. He opened the double doors.

The scent struck him in the gut. Iridescent bottle flies circled the hall. His eyes adjusted quickly, fixing on the light from the broken windows where they had fallen on the floor that had been black and white tile, now covered in dust and soot. He could see through the arch to the main drawing room, the receiving room, they had called it, and saw the marks of recent habitation. There was a pile of cushions and rugs wadded up in one corner away from the broken windows, in the shelter of a chesterfield. There were bits of paper on the floor, the corners full of screwed up pages from books that had been used, he guessed at a glance, for napkins, for writing paper, for other things. Newspapers were scattered over the carpets, with greasy bones and apple cores.

The heat and the buzzing made him drowsy, but he followed the scent. When he stepped into the hall, through the arch to the receiving room, it grew stronger, and the buzz grew insistent. The panelling was scarred with what looked like axe marks and knife marks and dark stains. It had been a beautiful room. Michael had often felt a little pulse of pride when he thought that it was his, partly. He could not see past the archway to the shrouded dining room because of the dark, and the brightness where he stood. The flies passed him, into the gloom of the velvet drapes. There was the dining table, still covered in a long white cloth and scattered with dishes, as though they had been taken up and set down again and abandoned months before.

He meant to go through the archway, but then the breeze changed direction, and he caught a lungful of the close, damp air from the dining room, with a stink so penetrating it brought fear to his legs. He tried not to, but he thought of the last night, the fire and the shadows and the Engine, and one hand went to his forehead where the skin still shone with burn scars. He turned back through the hall and out the double doors to the sunlight beyond. Once outside he meant to walk around past the dining room windows and look in, but found he couldn't, and while he hated the eyes of the house on the back of his neck, he hated even more the thought that he might turn around and see something, anything, a black adept standing motionless at one of the broken upstairs windows, or the pale, grey figure of Simon himself watching him run.

He ran to his cottage without looking back, for the first time grateful Simon had allotted him a spot so far from the manor. The narrow porch was covered in fallen needles and fir branches, but the windows were unbroken. When he unlocked the door it smelled lonesome, but it was dry, and the coffee tin still stood where he had left it on the shelf beside the little stove, and his muddy footprints were still on the floor. He pulled out a chair and sat at the table, looking out the window at the path past his front door, which wound down to the beach. It was overgrown on the verge. It wouldn't be long now. After all, he might know it was a path, but it was on its way back to forest floor, frequented by deer and cougars. It didn't take long, he thought, for the forest to rise up and swallow them down again, leaving nothing but the footings of old houses, and the line of a garden wall looming unexpectedly out of the forest along the overgrown path from the beach.

Anthea's city is milky and pale on a day in late winter, when the twigs are swollen on the scrub alders that grow in gaps along the harbour front, the water slack and oily around the wharves. The Prophet walks from the customs office to the gangplank of a westbound steamer. He carries a black valise of worn leather. His suit is a bare shade lighter than the mist that obscures the mountainside across the inlet. Even beyond the wharves the waves are sluggish, the dimpled surface of the water as close as the low sky. The grey hulk of his ship rests at her anchor. He pauses at the bottom of the long ramp to the second-class deck.

Up close, his hands are clean and yellowish and skeletal. The old-paper skin seems too thin to cover the long finger bones, as though it were a glove close to splitting; sometime it will fall away and show the desiccated workings of his left hand: the clotted blood, the brownish strands of muscle, and his overwrought nerves running from fingertip to brain. It is hard to believe this hand is alive, or that it could remain alive much longer.

When he showed his ticket and passport—Canadian—he did not speak, having nothing to declare. He does not speak now as he takes the first step up the long ramp. He should rest longer after each step. One hand whitens under the weight of his valise. The other hand supports him on the railing. The sun is higher, but from the second class deck it's hard to tell that the day has advanced.

Somewhere there's a steward who will help him find his cabin, but for now he is alone on the deck, the grey day around him brightening, but never approaching white or gold. He leans on the railing, his shoulders sagging under the immaculate lines of his grey suit. Beneath the fabric he wears a thin film of sweat like another garment; the parchment skin of his face shines with it. He won't set down the valise. It clings to his hand like a child, the bag a dead weight that numbs his fingers and makes deep, white cuts in his palm. It might be an anchor he drags after him. It might be his own heart made of cracked leather, and he like some older Magus gone out to hide it in the world, beating outside his ribcage in a seagull's egg or the red heart-wood of a Garry oak. Immortality requires that kind of sacrifice.

Looking at the ticket in his right hand, he walks down the long second-class deck. Someone has begun to swab the floor with seawater, so it glistens in the shadowless light, and in it he sees reflected a distorted bit of sky.

THE END

ACKNOWLEDGEMENTS

I want to thank my editor, Anne Nothof, for her good taste and patience, as well as Matt Bowes and Paul Matwychuk at NeWest Press.

I have borrowed—without permission—stories and lines from friends, so I thank Dean Ziegler for his squirrels, Jennifer Rempel for the KFC buckets, Eve Ojea for taking me to see Flamenco dancers, and Eileen Wennekers for a line of Menander's dialogue. Also, my brother leant me the title "Blueprints for Surviving the Coming Dark Times" from one of his own projects.

I am also grateful to Tina Northrup for her critical eye, and to my friends Catherine Greenwood, Heidi Greco, Holly Borgeson-Caulder, and Kimmy Beach.

Finally, I am grateful to my family, in particular Sharron, Ian, and Paulette, and my father, David (1944–2009). And of course Don Bourne, because he made me finish the story, when I might otherwise have given up.

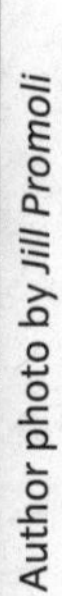
Author photo by *Jill Promoli*

REBECCA CAMPBELL

has had fiction and poetry published in *Grain*, *Geist*, *The Fiddlehead*, *TickleAce* and *Prairie Fire*. She has received a Masters in English at UBC and is currently working on her PhD. at the University of Western Ontario. Originally from Duncan, B.C. in the Cowichan valley, Rebecca now lives in Toronto, Ontario.

The Paradise Engine is her first novel.